Vague Semblances

a novel

Michael Cooper

SPUYTEN DUYVIL

New York City

I very much enjoyed and admired these poems—for their delicacy and tenderness, for the way they evoke the mutual permeability of person and world and person and person, for the delicate balance they strike between occlusion and transparency of vision. They remind me of Frank O'Hara's lovers "drifting back and forth/ between each other like a tree breathing through its spectacles . . ." Thank you for entrusting me with them.
 Ellen Levy

Michael Cooper is the poet of the little epiphanies of everyday life—a sensitive person who can find importance and beauty in what sometimes might seem mundane. Michael is not afraid to delve into sexuality, and often writes rather detailed poetry that mirrors the feelings and behavior of physical love. This is genuine poetry, but rarely obscure. This doesn't mean it's simple, or perhaps superficial. What he has revealed to me is only a small amount of what seems like a lifetime of writing and contemplating reality with a poet's eye.
 John Wherrity

I am eager to express my astonishment at Cooper's sensibility and love of language. Also his determination to see, feel, to squeeze, report, to blend, delve, to do all those things that celebrate noticing. I relish the bite and theology of a piece like "The Man Who Got Arrested for Impersonating the Deity." I thought I was reading Frost!
 Paul Bernabeo

For my son, Jonathan

Endless the series of things without name
On the way back to where there is nothing.
They are called shapeless shapes;
Forms without form;
Are called vague semblances.
Go towards them, and you can see no front;
Go after them, and you see no rear.

Tao Te Ching, Chapter XIV
Arthur Waley translation

PART I

"Pink elephants on parade!" cried the extravagant eggplant-eater, sifting through the rubble of his endless momentum, as the two-faced salamander rampaged through what was left of the wilderness. "Emphasize my cavity, you travesty!" demanded the mother-in-law of the laundry owner's manager. Well, you get the idea by now that this is going to be a bumpy ride.

You get two for the price of one, at the storage place's sale of abandoned goods. Safe harbor approaching, we get dressed for dinner with the captain. "You can save the caviar for tomorrow, Sally," quoth the tea dispenser's parrot, as they walked, amused, past the gaping gargoyles infesting the fringes of the cathedral, blue, in the evening light.

By now the characters in the story begin to reveal themselves to the headmaster, ensconced in the loneliness of his armchair, smoking a savory salmon in his pipe. "Open the curtains, please," begged the mistress of the house, collapsed on the sofa, which melted beneath her weight and tears. They might be preparing for an onslaught of muscle spasms in their backs.

"Don't look back," they warned Orpheus, as his eyes melted into pools of derision. "Take your socks off; I want to examine your feet," demanded the stern mistress who inhabited the first floor of the flooded apartment. He refused, on the grounds that his feet had not been washed for a week. Open sesame, and the thoughts begin again, at last.

I want to reveal, slowly, what happened to them all. It will take time, as slowly as an aardvark mounting its hairy mate. They open a can of soup, chicken noodle, for their illness. "Why do you always oppose what I suggest?" wondered the bread to the spreadable butter. I am merely the observer and chronicler of these things, after all.

Any resemblance in this work to persons living or dead, or circumstances beyond their control, is purely coincidental. The fiction of fiction. Squeezing the last bit out of the empty tube of toothpaste, he warbles and wobbles toward the empty kitchen. "There will be no supper tonight, children. We have no food," wept the father, emaciated, to his hungry progeny, gathered like figures in one of Picasso's Blue Period paintings, near starvation.

"Change the channel, Henry," begged his wife, her hair up in curlers for the night. Where are the lost children now? And is he even in the telephone book, anymore? Draining the dregs, the last sip of tea at the bottom of the cup, blue and white, Japanese, with stirring scenes painted on it, along with its saucer. Please do not give up on me; I have only just begun. So, open your eyes.

He wonders whether anyone really understands him; and so he writes on the walls of his room the random, obsessive thoughts which collide inside the walls of his skull, like a Bruckner symphony.

"Press on, you fools, for pity's sake," sang out the opera diva, enhanced by the rays of moonlight that followed their carriage everywhere it went.

Now we are in the thick of it. Just imagine, you and I, going through life together. Abandon all thought and conceive a tree growing inside your brain. It is laden with luscious fruit of a tropical nature. But he is still stuck inside the city, boiling like bagels before they are baked. The heat of the summer is stifling, and he has mushrooms on his feet where toes used to be.

"Cash in your chips now, and let's get out of here,"

declaimed the laden misfit to his brotherly lover. "I can't wait to tell you all about it when we get home," responded the golden triangle which overheard the entire conversation. Badgers even were concerned, and ruffled their back hairs in the furrier's red face. What will his wife say when he gets home?

"Please pass the sugar," asked the man on the stool to his neighbor, in the diner on the south side, at three in the morning, the night the Statue of Liberty suddenly melted into the water, dissolving slowly before the bespectacled enthusiasts, observing from a safe distance the remarkable proceedings.

Like a monkey on the shoulder of a sailor coming off the boat on leave at last, he heads for the nearest brothel; no, I mean the nearest church; no, I mean . . .

He gives someone a glass of cold water so he can get to go to heaven. "Why are there no windows in this house?" asked the young couple, house-hunting. "There are no windows in this house because the previous owner was blind, and wanted to save money when he built it, omitting the windows, which he could not have seen out of, anyway."

The opera singer makes her way across the stage, parasol over her shoulder as Madame Butterfly, as the cherry blossoms rain down upon her. Why do you ask me questions when I am in the middle of writing a novel? In the gloaming, oh my darling. Can of beans, for emergencies. Why not open one now; surrender, and eat them right out of the can, like Kerouac?

"If you offer me ten dollars, I will remove that stop sign on the corner." "Why would I want you to remove that stop sign?" The two figures turn into birch trees, right there on the sidewalk. No wonder your bread is baking. I asked him, but he refused to answer. Does anybody really care about anyone besides themselves, anymore?

They walk on together, like two figures from a wedding cake, groom and groom, surprising their parents and other relatives, dripping with buttercream icing on their fresh tuxedos. The parents bark like dogs, reduced to eating dog food. They need to be walked, to do their business. Why do I keep up with this? It is some deep, inner compulsion that drives me onward.

Like refugees, simply seeking a better life, instead of welcoming them into our homes, we demonize them, locking them up in detention camps, and sending them back to their own countries.

Dried persimmons, available through the mail, how wonderful. He is running out of steam, but feels compelled to continue, endlessly, until he runs out of steam. Seeking a better life; isn't that what all of us are doing?

Learning to be content with what one has. The sacred lessons of Life. The blossoms of my thoughts in wintertime, explode into fragments of word patterns, similar to normal speech, flowing through my veins, like blood, onto the keyboard, and thence to the screen, where I see my babies, growing before my very eyes. Thoughts in utero, waiting to be born.

I will write until the cows come home, he thought. Someday, I'll be a horse trainer, bringing my beauties to fields of sweet clover for them to munch. Where am I in all this verbiage? The omnipotent observer of my own existence. To tell the story that can never be told, like holding it in when you have to pee, but cannot stop what you are doing.

Lines follow lines, draining the excess, like cleaning out the drain basket in the kitchen sink: scraps of this and bits of that; remnants of meals eaten and forgotten. Into the garbage they go.

Double-space gives room for thoughts to bloom, into some hidden sun, a desk lamp whose light bulb never needs changing. Like my mind, he thinks.

How many pages make a book? It depends on the time and the season, and the mental state of the writer, and the availability of his Muse, enabling, inspiring, and allowing the work to come forth. It's like going to a fair, but not going on the rides, since they make you sick. Anxiety caught by the tail of his beautiful cat, wild once, now tamed at last. How will people, a century from now, think of poetry?

His stomach was bloated from constipation, yet he suddenly felt inspired and sat down to his Royal Standard typewriter, black and beautiful, and began to write. "What will the neighbors think?" wondered the lady of the house, still in her housedress, nonchalantly smoking a cigarette. Well, you can guess what happens next. "Don't fall off the roller coaster, darling!" advised the embarrassed teenager, about to go on the ride.

Exiled from his own life, he sought solace in his work, plunging headfirst into the Cave of Plato.

Nymphs dance in circles, around the sleeping boy, as he rests upon the mossy base of a golden tree.

"Wake up, sweet earthling!" they beseech him. Sleeping on, as though lost in dreams, he breathed peacefully, inhaling and exhaling, as his chest moved up and down.

"Please prepare tea, Martha," advised Madame, tending to her guests in the drawing room.

Whether or not their thoughts bypassed their conscious minds, emitting words over which they had no control, is a question whose answer may never be found. Going on impulse, though, they feed the vagrants bowls of muesli, with goat's milk and prunes.

"Why not collapse entirely, and refuse to move from one's bed?" Cousin Harold wondered. The family was concerned about his mental health. After all, he had attempted to acquire the gun that was kept locked in the cabinet, the key to which was kept hidden where no one could find it. "Collapse entirely? How Proustian," mused Mother.

Writing his brains out, he peeled away the unnecessary flesh, which kept him from moving easily about the room. Melting words appeared and disappeared as he typed them. Opening the window, the young housewife was pleased to see a robin fly to her nest, a fat worm in her beak, to feed her waiting chicks, beaks open, begging to be fed.

Visibly shaken by the experience, he exited the room, and went immediately to bed. What he did when he got there, one can only imagine. "Rockin' my soul in the bosom of Abraham," sang the blind Black man, a head of white hair and beard, just singing for the pleasure of it, outside the supermarket.

Well, a comforting cup of tea always does the trick. Opening the envelope, she read the letter inside.

Surprised to find that her best friend from college had just had an abortion.

Defrosting, frozen sushi for lunch. "Why not put your hair up in a bun, just for fun, hun?" I wanted to ask the waitress, but didn't dare. The clarifying thoughts break through the frozen ice of the lake, midwinter, Mallarme's swan floating, stuck in the middle. I open the envelope, or rather, she does, that woman who pretends to be me, rolling her cart down the vegetable aisle in the supermarket. What she finds inside will change her life forever.

Halfway through the cup of tea, he thinks of his late mother, melted into the earth by now. "Oppose the new rules for libraries," the mob shouted, where books are received, but not given out.

The children cry for books as for bread, as the librarians shred all the volumes in the collection. No one reads anymore, anyway. Books have been declared obsolete, people glued to their smart phones instead.

"What to do with the leftovers?" wondered Sarah, the cook. "Turn them into an hearty soup," suggested Martha, the housekeeper. He had always wished to be a lighthouse keeper, living a solitary life in the tower whose beams guide ships safely to harbor in the dark of night. Another invigorating sip of tea, reconstitutes the mind, awakens the body, refreshes the spirit.

One lone cigarette butt, curled up in the ashtray, somewhere in Pennsylvania, speaks volumes, louder than any words. Of course, there is the aftermath, wherein the participants remove their souls, undressing their psyches, parading around the room like pink elephants, for all the world to see. "Open the window, for God's sake, Henry," complained the aardvark chaperone, mincing his teeth, like there was no tomorrow.

Pools of blood gather amongst the startled guests, who proceed to evacuate the premises. No wonder, the house was bleeding, and the children were splashing in the lovely red liquid, until their mothers reprimanded them, and took them home for their baths. Why not talk about the woman who received the envelope, ready to open it? Alas, she has moved beyond our purview.

Squeezing the last drops out of the teabag once the cup is empty; this is what he decided to do with his life. Squeezing out the last drops of Life, like used-up teabags, sitting, lonely in their cups. Personify inanimate objects, he thought. Why not? I am as good at this as anybody else; in fact, this may not have occurred to anyone else before me, he opined.

Recognize the inherent souls of objects, supposedly inanimate, but really swirling realms of atoms, which our upbringing has trained us to see as a cup. It is in the emptiness of the cup that its usefulness depends, to paraphrase Lao Tzu. Why not strive for emptiness, to thus be filled again?

Charming young men entertain themselves on a sunny afternoon in May.

Coughing in the next room: the old man is dying.

There is nothing they can do to save him. His family has abandoned him to face death alone. "Today shall be my dancing day," he explains to the no one who isn't there. "Put a record on, Denis, the Sea Symphony of Vaughn Williams, please." He speaks to his long lost childhood friend, as though he were there with him.

With an albatross around his neck, he cannot put his head in the sand, but is forced to face life and death, head-on. To stare death down until it was no longer a frightful prospect, but a welcome haven and refuge for the weary end of a well-lived life. There, where no troubles can ever cause one harm, the dreamland of sleepy children. Returning to the earth from whence we came. What bliss.

So, our hero never appeared. That is why this is a different kind of novel. People come and go, appear and disappear, in the crazy dance of life. We are abandoned, but not hopeless, clinging to the source of all things, the embrace that includes everyone, all of us. He no longer felt ashamed of his particular inclinations, but had put them to bed, cozy under the covers, dreaming.

"Wake up! It's time to mow the lawn," proposed the familiar spirit, ensconced within his purple brain, out to lunch, no breakfast, walking on eggs, hangover, hopelessness. Why doesn't he just begin to breathe again? Each day is a resurrection, dragging ourselves out of the bed of sleep, into the new enthusiastic day which beckons each one of us to enter and fulfill ourselves.

His constipation was improving, thanks to the vast quantities of prunes he had consumed. There are few things in life as satisfying as a good bowel movement. So why not proclaim it? They walked around the park and finally sat down on a bench and listened to the birds chirping in the tree above them. He seemed embarrassed and couldn't talk. His companion responded similarly with silence.

I wonder what they were thinking? Strange fruit to be eaten in bitterness. Eating one's own heart, as Stephen Crane celebrated it in a poem. Why not change your attitude the way one changes one's underwear? A new attitude every day, consuming, energizing, explosive! I applaud these figures who inhabit my mind and fingers. Especially when there is nothing left to say. Say it again.

Speaking of explosions: what was that sound that

suddenly appeared out of nowhere? Enthusiasm unleashed from some unknown source, deep within the earth? The power of the sounds of language, as not just written, but also spoken word. He considered the implications of this idea. Wandering through the wilderness of your mind's eye's brain, I pick up where I left off with you, yesterday, barking up the same different tree once again, as usual.

Sitting at the typewriter, the keys begin to melt beneath his fingers. Upon close inspection, he finds that they have turned into black licorice. The Black ice-cream man from his first novel appears once again in his mind, haunting, poignant and invisible. Scooping out life from his truck, to waiting children. The ice cream is free to everyone, but the only flavor is licorice, according to custom.

Heroically, he rows out into the depths, evading conscious thought, as the stream surrounds him from all sides. Winding his way through the dense undergrowth, he perceives a hidden cave; whereupon entering, he finds treasure such as he never imagined in his wildest dreams. However, the treasure is guarded by a huge dragon, sleeping, with apparently no intention of moving.

"What are you waiting for?" asked the bronzed lifeguard, seated on his perch, above the sweating throng. So, he approached the freezing water, gingerly, hesitantly, putting one toe into the frigid lake, approaching it as one calling ceremoniously upon an old friend. Finally, he walked on through the water, until it was up to his neck, then plunged down his head into the green liquid, breathing heavily, and swam out as far as the eye could see.

Advancing boldly toward the mechanism, his shoes untied, he gasped, "My Muse has come back to me!" Sitting down at the typewriter, he saw the words on the page and merely typed them in. The power of water to solidify and inspire should never be underestimated, especially when it is in a pink water bottle. How water sustains all things, giving life and refreshment to everything. In his eyes, he was doing nothing wrong, and so refused to explain it to anyone.

His knees were wobbly, so he remained seated. Taking the wash out to hang on the clothesline, she greeted her neighbor, doing the same in the adjacent backyard. Wondering what to do next, he reserved the right to swim with an octopus, cavorting in the water like two schoolboys out for a swim.

"Where are you going?" she asked him. Refusing to answer, he put on his hat and walked out the door.

If you lived here, you'd be home by now: a good thing to offer guests, so they'd feel welcome.

The windows of the house had never been washed since they had moved in, twenty years before.

"Why not go fly your kite?" she suggested to the child, brooding over his Spaghetti-o's. "When your father comes home, we will have supper," comfortingly.

Don't look back, Orpheus was warned; Lot's wife looked back and was turned into a pillar of salt. Life can be so cruel, sometimes. "Keep going," said the zoo-keeper, as his young assistant left to go off into the world on his own. As I narrate this story, I am as amazed as the reader by what happens. The young woman with the laundry basket, off to do her wash, after a hard week of work.

Like playing Frisbee, you try to catch the object coming towards you. Don't duck; stand upright and blow your nose. There is nothing that can dissuade you from your task. Single-mindedness of purpose is required on the part of all participants in this experiment. Remove your shoes, but keep your souls on. You may need them later on.

Wondering where he was next to wander, he put on his jacket and hunting gear, and set off into the woods, his trusty dog leading the way. After about an hour they decided to take a rest, and he sat down on a fallen tree, noticing the fungi that proliferated on the rotting log. "Open a can of soup," she demanded, as the people melted into one another like fudge, congealing.

"Why is your mouth opened so wide?" he enquired of his host. "So I can drink and eat faster," was the reply. Going toward the coast, they meandered through small villages, peopled by plastic persons consisting of a variety of colors. They seemed to span the entire experience of human emotions, each one carrying a single feeling, saturated by it, engulfed by it, possessed by it, almost.

A variety of furry moths gathered each night at the front door, drawn by the porch light. He liked to go outside and play with them, making friends with them, welcoming them, talking to them.

"When we finally get to the coast, I am going for a swim," he thought, forgetting for the moment that he could no longer swim. This hurt him deeply, and his bowtie began to strangle him.

Going for his daily walk, each step sent a surge of pain through his back; nonetheless, he persisted in his routine. Made of rituals, his life was held together by them; the glue that holds it all together. Keep on task, he told himself, even when everything else in the world is going berserk. Especially then, when life is utter chaos, keep to the center, and hold fast to Life.

His friend, the radio announcer, plays Bruckner. Another day in Paradise with Dante. Wandering through the misty vales of mythic inventions, playing on the harp of Life, singing through the veins of blood which course through your body. Dancing with the moon, under the black, night sky. Taking a piss in the bushes where no one can see you, cicadas whirring away.

Suddenly, it's night, and you have to turn on the lights. He sits down and eats his soup. Pouring out his soul for two hours has worn him out. He turns to the typewriter on his desk. Pulling out a handkerchief he wipes his eyeglasses. Like playing a piece of music from the notes, he types in the words, as fast as they appear. It's no wonder he is a Servant of Love.

He would hear voices, howling, moaning, in the

night; he hoped they hadn't disturbed his new neighbor. He didn't know from where the voices came, but they persisted through the night. He wondered what they wanted, or what they were trying to tell him. He liked sneaking into the kitchen at night to eat ice cream right out of the container. The spoon kept dipping in for more. He couldn't stop himself until the entire carton was empty.

Don't look back, keep writing. That's what he tried to do, when no one was looking, when no one could disturb him. He cultivated an intense state of concentration, enabling him to reveal the words he saw on the page, so that others could read them too. His sense of purpose was immense , and he never forgot to wash his clothes once a week, like clockwork.

Meanwhile, back home, in another part of the country, she is taking in the laundry before it rains. No need to get them wet again, after they've been washed. Although the rain would give a beautiful freshness to my clothes and sheets, she mused. He was drying up like a prune, and offered his services to anyone who wanted them, but nobody did.

There it goes again: the telephone was ringing. He

didn't answer it, not wanting to interrupt his work, typing away until the cows come home. What was the point of it all? he wondered. Better not to think about such things, he concluded, always moving forward and ahead. Nothing could throw him off of his horse, after all he'd been through over the last several years. His unconscious mind led him ever onward, into the dark night of winter.

Standing on the railroad platform, he pretended to be going somewhere, when actually he was standing perfectly still, going nowhere. He walked very slowly; so slowly that people were annoyed and offended at him. Gazing downward toward the pavement, he was startled when suddenly a woman came charging at him, swinging her purse, with which she struck him on the head. He didn't even react, but kept on slowly walking, as if nothing had happened. This was a work of art.

Speaking of which, regardless of the level of enthusiasm on the part of the participants, the extras were added in the belief that something else would arise. In fact, what happened was a total surprise to everyone. He put on his hat and walked through the door, that is, through it. No wonder that the pigs were hungry, since they had not been fed in three days.

The chocolate bars melted in the cars, due to the extreme heat. No passengers were involved, and the chocolate was lost now, forever. The balloons flew up to the sky, taking the little boy with them, just like in The Red Balloon. Precious memories persist in his brain; he cannot forget what he has been through over the years. Why not start with the beginning?

What can be said of his childhood? "Don't bother to ask me," he retorted. Exasperated, he fell upon the sofa, and went immediately to sleep. Gathering in the laundry, the young mother prepares to go back into the house. The baby is awake now, so she will have to feed her. Taking out her breast, she nurses the baby closely to her heart.

In another world, what would you be doing right now? Perhaps the same things, but in another language. With stirrups on, he mounted the horse, who looked more like a zebra. The zebra was hiding behind the picket fence, for camouflage. Off they went, galloping through the fields and woods, in pursuit of nothing, just out for the joy of the ride. I wonder what he is thinking right now: maybe of toast with butter and marmalade?

Paddington Bear comes to visit the children who read about him in their books. They have an imaginary tea party together, and then he must leave. What a splendid time they had! But back to business: What were you thinking when you read this page of the book? Did the images compel you?

Did the narrative confuse you? How am I doing?

Entering the museum, they checked their coats and hats before going in. Browsing through the galleries, they found many objects of interest. But what were they talking about while they wandered through the halls together? He was fascinated by the vast array of possibilities posed by these many ancient objects. What their worth was? Their provenance? The date of their acquisition?

Like boiling water for pasta to cook in, his thoughts were of distant shores. When he returned home, putting his key in the lock, he entered and was amazed: the entire room was upside down, and he found himself walking on the ceiling. Luckily, the furniture on the floor was weighed down, and didn't come crashing down on him.

"Where do we go from here?" he mused, going out

of the door and closing it behind him. Mustering up his courage, he opened the door again, and the room was sideways this time, furniture jutting out into the middle of the room. "Well, I've had just about enough of this," he warned, leaving the room again, and trying once more. Thankfully, this time the room was normal, as it had been.

The cobwebs on the walls didn't bother him; in fact, he was rather fond of them. No one could understand this about him. Nameless, hopeless, wandering aimlessly around the room, he refused to sit down, out of fear that the chair might collapse beneath his weight. He turned on the radio, talk show, endlessly blabbering about nothing.

"What are your plans for the holidays?" she cheerfully inquired. "Nothing, absolutely nothing," he dejectedly responded. How can I impress upon you the level of despair he was experiencing? He was ready to give up on life altogether. His novel was going nowhere. No one will ever want to read it, he convinced himself. Nonetheless, he pressed on, working at the typewriter two hours a day.

What with the war on and all, the carousel was

shut down for the interim. The thousands killed, mercilessly, shamefully. The children go on playing, as if nothing were amiss. Oblivious to the incessant bombing all around them. When will these wars stop? What madness has infected those in charge?

The clown walks, melancholy, away, after the show for the children in the bombed out city. They were happy for an hour, before they go home to die.

Back to business. She was baking an apple pie, when the phone rang. "Hello, who is this?" but there was no answer on the telephone. Plastic and black, as she held the receiver to her ear, the telephone began to melt in her hand. Putting it down quickly, she noticed that it had dissolved into a small black puddle.

He was her special boy, his mother, dying endlessly before his eyes. A childhood of illness and remorse. His chest ripped open at four years old, for heart surgery. His mother almost didn't survive it, with illness of her own. His cousin, dying of leukemia, also at four, the same age as he. Darkened doorways that lead to endless nowhere, wandering on.

Meandering through life, he found solace in emptiness. Having been through every religion in the book, he had arrived at a place of peace within himself. Not needing any external group to validate him or legitimize him, he went on, a hermit, on his own. "Open a can of soup," he instructed himself.

Time to eat lunch. Now that he was back to three meals a day.

Morning used to be a nightmare, sitting in his chair in his bathrobe, reliving all the traumas of his life, over and over, again and again. Having gone beyond this, he now awoke with a start, ready to meet the day while it was still dark. He liked watching it get light out, the sun slowly rising and illuminating the world and everything in it.

One morning, he cheerfully emerged out onto the porch, ready for his daily walk, and slipped on the icy step, and fell right onto his tail bone. Ten days later, he had an intensely painful muscle spasm in his lower back, crippling him for a week. Spending his time reading, he went often to the typewriter, and clicked on the keys for two hours, to see what he might actually type. He decided not to stop typing to read what he had written, but went on, on and on, typing away.

"Enter, if you dare," warned the Guardian of the

Treasures. The captive audience moaned in disbelief. This tour of Hell was about to start off. Buttoning up their coats, as it had become suddenly cold, the participants in the tour bundled up, preparing themselves for whatever came next. If you were with them, what would you think you were about to experience?

Finishing up after supper, the single mother, puts her child to bed, reading him his favorite story, Hansel and Gretel. He is reading his experimental novel, Reap Violet Hiss, to inspire him before attempting himself to write. A cup of tea would be so nice right now, he thinks to himself. Marking his place in the book, he turns to look out the window. There are no stars out tonight.

In the morning, she wakes up, takes her coffee, and goes outside. The hills are rolling like waves in the ocean, and the landscape is lovely to look at. She thinks of him, no longer in her life, and wonders what he is doing right now. He has calmed down, at last, after the endless years of screaming in frustration at the moon, howling in despair, moaning in agony.

She doesn't know of his recovery to sanity, nor would she want to. They have both moved on, after an unhappy ill-conceived marriage. Now she was on her own, with the child to care for. He was alone with his obsessive thoughts, compulsive rituals, vagrant ways. It was left to them to determine their own lives, not looking to anyone but themselves to define themselves.

While the salamanders were sunning themselves upon a rock, he returned to his activities. There was nothing left to lose. He had tried every single option available to him. But what is the difference? No matter what happened, he would go on with his life, typing away at his invisible novel, filling in the words as he saw them. Nobody would believe this if they knew of it.

Rocking events protrude inside the brain of the recipient. Withholding nothing, he determined to not be dissuaded from his task. In the meantime, everything around him was exploding. Like a clean bottle of memories, he was entranced to leave the premises. Onward he went, into nothingness. But he was not lonely. The coughing from the next room interrupted his thoughts.

While the rice was cooking he prepared what was necessary for the rest of the meal. Opening his eyes, he saw before him a gigantic red cubicle which was occupied by a lone worker, slaving away at some unknown task. The receptacle was full of donuts, and his ears were ringing. The rice started to boil over, and awakened his instinct for survival. He left the room, exhausted.

Rescuing thoughts from the barrel of possibilities, they resorted to drastic measures. Why not open another can of thoughts? he wondered. The day had been extravagantly beautiful, too sunny for his taste, preferring as he did, dark rainy days, cloud-covered and anonymous. The bakery persisted in turning out sufficient goods for the populace. He wondered how long this could last.

"Wax the parlor floors, Martha, before you have your lunch," the lady of the house requested of her maid. The openings in the forest were inviting, so he wandering into the darkness of the trees. Having nothing better to do, he glanced at mushrooms growing on the stumps of fallen trees. Which ones were edible and which poisonous? he wondered, considering the risk of trying both.

She had put the child to bed, once again, and sat listening to the radio, knitting. The child slept and had a dream: He was wandering in a field of flowers, skipping along like a happy lamb, frolicking about. He woke up and was deeply disturbed to find himself back in his ordinary state and circumstances. Aware of their vulnerability, the flowers caved in on themselves, purposely shielding themselves in their leaves, until peace had been restored.

Violently seizing the oars, he rowed back to land, exhaling deeply while the water began to freeze around the little row boat. There was nothing to do but press on until reaching land, before mobility would no longer be a possibility. His constipation was finally relieved; the muscle spasm in his lower back has finally ended its painful visit. He ventured forth on his own, at last.

The dishes piled up in the sink, the recycling overflowing, he was drowning in his own life. He tried to catch up with all that needed doing, but he was always helplessly behind. Out on the lawn, people were screaming for no apparent reason, just a summer night in Hell, once again. Covering himself with his blanket, he resumed a state like that of a foetus, curled up in a ball under the covers.

Would no one come to rescue him from his despair?

Caught between a rock and a hard place, everyone experiences this trauma, that of just being awake in the world again, after the solace of sleep. While he slept, little elves invaded his space, cleaning up the dishes, the recycling, vacuuming the carpets, mopping the floors, putting everything away. When he woke up, he was amazed to find the results of this reorganizing of his life. He wondered how this had happened?

All the people went out to the harbor to see the ships come in. The children were especially excited at the sight of the huge clipper ships. Many people were there, and they expressed their desire to climb up on one of the boats, to inspect it. The lines to get in were so long, that many gave up, and simply went home. The characters in this story are necessarily obscure, since their forms are no longer accessible to me. I am making it up as I go along.

In the parlor, now that the floors were waxed, she served tea, to herself, and ate some delectable cakes. In the winter, when the roads are covered with snow, and movement is restricted, she would stay close to the fire, and read her ancient books. Anyone would do the same under the circumstances. The child was playing on the rug by the fire, warming himself in its hospitable flames.

Gum drops hanging from the ceiling gave a certain expressiveness to the room, and he found himself at a loss for words. A terrible thing for a writer. The words no longer appeared on the page to be simply filled in; he had to construct them out of his imagination onto the page. This was arduous work.

One must have suffered many days to write poetry, as Basho suggested.

Something about the cobwebs was so comforting, the presence of some spider long gone, left behind as a reminder of her coming and going again. The snow never came, at least not more than an inch. His friend called to offer consolation to him during this time of trial, having been sick with the dreaded disease, nearly dying, and no one to comfort him. Digging through life alone.

Allowing for reasonable excuses, they went on with their instructions, to carve away the extraneous elements of life, to dig down to the very bone, exposing the bare bones of existence, while the cigarettes smoke themselves, and the air conditioner hums its plaintive tune. He is writing a new novel, a sequel to the first, after forty-five years, returning to the source.

"Why not remember not to forget?" he said out loud. Remembering to take his pills, the necessary medication that keeps him alive, mentally and physically. Twenty pages into it, he kept writing, thinking of what to say, in the absence of any agenda. Working his brain until it buzzed. Opening the channels of perception into the realm of open possibilities.

They always did it this way, opening the channels of possibilities, at last, onto the field of their image-making, lost in the stars of endless night. Why they would do this is unclear, but they felt compelled to risk solidity in favor of flexibility. Closing their thoughts to anything but the present moment, they learned to be extravagant once again.

Chopping memories into pieces, and reassembling them into a collage of thoughts, encouraged him in his pursuit of Reality. Casting away extraneous things, he went to the heart of the matter, undeterred from anything but his obsession, bleak and buzzing, like a bee trapped under a glass.

"Walk in a straight line and do not stop for anything," instructed the Voice from Beyond.

Rebelling against any form of description, he exposed the thing itself, what lives between, within, and amongst us all, and all things. "Don't look back," the message on the wall warned. He refused to turn back, pressing on toward he knew not what. But, compelled to persist, he wrote on and on, refusing to stop until his work was finished.

This took the form of ejaculations of impulse, thoughts pulsing through his brain to his fingers, typing hysterically to keep up with his thoughts. The valve of the unconscious was open full throttle, and what came out, emerging from the eternal silence, was more than he had bargained for. He no longer had his wife or child, and was left to his own devices.

Warming up another solitary meal, he ate in contemplative silence, putting one forkful at a time into his waiting mouth, chewing and digesting each living morsel, until it became a part of himself.

Forgetting to close the window, the rain and wind poured into the room, as he rushed to the window to close it. There was nothing left of the meal, but bones and gristle on the empty plate of doom. What more could be expected?

The name Philippe Soupault, written on an index card to remind him of something. He couldn't remember what, exactly. The next day, having taken a piss, he sat down to work again at the typewriter. She had given up on life, neglecting to bathe or wash her hair. She had lost all hope, and had taken to drink. Barely able to care for the child, she hired a nanny, from her meek inheritance, so she could devote herself to relaxing.

What would become of them both, and the child? He was never permitted to see the boy, since the child's mother didn't trust him with her son. They never spoke anymore. The silence in this family was deafening. The child had begun to show signs of distress, developing several nervous tics out of anxiety. If only he could be a part of his child's life again! But she would not allow it.

Wait out the interval, and see what happens, like two ripe pears in a bowl, waiting to be eaten. His mind spun webs of words, meaningless, regardless, undressing language with polar wisdom, infatuated with the sun, collapsing amongst the lilies, exhumed like an inspected corpse, without any defense, or legal counsel. After all, it was his own life he was living, not someone else's.

Bring your own thoughts to this book, he imagined writing to the reader. Amidst the piles of books and papers, he dwelled in its midst, meeting his Muse every day for two hours. Not sure exactly what he was writing, since it mostly wrote itself. As his fingers clicked away at the typewriter keys, he felt a certain satisfaction, knowing the work was in progress.

Having immersed himself in the works of surrealism and dada, he sought to write in automatic writing, allowing his mind to bypass his conscious self, revealing instead the depths of the unconscious.

His mind would go in and out of sync; that is, sometimes he would write from his conscious mind, and other times from his unconscious mind. This pleasant variation of focus, he hoped, would engage the prospective, future reader in embracing the work as a whole.

All the literature he had absorbed and digested had become a part of his being and psyche. How would these influences issue forth in his own work? He tried desperately to find his own, unique voice. His poet friend had observed that, in fact, his "voice" had been consistent throughout his literary efforts, an observation that thrilled and terrified him simultaneously.

Had he, in fact, been one consistent person throughout his long life? Whereas he thought of himself as having led several lives in succession. So, the thought that he had in fact been present all along was a revelation. His voice, the same throughout his writings. How encouraging a thought that was! He had, in fact, lived several lives in one life, been several different persons along the way.

It was St. Valentine's Day, the anniversary of his mother's death when he was a mere fifteen years old, a tragedy that had haunted him his whole life. But now, he had gone beyond it all, moved ahead, with his dysfunctional, isolated existence. But, enough about him. Let's let the rainbows speak against the wall of hatred, and the doomed oppressors vacate their posts, immediately.

The narrator of this book is actually invisible. He cannot be seen or perceived. His omnipotence is questionable. He may have his own agendas, prejudices, impulses, which might disrupt the flow of the narrative. He will not speak of himself, except in emergencies. So, do not look for him, invisible voice that continues to write this book.

Outlandish, unscrupulous bandits had robbed him, although he escaped unscathed. Luckily he had reserves in the bank, so he recovered his finances quickly. But the trauma of being violated infected his unconscious mind; consciously, he had already forgotten the unpleasant incident, but his unconscious mind was in turmoil. Going for a walk in the park, he refreshed himself, invigorating, energizing his lazy limbs at last.

She absorbed her time knitting, and painting watercolors. These activities calmed her infested mind, going forever over the tragedies of her existence thus far. She lamented all that was lost, and needed someone to help her change her lightbulbs, that's how far gone she was at present. She never answered her telephone, so it was impossible to reach her. Her head was in the sand.

After all, what was lost is lost, and lamenting its loss doesn't help anyone. He had moved on with his isolated life, burning up the typewriter keys with his insane, wild rantings. Ostriches pull their heads out of the sand, and look around. The fast-talking radio announcer is concerned that the zebras are hiding behind the picket fences, all over town.

He would wrestle an octopus, if he could, or at least swim with one. This obsessive thought persisted to infect his weary brain. When there was nothing else to do, he went for a walk in the park, patting a friendly dog along the way. He felt vaguely human at last, breathing in the fresh air and enjoying the sunshine. People smiled at him, which warmed his cold, hard heart.

As long as children and animals trust me, I must be okay, he mused. Where have all the baby dolphins gone to play? Have you seen the arrested immigrant, beaten and tortured along the way?

Have you seen the thirteen thousand children killed in the war? Whose heart will bleed for this suffering innocence? The world whirls round its hectic pace, and no one pays any mind to these things.

Platypuses cavort together in the field, beckoning for food from the weary pilgrims who process through the bumbling town. The prize fighter is a vegetarian, surprisingly. The vestibule is empty now, they have all gone away. Intending to divert funds from one account into another, they forced clients to refuse their own funds. The economy was in a panic, and the Dow Jones was way down.

His meagre investments gave him comfort, in his advanced age. He had no friends, no family, not even an acquaintance to speak of. But he was never lonely, relying upon his imagination and ritualism to get him through the day. His daily walk helped him. The icy cold shower he took every morning bracing him, solidifying him, to meet the day ahead.

Venturing forth, she took her child to the park. She just missed seeing him, thankfully, since it would have been an unpleasant encounter. The child played on the swings, as she pushed him along.

There were toy boats on the pond, being sailed by small children. Then they went home again. This was an unusual outing for her, since she rarely left the house.

Imagination: what is it? What is it that keeps me writing this book, and keeps him typing away? Some inner compulsion, to say everything there is to say, but being aware of the necessary limitations such an enterprise entails. We press on, he and I, doing the bidding of our Muse. Amusing ourselves in the process, exulting in the ecstasy of language, at last.

He had returned to writing after an eight year

sabbatical: writer's block, you could call it. The devastations of his life had undone him, and he needed time to recover himself. The Wise Woman to whom he confided his struggles helped him to recover himself and his psyche. Her wisdom was like a warm, lovely bath, scented with spices and herbs.

He had felt it coming upon him once again, the urge to sit down and write. He could no longer hold a pen in his hand for long, due to his arthritis, so writing at the typewriter was the perfect solution.

He had never written directly on the typewriter before, preferring in the past to write in his illegible handwriting in numerous marble composition notebooks. These he would type up later on, to be able to present his work to others. It was a labor of love.

His writing was intentionally obscure, the better to confuse the prospective reader from knowing whatever he was writing about. The obscurity was a kind of shield to him against the world and its nonsense. He was hated universally, misrepresented by those with evil designs upon him. An object of derision and scorn. He had resigned himself to living his life as a hermit, dwelling deeply upon the mysteries of Life.

Heading for the hills, the rampant extroverts collide with a monstrosity of their own making. Sensible, like certain shoes, they wandered through the deserted fields of memory, discounting the cost of invisibility and its extravagance. Not dissuaded in thought, they began to perceive the inconsistencies of darkness with a yellow fork. Destiny had nothing to do with it, even though they wanted to succeed.

Nonetheless, they ran out of steam before reaching the goal.

I want to reverse life so that I will be getting younger instead of older, he thought to himself. And yet, he had embraced his aging process with open arms, enjoying the respect that strangers would give him, even women, holding a door open for him, out of respect for his age. The elongated necks of giraffes stretch out to full length to eat the tender leaves from the tops of trees.

Why wonder that the offerings of death instilled within my heart still burn with unceasing heat? he mused to himself. Open the doors of entrance, and engulf thyself in deep waters of contrition. Wend your weary way across the landscape that is melting into the waiting earth, and collapse into this dream of entrancement. Open the door and walk through before it's closing time. An overcoat and hat in winter is always a good idea. Wear it thick against the cold, impartial air that surrounds you.

Mistakenly, they asked for a raft to float across the river on; with sadness, they awakened the sympathy of the Watchers on the horizon, horizontally capsizing into bleak verticality, across the king-sized bed on which they floated, unabashed, naked as the day they were born. The vendors persisted in elucidating the dimensions of existence into colored paper strips, exactly where they wanted them.

Nothing could have been more absurd, actually.

Wandering on, endlessly, the clumped gaggles of people went morosely through the desert, entirely forgetting where they came from, processing with solemnity and pomp, as though nothing mattered anymore. Bleak, brief exhalations kept them going, sudden gasps at pretension's dismal doings, excused them from perplexing their minds' eyes from blinking. Overcast, the sky insisted on coming forward where it could be seen once more.

With a new clarity of purpose, he proposed to

continue whatever he was writing, explicit, indulgent, insensitive to collusion, purposed as if it were nonsense, exacting one's due in the form of caved-in chests of drawers, filled to overflowing with lingerie and other undergarments. The infections of destiny surrounded them on all sides, forgetting to watch the evening news, and proposing marriage to a beautiful cat.

A giant squid exuding its ink to defend itself. Basho writing a haiku, grinding his ink stone and making black ink. I, the narrator of this book, invisible, unscrupulous, inadvertent, distinguished, impress upon the reader how various, and vagrant, are the thoughts that come to me as I write these words. I will remain unknown, until the day springs eternal from the fountains of my consciousness. Really, the emphasis on art is entirely intriguing, from the vantage point of perception.

Tickling his funny bone, he laughed impulsively, and rendered himself instinct-variant, exuding the froth that bends all weary bones to excitement, drooling on as though there were all the time in the world. About-face, suddenly, turning toward the window, he coughed out a blob of phlegm, unsavory, and excused. His constipation had improved, thanks to a diet of prunes and raisin bran. Things were moving at last, thankfully.

In the interim, gladsome egrets resemble upholstery on a couch. Infested entrails curl around the starting point of the race. Two blooming pillars, wrapped around each other, engage in the endless civilization that obscures retinal vision. The farthings, on their way to exercise, demanded a total annihilation of all dissenters. There was nothing else to be done. They all went away, gloomily, convinced of their composure and excellence.

Solitary snails creep slowly along the way, leaving a trail of slime behind them. That is exactly how he felt about himself and his writing: He is a snail, leaving a trail of slime behind him. Will anyone ever even read this stuff? He wasn't concerned about this, and continued on as if nothing could ever stop him. In the meantime, countless grimaces overwhelm the station-master's brain. Better to stop before things get dangerous, he thought.

When the overblown entropy consumes vile laundry, you will inevitably succumb to stress and suffering. The agony of endurance, running the race set before one, only increases vital statistics.

Captivated by their own reflections, the populace convened for a special session, a meeting of the minds wherein they would establish and stabilize their wanderings once and for all. Conniving a scheme whereby all endings would become beginnings, he thought deeply on the implications of self-surrender in this way. Blooming voluptuously, the opulent flowers in the garden screamed significance, demanding the attention of those concerned. At the festival, several boys wound up drowning in the river, having been swept away by the current. Sadly, their bodies were never recovered. He put a record on the phonograph to play.

Preferring to work in silence, this was an unusual step for him to take. The Bach Orchestral Suites conducted by Casals provided inspiration to his mind. Variously listening, he pretended to be someone else, enticing romance through a tube of toothpaste. The bristles on the toothbrushes were lazy and limp, and needing to be replaced. He thought about this, and decided to do nothing about it.

Rising furiously, the mist exuded its sacred life onto the force-fed mutants, bearing down upon each other, casting away pride and controversy, enveloping mist that purifies sight and symbol. Captivated by the cloudy film. the envelopes, upon inspection, proved to be empty. Alas, nothing was found to substantiate the claim that malice had been afoot.

I wonder what all these emphases are about, thought he, whispering to himself politely. There was nothing to dissuade him from believing in the emptiness of reality. Cast away, like an old boot, he lingered in the vestibule of eternity, smiling halfway to the bank. Emptying his pockets, he found several small, smooth stones. He liked to hold them in his hand, to relieve stress. He liked their cold, hard feeling, squeezing his fingers around them.

Breathing heavily, she managed to lift the child onto her lap. He was a solemn child, unhappy and frustrated, neglected and ignored by his helpless mother. Random acts of kindness prevent obscurity of desire, opening new possibilities before our eyes. Remember to forget everything I ever knew, he advised himself, preparing to make a new beginning for himself at last.

Appalling, how people refuse to accept that other people exist beside themselves. The number on your ticket is what you will use to confirm the sale just accomplished. Proceed to the nearest exit, do not panic, do not run; proceed slowly and with confidence to the nearest exit. This is for your own safety and protection. We have an active shooter situation here, so please be careful. Collapsing on his couch, he quickly fell asleep until supper.

He had to cook for himself, so he could eat. He was not especially good at this, but managed to create something vaguely edible each night. She barely cooked at all, just feeding the child, and finishing his leftovers herself. This sufficed to keep them all alive, in one way or another. Food is as important as sleep, deep breathing is essential to bodily health. The state of one's mind is reflected in one's home. The environment one creates to live in is so crucial to happiness.

She had a trashy, redneck boyfriend, surprisingly, since she had always been a refined, sensitive soul. But he brought her some solace, bringing her the carcasses of dead animals he had hunted. So she would rustle up some squirrel stew for supper. The child ate everything she gave him, so eating was not a problem. She tended not to do her dishes, or to clean up after a meal, but left things piled up and rotting in the sink. There was nothing more she could do than this.

Emphasizing rationality, one begins to experience the profundity of Life, mesmerizingly beautiful, exhausting in its huge capacity, reflecting all that is and all that isn't. The endless way of all things, holding themselves together, an integrated whole, a being with multiple possibilities. After all, there were more sheep in the field than could be counted. But where is the shepherd to look after the sheep? Under a haystack, fast asleep.

The child had never been to school, what with his mother tending to him day and night as she was able. But he hadn't learned to speak, never mind to read or write. He was a solemn, silent child, awakening in his mother a tenderness that incapacitated her. She didn't know how to respond in love, so bitter was her cold, hard heart, from the misery that had been her life up until the present.

Bleeding hearts collude with one another to render useless the parting waves as they pass. Redundant telescopes produce infected garments, for the perpetrators of destiny to wear to their festive occasions. No one would believe the amount of garbage that was accumulated through the process with which they were engaged. Swallowing their pride, several representatives caved in on themselves, like tiny elves engaged in helping secretly.

What wonder then, that openings which take one across to the other side of night-time, ravage the pregnancy that is in progress, gestating the embryo, feeding the foetus, propelling through the emphasized desert, where playthings are tossed away, and no one enters backwards. Pleasing the mostly cruel companions, their wings were clipped and hair shaved off. No wonder no one dared to complain about anything.

Writing his four pages a day kept him busy. Coming up with ideas was dangerous; he would rather allow his unconscious mind to carry him away with itself. The birds in their cages sing their plaintive songs, appearing once a day to the visible realm, and disappearing after each singing. This was an unusual thing for him to believe, but there it was, right before his eyes. The birds gave him great happiness, as he would talk to them, and feed them.

He burned in his heart to see his child, but she would not allow it. What was so wrong with him that he didn't deserve to have time with the boy? This caused him endless grief and despair. He had had to learn to forget about it, since he had no power to change the situation. He steeled himself against the pain of Life, preferring to collapse into himself, and thus, arranging things in a manner suitable to his needs and passions.

Amphibious truckloads of chickens roll down the extended road toward the abyss. Not the abbess, notably. The dragons swirl in the depths, whirling in endless formation amidst th'encroaching chaos. Suddenly appearing, the playful dolphins wag their tails in happiness, but the buttered toast confides that it was cold. Taking exception to the general trend of things, one continued asking questions, without any answers.

He had a dream one night: He was in a field of tulips in Holland, windmills whirling round in circles. But suddenly, the flowers were all made out of butter, which melted in the noonday sun. He woke up in a sweat, panting, gasping for breath. He had not eaten that night, perhaps the cause of this nocturnal disturbance.

The empty organs pour out venom into the spotless eye of night. Since we have established that the envelopes were empty, what can be deduced concerning their purpose? Empty envelopes, empty vases, empty thoughts colliding like rampant rainbows, electrifying the wilderness until it's empty also.

Mainly concerned with the survival of their accomplishments, they went about their business as if nothing were the matter.

Cloud-dust wafted over the sleeping village, awakening him from his rest at last. Fondly, he thought of the day just passed, and how he had emptied his pockets to examine the several smooth small stones they contained. He was afraid to open his mail, leaving piles of it all around the house, unopened. Now and then, he would have a marathon, digging out from all his bills and junk mail. He never threw out anything.

Like blowing up a balloon, writing takes all your strength, taking your breath away. He understood this, and dedicated himself each day to his solemn, sacred task at the typewriter. The electrocutionist's picnic promises to be a captivating event, in which a storm will invade suddenly, sweeping away everything in its path. So run for cover, do not stand under a tree, for fear of lightning. An undercover cop, running for cover under a tree.

Captivating, like coffee ice cream, the underwear ran away with itself. Into the hinterlands we go, merrily capsizing like a swollen boat, or an aardvark lost at night. Poignant memories of the blast that shook our house once, or was it a brief earthquake? The room shook and moved before their eyes.

Comforting inhabitants move furniture around in the middle of the night, recklessly.

The narrator gets carried away sometimes, inventing noxious fumes which penetrate the neckties of the established partners in the firm of Watts, Watts, Watts, and Morgan, purveyors of fine goods from foreign lands. Discounts available for seniors, veterans, and active duty service people.

Asking for just a taste is like refining the fire of words to boiling point.

She had never toilet-trained the child, whose diapers needed changing on a regular basis. This she attended to stoically, bracing herself for the inevitable smells of decomposing matter. She had forgotten his age, which was just as well, since he defied all categories of development, living perpetually as a little child. Since he had never been taught to speak, he would make signs and gestures to indicate what he wanted. She had learned all his signals.

The child had a bad, rampant temper, and would burst into fits of howling and screaming for no apparent reason. When asked what was the matter? he would only cry out more painfully. She didn't know how to ease his discomfort, given his infantile condition. She fed, changed, and bathed him every day, since he was helpless to do these things for himself. Stranger things have happened, so this should not be a total surprise to anyone.

She amused herself, watching television while the child played on the floor before her. She rarely interacted with the child, leaving him to fend for himself, and amuse himself somehow. Theirs was a bleak story, largely left untold, due to the obstacles placed before them, insurmountable at best, disastrous at worst. Her family was far away, so she never had much support to help her with the child. Her life was bleak, in the little cottage where they lived.

Perhaps I will tell more about them in the future, but for now: radiant emphases persist in the palm of your hand, collapsing like buildings, demolished suddenly, crashing to the ground at once.

Had the people known what the purpose of existence is, they would not have wandered aimlessly through the wilderness, except for the mythology this provided scholars of the event.

Two pages typed. He would go on, slowly, enduring the silence out of which the words emerged, full-grown, onto the waiting white page. He was a good typist, fortunately, and could type as fast as his thoughts emerged, to catch them, like furry moths, on the screen door of the house on a summer night. Fortunately, he had everything more or less under control. He would take tea at three o'clock pm, with a chocolate covered biscuit, McVitie's Hobnobs.

Almost three pages typed. The literary Olympics in which he was engaged forced him to go beyond what he had thought were his capacities, plowing on through language into an oasis in the desert of refreshment, peace, and security. Swollen fingers, some allergic reaction to strawberries, perplexed him no end. He ran them under cold water at the sink; this seemed to get the swelling down a bit. A bowl of ice cubes came next.

Running out of steam, the pilgrims continued in their wanderings, looking for signs and miracles along the way. Death stalked them every day, along the route upon which they had set out. They huddled together against the cold winter blast. Stopping now and then to rest and eat some food, the little bit that they had. Flashing lights suddenly descended, surrounding them with violent sounds. It was a space ship, an interplanetary vehicle, in the field where they stood.

She had been to college, majoring in art history, although she never thought a moment about this subject now. She did her little watercolors, flowers mostly, and watched the child amusing himself. The redneck, trashy boyfriend would come to dinner often, and she would cook for him the dead animal carcasses that he brought her. It was a very primitive relationship, based on vulgar needs and wants, with no sophistication or brilliance to speak of.

Thoughtful alpacas chew their cud contentedly, as they graze in the field together. Thoughtful faces, betraying a sensitivity that is impressive in an animal.

Tender beings, feeding upon Life so beautifully together, a peaceable kingdom, envisioned by the prophet. He decided to clean up the house, doing the dishes, taking out the garbage and recycling, mopping the kitchen floor. These domestic duties gave him real satisfaction.

The flagrant vagrants again suit themselves with paper wrapping and cellophane and tape, conjuring leprechauns and lepers, their food festival, leaving behind all the mess they made. Laughing, they moved in concert through the village, entering without knocking. The procession was amazed, and relinquished all rights to future use of the material. Without looking, they moved steadily toward the center of the village green.

Gathering together to see what it was all about, the townspeople watched in amazement as butterflies flew suddenly out of a box, into the clear blue sky. The umbrellas were all open, nonetheless, against the possibility of rain, even though there was none. Time to take the temperature of the environment, the atmosphere, the sullen, sudden weather events that press upon us an obligation to look through the window before breaking it.

"The envelopes are on all the fruit trees," an obscure

phrase which he remembered from somewhere, lost in time, along with last week's laundry. Perhaps it was Gertrude Stein, of whom he had been always enamored. Fussing about nothing, he avoided doing what needed to be done, circulating in circles around the task before finally succumbing to doing it.

The silence surrounding him, he heard voices calling out his name, encouraging him in his quest for truth and reality. They call upon him to come with them, cavorting into the woods, to play with magikal faeries amongst the mossy fallen trees, dancing along to the piper's tune. But he could not go with them; he had grown too old, too set in his ways.

To even leave his house was an ordeal, dressing up to go out to the store for food, having to deal with the overwhelming sense of Reality, pressing its nose against the glass of his mind's heart.

The pilgrims chant as they process along the way, led by a flaming torch by night. They are content, not dependent upon any goal or destination: Pilgrims of the Present.

He followed the Complete Reality School of Taoism, emphasizing the importance of accepting what is, not trying to change it, but accommodating oneself to the patterns of Life. All the moments of his life, the little rituals and ceremonies, the blessings of objects and people, the endurance to run the race set before one, these things compelled him onward, hopeful in the face of hopelessness.

His little bit of wisdom strengthened him to overcome the traumas of his past, enabling him, through his work with the Wise Woman, to come to terms with and overcome any circumstance in which he might find himself. The herbs and concoctions she gave him were bitter to the taste, but long-lasting in their medicinal work. The bitterness of Life is what he contained within himself, working within him always like a burning coal.

Opening the letter once again, she found a note in it this time. Opening it, she began to read.

Someone had left her a small fortune, her father who had recently died, and she and the child could now live in the style to which they would so easily become accustomed. There was no way to communicate this to the boy, but her enthusiasm was contagious, and because of this, the child burst into endless fits of laughter.

Rolling thunder advanced upon the village, accompanied by occasional lightning. The child was frightened, so she tried to comfort him in his animal-like reactions and mood swings. No one could predict what his mood would be next. The storm poured down rain and hail, winds sweeping things away, the creek flooding, the streets covered with water.

Entropy infected the citizens, propelling them into savage remnants of further discussions about the weather, depending upon the time of day, season of the year, cycles of the moon. He felt susceptible to these subtle influences, attuning himself to the rhythm of the planets in their wanderings. Many brave men had tried before him, and women too, to climb the vast mountains of vain settlements where the fool dances upon the hills.

The other children in the village wondered about the child, kept indoors all his life, never meeting another child to play with, alone with his mother day and night. The people grew suspicious of the mother, alarmed that she would keep the child from normal growth and development. But this was her way of assuring that the child would never leave her. So she kept him tight within her grasp at all times, never leaving him for a moment.

The symmetry of the situation is invisible; playful salamanders sun themselves upon the hot rocks in the bright sunshine. Hippos play in the river, elephants washing themselves with their trunks. And even mighty horses, round the entire property, stroll along like eggplants in the noonday heat.

You wonder who I am, but I cannot tell you, since I don't know who I am myself.

Thus, the omnipotent narrator pops his own bubble, revealing himself as invisible once again, in case anyone has particular concerns to be addressed. Warranting intervention, one must come to terms with reality as an hypostatic union, in which all things cohere and maintain themselves. Can you hear me? he asked himself one evening. There was no answer forthcoming, after a long, pregnant silence.

The dream of tulips and windmills in Holland returned to him time and again. What did it mean? Should he take off on a trip to the Netherlands? Or merely stay put where he belongs? He had not had a real vacation in years, limited by his age now to driving locally only. He liked his solitary life, no one to answer to or take care of, only himself to tend to. This was a comforting feeling for him.

Like dredging for oil, he dug down deep within the well of his unconscious mind, giving vent to uninhibited, unabashed spontaneity as he wrote down these rampant thoughts on the typewriter. This gave him immediate duplication of his instincts, right onto the waiting white page of paper. Focusing on this effort took great resources from the depths of his being.

He had recently been taken under the wing of a poet even older than himself, who had encouraged him in perpetuating his singular voice in his writing. He had recommended him to his publisher, who had decided to take him on, publishing his experimental novel, Reap Violet Hiss, forty-five years after its writing. This was a great boon to his ego, crippled as it was by years of neglect and lack of recognition.

He had written all his life, accumulating eighteen manuscripts awaiting distribution out into the world. He had written faithfully, extravagantly, and wondered what to do with all these words? His editor had expressed an interest in publishing his first book of poems, Fresh

Window, and he eagerly awaited news of its production. Was he now to finally get the recognition for his work for which he had longed and yearned so many years?

His work was intentionally obscure, disguising what he really felt and thought with a garble and gaggle of meaningless language, posing as fiction and poetry. Now he was writing his second novel, and waited with baited breath to see the next sentence that would come out of him onto the paper page.

He longed for the child, pain-stricken that this boy was not accessible to him at all.

The owners of the club went off to Florida, and the opening was postponed indefinitely. More patrons went next door to the local bar to quench their thirst and frustration. No one obliged each other by introducing a captive audience to applaud the festivities, abounding throughout the carnival. Mardi Gras on parade, floats with muscled men cavorting, costumes outrageous and flipping sentences.

Why they would go on like this was beyond reasoning; their efforts were controlled by some external force, moving the pieces of living things as on a chess board. The people moved from one space to the next, moved by invisible hands that manipulated the pieces to its own purpose. He was thirsty, and drank a sip of the cold water he always kept near him, to refresh his mind and body.

His persistence was commendable: he never let up for a moment, draining the dregs of his imagination until there was nothing left to draw upon. Then he would stop, and not even read what he had written that day, or any other day. Merely moving on ahead, never looking back. This is what he found so fulfilling, to make a composition of words on the white paper page, for posterity to enjoy, giving him much hoped-for posthumous fame and recognition.

Nothing much ever happened in his life, so he had very little to write about. He would let his imagination run wild, inventing stories and episodes that were both thrilling and confusing. He felt that no one would ever be able to understand his work, as though he were writing in Chinese for an audience that did not speak the language. Idiosyncratic fragments, too obscure, too precious to relate to anybody but himself. Assured obsolescence.

He had worked diligently, over the three years he had

been in consultation with the Wise Woman, producing the eighteen manuscripts. Originally handwritten in marble composition notebooks, in his illegible penmanship, he transcribed each one into freshly typed pages. All this in two years of typing, forcing him to go beyond what he had previously thought were his own limitations.

Dead roses, piled up mercilessly upon the antique books which resided on the old pump organ. Flowers of evil, putrid and pungent, which he savored in their lifeless beauty. He always had fresh flowers, which would, when they had withered, be brought to the display on the organ for future appreciation. He could not bear to throw them out, but compulsively kept them all.

Extravagant hairdressers parade down the boulevard on Hairdressers' Appreciation Day, flaunting their scissors and clippers like passive weapons. The children were confused, afraid instinctively of scissors and haircuts. The mothers tried to console the children, but they were inconsolable. Moving on from there, they gathered up the kids and went home.

She painted watercolors, mostly of flowers which she

gathered from the wild fields outside the village. She would bring the child with her, and he would try to eat the flowers, which she did nothing to prevent. Where were the pilgrims now? Climbing the rocks on the land jutting out into the sea. They gathered snails just for the fun of it, before moving on along the seashore. Leaderless, they moved as a mass, one gigantic body, whose limbs were at unity with one another.

He had sent the child gifts, most recently a jack-in-the-box. This was an antique, vintage item. But it turned out not to even work, and was very dirty. So she threw it out in the garbage. He never knew what became of this well-meaning gift, so the fact that it was garbage never reached him. She usually refused the gifts he sent for the child, depriving him of many nice things.

She and the child would work on art projects together, drawing pictures with extra large crayons. The child's drawings never represented anything, but were mere scribbles of a twitching hand, drawn in haste without any thought at all. She drew simple scenes, a house with a tree, a swing, flowers growing all along, a smiling sun, and a little cloud.

Eating his raisin bran, he dribbled milk down his

chin onto the lapels of his flannel shirt. This was an occupational hazard which seemed unpreventable, even with the best of intentions. He drooled on occasion, when he ate, unable to keep the food in his mouth long enough to swallow it. As he had no one to impress, he didn't worry about his drooling.

Sounds from the other room, doors opening and closing, footsteps on the staircase, what was happening? Was his imagination running away with him at last? Was he to lose the little connection he had with reality entirely? Tenuous as a spider's web, his link to Life, but resilient in times of trouble. He had worked hard with the Wise Woman to achieve Reality awareness.

Living the kind of life that enabled him to be sensitive to everything around him absorbed his days and nights. Complete Reality was his goal and purpose; he would settle for nothing less. The piles of books which surrounded him were living testimony to the larger purposes of existence. He had absorbed much knowledge through his voluminous reading, clarifying for himself what he must do with his life at any given moment.

And now, a word from our sponsor: Fluttering

rainbows disintegrate, dissolving into perfect angels, creamy white, with peanut butter filling. For good measure, please do not forget to remember your umbrellas, in case of unwanted precipitation. But he loved rainy, gray days, since these suited his temperament more than bright sunny days. Not that he was gloomy, but he had a certain seriousness and solemnity that commanded respect.

This, however, he rarely received. His book had sold poorly, being too esoteric for the average reader of romance novels, or popular fiction. He was now writing, he thought, a new novel. It was still in its early stages, moving slowly like an elephant, from his mind onto the page. Allowing for influences beyond his control, he swept the floor and sat down to work.

Oblong entities exude violent thrusts into the mouth of night. Similar vestiges of hopelessness convey the thoughts of luminous noses, entering entirely into the frame of reference that had pressed itself upon one so firmly. Those Who Know let on that they were just pretending, never intending to move along so freely without the conventional restraints.

Moving slowly like an obelisk, camels proceed

through the desert of their minds, entering hesitantly into the Dangerous Zone. Mushrooms grow, phosphorescent, in a plethora of colors, on the mossy fallen trees in the forest outside the village. He liked the danger of picking these, not knowing which were edible and which poisonous, a kind of Russian roulette he would play with himself.

But it has all been said before, but maybe not. After all, the particular arrangements of words that he wrote had never occurred before in this precise form. A unique utterance, like those of the Oracle at Delphi. Prophetic utterances, poems in prose, sighs and moans too deep for words. The outlandish octopus presses the point home with passion and verve.

Open wounds still bleed: the thoughts of angels press themselves upon us, waking us from the uncomfortable sleep of deathliness. Awake at last, we learn the phrases of eternity, waltzing through the endless wasteland, thoughtfully awakening our unconscious mind, to productivity. The allowance made for frantic antics wastes time and money. Much more could be done with so little, really.

She would take the child down to the seashore,

where he would play in the sand, and collect seashells and small rocks, and pieces of polished glass. These were adventures for both of them. No one was on the beach that morning. So, they had the peaceful scene to themselves. She had brought lunch along, which they ate with enthusiasm. Then they just looked out at the sea, she with her arms around the child, whom she loved, despite her usual inability to show it.

He took his tea methodically, a ritual of peace, a haven from the tumult of the storm of life, an interval of solitude, to which he looked eagerly forward. He had regulated his existence into compartments, convenient units of experience, which gave him great assurance and comfort. Few people passed through his life, living off of his pension and social security as he did. He found it better not to have too many people in his life. It always ended badly.

Monstrous aberrations intrigued the vestal virgins to launch into space, expelling major disasters through a tube or funnel, into the depths of the mechanism. There seemed to be no way out, so they settled in for a long winter's nap. Previously, in the same vicinity, wolves devoured the chickens in the barnyard, one too many times. They could not be kept out. Instead of wasting time, they set out to invade the premises once again.

The bird was chirping. He wondered what the sound was, since he had never heard anything like it before. The bird was singing some enchanted song, fluttering notes like seeds planted in the earth. He felt like a summer solstice in his bones, even though it was mid-winter. Trying to explain what he was going through to anyone would be impossible. Captivated by circumstances, a prisoner in his own life, something in him yearned for something more.

He could not even explain it to himself; the wounds that had been festering for so many years had been opened and cleansed by the Wise Woman. Her tender healing touch restored him to himself. Yet she would always say that it had been he who had done the work. He would drive through the countryside to visit her, Amish buggies riding along the way.

What happened between them remains unknown to any but these two. Leaving the Wise Woman, after an hour with her, he couldn't remember his troubles; a certain freshness was about his mind, a clarity and lightness, as if his feet were three inches off the ground. He could almost fly away home after these sessions, not needing his old Cadillac to get there.

Taking a break from writing, he took time to put the chicken thighs into the oven, seasoning them first, and cutting away the unnecessary skin. Cutting up turnips to boil for supper. His humble meal, eaten with thoughtfulness, alone, as usual. He kept the radio on while he ate, listening to the thoughtful commentary. First, though, he would feed the birds and the cat. Then he would eat.

The solemn rituals of meals, mystical, fire and food combined to cook, something very primitive, something in our bones, some ancestral memory engrained in our brains. We relive the ritual every time we prepare and eat a meal. Focus on the food, his brain said to him as he ate. Eating with the birds, together in the dining room, was always a holy occasion. They ate together, he and the birds, with the cat in the kitchen in her corner.

Throngs of savage infants marauded through the village, slicing their way through the dense undergrowth, and not stopping. What he thought about that day was a mystery to him; he couldn't remember what he had thought about. Taking a long drink of ice cold water, he began to remember. He had thought about suicide, how he wouldn't, couldn't ever do it. Even at his worst moments, he managed to pull himself out of the hole he was in, and breathe again.

He liked that the chicken was in the oven cooking while he was writing; an interesting simultaneity of events, with deep poetic meaning. He was cooking his novel on the typewriter, while the chicken was written in the oven. What a marvelous state of affairs! Thankfully, at the moment there was peace; everything was under control, at last.

Plastic containers float, polluting the waters of ancestral lands. The outrage of the environment concerned him, although he didn't know what to do about it. He meticulously recycled everything, kept a compost pile in the backyard, used only cold water, flushed only for solid waste, tried to conserve energy, be a responsible citizen of the earth, which made him feel good.

When it was time to write, floods of endlessness came crashing down upon him, waking him from his reverie with sounds of crashing cymbals, exploding cannons, trusting simple things, asking simply to live. He felt the pain of the world, its suffering, hunger, homelessness, illness, death. His heart bled for the suffering of the war, helpless to do anything but grieve.

A Turnip Symphony: a salute to all root vegetables, so edible. Dark, from the bowels of earth to your kitchen, just in time to be cooked and eaten! Wondrous carrots, turnips, rutabagas, parsnips. All very yang, and alkaline, good for the bones and digestion. We boil them until tender, then add butter, salt and pepper, parsley, hot to the table, to be feasted upon by hungry feeders.

The brain presides over the body, lest the body preside over the brain. He followed a strict regimen, an austere, spartan lifestyle; an "ascetic aesthetic" of his own devising. No one knew about this; it was his secret lifestyle. Only washing and showering in ice cold water, taking his walk every day in all kinds of weather throughout the year and its seasons. At his age, he was pretty fit and healthy.

He compartmentalized his day, chopping it up into convenient units, digesting it like Digestive biscuits from Britain for his tea. He had been to the doctor, the dermatologist, who also went to the Wise Woman.

She froze off two precancerous growths on his head, examined his horrid toenails, and gave him a shot in the buttocks, to hopefully grow hair.

The compartments in his day were lined up in a row, like building blocks for a child's playtime. He liked their clean, crisp units, dividing life into digestible bites, so no one need be overwhelmed by circumstances beyond their control. Boiling the turnips, root vegetables, like in Godot; Didi and Gogo eat them out of their pockets, a spare radish is cherished like a gift.

Misfits, nondescripts, antelopes, converge upon the village green, conveying the sentiments of many of those concerned. They wallow in the mud together, like people always do, preferring to be dirty rather than clean. Public mud ponds, where people can play and romp in the mud. A new fad, a new sensation! Mud festivals all over the place, drowning in mud, together.

"Damnit," he said; he had to pee again. His frequent urination was better under control, since his doctor had put him on two medications for this problem. But it always interrupted his flow of thought, having to begin where he left off after he went upstairs to pee. Oh, the simple pleasures of life, nothing like a good piss to make one feel happy and relieved. It was the only thing his penis was good for anymore: urination. Having given up on the possibility of love, never mind sex, years ago, this flaccid member that dangled between his legs was as useful as a vestigial tail.

The name "Philippe Soupault" on an index card still intrigued him. He had digested several of this author's surrealist works, notably *The Magnetic Fields*, written with Andre Breton. This unique novel is the precursor to his own Reap Violet Hiss, prefiguring what he was to do one hundred years later. Strange juxtapositions of images, startling revelations, unreal events which emerge out of the depths of the unconscious mind of the writer.

He wondered what this connection was, this name that coursed through his brain like a river overflowing its banks. He ran to the window and looked out, expecting to see something unusual. But there was the street in front of his house, the neighbors who never spoke to each other. Except for one new neighbor, a young woman to whom he gave his first novel, to welcome her.

Like a river overflowing its banks, that was what his

writing was like. He enjoyed writing at the typewriter; the beautiful blank white page of paper slowly filled up with words, so many endless words.

"The envelopes are on all the fruit trees." He had remembered that yes, it was Gertrude Stein, in Four Saints in Three Acts, the startling opera that entranced him in his youth.

This sentence was pregnant with meaning to him; envelopes on fruit trees? How utterly fabulous, he thought. He could imagine harvesting envelopes from a tree in his garden, how convenient, for all those letters he never would write. Envelopes like lemons, growing spontaneously, delicious to lick when you close them. The lemon flavor lingers in your mouth, like a ripe avocado.

Mixing in images taken from nature, vegetation, plants, edible things, added a certain festivity to his writing. He would suddenly invent characters, scenes, dialogues, like operas within a novel. They would appear and disappear, melting into the paper like fresh laundry, waiting in the clothes drier to be taken out and carried upstairs. All these poured out of his fingers onto the clicking keys of the typewriter, miraculously flowing like blood onto the page, his blood.

Going to the Wise Woman for the first time in a month, since he had been sick and fallen and been robbed. They had been talking on the phone in the interim, but there was nothing like seeing her in person. He drove contentedly through the snowy fields lining the country road, horses and goats along the way. He listened to Brahms, The Alto Rhapsody which he dearly loved, and then the bright Serenade Number 2, one of his favorites.

The meaningful, mystical time they shared together was always deeply rewarding and profound. Dissecting the body of human experience and reassembling it, cleansed and stitched up nicely was a great work, which they did together, he and the Wise Woman. On the way home, he would always stop at the Amish store, to buy fresh cold cuts and produce for his weekly food. The Amish girls were so sweet and pure, innocent and joyful.

His one friend would always call at the most inconvenient times: when he was with his Muse, when he was making supper, when he was out for an appointment. He enjoyed his conversations with this friend, his only one, but at times the friend could be depressing, always moaning about the state of the world, about the atrocities of the war, about the government, and those running for office.

He was aware of these things, and kept abreast of the news, watching the Arab news channel in English, to keep his perspective on the war and world events. He felt compelled to be aware of the suffering of the world, embodying in his consciousness the pain experienced by others than himself. He was committed to the way of Compassion, having made a vow to Avalokiteshvara when the Tibetan monks had come to the small nearby city several years before.

He had gone in his black cassock and cape, having been an Anglican priest in his previous life. He intended to make a statement about himself, submitting to the ritual and ceremony of the Buddhist monks, with humility and faith. They placed the blessed white scarf around his neck and he felt a wave of warmth, a profound peace, flood through his being all at once. The others gathered there seemed surprised to see a priest attending such a ceremony.

But he had reached a point of universalism, acceptance that all ways to the Divine were the same, equal legitimate possibilities for living a fulfilling life. And yet, he submitted to none, although he clearly had. His life as a priest was a fulfilling failure, a series of disastrous, beautiful experiences, through which he was continually misunderstood and misrepresented, making him always the object of scorn, suspicion, and hostility.

He had left this all behind twenty years ago, after the scandal that ended his last parish ministry. This he never spoke of, nor even thought about anymore. He had been mistreated and cast out, having accepted his homosexuality after years of denial. This was a cataclysmic explosion, when his wife decided to "out" him to the parish. Ironically, he had been faithful to his marriage and priesthood, nonetheless he was expelled as if he had not been.

After several attempts at love, all of which were illusions, he had given up on such possibilities. The irony was that, now he was celibate, after all that being thrown out for being homosexual, all for nothing. Nonetheless, he was content in his being, feeling very much at one with himself, not needing any external validation or approval. He lived his life as a Taoist hermit.

He aspired to be a sage, following closely his Tao, with each tentative, thoughtful step. Being mindful and centered, so as not to be thrown off his horse by anything. He had survived being robbed, the disease, the fall, the muscle spasm, and still he was intact. He was humbled by these experiences, and brought back to a remembrance of his purpose. Indeed, he had begun his new novel in the midst of terrible pain and despair. It provided him a much needed outlet of expression.

The drive through the snowy fields was exhilarating: the endlessness of the fields on either side of the road, the fact of very few cars along the way, the beautiful old barn, so full of soul, which he blessed as he drove past it, giving him joy in his heart. He was blessed to be a blessing, sharing the Tao with everything in his path, recognizing the perfection in all that is, and all that isn't.

He blessed things for a living: acknowledging their usefulness, recognizing the divinity of inanimate objects, thanking the pot for its useful service, embracing the teapot for its daily use. This was his way of staying on the Way, the Tao that held his life together all these years. As he looked back on life, he had a certain bittersweet sorrowful joy, a satisfaction that he had always done the best he could. No doubt, there were many who disagreed, but their opinions no longer hurt him.

She was a committed, fundamentalist, evangelical Christian. The fact was, that she no longer went to church, or had any contact with fellow believers. Isolated with her beliefs in a vacuum, her faith began to falter. How could she believe in a God who had let her life be so miserable? She wrestled privately with her demons, and could not talk to anyone about this. Her reality began to melt away, and the bare skeleton of her being began to show itself.

The reality of her private life with the child was stifling at times. The brief relief which her unsavory boyfriend gave her didn't last very long. She had an emptiness, which her faith used to fill, but no longer did. Questions concerning beliefs assaulted her, and she was alone with these torments. This is why she had taken to drink, every night, glass after glass of cheap red wine in a box.

She would fall asleep on the couch in front of the television, and would have to get up to go to bed.

His mind had run dry; he only thought in abstract concepts, and had lost touch with tangible things. Even though he had followed his path, there was something missing. Perhaps it was the human element. The phones across the country weren't working, so he couldn't talk to his friend. This left the day feeling empty and useless. Caught in his own trap and cage, of his own devising, he inhabited an inhospitable world, with his home as his haven.

He had surrounded himself with beautiful things, artwork and endless books, decorative furnishings that lent an antique quality to his home. It was his museum, and his tomb. He intended to die there one day, in his bed, at peace with himself and Life. He had no fear of death now, although death had haunted him all his life. He had to stare it down, until he could see and perceive death in all its mystical beauty.

He looked forward, one day, to returning to the earth, to the Tao, becoming one with all things as he had been before his birth. A cessation of all striving and struggle, a hoped-for harbor in the midst of life. He no longer believed in a personal God, thinking it absurd to personify Life; he found comfort in the Tao, that which holds everything together, which cannot ultimately be named.

He had ceased to believe in the "soul" as an entity separate from the body, which existed before life, and which continues after death. This concept he attributed to Plotinus, and through him into Christian theology. He knew, from his Jewish background, that Jews believe in a single, psychosomatic being that is a human, body and mind united in a single organism.

He knew also, that Judaism generally does not believe in life after death, but has the comforting notion of "resting with one's ancestors." He could use a rest, although his whole life was a rest. Retired for twenty years after his cataclysm, his time was his own to devise. He kept his routines and rituals strictly, as if his life depended on it, which it did. He knew that he needed structure, so he followed his rigid schedule religiously.

Meanwhile, the pilgrims had reached the grotto, the shrine that was their first stop on their pilgrimage. They knelt in the night air, rapturously, candles burning, and ecstatic smiles on their tear-streaked cheeks. He knew nothing of this, and wouldn't have participated if he had. The townspeople tolerated this display of religious enthusiasm, because it brought business to the village.

Nearby, flaming torches burned, foxes were released, the hunt had begun. The hounds melted into the hillside as the horses fell on top of one another. The entire scene was a mistake, and had to be performed all over again. Was this a movie set, or the setting of a novel? The story continues, regardless. Infants crawl through the wreckage, incurring the wrath of the undertakers.

Several vegetables got wind of the announcement and rebelled against their storekeepers, marauding like a mob, to tackle and attack the owner. He struggled for his life, and eventually succumbed to wounds. In the middle of the night, rude awakeners disturbed the sleep of the populace, pouring molasses on their cars, and feathers from a pillow. These pranks were not appreciated.

Over the telephone, he heard his friend's voice. Apparently, service had been restored. Communication was now possible, although he had to call the friend back, since he was writing.

"Cash in your chips" was the announcement made at the casino in Hell, where the ramparts' red glare overwhelms the possibilities of enthusiasm, over the counter.

Yesterday, they might have come back again, but they had lost their way home. Foundlings flounder through the jungle, running backwards to attain the useful goal. The funeral director who lives down the block will help him one day with his death plans. He hopefully planned his own funeral, with pertinent texts and music to soothe the day.

Thankfully, he planned on living a very long time, so he was in no hurry to finish things, but took his time, methodically working away at all his tasks. He believed that if he was faithful to his work, it would ultimately be discovered, recognized, and published. This had in fact happened. And it was utterly exhilarating for him. He was humbled and moved deeply by this success.

He had given away all his copies of his book, awaiting a new shipment of them coming soon. He liked giving them away to significant people in his life, people who had been a help to him along the way. Hoping they would read his book, he wondered how they would deal with it, "difficult" as it was. But he was delighted that they could make sense of it, rolling around in his words.

He had given up cigarettes three years before, substituting vaping nicotine instead. This came in delightful flavors, pleasuring his palette, and awakening his mind, without the cancer. He also had his medical marijuana, which kept him content and at peace. He never touched liquor, and hadn't for many years. He liked it this way: his mind was his own, awakened and alert.

He had to type his four pages a day, this was how he defined his existence. It was how he fulfilled his responsibility to his Muse. And he found deep satisfaction in this obedience. Almost time to make supper again, the daily ritual of fire and food. Feeding the hungry pilgrims in their grief. Feeding one's own stomach. He ate out of guilt, knowing how they were starving in the war.

He had begun reading How To Write, by Gertrude Stein. At her most difficult, her incomprehensible writing, presumably to teach one how to write, was a delight to him. He found such pleasure and satisfaction in her dense, mellifluous language. It would be this book that would teach him how to write, from the source herself. He would learn a new way to use language, as he assembled his thoughts and ideas in his writing.

Startled into wakefulness, the envelopes on the fruit trees blossomed, giving forth an exquisite scent, poems pouring out of them, haiku, for the digestion. The cataclysm had abated momentarily, and everyone picked up their things and walked out the door. Help was coming in the form of diseased members, coughing up phlegm into their waiting handkerchiefs. The disease was rampant.

He had gotten sick, and thought he was dying, not knowing what was happening to him. He finally found out that he had the disease, which he had taken for a mental breakdown after he was robbed. He ached all over, especially in his legs and head. No one to help him or take care of him.

He had recovered slowly, and began his daily walks again. Slowly he built up his strength.

The traumas of being robbed, catching the disease, falling on his steps, having a painful muscle spasm, all contributed to his weakening. The wind had gone out of his sails. He began in earnest to recover himself. Keeping to his responsibilities helped him to recover. If only he had more people in his life, he would be surrounded with love and support. But this was not in the cards for him.

Weaklings rampage through the library, eating books, and devouring newspapers and magazines. They do not stop until everything is eaten. This strengthens them in their pursuit of their destiny. Like a dream, where you are making or trying to make a phone call to someone who never answers. You don't know who this is, or why you are calling them.

Like force-feeding someone on a hunger strike, the invading armies took captives prisoner, and locked them in cells for interrogation. There were merciless beatings, torture, degradation. And the world chose to look away. His heart bled daily for the suffering of the war. 30,000 killed, 15,000 children dead, 1,000 infantile amputations, mostly without anesthetic.

He could barely focus on his writing. The pain of the world ate away at his heart. He watched the news for an hour a day; this was all he could handle of such suffering. He amused himself with music, reading, eating, cooking. There was much to Life yet to be experienced. Although he lived in a vacuum, in emptiness where he was happiest.

The weekly, Friday ritual of sorting out his pills for the week came suddenly upon him. Opening the jars of medication, he placed each pill gently in their compartments, neatly arranging them to get him through the week. He was thankful for his pills, his little friends, who helped him through the days. He took numerous vitamins and supplements also, which filled out the pill boxes nicely.

Gluing together the pieces of the jigsaw puzzle, the children advanced their agenda, peeling away thoughts like lemons, to quote a phrase. The incipient monsters gather ceremoniously upon the rocky shore, testing their test tubes with valor and anticipation. Never were such beings assembled in one place. To do their work, monstrous work, was their purpose and intention.

Cavorting like various fruits, no one entered the amusement park after dark, for fear of ghostly presences, alert in the night time for revels and torment. Making out on the lawn, the teenagers got caught with their pants down. Everyone ran for the hills, exploding parcels along the difficult way. All seemed certain of their wintry thoughts, frozen mid-stream, like apricots.

Indelible memories persist like waiting vestibules, melting and frozen, dark and whitely, pressing on with vigor toward the empty rainbows colliding with scissors. Cauliflower steamed tends to crumble.

After all, it was the thought that you had before you read this, and the thought you are having as you read this, that really counts in the end.

Patriotic citizens parade sideways through the vacant streets, enduring the hecklers who taunt them along the way. You should not have forgotten to message your thoughts to the writer, but he would wonder at the amazing things you think of. Asking the thoughts of a stranger would be interesting. What people think about while they are going about the tasks of the day. And never forget to stop at stop signs.

He wanted to go on writing for another half hour, but he couldn't think of anything to write. Almost time to make supper, angel hair with garlic, herbs and grated cheese. He strained his brain to think of meals to make. It was challenging just cooking for himself. He had to make small amounts of food, just enough for one meal for himself. He liked cooking, and enjoyed eating the food he cooked.

His dark secret: he had three daughters from a previous marriage, none of whom spoke to him.

This was a source of extreme agony for him. His heart was ripped out of his chest over this tragedy.

They would speak to him now and then, but would always wind up getting angry or annoyed at him. He had always tried to be a good, loving, nurturing father to them, but nothing seemed sufficient for them to retain good relations with him.

He was just too much for them to deal with. It wasn't his fault that he had had such a horrible month; he had told them of his misfortunes, but they just didn't seem to care. When he claimed that he deserved better than this, they expressed their belief that he did not. Shattered by this rejection and abandonment, he drew upon deep resources of his being, not to come utterly unraveled over this.

His work with the Wise Woman had steeled him against such onslaughts of hostility. He was grounded in his being, in his Tao. Not even this disappointment would undo him. Faithfully persisting, he went through his days, not allowing himself to think about unpleasant things, but shielding himself from the harm that hostility could do to him. He was secure in himself. He had been the best father he could be, and if his daughters didn't need him, he would go on without them.

Hearkening to the beat of a different drummer, he went about his days mindfully, intentionally, doing the best he could. He found meaning in even the littlest tasks, tiny moments that would seem insignificant to most people entranced him, like a good, old black and white movie. Opening a can of beans became a solemn ritual. Waking up late today, at 6:30 instead of his usual 5:30, he didn't have time to read as he usually did.

He had to make fresh coffee, since what was left in the pot was from yesterday, undrinkable and flat. He put the heavy cream into the coffee, watching the dragons form and swirl in the abyss of the brown liquid. Then the first sacred sip, touching his lips, awakening him to the day, embracing his thoughts and body with comfort and encouragement. He only had one cup of coffee now, having previously had six cups a day.

Now he only drank water, beautiful ice cold water in his special pink plastic water bottle. He loved the invigorating sensation of the icy water filling his mouth and flooding down his throat. He had been to the vape shop, and was recommended a flavor that was predominantly pineapple, his favorite. Milk and cider and flowers at the supermarket. He always had fresh flowers in his kitchen on the island.

Vague semblances, of his previous book of poems, fluttered about his head, confessing rumors that no one believed anyway. The remnants of divisiveness invaded the arctic caverns about which the infested rumors fluttered, like butterflies. No one believed anything anymore, and the churches were all closed for repairs. The congregants melted into their fears of death, with no escape.

He had come to see that the world religions came about as an antidote to death, telling their believers that, in one way or another, they could elude death, and their souls would go to some heavenly paradise, or be reincarnated in another form and shape. It was, in fact, his lifelong terror of death that had led him through his spiritual quest and journey.

The Church had provided an easy answer to this problem: Trust in Jesus Christ as your Lord and Savior, and get to go to heaven! What an amazing deal! But it nearly destroyed his life. His vision of Jesus one morning as he woke up in a pool of his bodily fluids was a drug and alcohol induced delusion. Yet he found in Anglicanism the answers to all his questions. He did not know at the time that he was being brainwashed and initiated into a cult, a very established one at that.

And yet he was captivated: the gothic architecture, the Tiffany stained glass windows, the choir of men and boys, the canticles sung to Anglican chant, the incense, the rituals, the ceremonies, the dignity, all a pompous show, signifying nothing. His sermons would ramble on, leaving the congregation lost in a mist of words, a pantheistic vision of the divine in everything!

He had returned to contemplative practice, drawing upon the Pseudo-Dionysius, the Cloud of Unknowing, Julian of Norwich, Hildegarde of Bingen, Meister Eckhart, combined with his growing interest in Taoism and Buddhism. He led a School of Contemplative Prayer in his parish, drawing participants from a wide range of religious, and nonreligious backgrounds, to practice meditation in the medieval Christian tradition.

A faithful little flock would come to these gatherings. He would teach from the contemplative literature, and then they would practice contemplation. He would ring the Sanctus bell to begin and end. They would then do a walking meditation, slowly moving, mindfully, up and down the center aisle of the church. This was a beautiful thing to do together, nonetheless, the parishioners were alarmed.

What was this new teaching? Was this some occult practice, forbidden and dangerous? When he appeared on the front page of the local newspaper in his black cassock, cape, and skull cap, seated on his meditation cushions, the community went into panic. How could they stop these pagans from entering their holy place, violating its sanctity?

And he was teaching that contemplation was the way to salvation, union with the divine, holiness in the moment, experienced reality of transcendence in the immanent present. Not some mere lip service to creeds and doctrines, but entering into the reality of Ultimacy oneself here and now. This was very threatening to many of the parish. They were set in their ways, and were content to have their little bit of religion, dished out in bite-sized portions one morning a week.

The tragedy was, that his "little flock" of true believers who had entered onto the mystical way with him, were only a small minority; the others would prevail one way or another. Several had left the church, taking their money with them, and worked remotely to find a way to get him out of the church. When his wife finally broke down, revealing his homosexuality to another parishioner, they finally had the weapon they needed to drive him out of town.

By the next morning, the news of his "outing" had reached through the diocese and village. A stalwart parishioner circulated a petition for his removal throughout the town, accusing him of "conduct unbecoming a member of the clergy." There had been no such conduct! The bishop was brought up to meet with the vestry, to secure his removal. The Standing Committee of the Diocese would meet to seal his final censure and inhibition.

He was given one month to move out of the parish rectory, where he lived with his then wife and three daughters. He escaped to the next town, fearing for his life, exiled from his marriage, children, home, vocation and ministry. He was inhibited from exercising his ministry as an Anglican priest, withdrawing into a hidden, contemplative cave, to lick his wounds and recover his psyche. His daughters had also suffered through this, having it known about their father throughout their schools.

If only the priest who prepared him for entry into the Church had not told him that he would have to renounce his homosexuality or bisexuality, as these were incompatible with the Christian life. Instead of bringing life to him, this only brought death. He thought Jesus would free him of this inclination, and trusted he had been healed. Thus, he proceeded to lose all his hair, in circular patches, looking like a chemotherapy patient. His alopecia had resurfaced.

The internal turmoil this created in him was immense; he was split in half, believing he had been "healed," and at the same time being tempted constantly by his true inclination. He took out his anger and frustration on his wife, screaming at her for hours at a time over the slightest little thing. His daughters would cower in fear in their rooms, while he would vent his spleen.

No doubt, this was part of why they did not speak to him now, traumatized by his insane ravings, the memories of which persisted in their brains. Could they ever forgive him? The fact that he had been diagnosed with Complex PTSD did not excuse him. But uncontrolled screaming is a chief characteristic of this disease. He had tried to explain this to them, that he literally was not in control of himself, captivated by this illness.

His tumultuous relationships throughout his life had been crippled and warped by his unfortunate sickness. This was why he kept to himself now, more than ever. Relationships of any kind just never seemed to work for him. Now he had one friend, and that was comfortable and practicable.

He valued this friend as a sounding board for his thoughts and events. They had a sympathetic friendship, which brought them both comfort and reassurance.

But he had nurtured the daughters from their birth through their childhoods, teaching them to talk, to read, to write; reading them stories he had collected into a major gathering of children's books. He read them The Real Mother Goose, singing the rhymes to tunes he made up himself, simple folk ditties that delighted the girls as he sang to them.

The Beatrix Potter books, with all his special voices for the characters, funny, satirical British accents to emphasize and enliven the stories with fierce whimsy and fun. The real Pooh books, the stories and the poems, were treasures to be cherished. The Rutabaga Stories of Sandburg, The Just So Stories of Kipling were also valued delights.

Such nurturing, nourishing love, to lead to such a pass as this! The silence of their voices was deafening, and he had to steel himself with all his strength to withstand and bear it. He saw this as a terrible betrayal and abandonment. And he could not wrap his brain around it. Why did they have such hostility toward him, nearly a kind of hatred?

He had apologized to them and to their mother, and hoped that this would lead to better relations between them all. But nothing seemed to change. He had given up on them, and released them to Life, to provide for them, and lead them, one day, back to him again. There was nothing more he could do about it, so he accepted the situation that he could not change, and went on with life.

Still, the violin lessons for the eldest daughter, the ballet lessons for the middle girl, and the tennis matches for the youngest, haunted his memory with visions of happier times, when life was young and there was still hope for the future, and enjoyment in the present. Those bittersweet memories consoled and tormented him simultaneously. He tried not to think about upsetting things, but now and then, they would return to him, like a strange dream.

She had agreed that the child could live with him. He took his son to his bosom, and dedicated his life to training the child. He had never been taught to speak, read, or write. He still wore diapers, and needed to be trained in all these things. Being prone to fits of passion, rage, and anger, the child presented a serious challenge to the father. But he took this on willingly, and set himself to train the child to be a human being.

Learning to talk, the child formed words slowly and carefully, listening to the father as he patiently spoke each single word. The process was arduous, and time-consuming, but he could think of nothing more worth doing with his life. This gave him little time to write, which he had to do while the child was asleep. This was his time to contain himself, to reassemble himself, after the chaos of the day.

Mornings were the worst time. The child was like a raw wound, bleeding emotions, panicking over any little thing, being thrown into a tumult too easily. He had to stabilize the child, encouraging him to grow up into a proud, young person. He tried sending the child to school, but there were always problems. The child could not seem to learn like other children.

Doctors, therapists, social workers were consulted, to determine what the child was capable of doing and being. Tests were administered, and the results pointed to an incapacitated child, whose development had been stunted and compromised. The mother's neglect and abandonment of the child had caused him profound distress. The father would have to be both father and mother to the child.

Their life together was alternately peaceful and tumultuous. The child, now talking, bemoaned his painful lot in life, complaining of his misery to his father, who felt helpless to change anything. They were joined together at the hip, not being sure of where one ended and the other began. They knew each other's thoughts before speaking. They cultivated depth of experience between them.

She now, alone, could revert into her depression, solitary moans too deep for words. She had been a modern dancer, taking lessons and performing with a small dance company. This had given her much satisfaction. But that was long ago. Now she didn't dance, but sat on her couch, wrapped in an afghan, watching television, meaningless television, endlessly.

She had little contact with the child then, embarrassed for him to see her messy house, which had gone to seed, blossoming garbage and recycling all over the kitchen, dishes piled up, waiting to be washed. A refrigerator filled with half-rotten food, bursting at the seams. A freezer so packed and frozen over you could not tell what was in it.

He liked living with the child, whom he thought of as his "little puppy dog," endeared to his heart, despite the overwhelming challenges of life together. The child had to learn how to eat with a fork, knife, and spoon, and to observe certain minimal table manners. Often food was spilled and overturned, needing to be cleaned up. But most of the food went into the child's waiting mouth.

He now had to cook for two; this gave him more incentive to come up with creative meals.

The child ate most of what he cooked, refusing to eat fish. This was a source of great grievance to the father, since he loved cooking and eating catfish. Tonight it would be the steak he took out of the freezer that morning. This would be sufficient for them both.

He had to do everything for the child, who was not

inclined to help with chores around the house. He had accepted this as his karma, that the child's care would occupy him for the rest of his natural life. This gave him a real purpose and incentive to try his best to make a life for the two of them, together in this old house of theirs. This house which had become their home.

She had grown up in a big house that her grandfather had built. Her mother proceeded over the years to fill the entire house with garbage. She forced out her husband and children, who could no longer live in such surroundings. There was a path a foot wide, surrounded on either side by piles of boxes and newspapers piled up to the ceiling. This path led up the stairs to her mother's bed, where the old grandmother lay, deluded and senile.

The kitchen was filled with rotting garbage and cast-away food. It would take all day to prepare a meal, with them waiting anxiously on the balcony to eat. Her mother was utterly dysfunctional, never showered or bathed, never changed her clothes. Just as she had turned out to be presently. History repeats itself in families, the dysfunction of parents passed on to their children, like a Greek tragedy.

Like finding the perfect letter to correct a misspelled word, life goes on, despite our failures. The characters in this novel present themselves to me as I write about them, giving me a sense of who they really are, and what they are about. They are so like real life that I begin to wonder whether or not they exist? In reality, everything exists, so in fiction, everything exists.

Blooming flowers, exuding their potent fragrance, speak in syllables, audible only to the sensitive ear, preferably equipped with hearing aids. The syllables for words, which send out obscure messages, like telegrams, expressing cosmic thoughts, melting into vocabularies of unheard tongues. Lashing out like lightning, they suddenly appear and then disappear at once.

Freshened memories, dividing like rainbows, mix entropy with distinctiveness, forming a performance of disconnected episodes, which tremble like moths fluttering around a porch light that has been left on for too many days. Has the neighbor abandoned his house? His wife left him for his best friend, he lost his job, and disappeared with his four-year-old son into the night. What has become of them? A mystery in the neighborhood.

Entering backwards, the letters of the alphabet dance in concentric circles, advancing their plan to dominate the world, one poem at a time. They would infect and infest the brains of waiting writers, with visions of contentment and abandonment. No one listened to them anymore. So the letters marched off in formation, taking their business to the next town, shaking the dust off of their feet.

He had written for almost two hours, completing his appointed portion for the day's work. This gave him a feeling of real satisfaction, knowing that he was writing his best work. Slaving away at the typewriter, the keys danced beneath his fingers, expressing his moods and ideas in concrete terms. Sixty-four pages, and counting. He had really brought about what he had planned for.

The work was taking shape, and formed itself according to divine commandments, led mystically through his writing process as if led by some unseen hand. Drawing him ever onward, he kept his nose to the grindstone, writing his brains out day and night until the work was finished. It must be as long as his first novel, and as good and rich in diversity of material.

Sleeping, the child found solace in slumber,

dreaming of a better life for himself. The father ached in his being, to give the child a way to find happiness. His heart bled gobs of clotted blood for his only precious son. He gave everything he had to him, and made his child's happiness more important than his own. He did everything for the child, helping him to slowly grow up at last.

Like looking out a window in midwinter to see if there is snow, he looked toward the future, unknown and unprepared, for a vision of what their life might be like together down the road. Would it ever change? Would it ever get better? These thoughts impressed themselves upon his consciousness, awakening him to possibilities beyond what either of them might ever have hoped for. This consoled him, as they lived their desperate lives together.

The fact is that he was writing a novel about the same things written in this present book. This may seem surprising, but in fact, it is the most normal thing possible. There is a fearful symmetry in all this, somehow bleeding between reality and fiction. The boundaries are increasingly blurry, and no one knows anymore which is the right and which the left. So people moved slowly, rethinking their motives and hesitating at every step.

I, the omnipotent author, am writing a novel about someone who is writing a novel about the same things this novel is about. Does he know that I exist? That I am writing about him? That I know his thoughts, his every move? Would it matter to him? Does it matter to me? I am the invisible voice that speaks these words, anonymously, having gleaned thoughts of them.

I shall reveal nothing of myself in all of this, preferring to keep a safe distance between myself and the prospective reader. I will not write about myself, or anyone close to me. What I know about the people in this book I will not hesitate to reveal, in all its gory glory. That is the task I have assumed. It has been given to me to pursue this work, and I shall see it to completion.

He wore brown Birkenstocks, black socks, boxer shorts, corduroy pants, black long sleeve tee shirt, and a plaid flannel shirt on top. He had misplaced his characteristic black beanie. He liked the look he had cultivated, the esoteric poet and writer. He wore round tortoise reading glasses, which he fancied made him look like Anton Webern. He adored this composer's minimal music, barely audible at times, then suddenly violent. His kind of music.

Flashing lights blink, emphasizing the difference between black and gray, turning to white, in the envelope of night, surrounding the excess crowds converging upon the village green. Passers-by laughed to see such sport, and the dish ran away with the spoon. The envelope of night is opening, revealing hidden thoughts and desires, which converge upon the sleeping victim, surrounded by flaming torches. They will peacefully pass by, giving their blessings upon this chosen one.

Sipping his three-o'clock tea, he was invigorated, while the emphases of delusion granted perfect perception to the deluded masses, wandering hopelessly on. The pilgrims persisted in their bleak rituals, contorting themselves into the shapes of the letters of the alphabet, spelling out mystical words signifying nothing. He knew nothing of all this, nor would he have cared if he did.

Palliative care was provided to those in serious need of help, and the ambulances brought a steady stream into the hospitals. This was the endless war, drooling endlessly on, with no hope of relief. The million and a half people who had gathered in the city for safety were now at risk of attack. What could be done to protect these people? To where could they be moved safely?

After his cataclysm, once the marriage had fallen apart, he had "played the field," as a newly freed man. Following his particular taste, he pursued unhealthy relationships with younger men; in these, he was often easily taken advantage of for drugs and money. Infatuated easily by a pretty face, he fell for these unworthy recipients of his love, and was tragically mistreated.

It was through these encounters that he fell into the use of drugs; first marijuana and hashish, then cocaine, heroin, methamphetamine, et al. It was particularly with his one young companion that he entered into the use of heroin. It was a religious ritual they performed together, the companion administering the injection into his arm.

He would swoon as the drug entered his vein, and collapse into a puddle of pure bliss. But this companion eventually got him addicted, and their use became daily. He wrote a poem about this:

LOVE
My bulging vein
waits for you
to plunge
the needle in.

The erotic component of this was unmistakable; the ritual usually involved sex in one form or another, and the entire situation was utterly unsustainable. Thankfully, this companion went elsewhere, and left him to recover his life again. He was prone to unhealthy relationships, where both parties took advantage of each other, out of their own interests.

After several of these disappointing heartbreaks, he had renounced love in all its forms. Only for his son would he harbor such caring emotions. He had given his love away too many times, and gotten only grief in return, mingled, no doubt, with occasional moments of ecstasy. Was it worth the trouble? He had decisively decided NO!

He would guard his heart, and keep it to himself and his son. His middle daughter had become very hostile to him, calling him and screaming at him for a half an hour. This was terribly distressing to him, and he decided to cut off communication with her. Then he decided to write her a letter, telling her how he felt about the situation. She wrote back a very hostile note, saying that she needed to protect herself from him. He had needed to protect himself from her!

His daughters were a source of endless distress to him; they refused to have any contact with the son, who had grown up now, and as a teenager, had become addicted to methamphetamine. His father struggled to help the boy, but nothing seemed to work. The boy had found a synthetic happiness, which nothing else in life seemed to give him. An artificial paradise, shot into his veins, or smoked out of a pipe. The boy had gotten to such a pass that he could not even shoot himself up anymore.

This useless addiction infected their life together like a cancer, slowly eating away at them both. He was in despair, not wanting to evict his son, helpless as he was. So they soldiered on together, making the best of things as they were. Trying to construct a life together, based on more than intoxication with illegal substances. There had to be more to life than this.

The methamphetamine helped to boy to feel almost human, which he never did feel without it. His mood was usually so low that the meth perked him up, enlivening his mind, awakening him again. He desperately needed to find a way to feel human without this dreadful drug. It had taken over his life, and the life of the father, since this is what they lived with.

The father had recovered from his drug use, and encouraged his son to do the same, and finally "get clean." The boy had made several attempts at this, but always wound up relapsing. The father was determined that this would be the end of his active addiction. He would insist that the boy quit and get clean. The boy wanted to do this, but didn't know if he could manage it.

They would struggle through it together, the father never wishing to abandon his son, as his own father had abandoned him. After his mother's devastating death when he was fifteen, his father wanted to remarry; but his prospective wife refused to marry him if his son was living with them. So, his father sent him out into the world at seventeen, totally unprepared to face life on his own.

He resolved that he would never "throw out" his son, his beloved only-begotten son. He would never traumatize a child the way he had been traumatized by his father. Blank checks handed out to strangers in the middle of a snowstorm. Arranging tables for the community dinner. Taking out meals to eat at home. The church suppers. How Sunday mornings were a preparation for church, dressing the children to appear the perfect family.

Now Sundays were a quiet contemplative time. "Sunday Morning" by the Velvet Underground was his favorite song, expressing the languid, liquid quality of this early time of day. No longer would this day revolve around the celebration of mass, with all its preparation. No longer would he need to prepare a sermon to deliver to the hungry throng. His time was his own now, and he answered to no one for his actions, apart from his own conscience.

His journey through religion was transforming. Raised in a secular Jewish home, he early had a spiritual hunger. His experience of the Reform temple where he was to be bar mitzvah'd awakened something deep within him. The prophecies of Isaiah spoke deeply to his heart. He entered into his preparation with an open mind, finally the day arrived, and he would be a man.

He would pursue his background as a young adult, discipling himself to a kabbalistic rabbi. The mystical teachings stirred him, awakening more of the Divine in his life. He also practiced zazen at the Zen Center, and found significant meaning in this study. His mind was wide open, and he would forget about religion, then start up again. His life as a bohemian young poet consumed him.

Then his foray into Christianity, studying at the Near Eastern Studies Center at the university. Reading the gospels for the first time. Coming through this to believe that Jesus was the Messiah. Then having his vision of the risen Lord one morning in his bedroom, as the sun was rising. Was this an illusion? A remnant of his previous night's debauchery? The result of combining medication and liquor?

Whatever it was, this was his moment of conversion. His Damascus Road moment. This led him on into reception into the Episcopal Church, baptism, confirmation, marriage, then ordination into holy orders. He was a zealous, obnoxious convert, all the worst characteristics that Christianity can produce. He burned like a blazing fire, and was raised up early in the church as a lay leader, teaching, leading a prayer group, and eventually even preaching.

He went back to college to finish his degree, so he could go on to seminary. He loved his studies in college: English poetry and Classics majors with a minor in Religion. He studied Greek and Latin, arduously, struggling along the way. He worked his way through this all, slaving away at the local Copy Center, xeroxing manuscripts for all the famous writers and poets who lived in the village.

Going on to the seminary, after graduating magna cum laude, he pursued studies in Greek, working through the epistles of St Paul. He delved into the "new criticism" expanding his perspectives on the issues of scriptural studies. He was alienated in his seminary, by the radical theology and chapel services, which he never once attended. Filled with evangelical fervor and zeal, he was confounded by these people who seemed not to believe the Christian faith anymore.

Defensive in his beliefs, he did not make many friends during this period. He clung to his faith with bloodcurdling terror, as if his life depended on it. Swallowing the whole package of orthodox doctrine, he was brain-washed thoroughly, equipped to be a spokesman, or salesmen, for this used religion. His ordination in the cathedral as deacon and then as priest were pivotal moments for him.

Prostrating himself before the high altar, he utterly gave himself to his vocation. He would go on into several parishes, where he was inevitably met with hostility and suspicion. How could he be Jewish and a priest? Was he really a Christian? Didn't he seem rather gay for a married man with children?

These tenures, though rewarding, were inevitably failures, from which he was removed by a bishop, or by circumstances beyond his control.

And then there was his very suspicious appearance: hairless on head and body, big nose sticking out like a beak, sunken-in chest, skinny with a bulging stomach, causing him to appear like some strange, awkward bird. And then there was his speaking voice, subtle, slightly effeminate, soft and reassuring. This alone had caused them fits and seizures. He would drone on and on in his spontaneous sermons, way above most of their heads, to an uncomprehending, baffled congregation.

And then there was his practice of Anglo-Catholic liturgical traditions: chanting everything possible, incense wherever possible, mystical visions while he celebrated mass, enwrapping him in a misty cloud; he was out of his body as he censed the altar, moving gracefully around in a circle.

His faithful few loved the solemn ceremony of it all, but the majority just didn't "get it."

How beautiful and sad it was for him to remember those days now. It seemed like another life, which it truly was. His cassocks, albs, and vestments were neatly stored away in the attic. It had been some twenty years since that all happened. And he had moved on completely. One nice thing occurred: He heard about the new woman bishop in the diocese, and decided to contact her. They had a very moving phone conversation together.

He told her how he had been cast out of the parish after being "outed" by his wife. There were other reasons presented at the time for his expulsion, but the real reason was his homosexuality. The bishop expressed sorrow for what had happened, and the way he had been treated, and put him back on the rolls as a retired priest in the diocese. This was a very moving recognition and acknowledgement, and he expressed his gratitude to the bishop.

Not that he would ever function again as a priest; he had left the Christian faith and found a hospitable home in his philosophical Taoism. Although no longer believing in a "personal God," he nonetheless maintained an active, disciplined life of prayer. He saw no contradiction in this, and found that his prayer life transformed him, increasing his compassion, as he prayed for those he cared for. He employed Taoist versions of Jewish, Christian, and Anglo-Catholic prayers in his devotions.

Uniting himself with his Tao, in the early morning, strengthened him to face his day ahead. He would read haiku, Chinese poetry and prose, and Taoist readings. This early morning time was precious to him, with his cat lying on the adjacent chair, faithful companion always. He had found the cat, as a tiny kitten, meowing at his back door. He trapped her and trained her, and now she was a perfect companion. She always kept him company. He believed she was his Muse.

What happenings would transpire before the envelopes blossomed again on the fruit trees?

He waited in expectation for the first fruits to reveal themselves. The words that the flowers cast out were cryptic and mysterious, like those of the oracle at Delphi. He saw himself as a kind of oracle, filling in the words as they appeared on the page, telling the same stories that are being told here.

Of course, he told them in his own unique style, words strung together in incomprehensible sequence, blurring the eyes to read them. A telephone rang; he answered it. It was her, checking on the boy. Her son had given up on her, believing that she didn't want to see him. Maybe something in her longed for the boy, alone as she was in her despair. Her boyfriend didn't help matters.

She knew of the boy's addiction, and was wary of him now. She didn't understand why he did this, and was profoundly disturbed by her son's addiction. So she distanced herself from him to be safe. She had trouble dealing with people's problems, and was threatened in her sense of security by anything outside the normal. So she kept to herself. Perhaps the boy could visit some time.

Silence. The golden moment. Transfigured by the

rampant thoughts of solitude, invading the mind of the writer. He wrote in total silence, allowing himself to be receptive to what his inspiration gave to him, writing the words on the page as if led to by some unseen force. This was really his unconscious mind asserting itself, writing as if automatically the words that he was given.

He was reading Gertrude Stein's book, How To Write; a compendium of advice from the mistress of language herself. Written in her most "difficult" style, she strings together sequences of seemingly unrelated words into pure poetry of language. This was intended to show how to write: teaching with her inimitable style what she is setting out to teach.

Reading this book entranced and enchanted him. Sometimes he thought that he was on the verge of losing his mind reading it. He wondered if Stein had been entirely in control of her faculties. He remembered a W C Fields movie, where the famous comedian reads a poem by "Gertrude Smug," in obvious imitation of the great author. This had amused him to no end.

He had received his next shipment of his first book, Reap Violet Hiss. The fresh copies looked so beautiful and black, with their bold cover design and cryptic content. He could now have a book signing at the local historic bookstore, where he knew his friend who was trying to help him. He had given two public readings from his work at the local library that winter, stepping out of his usual shell for a moment or two. These were gratifying events for him.

He was such a private person, living in his cave with his son, that the two of them had little contact with the world outside of their home. His friend would call every morning like clockwork, droning on about the misery of the world. This friend was going on a cruise with his wife, and would be away for ten days afloat in a boat in the Bahamas. They would still be able to talk every day though.

A transparent novel with wings floats through the air above my head. Speaking in tongues, the words emerge like birds and flutter their wings in the open air. Vessels of mercy crack through the hard, frozen insistence, melting it to drool down the chin of the writer. The carousel is a merry-go-round, circling endlessly, the horses going up and down. Tribes gather to inspect the facilities.

To get back to the beginning is what everyone wants.

Instead of moving forward. Like leprosy, evil portends a universal disaster, plaguing the filters that pretend to invert the claustrophobic memories that persist on Wednesdays. Breaking through the barriers, one may exude simple things that transform into opulent blossoms, withering on their stems in the night.

Dancing, colliding universes beckon one onward into the avoidance of obligations, casting profanity to the wind, wishing like apricots, pressing into desperation, oracular voices protruding, seldom-entered rooms that are covered with cobwebs. Despairing of what to wear tonight, one goes naked, one goes wearing clothes upside-down. You get the idea.

The photographic prints live quietly in a box, waiting to be remembered by him. The pears are no longer in the bowl, having been eaten. "Just as we care for what is, so we should care for what is not," to paraphrase Lao Tzu. "Being depends upon not-being." Sound advice concerning nothingness.

He caught one of the dragons in his coffee from the swirling cream, and rode its back around the room.

Fluttering rainbows bounce around the kitchen, refracted through the crystal that hangs by the window.

The sun-catcher, stained glass, with a smiling sun in the middle, and the evil eye hanging by a thread. The microwave that beeps by itself for no reason, asserting its existence. All the effects and furnishings that make a house a home. He lived in his house with his son.

What are houses? Rectangular buildings that people live in, alone or together. He lived in a small village with many houses. Most of the people rarely spoke to each other. He knew the people across the street to wave "hi" to, that's about all. His one neighbor had vanished into thin air with his little boy; his new neighbor was rarely home, working hard as a physical therapist at the hospital.

Theirs was a big, old house with many rooms. Two of these were just taken up with storage. The other rooms were interestingly decorated, and created an unusual quality to the home. Vague semblances floated through the air, filtering blessings upon the sleeping father and son. Shattering all illusions, these dreamlike phantasies lingered lovingly over their heads.

Saturated extravagance bled lustfully into the waiting mouths of the gathered throng. Their eager impulses lashed them together like a symphony of complaints. Rummaging through the various garments that had been cast away, they looked for wings to fly with, but didn't find any. The morose pilgrims vanish conspicuously, into the waiting vestibule of night.

He thought he was losing his mind. Pouring himself out onto the page in the typewriter, until he could barely breathe. He had broken into a sweat from head to toe; this kind of seizure attacked him now and then, when he had consumed too much marijuana. He thought he was going to pass out. Wiping himself down with a towel, he opened his shirt to cool himself off.

Lugubrious counterfeiters rescue the hostages from the bank, evicting themselves from organized crime with a flourish. When they went away, there was nothing to come home to. Playing a symphony in his mind, he plays all the parts of the orchestra, recreating the sound of the music in his brain. He liked playing his old phonograph records, with their crackles and pops. There was nothing else like it for comfort and a sense of peace.

Wagging tails of dogs and cats. Fluffy figments of the imagination, dancing backwards through the cloudless sky. Open wounds, bleeding from the suffering of the world and the war. His mind, a broken vessel leaking water. The steady drum beat of the antagonism run amuck. Bodies blown to bits. Children orphaned, parents childless. Old people homeless. The disabled without hope.

The wars were all pointless, vain ventures into absurdity. He could not stomach any of it. He felt a heaviness in his chest, like someone was beating on him. What was this strange sensation? Had the war taken over his mind to such a degree that he could not function? His was a sensitive nature that suffered fools endlessly, having made poor choices along the way.

Now, he found meaning in the compassion he cultivated for the suffering of the world and the war. Participating in the suffering of the world made him a citizen of the world. He embodied the pain and death in himself, taking it in and cleansing it, spiritually. He was a vessel for the healing of the pain of the world, and he knew this early on.

This gave a greater meaning to his life than it otherwise would have had. Watching the news, he had to guard his emotions, lest he fall apart at the seams, unraveling in agony, vicariously suffering. His back was hurting him again. Tomorrow, at the chiropractor, he would find some relief, he hoped. He had bought seven bottles of kosher grape juice on sale, none of which he could open. So he brought one to his chiropractor, who was strong enough to open it.

The chiropractor had become a good friend, and this man helped him with his recycling, taking it to the place with his own son in his truck every three months. This was a great help to him. The chiropractor had done many favors for him, and was always ready to help him out. This was a great comfort to him in his old age, advanced as he was at this point.

Pain searing through his upper body, gas or some indigestion? He was almost through writing for the day, and was visibly slowing down. Ideas had stopped coming, he was running on empty, with still a long way to go. The merciful end of a good day's work, so satisfying. Although he wondered what it would ever lead to? Would it ever be finished? Would the endless narratives ever be complete?

Wringing their hands, they moaned, "It's sad, so sad . . . " Revving the motor, they prepared to take off. Into the sky with their airplane, they wandered off into the clouds. Passers-by waved as the planes took off, flinging their handkerchiefs in the air. The pilots were young, and this was their first flight unaccompanied. They soared up into the sky with fearless thrusts.

"Tell you it's just plain sad . . . " Singing like birds, the thoughts of them were gathered like bouquets of flowers. Entering the castle grounds, the pilgrims moved ever slowly, entrancing the leaves on the trees to flutter in the breeze. Grabbing their purses, the ladies exited the room, going to powder their noses. Flaking like fish, they undid their blouses and flashed their breasts.

The chiropractor had adjusted his spine where he had had his muscle spasm, releasing a huge amount of tension. He was very tender after this, and the chiropractor opened the grape juice. "Go home and write," he had told him as he left the office. How encouraging! Yes, he would go home and write, working away for his required two hours.

His son didn't like it when he was working; the boy hated to be alone. But most of the time he respected his father's need to write. He had never read any of his father's writing. Only his middle daughter had, and now they were not speaking to each other. How tragic a loss for both of them! He wrote on anyway, regardless of the circumstances. It was like his morning walks, throughout the year, in all kinds of weather, invigorating him, energizing him.

He had given up swimming. This had been a central part of his life, swimming from May through September, in the little creek by his house. He would enter the freezing water slowly, until it rose up to his waist, and then he would dunk down into the water three times, reliving his baptism every day. He would swim vigorously across the creek, forwards with breast strokes, and then would turn around at the far side of the creek, and swim backstroke to the other side.

This went on from early spring into early fall, every day, twice a day, morning and afternoon.

He would go into the freezing water in September and even into October sometimes, braving the creek when no one sane would do it. He steeled himself against the cold, defying the elements by his bold asceticism and spartan lifestyle. But the effort had become too much for him. He had trouble navigating the steep hill he had to descend to get to the water.

He would slide down on his backside and would be unable to get up again. So he finally gave up, and admitted to himself that it was time to stop. His advanced age had caught up with him at last, limiting what he was able to do. He accepted this, and embraced his aging process, enjoying getting older, and the occasional respect it offered him.

He accepted the fact that there were certain things he could not do anymore, and gracefully adapted his life to accommodate these changes. He took care of himself, and tenderly tended to his needs, emotional and physical. His son was a sweet boy, with many problems. The father devoted himself to nurturing his son into the ways of life. The boy was growing up. He rarely wore diapers anymore, but occasionally would put one on for comfort.

The boy would watch cartoons, endlessly. Mindless, infantile humor that captivated his attention. In many ways, the boy was still a child, never having fully grown up. The father tried to understand this, and meet his son where he was, since that was the only place he could be. They journeyed on together, and they were inseparable.

His youngest daughter was the source of his greatest pain; she had stuck with him throughout the years, but had grown increasingly difficult. She would be speaking to him one week, and not speaking to him the next. She would walk out on the father and son in the middle of a visit, suddenly leaving the house without explanation. She had complained that her father was too much for her to deal with, and began to distance herself from him and her brother. Now she was not speaking to them.

This caused him immense suffering. But he managed most of the time not to think about it. He kept his head above water, finding strength in his Tao, and in the work the Wise Woman had done with him. How did he keep from breaking down over this? He had had several mental breakdowns in the past, over the daughters' absence in his life. He would not "fall through the ice" over this again.

His mental breakdowns were severe, lasting usually three or four days. During these episodes he felt like he was dying, literally. These moments lasted forever, and he felt no way to escape them. He would ride it out, medicating himself against anxiety, riding it out until it finally subsided. He had not had one of these episodes in a while. There was the brief one over New Year's Eve day, when he realized that none of his three daughters would be calling to wish him a happy New Year. He collapsed.

His daughters would gather together for holidays with their mother, to which he and his son were not invited. The knowledge that they would all be celebrating together without them was devastating to both of them. They felt bereft, abandoned, forsaken, alone. Holidays for the father and son were solemn occasions. He would prepare festive meals for the two of them to eat alone together. They would survive somehow, if they cared for one another.

His new novel obsessed him. He thought about it day and night, and could not wait for the next day, when he would return to the typewriter again. He was writing the story of his life, disguised as a fictional character. His wife was in it, and the children, his son and wayward daughters. He rethought his entire life as he wrote his new book. Everything was up for grabs, and he left nothing out.

He wondered whether his editor would like this new

book and want to publish it. It would take him at least a year to finish this work. He was in no hurry. Taking his time, he figured out what he wanted to write, and tried his utmost to achieve this goal. He was wide awake now, after his tea, and ready to pursue the great work again. This would offer him satisfaction and encouragement.

Entering the gallery, the assembled throng looked at the works on display. Paintings and sculptures from the dada and surrealist movements. He wandered through the rooms, entranced by the hallucinogenic works that seemed to defy all logic and sense. He liked the crazy emphases of their objects, resonating with intricate details of how to make a work of art.

Upon returning home, he found his son playing on the floor with toys. The boy still liked to be a child, and had a very childlike demeanor. His innocence was deceptive though, for his was more sophisticated than he let on. His hysterical histrionics were a lot to deal with, unnerving the father and disturbing his peace of mind. The boy would explode suddenly, over nothing, and would take a while to calm down again.

He longed for a peaceful life and home, without the violent mood swings to which his son was prone.

Would the boy ever get into the counseling for which he had been on a waiting list for a year?

They hoped for this, since there was a woman at the doctor around the corner who could help the boy.

But it was taking forever to get in to see her, causing the boy extreme frustration.

The father talked to the Wise Woman about his son. She tried to advise him what he should do and not do. They put their heads together to find a way to help the father and son, but nothing ever seemed to change. There was some improvement in the boy's behavior, but he was only happy when he had his drug. His "connection" would be going into rehabilitation tomorrow, then moving to the city, and he would not be able to get his methamphetamine anymore.

The father had found his black beanie, which he wore to contain his thoughts. Underwear exploding, parchment ventricle, obsessed vagrants, flagrant in their receptivity. The owner goes to the store to make sure it has not been robbed. The night, melting like dissolving rainbows. His "trigger finger," causing the middle finger of his left hand to clamp up, curling in on itself. This made typing very difficult for him. But he soldiered on, nonetheless.

Empty memories, his eldest daughter who had not spoken to him in eight years. There was the one brief dinner together when she came home to see him. A very awkward time in the local brewery and restaurant. He had asked her why she hadn't spoken to him in four years. She refused to answer.

He pursued this in a letter after she went home, asking for an apology for the suffering she had caused him over this period. No response was forthcoming. Four years more of silence.

He had no way to reach her, not knowing her address in another state. She had him blocked on her phone, so that was not a possibility. He had had a special relationship with this, his eldest daughter. They had shared so much together: the love of all the arts, their shared birthday, their passionate, creative Taurus nature. She had studied the violin, and was very talented. They had played together, him on his cello, at one of her violin recitals. This was a pure joy, and a fond memory.

He had blocked her out of his mind, to survive her silence. But recently, he had begun to embrace her in his heart, again. He had his youngest daughter bring her his book, and the photograph he recently had taken of himself, gloriously smiling with his new wispy whiskers. He had hoped these would warm her heart, and return her to him. He prayed for this every day, but no response so far. He waited for her call with baited breath each day, but it never came.

Castigated castrati roamed the desert, seeking refuge from the sandstorm of life. Singing in their golden tones, they rummaged along, despairing for their lives. Plastic pollution in the oceans, bizarre erratic weather turning from winter to spring from one day to the next, then back to winter again. The earth was dying, and no one did anything to save it. This caused him considerable grief.

Frozen embryos, with their fertilized eggs, were declared to be children. Abortion had been declared illegal, and women and girls were given no choice but to have a "forced birth." The government had outlawed birth control in any form. Women were housed in camps and farmed like cows, turning them into "baby machines" against their will. The degradation this produced was immoral.

Open-air vestibules with contorted remnants,

cavorting into invisibility. The round movements consisted of used tea bags, and empty biscuit boxes. The rhymes were busted, and contrary to logic, pierced the veil of the Temple, rent in twain. Vestiges of conflict evoked a somber remembrance, colliding into infinite space, without opening the window.

Into the realms of sense they wandered, fulfilling the destiny of an albatross, relinquishing any claim to obsolescence. Returning the other way, the infected souls proceeded to disrobe, causing a cacophony of distinction. Wandering thrusts made every effort to oblige the citizens of their rights, discussing this on an oblong table laden with rotten food.

Distinguished members fulfilled themselves, by talking on the phone to no one. The oblique reference here was to the box of toothpicks, situated in front of the photograph of his youngest daughter as a baby, looking out the window from the rectory to the church, photographing her from the back, showing her looking out the window. This was a mystical image for him, one of transcendence and deep meaning.

There were eight hundred toothpicks in the box, for which he found various uses. Laboring on, the gathered emptiness went suddenly inside-out, walking through the door into the next room. It was time to take out the garbage, almost overflowing. Strange emptiness persisted in flavoring the unusual temptations with unusual flavors, inconsistently.

Talking about the bedrooms people sleep in: the melting bodies rest comfortably within their electric blankets, rotting slowly in their underwear. Grim sights alarm the waiting insistence, draining it of all its emptiness, like meat put into freezer bags, letting all the air out before closing them. The trip to the Superstore, gathering up groceries by the armful, vegetables, fruits, beautiful fresh meats and fish. He wandered through the aisles as if visiting a museum, admiring all the choice foods.

Listening to Glenn Gould play the *Well-Tempered Clavier* of Bach as he drove along, he was thrilled by the incredible playing and music, and the beautiful landscape through which the highway carved its way. Fields and trees, farms and orchards, into the country as soon as he left the village. He enjoyed a ride through the countryside; it refreshed his spirit, and brought him out of his head.

Motorized wheelchairs gathered for the protest against the war. The shouts were insistent, the people calling on the government to end the war. But no one was listening. Yesterday, over a hundred people were killed as they gathered around a truck carrying food. They were desperate to find some food for their children, and the army just started shooting at them randomly. The hope for food turned into a bloodbath for hundreds. The wounded survivors told the story.

Bloodlust, greed, and vengeance; hatred of "the other" run amuck. Villainy at the highest levels of government. Untrustworthy custodians of peace. Fathering-on their intentions by sending weapons to the warmongers. Insanity on a mass scale. No hope of survival. Nowhere is safe. There is nowhere to go.

And yet, the army continues to slaughter civilians, as they seek to kill their enemy. Merciless slaughter.

This is why the inheritors of claims devote themselves to opening the sandbox of exoticism. The telephone rings while he is writing, but he doesn't stop to answer it. Because the fingers of the writer are clamped up with his arthritis, and he can hardly type at the typewriter. He had significant trouble during his cello practice yesterday, with his finger clamping up.

He had played the cello all his life, and this was a huge part of the person he was. He still had the same cello his parents had bought him for his bar mitzvah. It was a German instrument, nearly 150 years old, and very precious to his heart. He had played in the local symphony for 24 years, until his retirement three years ago. He left to work on his writing and poetry, producing the 18 manuscripts in two years, from his endless marble composition books.

But the cello gave him great joy. He played for himself and his son and his dead parents, who had always encouraged him with his cello. He had his weekly ritual: playing through all the scales and arpeggios, then his favorite etude, the slow movement from Schumann's Five Pieces in Folk Style, then one of the Viola da Gamba Sonatas of Bach. What sheer bliss! He played baroque music with a baroque bow, gut strings, no endpin, balancing the cello between his knees so he could dance with it.

This peculiar effort at "authenticity" of playing had been adopted by him many years earlier.

He found it deeply gratifying and inspiring. The

baroque bow was especially suited to this music, and enabled him to bounce and dance on the strings with lively movements. Going from playing every day for three hours to learn his symphony music, he now practiced once a week for an hour. This suited him well, and gave him the ability to prioritize his focus on his writing and poetry.

His son was also homosexual, surprisingly to the father. He had known from an early age that this was his nature and inclination. This formed a deep bond between the father and son, understanding such an intimate part of each other's being. The mother had responded with hostility to this news, blaming the father for the son's "sinful nature." Her biblical faith demanded that she not accept this news, but continue to pray for her son's "healing."

The boy was deeply hurt by her insensitivity. He felt rejected by her, abandoned when he most needed her. This caused him to be uncomfortable around her, because he felt that she was judging and condemning him. Their visits became more and more infrequent as a result of this. She rarely reached out to the boy, and was very awkward when she did. So the boy avoided his mother. So sad.

Suddenly, he was bleeding. When he got to the store, he saw the blood on his left hand. The father was vulnerable, apparently, and prone to strange, unexplained injuries. This was on the hand with his trigger finger that always clamped up. This hand was in bad shape, truly. He struggled to type at the typewriter. He wrote on an old, beautiful, black Royal Standard, giving him a sense of history as he typed. This gave a deep meaning to his work.

Stranger things have happened. The court adjourned for the day, including the strangers who came to observe the proceedings. Melting chocolate caved in on itself, applauding the various terms by which things defined themselves. Rushing for the door, the inhabitants construed the episode that flavored the proceedings, galloping across the river in one fell swoop. Nothing was left to chance.

He could barely type, what with his finger clamping up. The villagers consorted to relieve the depth of calling for the afterbirth, recklessly invading the space between their eyes. Nothing proved more interesting and absurd than the force-fed orangutans, dancing between the branches of their tree. Most people believed the reports of loose diamonds sitting and melting in the snow.

The undertakers gathered in their lodge, inquiring after the obsolescence of entropy in the wings. No one believed the story about the kindergarteners who slept for a week, following their story time. Pressing the issue, they ventured forth into the night of dreams, invading the space they never occupied before. Following their instincts, they ate locusts and wild honey, like the Baptist.

As was said before, he wrote until the cows came home, chewing their cud. He had put a bandage on his cut. He would make a meat loaf for their supper, a favorite of the boy's. The boy had eaten half of the Hobnob biscuits which he had just bought for his tea. The boy could not resist sweets, and usually ate all of them before the father could even get any.

The boy now insisted on sitting in the study while the father typed. This was a challenge for him, to concentrate on what he was doing, with the boy moaning and murmering in the room with him. Now the boy was in the living room, just outside the study, moaning and wondering what he should do next. Nothing left the remnants of existence to their fallenness. Rapidly dissolving, they further expanded their venture, until it was fulfilled.

Collapsing roofs alerted their inhabitants that the world was about to end. Or was it about to begin? Struggling through the vestiges of time, everyone applauded the efforts of those concerned to alleviate poverty and hunger. Why would they remove the rooms they lived in, thoroughly speaking?

Electricity flowed through their veins, and nothing would stop them now.

Queer boys enjoyed themselves, collapsing in the parlor. Vague semblances, again, walked through the doors that had been locked against invasion. Parting the curtains, they looked outside. There was nothing left, it was all burned away. The fires had consumed everything in sight. There was nothing left but ashes, smoldering away. The gumption that they had lost was now dangling from a thread between their eyes.

"Ave Maria!" they sang, as they floated off into space. No one remained after this display. The servants were released, and the opera singers ventured off into the distance, complaining of toothache. Perplexing foreigners walked among the villagers, asking peculiarly interesting questions in broken English. The villagers were entranced and charmed by their innocence.

Favoring the outsiders, the insiders turned inside-out. Flavoring the entrance with vibrant exits, they moved entrancingly through the various rooms that had been designated for inspection. There were entrances and exits, marauding over the broken glass. Calling for reinforcements, the police rounded up the hardhats, collapsing them into particles of dust, scattered to the wind.

Walking furiously, like a Verdi opera, they entered into the private grounds of the castle. Having gone to excessive lengths to prove a point, many members disabused themselves of foreign languages, singing in tongues of their own devising. Gallumphing through the house, they indicated that nothing was beyond consideration. Everyone wore white, shining garments, whiter than any fuller could bleach them. And they rounded up the extra investments to dissolve.

White-washing the obvious, there was room for disagreement, but not for long. Objections were rejected on sight, and the caved-in thoughts exerted considerable influence upon their minds. No one thought differently concerning this, and they all applauded once the music started. Forgotten dreams were revived and taken out to lunch. Many proved their stupidity by acting like they were someone else.

No one thought this peculiar, lying as they were through their teeth.

He listened to the opera on the radio through the static, a recording from sixty years ago. He adored opera, and listened to it on the radio every week. He loved the intensity of emotion portrayed in opera, and found deep satisfaction in listening to it each Saturday since childhood. The static and crackles seemed to add a certain authenticity to the ancient recording. He listened through the static.

Evacuating adolescents coughed, as they rode to their grandparents' houses. The chiropractor who called to see how his back was doing, after the intense adjustment the other day. This was very kind and caring of him, and his back was feeling better. Growing like leprosy, the invaders caused considerable confusion and distress. The people could not get their boots on, so they left, barefoot.

Collapsing like a house of cards, they went backwards, moving in circular motions, excessive breathing complicating the entrance of deception, unawares. The pilgrims had collapsed into themselves, and talked to each other in sign language. Talking this way gave a break to their mouths, which were occupied in chewing sugar cane. They liked the sweet taste of it.

Peopled like angels, they fluttered away in the dust, enraging the observers to a panic. No one accepted that there was no water anymore. The villagers had been desperate for water, and there was no end in sight. The thirsty inhabitants chewed leaves of weeds for some moisture. In the war, there was no food or water, no medicine or fuel, the people ate cactus leaves for want of anything else.

Seventy of the army's hostages were killed by the army's own bombs. The situation was hopeless. Food was dropped from airplanes to feed the desperate populous. But this was just a drop in the bucket. 500 trucks a day used to enter the territory before the war started. Now only a couple of dozen entered daily, depriving the citizens of much needed humanitarian aid. How would the parents feed their children? Babies were starving to death without milk or formula.

Asking no questions, like stepping on sandwiches, contrary to the prevailing opinion, most thought that the damage had already been done. So they steeled their flanks to surge into the forest, hunting for mushrooms. The fancy that had taken them wore itself out quietly, and retired to the top of the tallest tree, where it was shot down by the police.

Varying speed turntables evoked the sounds of the spheres. The captives were entranced and lulled into submission. 7,000 civilians had been captured by the army and now languished in prison. Tortured, beaten, barely fed, even children had been detained, and women. Mostly young, single men.

And the army had attacked another food convoy, killing at least eight people, and wounding dozens.

Everyone celebrated amidst the dying, and tried to observe their holy days and fasts. The people were strong, and even though their plight was desperate, they had not given up hope. The resistance had first attacked the occupiers' country; but the army's response was totally disproportionate, having slaughtered 30,000 civilians, and wounded 70,000. Another 10,000 were still buried under the rubble. 15,000 children dead, and 1,000 infantile amputations, mostly without anesthetic.

But what would the lonely platypus do, wandering on through the night, without a home?

Saving grace of the emphasis on beauty in the face of ugliness. He tried to make life beautiful, in the midst of the chaos he lived with. Little moments of revelation, even in his house with his son. Illuminated hours, fixed as if carved into stone, tablets of meaning and significance to be studied.

His friend had come to brunch on Sunday, lox and bagels, their favorite. The friend talked on and on with his mouth full of food about the most depressing things. But their visit was redeemed after the meal, with reminiscing about their academic careers which both had enjoyed tremendously. The friend and his wife would be going on a cruise to the Bahamas, concerning which the friend had considerable anxiety. He hoped that his friend would survive the trip.

Speaking of furriers: walking into the dressing room, he tried on various clothes; this was years ago; switching back and forth between the various garments, unable to decide which ones to buy. He left the store without anything. This was typical of him. At a store, he would usually leave without purchasing some item that he really wanted, only to obsess about it, and return to the store later to buy the item. Some social anxiety that caused him to psychically clamp up in stores.

The empirical evidence for the seizure of goods has grown corrupt. The believing remnants exposed their vulnerabilities by reading blank notebooks, upside down. This habit cultivated obscurity among the readers, allowing them to imagine nothingness, captured on the unprinted blank page.

This calmed the wayward pilgrims, filling their busy minds with beautiful silence.

Stories about him circulated through the village. They had not forgotten his disgraced removal from the next town, many years before. He was the eccentric, old, queer poet and musician who had once been a priest, had a family, a career, and a life. All that had been taken away from him, but he no longer bemoaned the curse of Fate which had previously plagued his life.

He had found a kind of sanctuary in his home with his son, now grown. A haven from the storm of life, a save harbor where he could be at peace, as long as his son's temper and addiction were under control. The boy had gotten his last bag of methamphetamine, and would no longer be able to get any more. He would have to face his withdrawal bravely, and not succumb to using again or going crazy.

The father began each session of work reading the previous day's writing, to see what he had produced in his unconscious state of mind. He was always surprised at what he had written, seeing that it was amusing, worthy, and useful to keep, and to keep on writing it. Inspiration came naturally to him, and he was able to put himself into a state susceptible to divine influences. This was a mystical state.

He had cultivated and aspired to the state of a Taoist sage and poet. He emptied his mind on a regular basis, and made room for inspiration to enter in and do its work. His cat was his Muse. The cat thought that he was her mother. He thought that she was HIS mother. They had a deeply sympathetic relationship. She would stay all day in his bedroom, ensconced in his favorite chair. She only came down for supper, and to watch television with him.

At bedtime, his cat would join him in bed, cautiously coming closer to him. He would pet and stroke her, until she finally would come right up to him, and place her paws on his shoulder and cuddle with him for quite some time. This had utterly disarmed him the first time she did this, and he was so deeply moved by this tender, loving gesture, that tears welled up in his eyes. Sublime moment.

The boy's birthday was coming up, and he wanted to go out to a restaurant for dinner. The father would do all he could to make a special birthday for his son. He was to visit the Wise Woman that afternoon, but would speak with her on the telephone instead, not wanting to leave the boy on his special day. The organ played on, dramatically, emphasizing the breadth of its possibilities, powerful and overwhelming in its depth.

Walking through the woods, now becalmed and peaceful, the pilgrims ceased their protest, and eventually caved in on themselves, depopulating their own numbers. The flagrant vagrants proceeded into the castle grounds, exhibiting their talents, parading like it was a festival. Under their coats they pulled out dead chickens, ready to be plucked and stuffed.

He had caved-in on himself years earlier, hopeless after the abandonment by his daughters, the breakup of his friendship with his young companion, and the recovery from his heroin addiction. He caved-in on himself and gave up on life. He didn't clean his house for six years, or write any poetry or prose. He would wake up, afraid to get out of bed and face the day. He would sit all morning in his bathrobe, drinking coffee, and reliving all the traumas of his long, arduous life.

The death of his mother especially haunted him, sudden and unexpected at his tender age of fifteen. She had been in and out of hospitals for years, so he didn't think anything of it when she went in again, suddenly. His mother had not known that she had cancer; this was in the days when the word "cancer" was not even spoken. Only her husband and brother knew of her illness and how severe it was.

So when his father suddenly walked into his room white as a sheet, saying "You'd better get up," he looked at his father and knew she was dead. Not a word was spoken of this. He heaved a huge breath and fell out of bed, curling up in a ball on the floor. He breathed deeply and found some assurance in himself that his would survive this, and go on to live his life.

But the trauma lasted his entire life, until he went to

see the Wise Woman. She knew how to heal his broken heart, applying deep medicine and incantations, to restore him to his right mind again.

The trauma and pain went away, and he was no longer captivated and haunted by his mother's death.

He had a sense of her presence in his life, a living presence that was more real than most living people.

It was his mother who had instilled in him the love of poetry. During her extreme illness, he would walk to the library, and bring back books of modern poetry that she loved, e. e. cummings and Marianne Moore. These precious poems they would read and discuss together, the mother lying in her bed, and him sitting on the bedside. These were blissful moments, and blissful memories for him.

His mother had had polio as a child, and one of her legs was deformed, and she walked slowly, with a limp. She wrote light, humorous, occasional, rhyming verse that used to amuse the family and friends to no end. She was a natural comedienne, and was always the life of the party. She loved classical music and the ballet: she actually took him to see the Royal Ballet with Nureyev and Fontaine. Perhaps she loved ballet because she would never be able to dance it.

His father had been an artist, trained at the Academy in the city. He produced the most wonderful paintings and sculptures, which the poet now had in his home. His father had been a quiet, sensitive man, who took his son to the opera, museums, and concerts. When they drove together in the car, they would play the classical music station, and they would try to guess the composer. They also did Japanese sumie ink painting together, watching a television show that taught it.

Slipping on a banana peel, the entertainer proceeded to tell several offensive jokes. Nobody was laughing. When he threw up all over himself, the audience walked out in disgust, demanding a refund. When lunatics emerged, laughing at themselves, the carpet was rolled up, and everyone began to dance. As there was no music, this didn't matter to them, and they cavorted amongst themselves.

The carpet had pink flowers on a pale green background. He had had two beautiful real Oriental carpets during his marriage, but his wife insisted on keeping both of them. He regretted this terrible loss. But he had carpets that came from the Irish Embassy in the city, which had been given him by a friend years before. These, with their brown and black geometric patterns on a cream background added a touch of dignity to his home.

He was having work done on his old house. He had had his bathroom painted espresso brown, and was having new flooring installed. But to do this, he had to have his old claw foot bathtub moved out of the bathroom, so the flooring could be put in. This was going to be a huge disruption to the household. Roofing work was also being done, and his collapsing porch ceiling needed to be fixed.

Slightly distracted by all this hubbub, he largely kept his wits about him. It was nice getting things fixed; there was a sense of improvement and progress. Refreshing and caring for his home.

The contractor who had been working on his house was a kind, gentle person, and it was really very nice having him working in the home. They had become good friends. He had given him his book.

Still, the inverted remnants disturbed no one, going about their own private business as if they had the right to. They bent themselves into shapeless forms, biomorphic shapes like those in the sculptures of Arp.

Revealing their true natures, overtures were played, entrances and exits were strictly timed, and no one revealed more than was decent, operating under a misconception.

Fluttering rainbows extracted vague essence from the flowers of evil, depending upon one another for support and encouragement. Thank you to all who came out to celebrate. It was a perfectly lovely affair, and everyone was very well pleased. Undergarments were worn on their heads like hats. The parade moved slowly and intentionally through the deserted streets.

A bird was chirping outside the house. The workers had left, after inspecting the collapsing porch ceiling. Extra special inventions were removed from circulation, due to safety concerns. His new friend had called, who was trying to promote his work. This friend was trying to help secure him a reading in the city at the Poetry Center, where he used to read as a young poet. This would be great.

He had even purchased his outfit that he would wear if he got to do this reading. A beautiful green corduroy suit, with a blue and green checked shirt. This would be an historic return for him, a sentimental journey of a real and vital sort. This would be an acknowledgement and recognition of all the hard work he had done over so many years, writing his heart out in eighteen manuscripts. What evidence of a determined spirit, an unconquerable soul.

Vestiges of memories collapsed into a pile of useless thoughts. Running on empty, they persisted until they had used the last drop. The drop-off center was on suspended animation, and no new offerings were being accepted. So most people went on their own, hoping to obtain what they needed. On par with the excellence of His Excellency, the orphans were diapered and fed.

Vaguely indicating their preference, the gathered throngs proceeded to invade the castle grounds again, hoping to see the ruler to whom they would express their demands. He was taking his bath, and could not meet with them, alas. Intricate signs designated openings and closings whereby they could meet themselves along the way, recognizing each other as they passed.

Endless overtures were played by the brass band on the village green. The envelopes had once again begun to bloom on all the fruit trees: poetry was in season again. The spring had arrived at the beginning of March, peculiarly. It was the climate crisis and global warming. They had been warned against this terror, but merely enjoyed the sudden spring-like weather, without thinking.

Entering backwards, they processed like a flock of canaries, into the waiting chamber. There, was a display of artifacts from Mesoamerican antiquity. Everyone began to eat these, munching and crunching on centuries-old antiques. When they had satisfied themselves, they disgorged what they had eaten, and ate it back up again. This terrifying spectacle went on for weeks.

What would happen to the broken bottles, scattered all over the grassy lawn? The cows would hurt their hooves, they thought, concerned about bovine injuries. The balloons took off, carrying a little child up into the air with them. The crowds remembered the precious moment in The Red Balloon, and wondered that this was happening to them now. The child happily rose up into the sky and vanished from sight, eventually.

Saturated with bacon fat, the trumpeter played Taps, and the crowd bowed solemnly. No one wanted to be photographed, since their hair was undone. The entryways were blocked, and the sound of piercing screams reached the ears of the judges, who declared the president immune from prosecution, enraging the mobs that rampaged through the city streets.

He tried to work, but his ears were buzzing. His hearing aids had picked up distant sounds; he could hear from miles away, the chants of the revolting masses, swarming the capital, and advancing upon the center of the city. They were determined to unseat the president. Their rage was endless, since he was supporting the war and its genocide.

What would happen if the glue was unglued and everything fell apart? The screws unscrewed and then screwed on back again? He believed in his Tao, holding it all together, and went on with his life, oblivious of the troubles of his life. He had a strong center, out of which he emanated, circling around in perfect formation, reliving his life, and living it again.

So, the thoughts continued, until they burned a hole into the system of citizenship, calling out for justice and peace. The hope of the nations depended upon this. The government had failed its people. The war's misery went on relentlessly, babies dying of malnutrition every day, two dozen by now. His government was supporting the war in this time, and he felt outraged at this injustice.

The president was sending bombs to the war, to slaughter more innocent civilians. And money for more ammunition. They were on the wrong side of history, and there was nothing he could do about it, but hope that the president's mind would change. Otherwise, the war would go on for years. He could not bear the thought of this, but felt helpless to do anything about it, sadly.

The distant music was mystical and consoling. He had been to the doctor who had given him an injection into the palm of his hand, to heal his trigger finger. The doctor had sad that it would "feel like your hand is exploding." And it rather did, although it was not terribly painful. It was a very intense experience, though. He trusted his doctor implicitly and knew it would be alright. He now already felt much better. The finger was still a bit stiff, but it was no longer cramped.

He was able to type much more easily now, and began to write his daily quota of four pages. This would bring him to one hundred pages, a milestone in his literary career and aspirations. He had run two hours of errands that morning, and felt glad to get out of the house for a while. His son was sleeping, avoiding life as usual, so the father would not be missed.

He enjoyed driving his old plum purple Cadillac here and there. He played beautiful music as he drove through the country road, passing gnarly old trees, a tractor in a shed, a pond. He imagined himself as part of some wonderful ballet, driving gracefully along with style. He was in his own little world in his car; he liked the size of it, that it was big; he loved the buttery smoothness in its drive.

In his camel hair coat and tweed hat, he looked rather distinguished. People wondered who he was. They all knew him at the bank and the shops. He was a peculiar, familiar presence. He rarely left the house apart from his morning walks, and only went out for appointments and food shopping.

He led a spartan life, enjoying an ice cold shower every morning. He found this invigorating and energizing, a manifestation of his "ascetic aesthetic." Whitman had advised cold bathing, especially for men, and he took the great poet's advice. Reading Leaves of Grass had changed his life completely. He was especially moved by the Hymn to Death, celebrating the reality of life's end.

Whitman has a bird sing this hymn, in which he extolls the all-embracing nature of Death, submitting to its ultimate grasp of each of us. When the father read this poem several years before, it freed him of his white-knuckled terror of Death. He hoped to have this poem read at his funeral one day, if his daughters ending up attending. He also wanted a poem by e. e. cummings and a chapter of the Tao Te Ching. But would his daughters even come to his funeral, or refuse to, to avoid their brother?

He thought about this, on occasion: What if he got seriously ill, and needed hospitalization? Would his daughters even care? What if he was on his deathbed? Would they come to be with him? He looked forward to dying peacefully one day in the distant future from his own bed. How beautiful it would be if his children were all there to be with him as he departs this life. But they might not be. These were not morbid thoughts to him, but dealings with Reality.

Sudden thrusts of emotion, breaching trust,

enveloped the village. Owners of the shops knew what to do in emergencies: shoot to kill. Guns had proliferated to such a point that everyone had one, except for the father and his son. They refused to succumb to such vulgar barbarism. Life is like Swiss cheese, he thought: It is in the place where there is nothing that the usefulness of the thing depends, to paraphrase Lao Tzu.

Blessed nothing! How wonderful, he mused, that emptiness is just as important as fullness. He loved emptiness, and silence. He usually wrote in total silence, finding this quiet space suited for his mind to be susceptible to unconscious thoughts. With these he filled his pages, writing his book which was dealing with the same material that is presented in the present volume, curiously.

Vague semblances once again, as always, "scent the air with sacrificial wounds," to quote a phrase of the poet's. Marauding bands of youth, like stray mangy alley cats, roamed the empty streets all night. Blowing away dandelions that had gone to seed, they infested the realm of the possible with unknown possibilities. "Vague Semblances" was the title of one of his books of poems. The title haunted him, like gas after a very large meal.

Open the book and read, he thought, as he opened his ancient copy of Dante's Divine Comedy.

He had only two more cantos to go, and he will have read the entire six hundred pages. He read this book every morning at eleven o'clock, in his bedroom, surrounded by windows, with his faithful cat by his side on the adjacent chair. This reading was extraordinary, traveling through Hell, Purgatory, and finally to inhabit Paradise. Although he rejected the cruel theology of this work, he had thoroughly enjoyed the journey with Dante, Virgil, and the radiant Beatrice.

The boy had gone for a haircut, in the village, with twenty dollars his father had given him. This was an unusual thing for the boy to go out on his own, walking all the way to the barber shop. He didn't like walking through the town, which he hated. The boy had no friends, and no one but his father in his life. He felt constantly lonely and hopeless. The father prayed that things would get better for his son. He wanted his son's happiness more than his own.

Open invaders wrested Fate from obscurity, calling

upon their stagnant memories to stop their vital signs from disappearing. No one could refuse this treatment. They were told it was "for the best."

Experiments were done on unwilling patients, exercises in genetics, attempting to produce a superior race. Minorities were forbidden from bearing children, in an attempt to ultimately wipe them out.

Getting closer to the end, they huddled together against the encroaching cold. Yearning to breathe free amidst the war, the populace was shocked when the president airdropped packages of food into their midst. This was a mere drop in the bucket, in no way sufficient to their needs. The army had blocked shipments of food, water, fuel, and medicines to the besieged territory for five months. The people were literally starving to death.

Open wounds expose the need for deliverance. Clapping hands deny the devastation of the imbeciles. Operating rooms turn into carousels, and instead of performing surgery, everyone goes for a ride. The children play in the bombed-out playground. Overtures again, through the loud speakers, endlessly playing on. The band is made of corpses, playing on brass instruments.

Unfortunate events preclude the possibilities of idiocy and its artifacts. He loved quoting himself, from his poems, in the midst of his new novel. The breadth and depth of his work was startling. Even he could not believe how much he had produced over the years. He believed that if he stayed faithful to his work, it would one day be recognized and published. And this had finally happened.

Parked cars are torched and burn and melt in the sunshine. Police are too busy eating their lunch to even care. The police were not well thought of, since they had shot numerous young males of color, and murdered them in other ways. Suspicion was heavy upon the police. They rarely responded to emergency calls, and if they did, they would always escalate the situation until it turned violent.

No one even bothered calling the police anymore, because they always made a situation worse.

Crime was rampant and out of control. People were afraid to leave their homes, and only dared to for an absolute necessity. Children were afraid to go out and play with their friends. Drive-by shootings were common, and many children had lost their lives in this manner.

Hooray for the penguins, persisting in Antarctica, with the ice melting beneath their webbed feet, he pondered. What more could be done to stop the ice from melting? The glaciers? He wondered. The earth was dying, and nobody seemed to care. He worried deeply about the climate crisis and global warming, which the government seemed to ignore with a vengeance. It was too late to save the planet, which was slowly burning up.

Enough of that. In the meantime, pelicans paraded down the alleyways, looking for fish. They finally entered the supermarket and devoured all the fish in the store. Nobody seemed to mind, and they thought that the pelicans were cute. Zombies drank the blood of the gas station attendants, and proceeded to eat the pelicans. Again, nobody seemed to mind. Things had gotten that bad.

When the entrances got confused with exits, people were trampled to death. And in the war, people were shot at and trampled to death, trying to get food from the humanitarian aid trucks. Nursing mothers had no milk for their babies. And there was no cow's milk or goat's milk available either. The animals had all died.

The people wandered the bombed-out streets looking for anything to eat, some water to drink, a bathroom to use.

Rampant diarrhea infected thousands, and there were no facilities in which to relieve themselves. So people did it right out on the street. They had no shame anymore, and their dignity had been crippled severely. A proud people, they had endured many wars. The army had occupied their land and driven them out. They were refugees, exiles from their own homes and land. Because of this, they yearned to return to their land. In the small bit of land they occupied, they were bombed daily.

He had been to see the Wise Woman, enjoying his ride through the countryside: baby goats, horses, his favorite old gray barn, ancient now and no longer in use. She had been pleased to hear of his reaching one hundred pages in his new novel, saddened that his three wayward daughters were no longer speaking to him, once again. They talked about his son, how he hoped the boy would finally give up his eight year methamphetamine addiction.

Processing slowly, the writhing throngs met their

own match. The firemen turned their hoses upon them, drenching them all from head to toe. They didn't care, but pressed on, lighting fires with tires, smashing shop windows, looting the stores of their goods, rampaging along like it was nobody's business. The box of toothpicks in front of his youngest daughter's photograph. The baby goats, huddling together. The picture of Life that revealed itself to his eyes every day.

When he came home from the Wise Woman, his son had just woken up, and wanted to wake up in the study, asking the father to forsake his work for an hour. So the poet went to watch television about the war, but the son was disturbed by the television, and had a little fit over it, and finally went up to his room to go back to bed again. So the father could work on his new novel, after all.

His book had characters drawn from himself, his son, his former wife, his three daughters. He used his imagination to transform these people into a fictionalized form. His characters resembled these people, but were no longer them. He had transformed them into literature, and saw this work as a mirror into his life and reality. Sometimes the border between life and art began to dissolve, and he didn't know if he was himself, or his character.

Sometimes he thought that he was close to losing his mind, somewhere inside his new novel.

He felt this way when he was reading Gertrude Stein's book, How to Write. It was surely teaching him how to write in a peculiar, particular way, stringing together seemingly unrelated words and spinning them into a musical fugue of words, more abstract art than realistic.

He tried to do this in his new novel, alternating between abstract and realistic styles at will. He had done this in his first novel, Reap Violet Hiss, with considerable skill in his tender twenties, years before. His new novel began very abstractly, and finally crystallized around the main characters and their stories. More abstract interludes were scattered throughout the manuscript.

The boy was miserable, half of the time. It was very hard for him to be without his drug. He had to learn to survive without it. His son's addiction had wrecked their home life for too many years. The boy would have to learn other ways to be happy, without his usual way of happiness. There were so many ways to be happy, if only he could find them. The father prayed every day for this.

He had had another friend, whom he knew since the days of his church, which this friend attended. They had met at a bookstore, and he went up to this fellow, since they were both dressed in black and had no hair. He thought that they should meet. They became friends, and this man attended his church for a while, until his cataclysm. They remained friends, but this guy always created conflict and negativity, criticizing the poet.

This friend especially hated his first novel, claiming that it was incomprehensible, irrational, illogical, and irrelevant. His criticism and attack were vicious and merciless, and the poet was deeply offended. This was his precious novel, and it was like his child. He defended his work, and cut off relations with this friend. That was very sad, since they shared so much in common.

The friend had made attacks like this before: claiming that the poet, having an affair with a young adult man like his companion, was the same as if he were having a relationship with a child. He stopped speaking to the friend after this. He gave the friend another chance. Then, the friend attacked the poet's son, verbally assassinating him to his father, in the most cruel, uncaring way. He broke off relations again.

But condemning his novel was the last straw. The friend had looked forward to reading the novel, but his reaction was absolutely hateful and poisonous. The poet would go on without this false friend. But the poet missed him, and their endless rambling telephone conversations. The friend was a musician, an artist, and had written poetry. They shared a common interest in the same writers, poets, musicians, composers, and artists. So, losing this friend was a significant loss.

He had no one else with whom he could discuss the arts. His one remaining friend seemed not to have much interest in such things. And they mainly talked about current domestic and world events, consoling one another about their common pain over the war. They processed the latest news together every day, and shared a common viewpoint about these events.

Now the friend was going on a cruise with his wife. He had to drive to the city, stay overnight in a hotel, and board the ship the next day. The friend was nervous about this cruise, and wasn't sure whether he even wanted to go. His wife was feeling similarly. But off they drove, across three states to get to the city. The poet hoped that they would make it okay, and not have any trouble.

His son would go crazy over the slightest thing. If he did not get what he wanted when he wanted it, he would throw a fit. This unnerved the father to no end. He wanted and needed a peaceful home, out of which he could live the life he needed to live, and do his writing. But the chaos was enveloping him, cruelly bruising his mind and body. Overturning the apple cart over anything, the son missed calls from doctors, thus missing appointments.

The boy still had thirteen people ahead of him on the waiting list to see the counselor around the corner. He had been on the waiting list for one year already. The boy desperately needed some help, and this woman was wise and capable, and could free him from the bondage of his problems and misery. This was an encouraging sign, and perhaps the boy would get to see her by the summer.

Two small children were pulled from the rubble, after a bomb blast from the army leveled on an apartment house in the war. This was a miracle. A woman was blinded by a tear gas canister thrown in her face, and went on to be a senator, working for the working people. Gangs marauded through the streets, freeing all the prisoners in the jails, insisting that the president resign. The people were terrified to go out of their homes. The border had been closed again, and the airport was under attack.

The flagrant vagrants moved precipitously across the field of vision, eliminating any need for barter or exchange of goods. Servants left their jobs, rebelling against their masters, who would now have to fend for themselves. Apples that grow on trees coughed up a stench like that of rotting fish, and rejected any parlance that would excuse them. This was very inconvenient for the firemen.

Actualized daydreams made their presence known, like a roast beef sandwich, or an order of ventilated off-springs. Relying on their own instincts, they breathed a phosphorous fume of purple, elliptical rainbows, electric toasters, sandblasted buildings, forgotten memories. The memory of gloves. Chinese fans protruding against the night sky invisibly.

Taken separately, the envelopes contained false

visions of death. So, caution was taken in opening them. Eating their own eyeballs, the exterminators produced more rodents and roaches, collapsing into a puddle of their own remains. Forgetting to tie their shoes, they tripped over themselves and forgot again. Precious thoughts conflict with Reason, inevitably speaking.

Nonetheless, forgotten were the obligations conflicting with their purpose, so they exited the entrance, fluttering away. The rowdy teenagers, set on their design, flattened the bread that was rising, to keep it from baking properly. Their noses were running and they had no tissues, so they wiped it on their sleeves. No one was looking, and their parents had gone out for the evening.

He had talked to his woman friend, with whom he had not spoken for two months. When he told her that his three daughters were not speaking to him again, she attempted to justify their unconscionable, hostile behavior toward him. She said that he was "overwhelming," and it was understandable that his daughters found him "too much to deal with." He was very disappointed in this woman, who seemed to have no compassion for his suffering, excusing his daughters as she did.

He wondered whether his several friends to whom he had sent his first book had read it. But he was afraid to ask them, fearing that they might not appreciate his novel, or understand it. This was a "difficult" work, written in abstract language, like an abstract painting. He had cautioned them that this was not like an ordinary book, but required intense reading by the reader.

He hoped that his book would be a success, but it had not sold many copies yet. He desperately wanted to be read: it was the fulfillment of the process of the novel, coming into being, discovered after 45 years, and published at last. He believed in his book, that it would one day be recognized as a significant contribution to literature and the arts. He hoped it would take its place among the great books of the previous century.

Like "peeling away thoughts," he delved deeper into mystery in his new novel. For the first time, he was writing about definable, recognizable characters, with narrative connecting it all together. His unconscious mind was an endless well of images and ideas, giving him material that he didn't even know was there. Words danced in his brain, exuding meanings that were new and fresh every day.

He was the channel of his own spirit, speaking in language that was hard to understand. He was true to his Muse, amusing himself as he wrote. He was amused, in language hard to understand. What language was he speaking? Some unknown, dead tongue, forgotten for centuries, which he revived?

Writing was his chief amusement, along with his cello, and he loved doing it as often as he could.

His son, infantile emotionally, compulsively masturbated in the study, where he kept his pornography. This kept the father from doing his writing when he wanted to. So he watched television, until the son admitted that he was unable to achieve his goal, and had given up. The boy was lonely, and desperately wanted a friend, someone to be in his life besides his father. But no one wanted to be his friend. He was utterly bereft of hope, and wanted to die.

The son longed for a boyfriend, a partner with whom he could share his life. But no one seemed interested. The boy's manner confused people and put them off. They instinctively felt that something was not right about the boy. His problems and challenges oozed from his pores, and were visible to other people who didn't even know the boy. This left him alienated and isolated.

Young pilots on their first solo flights melted into the clouds and were never seen again. The parents grieved their sons, lost in the fog of the sky. Hamburgers were grilled to console them in their loss. But no one was able to keep any food down. They disgorged their meals and left to go home. Unable to contain themselves, they poured out tears into waiting glass bowls, to drink later on.

Enveloping memories, grilled like hot dogs on the Fourth of July, cascaded down the chute.

There was stardust in the eyes of the beholder, and the moon was full once again. Vampires and werewolves were nonexistent, luckily for the villagers, and no one was conscious of clouds in the night sky, where the Northern Lights were displayed for all to see.

Crippled children were laid down to rest. The handicapped demanded their rights, threatening to blow up the Capitol. Blacks and Latinos loved each other, but cared about the terrible oppression they suffered, forbidden from procreating until they would eventually disappear. Poverty was rampant, and children were going without food every day. Most of the schools had all been closed, since education was now forbidden beyond elementary school. Some parents taught their children secretly, fearing the censorship of the police.

He had had another friend who never reached out to him at all. He had to initiate any contact or conversation, and this friend would not respond to messages he sent. He had pointed this out to the friend, feeling that he was doing all "the work" of the friendship himself. But this friend got angry at him for saying that he was not responsive, and insulted him. So he had to break off this one-way friendship.

This was sad, since this friend had baked him a beautiful birthday cake on his birthday, and had been very kind to him, also giving him a lovely vase which he had made. But a friendship takes commitment by both people, and he never felt anything coming back to him from this friend. He had even tried to "make up" with this friend, but there was no change in his behavior. So it ended.

Vague semblances startle the sleeping giants in their rest. Upon waking, they look for food, and are violent when they don't get any. The villagers were afraid of them, and brought them offerings of food so the giants wouldn't eat them. In the absence of a giant-killer, they had learned to live together.

The giants were mostly peaceful creatures, and kept to themselves, largely.

Where were the sleeping villagers while this was going on? Dreaming in their bedrooms of cats chasing butterflies in a beautiful meadow on a summer day. Thoughts dissolved and then re-formed to turn into ice sculptures on the village green. No one resented their presence, but received them as visiting royalty in their midst. Coughing suddenly, they woke up and discovered themselves in their beds.

Welcoming the new day, the bird began to sing, like a rooster crowing, announcing the dawn.

He loved his birds, one parakeet and one cockatiel. He talked to his birds, making friends with them, and thanking them for coming to live with him. He also thanked his orchid, blossoming at last. The flowers cheered him up, and gave him hope for the future. He loved his beautiful green plants, and lovingly watered them and cared for them each week.

He revved up his energy level with some marijuana, and set out to clean the cat's litter box and the birds' cages. This was like the Labors of Hercules for him. Breathing heavily, he emptied the old litter into a plastic bag, took the litter box upstairs to the bathtub to rinse it out, came back downstairs, filled the litter box with fresh litter and replaced it in its spot in the laundry room.

Continuing his tasks, he proceeded to clean the birds' cages, discarding all the uneaten seeds and husks into a waiting plastic bag, hanging from the cockatiel's cage. The birds were freaked out by this housecleaning, which they desperately needed. Feathers all around, fluttering in the air, he cleaned out the cages and put fresh newspaper on their floors.

Then having to take the two bags of waste out to the garbage. What a sunny spring-like day it was, and only the beginning of March. He had been taught that "March comes in like a lion, and goes out like a lamb." But this March was coming in like a lamb already. This was more evidence of the climate crisis and global warming, but everyone said "What a beautiful day it is today!" ignoring the horror of the situation.

The president had said in a speech that he would build a pier so ships can bring humanitarian aid to those suffering in the war. The army had refused to let in no more than a couple of dozen trucks a day, delivering aid, starving the captive people in the besieged territory to death. The president clearly was courting the hundreds of thousands who refused to vote for him in the upcoming election, due to his support of the war, sending more and more weapons for the army to use to kill more civilians.

The president seemed to be talking out of both sides of his mouth, or out of two mouths. At the same time, sending bombs, and also sending humanitarian aid. This schizophrenic agenda disturbed the poet to no end. He couldn't bear the thought of all those who had died and been wounded; all the children slaughtered or orphaned, or having had limbs amputated without anesthetic. He felt the pain of these suffering people as if it were his own.

He could only watch the war on television for one hour a day now. At the start of the war, he was glued to his television all day, not believing the horror he was seeing. Bombs exploding over hospitals, schools, aid organizations, mosques, churches, apartment buildings, homes. The attacks were relentless, revenge for the resistance's attack on the colonizers, which had killed 1,200 people. The attacks of the army had slaughtered now 31,000, including 15,000 children, a disproportionate number.

The war was tragic and part of a larger problem. The people who were being attacked had been driven from their land 75 years earlier, when the army drove them out. They had sought shelter in this small territory where more than two million people lived. Now they were being driven out again, having to flee their homes, which were under attack, and head south in the territory.

Homeless refugees, they set up makeshift tents to dwell in through the war. They had no possessions, having left everything in their abandoned homes. The children had nothing to play with. There were no bathrooms. The dead lay ignored on the streets. The hospitals had mostly closed, and the few that were still open had no supplies and could not properly treat the wounded.

"Cry out, O earth! Ye gods, give ear!" he had suddenly thought. In despair he cried out for help for all those suffering in the war. Weeping in his heart, he got back to work again. His tea and biscuits had invigorated his mind and body. The son was in the living room watching horror movies. The boy loved very extreme music: black metal and death metal, with intense screaming, howling, and groaning.

This music enabled the boy to vicariously let out his anger, allowing the "harsh vocals" to exorcize his anger and rage. The father had learned to deal with this hysterical music, and even liked some of it. The boy loved to play his music for his father, and enjoyed sharing what he loved. This was a challenge for the father, to endure this assault on his hearing aids. But he was very Taoist about it and took it as an always new experience, stretching out his capacity.

It's time for a word from our sponsor: Infected earthworms cavort inside their mason jars, expecting to be bred for experimental purposes. The technicians wore aluminum foil suits for protection, and waltzed around the room in circles. Forced births were the norm, and anyone who resisted were strapped down and held captive until they delivered.

He kept vegetables and cider on a table on his porch, having no room in the refrigerator. Turnips and beets from the Amish store on the way home from the Wise Woman. They always had enough food to eat, and the father was good at planning a variety of unusual meals for their supper. He made Indian curries, Chinese stir-fries, Italian dishes, Jewish meals, and ordinary American food. He planned each meal in the morning, taking out something from the freezer to thaw for supper.

The air balloons wafted across the clear blue sky, off into the distance. The meals left out for the homeless melted in the afternoon sun. The homeless were on hunger strike, demanding adequate housing. They refused to eat food until their needs were realistically met. They camped out on the village green, to the dismay of the villagers, and set about to make homes for themselves right there. No one attempted to stop them from doing this together.

He worked on his new book every day, never taking a day off, as his son would have liked him to. He kept a tight schedule throughout his days and nights, adhering to his pattern of doing things.

All the little rituals and details of a day. His life was ordered by keeping up with all these details. This is how he held himself together, having an ordered, peaceful schedule for himself.

Waking up at 5:30 every morning, he enjoyed these early hours in the dark. He loved watching it get light out, through the window in the study. This was always a very exciting event for him. He spent the early hour reading, these days How to Write by Gertrude Stein. He loved waking up to her mellifluous language, as absurd and always intriguing as it was. It was a pleasure, as she would say.

He then went upstairs with his coffee for his devotional readings and prayer and meditation exercise. This quiet, beautiful time strengthened him to face the day, and prepared for whatever might come. His cold shower followed, then his toilette. He gave great emphasis to his cleanliness and personal hygiene, and loved washing his face in his blessed ice cold water. He had his best prayer time in the ice cold water of the shower every morning.

Putting on his artificial body parts (his eyeglasses, partial dentures, and hearing aids), he was prepared for the day. Now to get dressed, clothing himself like a king getting ready for court, he gently put on his garments, lovingly, one at a time, then finally his shoes. His watch, bracelet, and wallet on, a spray of his favorite "Black" cologne, and he was ready to go.

Pigeons gathered on the village green, hoping to be fed by the hunger-striking homeless, who had no bread to give them. Plastic tubes ran down the sides of the mechanism, churning away like humidifiers in the desert. The families of the hostages were demanding their release. The resistance and the army had been unable to reach a deal for a ceasefire. The suffering people were paying the price.

He finally had a hole in the right elbow of his black and grey flannel shirt. This always happened, as he would lean on the walls of the stairwell, in order to balance himself, since there was no bannister.

He wanted to have one installed, but had just spent a great deal of money on his laundry room and bathroom renovations. So the bannister would have to wait. So the inevitable hole on the right elbow was a yearly occurance; every winter this would happen to him. So each year he would have to buy new flannel shirts, his favorite thing to wear in winter.

He had spoken on the phone to one of his oldest friends, a 90 year old artist and writer to whose children he had been nanny, and to whose husband he had been a young lover 50 years before. She had ordered four copies of his novel, to give to her now grown children and to her gallery owner. She was going to send him her new book, a coffee table work from years before. She was excited to hear of his new novel, and impressed at his disciplined schedule.

They had only discovered one another a few years earlier, and were delighted to be reunited. They loved one another dearly, and had many fond memories between them. He had connected with her grown children also, and they were very glad to hear from him. They had all been together many years before, and had lived as a family together in their townhouse in the city where he had grown up.

He was so young then, and open to all new experiences. With his long blonde hair hanging down, baggy white pants and old man's white shirt, he looked like some strange, exotic bird. He was a tender, sensitive young person, and flowed from one moment to the next with grace and confidence.

He had gotten involved as an "enfant terrible" in the downtown arts scene in the city.

He was sure to appear at the right gallery openings, parties, concerts, dance performances, poetry readings, and other events to be in the eye of the cyclone. He met all the right people: those artists, poets, dancers, film makers whose work he admired. Some of these were already famous, or went on to be. He gave poetry readings at the Poetry Center, and mixed media performances of his music and performance art.

He went to a party at the home of a well-known publisher of avant-garde literature, and ended up talking to him after the party and stayed the night on his couch. In the morning, he was enchanted to meet the young twin girls and their mother. This publisher pursued him, and he became this man's young lover. They lived in another state, up north near the border, and he became nanny to the twins.They became an unusual kind of family, with him as "personal assistant" to the man, doing for him whatever chores and errands needed doing. His chief pleasure was caring for the girls, playing with them and reading to them. They loved when he read to them from Gertrude Stein's book, The World Is Round. What lovely times they all shared. It was then that he wrote his first mature poems.

This publisher had an indoor swimming pool and sauna. He would love to go in the sauna, get very hot and sweaty, and go roll naked in the deep northern snow. The sight of his corpulent body playing in the snow was a sight to behold. His two huge white dogs would roll in the snow with him.

They finally came to an end, and he returned to his apartment in the city.

He had a mentor, a well-known poet, whose personal assistant he became, as well as nanny to the poet's children. The poet's son had read Moby Dick at six years old. His daughter was magical, and loved to dance. The poet was very wise and deep, and he learned much from this precious mentor.

The man encouraged him to write, and came to his poetry readings to support him.

They were not lovers; he had not wanted to spoil their sacred friendship, and the purity of all they shared together. This poet's wife had abandoned the family and left the poet to be a single father. She was an artist, and wanted her freedom, so she just walked out on them. He was friends also with this woman, who was very peculiar and impulsive. And he never understood how she could have left the poet and their children.

He had spoken on the phone with another female

friend, whom he had known since his days in his parish. She used to attend, and was one of his greatest supporters during the cataclysm. They had remained friends, although the woman had moved to the capital of the state. She had become the Wasp Woman. On her balcony, she had become friends with some wasps. She fed them honey which they loved to eat. They would even come on her finger to eat the honey from her hand.

There was something magical about this woman: she had the wisdom of the earth. A deep knowledge and spirit that attuned her to the movements of nature. She talked to these wasps, and sensed they were hungry, so she fed them. She sensed that they had come into her apartment to seek shelter from the cold and hibernate for the winter. So she welcomed them into her home.

This woman had a cat who died. This was a huge crisis for her. She had been so close to the cat, and was devastated by its death. Recovering eventually, she adopted two young male cats, who had been wild, and was training them to grow up into nice cats, which they had never been able to do.

It was wonderful how close she was with these animals, who were more than animals to her.

Floating vestments wafted through the silent air, the clothing of clerics who had abandoned their posts once religion was abolished. Empty garbage cans blew down the empty street. Chosen tokens of parleyed agreements were damaged by the frozen cartons of raw flesh, cascading down the slopes of the grim mountain. Thoughtful gifts collided inside the hospital, draining their blood like a gas stove and oven.

Tender shepherds voice captive praise for the pink elephants that retired after the parade.

Putting on thick mascara, the women asked for entire boxes of pasta to be planted into their skulls.

Anteaters danced upon the surface of the moon, glancing in the direction of earth. Asking questions that have no answers, they placed dominoes upon the table of glass. The direction was the same, and the mother of the children lived out back in the studio.

The rain was pattering down upon the waiting earth. He could hear it through the window by the desk where he was typing. Sudden thrusts of iron pierced the entrance of affliction through the throat. Western ideas collide with Eastern thought, he considered. He was amazed how different cultures have their entirely unique world view, self-understandings, stories about the origin of the earth.

He was reading (having finished Dante) the Metamorphoses of Ovid. This Latin Roman writer dwelled upon transformations of one creature into another. He has his own Creation story, and even a great flood which destroys the earth, except for one couple. The miraculous way the earth is repopulated is told in vivid detail. The similarity with the Hebrew Scriptures version interested him greatly. He wondered if there is some universal mind, as Jung had claimed.

Rabid zombies walked toward the hunger-striking homeless on the village green, suddenly appearing out of nowhere. The homeless were not going to leave their encampment, so they chased the zombies away with flaming torches. The hunger strike was not going well. The pilgrims kept offering them home-cooked meals, which they systematically refused to eat.

Captive leeches cling to their jars. The bell tolls the quarter hour. No one moves in inch. Suddenly, everyone is frozen stiff and cannot budge. The firemen pour water from their hoses to melt the ice and release the frozen people from captivity. Slowly they begin to thaw. They celebrate their freedom by eating all they can eat.

The village came up with a plan to house the homeless in abandoned homes, of which there were many. They set out to renovate and restore these homes, so the homeless could live in them.

The whole village got behind this effort, conscious of their responsibility to help those in need, especially with the war going on. The homeless were thrilled to have places of their own, at last, and everyone was very well pleased.

His 90-year-old friend had published a book, based on material that she and her former husband (whose young lover the poet had been) had put together many years earlier. She wanted him to have this beautiful coffee table art book, but the price was more than he could afford. So, he negotiated a price with her very generous gallery dealer and publisher, and he was able to get the book for a price he was able to afford, having been through financial difficulties of late. He would treasure this book.

He had also sent to this woman some early poems of his own. He also sent them to her publisher to enjoy.

He hoped that they would enjoy his poems. Three of his earliest poems, and one very long, epic poem, A Poem About The Paint That Is Peeling, which had been published and then lost for 45 years. This poem had been recently discovered and returned to the poet with great rejoicing. His poem had come home to him at last.

He had read this epic poem at the Poetry Center in the city in his youth, to considerable acclaim. In fact, he had a certain reputation as a poet in his younger days in the city. He was known for his dry, reading style that allowed humor to be expressed with solemnity. However, one fellow poet had, alarmingly, accused him of writing "fake poems." This disturbed the young poet terribly, and he didn't know what to make of this criticism. It seemed to write off all his years of poetic effort.

He had always believed in his work, and gave himself to its production with all his being. In his younger years, he had really lived as a full-time bohemian poet. But what with his religious conversion, marriage, children, parish ministry, he was sidetracked from his vocation as poet and writer. He prepared sermons instead of poems. There was the one time when the British string quartet whom he knew, came to his church and played the Seven Last Words From The Cross of Haydn.

The poet had written a cycle of meditative poems on the themes of the Seven Last Words, and read these, with the quartet playing each movement of the piece after he read each poem. This was a major event, and the church had a full house of concert-goers. The program was a huge success, and a reception followed in the parish house. He had also given a concert in the church with his baroque ensemble, which was very well attended also.

But his writing had become a solitary act, a devotional exercise that was entirely a very private matter. He wrote for years, by hand, in his marble composition books, accumulating eighteen of them. These he gathered and kept as precious manuscripts, to be one day dealt with. He had played cello with the local symphony orchestra for twenty-four years before retiring to work on his writing and poetry. Retiring, he had produced and typed up the eighteen notebooks in two years.

Performing in the symphony had been a great joy for him, although it was a labor of love. He needed to practice his cello for three hours a day to learn the music the orchestra would be performing at its next concert. He had to work hard to be able to play this challenging music, spanning the full repertoire of a symphony orchestra. He began to be intimidated by the young music majors who came to play with the group; they were so much more technically capable than him, and he couldn't keep up with them. Also, he could no longer drive at night, being unable to see the road.

This was part of why he retired. Also, the music they were playing had become increasingly difficult, and he could no longer justify the amount of time he had to prepare the music. The poet wanted to work on his writing. So he sent a letter to the members of the symphony announcing his departure and the reasons for this. He was honored at the last concert he attended, when the conductor called upon him to stand up, and recognized his 24 year accomplishment. The audience gave him two vigorous rounds of applause as he happily waved his hand to them. This was a beautiful moment.

The poet had spent his life reading poetry: traditional verse, but especially the writing of the preceding century. He loved the modern, avant-garde poetry and fiction: experimental writing like his own, which inspired him tremendously. This writing moved him with its unusual use of language. He loved the "modern" writers, who were no longer modern at all. Many of them were a century old: James Joyce, Gertrude Stein, the dada poets and the surrealist writers: Cocteau, Breton, Eluard, Aragon, Soupault. He loved also the older French poets: Baudelaire, Rimbaud, and Mallarme.

These poets and writers wrote "abstract" works that used language and thought in unusual ways. Their bold, iconoclastic writing broke all the rules of literature, breaking out into the previously uncharted territory of the unconscious mind. New forms were developed, with a new freedom of expression. Pound, Williams, Stevens, HD, were all heroes to his thinking, and helped him to grow in the knowledge and love of poetry, and to find his own voice and keep it.

The old poet who had taken him under his wing had told him that he saw that the younger poet had demonstrated one consistent voice throughout his body of work. This amazed him, since he had thought that he had been several different people throughout his long life. But this was a revelation!

He had, apparently, been the same person throughout his long life. How amazing.

And he had written in a number of different styles and manners, so the observation that he had a consistent voice, even through such a wide variety of writing, was remarkable to him. He was grateful to the older poet for sharing this insight with him. It changed his perception of himself and his work, and affirmed the consistency of his efforts. The poet found himself believing in his purpose, and was profoundly encouraged to keep on with it every day.

He had studied the cello from twelve years of age, and fell in love with it immediately. Having watched Casals' Master Classes on television, he knew this was the instrument that he wanted to play.

He took lessons from a local cello teacher, and played also in school. He performed at a school concert, playing two pieces by Tchaikovsky and Granados. He parents were so proud of him that day.

He went on to study at the high school dedicated to students of music and art. He had to travel one hour each way on the subway, lugging his cello, to get to this school in the city. He played in the all-borough orchestra, and the all-city orchestra for students, and they played at the major concert halls.

He began lessons with a new cello teacher in the city, and counterpoint and piano with another.

Playing more advanced music, he also played with a string quartet. But after his mother's death his life fell apart. He was no longer able to concentrate on school, and finally dropped out. He stayed in touch with his friends, and spent his time reading and drinking his father's vodka in his bedroom.

It was during this time that he and his father had difficulties, and argued often.

He was working on his music and writing and reading, and he determined that he would be a poet and an artist of literature. He was in the young composer's group at his private music school in the city, and they gave a concert of their works. He produced an event involving radios, loud speakers, scents, and it was a full sensory experience. The audience was surprised, and didn't quite know what to make of this. But he and his friends had fun performing this piece

Blasting emphases gather in the confines of the room, winking at each other, and plotting to strip the fruit trees of their envelopes. Waiting for the spring, the flopping winds blew across the field of perception, invading the unconscious minds of those who were waiting. Clarified thoughts, like butter, remained at the exits, while flippant elves maimed each other severely. Amplified dreams awakened blissful romps through the woulds.

Carefully pulling back the extra film from the covers, wishful membranes balanced balls on their exit chutes. Weathering the fall of dice, playful seals dived for luminescent fish. Squeezing out their eyeballs, ventilated parsons ate jellyfish, cold and raw. Captive artichokes resisted the strong winds that blew wildly in their minds. No one resisted the cavorting boys with their blue electric penises.

While indulging in mindless drivel, they refused to read books, since these had been forbidden.

People watched the state television day and night. Most had televisions in every room of their homes.

The poet watched the Arab news station, in English, for its coverage of the war. This was the only station allowed into the besieged territory; international networks were forbidden by the army.

One hundred and fifty journalists were killed covering the war. Two hundred aid workers had been killed. The poet watched this coverage of the war with deep passion in his heart. He bled internally for the death, pain, and suffering of the innocent people there. He felt like it was happening to himself, and significantly, it was. He entered into the experience of the war: the starvation, the maiming, the hopelessness.

He had spoken to his son's mother; he wanted to tell her about the daughters not speaking to him or their son. She said that she would pray for him. This was one of their more civilized conversations of late, and she genuinely seemed to care about the pain he was suffering over this situation. He pointed out to her that their son didn't feel comfortable going to her house, because he felt that she didn't want him to visit there. To this she made no response, but said she would see her son on his upcoming birthday.

The poet had thought that he had lost twenty pages of his new novel. He went into a panic, looking everywhere but couldn't find them. After almost giving up, suddenly there they were. He was desperately relieved, and started in on his work for the day immediately. He was a poet who had written a novel, not a novelist who wrote poems. He had one novel already published, his first book of poems on the way, and he was writing another, new novel.

Escaping things transformed into other things: people into trees, trees into people. Nothing was the same for very long. Extra thick dreams changed people into poems. Where the thickness was, there also was the answer to the question. Pressing on their mouths, they were unable to speak for a minute.

This disorientation continued until the cows came home from their field.

The winds blew fiercely, blowing the envelopes off of the fruit trees, containing their poems. The villagers ran after the scattering envelopes as if they were some lost treasure. They ate the poems after reading them, ingesting their words like food. The flagrant vagrants were happy in their new homes. The rampaging boys had returned to their home, and were recovering from their efforts.

The poet had swept and mopped his kitchen floor that morning. This gave him a great deal of satisfaction. Seeing the results of his effort was gratifying to him.

Tangible results were as useful as metaphysical ones, he thought. Although he was rather of a mystical nature himself. Still, he moved awkwardly through the physical world, as though a foreigner from a distant country.

A stranger in a strange land, he had always felt different. An alien, the "Space-Jew-Faggot-From- Mars," as he thought of himself, and how he thought other people perceived him. He had never felt at home in the world, but as though he were some different species. He had never felt like a boy or a man; nor had he ever felt like or wanted to be a girl or a woman. He was an entirely different creature, spanning the genders and transcending them, containing all orientations within himself.

"Behold, I have become all things to all men," had said St Paul. This seemed to apply to the poet, and he reveled in his marvelous ambiguity. He was not a traditional beauty, but a more exotic kind. And he had come to terms with his unusual appearance, and rejoiced in his own unusual beauty. Not conceited, he just felt that he was at least as good as everyone else, if not better.

The poet had been emotionally challenged for most of his life. He had been in counseling as a child, from age eight until fifteen, when his mother died. Peculiarly, his father and counselor decided to remove him from counseling. This, after the devastation of his mother's sudden passing, was a terrible blow. His counselor had been a lifeline for him through his childhood and adolescence. This seemed to him, in retrospect, a very cruel decision.

This left him without moorings in the world, hopeless and without help. He fell through the crack that this created, and no longer could function as would have been appropriate to his age and academic standing. He could no longer deal with school. In fact, he had always excelled in the subjects which interested him passionately: English, Art, and Music, and merely passed his other subjects. He couldn't be bothered with anything he wasn't interested in.

After dropping out of High School, he decorated his room. Taping aluminum foil to the walls, he also hung opened dry cleaning bags from the ceiling, to create beautiful, puffy pillows. He brought home from the vacant lot across the street a broken tricycle, a long rusty pipe, and other discarded objects which he claimed as "art." It was this, and his staying up all night reading and drinking vodka which led his future stepmother to refuse to marry his father if he was going to live with them. So much for art.

He would wander along the side of the highway picking wild flowers, really weeds. These he would happily bring home to place in his room for decoration. He would take long walks at night, when no one was out or around. It was then that he began to be "a solitary," living his life by his own rules and instincts and needs. He would answer to no one but his inner conscience, which would lead him through his long, varied life.

The young poet had written to a famous composer whom he greatly admired, and wished to disciple himself to this great man. Suddenly, out of nowhere, the composer called him, inviting him to come visit at his home in the woods. The young poet was thrilled out of his mind! He took the bus up to see the composer, and they spent the day together. He showed the composer the music he had been working on, and they went hunting for mushrooms.

They had dinner at the home of an elderly, eccentric

Hungarian artist who cooked the mushrooms and made dinner. This would be the first time he ate wild mushrooms and artichoke.

This artist was marvelous, and most unusual. She had a huge head of fluttering white hair, and made art out of objects she had found: some from nature, some domestic.

This visit to the composer changed the young poet's life. The composer mentioned people he should meet, which opened up the entire community of the arts to him. It was through the composer that he met the most influential people in his life; people who had studied with the composer years before, and had been greatly influenced by him. These people became his new family.

Radical lesbian feminists and avant-garde artists in various media were the people he spent time with back then, as a young poet. No doubt, he was seeking a father figure in the three older men to whom he became disciple. To two of these, he had been their young lover. This might seem unusual, but it has parallels in many ancient cultures, particularly in Greece and Rome, as well as the samurai tradition in Japan. A young man discipling himself to an older and wiser man and submitting himself as his lover.

He learned so much from these older men, and entered into his life with them with enthusiasm.

Had he been taken advantage of at such a tender age? No one can say for sure. The difference in power between them was significant, but this is what attracted the young poet to these particular men. He gladly submitted to their teaching and influence, as well as the carnal desires of two of them. The young poet found deep meaning in these relationships.

How interesting then, that the poet, after his two marriages, in middle age, would find himself in relationships with younger men. Fully grown, not children, these attracted him by their winsomeness and youthful vigor. Their minds were open to his influence and love. He enjoyed these relationships and encounters, always wanting to get to know a young man, to talk together endlessly, getting to know each other, and, on occasion, pluck the fruit of love together.

However, these relations often involved the poet being used for money and drugs. He was also robbed numerous times: his mother's precious jewelry was stolen, including a strand of real pearls; his eldest daughter's violin had been taken, tragically. This instrument had been from her great grandmother's house on the island, and been restored and cleaned up for her to use. An entire safe was dragged out of the house by kids looking for marijuana, which wasn't even in the safe, thankfully.

The white page of paper in the old black Royal Standard typewriter. The bits of turnip coagulated in butter on the plate from last night's dinner. The ectoplasm stuck to the walls of the shower in the bathroom. Stray toothpicks, an orange bottle cap, a cough drop, a cigarette lighter.

Their favorite pasta: angel hair with olive oil, garlic, herbs, and grated cheese. The sudden silence.

Adjusting his margins. Beginning to write.

He was intrigued by the image of the bits of turnip on the plate: a gelatinous mass that had solidified in its butter. The remains of the turnips, white and purple, which he had purchased at the Amish store, coming home from seeing the Wise Woman the previous week. Their beautiful colors and lovely round shape entranced him. These he would wash, slice into thirds, and then cut those into thirds, ending up with nice, even cubes.

Boiling them in water, they were then drained

and buttered, salt and pepper and parsley added, and taken hot to the table. His son loved these turnips, so the father made them often. They were the perfect accompaniment to the baked chicken breasts he had also cooked that night. The father and son ate well: he, with guilt over those two million starving in the war. But not eating would not help those poor people, so he made a contribution to the aid organization trying to help them.

Suffering succotash, entering the ambulance, walking backwards, the antelope advanced on three legs, hobbling. The new young mailman who brought his package, containing the blue and green checked woolen trousers he had ordered, was beautiful. Although he had renounced romantic love, he still instinctively felt moved by beauty in all its forms. So the new mailman was a delight.

Stepping lively, the orchestra prepared to perform, even though there was no audience. The newspaper had printed the wrong date, so nobody had come. The musicians decided to play anyway, just for the enjoyment of it. They played the entire program, even taking an intermission. Slowly, various birds began to gather, listening to the beautiful music. Small animals poked their heads out to hear the amazing sounds. Deer, bunnies, butterflies came out of their hiding places to watch and enjoy the new sounds they were hearing. The orchestra never knew they had an audience, never having looked up.

The cobwebs on the walls. The ashes on the table. Stuck like a duck. Emphasis on duck. Like his poem, Ducking. He wrote abstract poems, which only occasionally hinted at reality. But these poems and his novel could be read by anyone, he believed. He had receive the first "proof" of his book of poems, and the design was wonderful and very bold, yet sensitive to his work. He looked forward to this new book coming out soon.

When his eldest daughter was learning to speak, she would see a pigeon in the park and gleefully shout out, "Ook! Ook! Ook at da guck!" calling all birds a duck. He missed this daughter terribly. It tugged at his heart. His youngest daughter had given her eldest sister his book, and a recent photograph of their father. The middle daughter had spoken to her sister about how well their father was doing, and all the good things happening in his life.

The father waited patiently, praying and hoping that this daughter would return to him and call him on the telephone. In her teenage years, she had given him a beautiful book, which he called The Japanese Notebook, because of its calligraphy on the cover of the character for "moon." He had written many poems in this notebook, especially as he was starting to write haiku.

This daughter had written her father a four-page love letter in this notebook, praising him for all his virtues. What had happened to those feelings? Where did they go? They had not spoken for eight years, apart from their one ill-fated dinner five years earlier. Shortly before this daughter broke off contact with her father, he had purchased a white linen suit at the upscale department store to wear at her graduation from graduate school. But sadly, he was uninvited from going. This had broken his heart.

The poet had tried to love all his children equally, when they were willing to accept his love.

But naturally, perhaps, as is the way of nature, he had a special bond with his eldest daughter, his first child. For the first time he got to change diapers, cuddle and play with her, be silly and have fun together. For the first time he had enjoyed the adventure of teaching a child to talk, to read, to watch her learn to walk. To read her classic children's stories and poems.

But he went on with his life, trying not to think about his eldest daughter. It was too painful to think about her. But recently, he had embraced this daughter in his heart again, ready to receive her back after all these years. He could feel her taking baby steps toward this goal. He could feel her opening up to caring about him again, and, in time, being reconciled to him at last. He could now pray for her.

Like superheroes, the firemen grilled halved chickens for their annual barbeque benefit. On the village green, all the villagers came out for this pleasant event. Miraculously, after the pastor prayed a blessing, the chickens reunited their halves, grew back their feet and heads, shook off the barbeque sauce, growing feathers, stood up and attacked the villagers. The flagrant vagrants tried to fight them off, but only got bitten and clawed in the process.

The villagers ran off to their homes, bleeding and shaking with terror. The chickens ran off into the country, and were never seen again. It was an effort for the firemen to clean up all the mess, what with feathers and barbeque sauce everywhere. Everyone had to improvise supper that night, mostly eating leftovers, or frozen pizza. The village recovered and peace was restored. The flagrant vagrants were bandaged up at the hospital, and soon recovered.

The poet had always felt out of place in the culture in which he found himself. He thought that he belonged to another time and era, the previous century, actually. He had never adjusted to the new century, and read only dead authors and poets. There were only two exceptions in which he read living authors: A S Byatt, whose Possession he had adored; and Umberto Eco, whose The Name of The Rose had made a deep impression on him.

He did not identify with the popular culture of his day, movies, music, art, dancing. He lived in his mind in another era, when things still had meaning, when people still had feelings, when everyone seemed to care about each other. And the arts, in all their forms, had reflected these concerns. The country seemed shallow, and mindless, materialistic, superficial, cynical, arrogant, self-centered. This was also why he felt like an alien, safe in his house.

The poet tried to see beauty and meaning in everything in life. He valued the most mundane events and actions. He had written a haiku the other day:

The birds are singing,
in the darkness of morning:
emptying his bowels.

The poet valued his morning defecation as a holy occasion. He had a rigorous regime to maintain his intestinal and digestive health: the poet took fiber capsules made from psyllium, and probiotic gummies, which helped him maintain regularity. Like clockwork, early in the morning, he would feel it coming, and go to relieve himself.

What a wonderful moment this was: a miraculous event! An incredible release and relief, the closest he would ever come to giving birth. A sense of accomplishment enlarged his heart as he gazed at his creation in the white porcelain bowl. A sense of pride; after all, this is a baby's first creative act, and it stays with us throughout our lives. Why not make the most of it? he thought. So he reveled in this simple biological act, as if he had written a beautiful poem on the toilet that morning.

Floundering like halibut, the exterminators sucked tubes of plastic, and emptied their armpits of all extraneous additions. Parcels of vain strivings tied emphasized their unusual attributes, to the various entities that were present. "Anybody can do that," offered the mayor to the gymnasts. The full-throated contralto poured gasoline on the albatross, who flew away before she could light the match. No one applauded her performance art display.

Kindling wood was gathered for the bonfire of the vanities, in celebration of the onslaught of spring, having come a week early this year. They tore apart phone books to place on the fire, tossing them onto the waiting flames with precision. Talking amongst themselves, the villagers pursued forbidden topics of conversation. The Communication Police regularly eavesdropped on private conversations, tapping all the phones of the village.

If they heard anything amiss or forbidden, they

would break into the conversation and impose fines on the callers. So people were afraid to talk on the phone. Finally, they stormed the Communications Station and burned it to the ground. At last, they could talk on the telephone in peace.

Friendships were discouraged, and the only way people could maintain contact was on the phone.

The Relationship Police investigated any forbidden relations, imprisoning those who were "caught in the act." Intimate relations outside of marriage were forbidden, and birth control was illegal, for married couples. People had so many children they didn't know what to do. So many mouths to feed, diapers to change, homework to check. Couples were overwhelmed and children were neglected.

Vain strivings melt their oval-shaped parcels, laying slices of raw bacon on them for amusement.

Captive felines wander off into the woods, un-house-broken once again. Your thoughts turn into furry moths which fly through your memory at twilight. Feverish thieves counsel one another concerning the burning house across the street, having planned to rob it. Their disappointment was extravagant, and they ate Chinese noodles with chopsticks, on the patio at night.

The poet let his imagination run wild, rampantly exuding each word, one after another. This journey of language transformation was his entire purpose in life. He was almost finished reading How to Write by Gertrude Stein. He read this in the early morning, when it was still dark out. Letting her words be the first thing he engaged in each morning left him open as a sponge for her to do what she would do, and he would eat it up with a spoon,

Stein's writing made his own seem comprehensible. She was so wonderfully obscure that he had no idea what she was writing about most of the time. But the poet loved reading incomprehensible writing and poetry. This made his overactive brain buzz, since he came out of a tradition in literature which proclaimed incomprehensibility as a virtue in writing. This may seem peculiar, but it was his background, his present, and his future.

The poet took a walk every morning, all year round, in all kinds of weather. The walk cleared his mind and invigorated his body, so that he was prepared to face the day ahead. He enjoyed these walks to no end, and almost never missed a day. He liked breathing in the fresh morning air of the village, and walked before anyone was about. He like seeing the same houses, dependable in their presence as mountains. He blessed his neighbors along the way, praying good things for them.

This walk always followed his breakfast of Greek yogurt and mandarin oranges each morning.

Upon returning, he would change out of his sneakers, and put on his favorite Birkenstocks. He would then go downstairs and feed his precious birds, whom he would talk to each morning. Then, he would take his pink water bottle and go into the study to imbibe his morning marijuana. This calmed his spirit and mellowed his mind from its sharp edges. The indulgence would last him until after lunch, and he was ready to face the day.

Outlandish sailors roamed the forgotten piers, looking for love. Extra heavy tears poured down the face of Time, as wrestling orphans gathered in pools of blood. Remembering to turn out the lights, the meaning of the text was forgotten for centuries, and no one dared to open this book again. Staying on top of the situation required knitting skills, plumbing abilities, and more ectoplasm.

Because of the situation, the purview of things transformed into thoughtlessness, exuded like sap from trees in spring. Coughing, they opened their minds, and forgot what they were doing. Playing games together, they pretended to be a family, collapsing like a pile of dominoes on the kitchen table.

Various accusations conferred acceptance upon the newly arrived immigrants.

The last thing that anyone needed: a fix for an addict, a supermarket transformed into a way-station for travelers lost in a strange country. The faucets were leaking, and everyone had to go to the bathroom at the same time. They lined up and waited, clenching their sphincters, to hold it in. One had an "accident," not being able to wait any longer. This was an old man, who broke down in tears after it happened, so humiliated did he feel.

Ancient Greek and Roman plays were offered at the local theatre, and the villagers attended with great excitement. But they were dismayed and confused when the plays were performed in ancient Greek and Latin. Most of the audience walked out, but the poet stayed, recalling his Greek and Latin from his college days. The plays were performed impeccably, and the poet was very well pleased.

Octagonal spikes protruded from the ice trays in the freezer. Portions of emptiness wandered through the streets, looking for someone to eat them. Useful messages were sent from one end of the village to another, expressing condolences for the death of Life. The messengers retreated to their caves, to squeeze out of rocks the milk of giraffes. Piling up around the edges, mildewed hay fed the cows of destruction over their dead bodies.

Useful as they were, the fingers of the secretaries had trouble typing. The heir apparent would never agree to let the clouds for their raindrops on his birthday suit. Pencils were always ready to work, inhaling the fumes of sawdust that followed them wherever they went. Coal was reinstituted as a source of energy, and oil was the only alternative. Natural gas had been outlawed, as being too much cheaper than oil. The villagers struggled to pay their bills.

The poet had been to the doctor for his annual checkup that morning. He had given the doctor a copy of his novel, and the doctor was very impressed. The poet was in excellent health, and his doctor told him to "keep writing." This doctor was a very caring physician, and the poet trusted him implicitly.

He had a very reassuring, encouraging manner, and the poet always looked forward to seeing his doctor.

The poet told the doctor how he was having trouble playing his cello, even following the injection for his trigger finger the past week. It was a struggle to play, since his middle finger on his left hand was still not fully functional. This finger, along with all the fingers of his left hand, fingered the notes that he played. The second finger in the fingering scheme needed to move quickly and dance over the strings. But this was painful to endure.

So his doctor was going to refer him to the hospital, where they might be able to help him.

This hospital was in the town of the Wise Woman, and he had been to this hospital's clinic before, to have a growth removed from his cheek. The doctor said they may have other treatments, other injections, or even surgery. The poet shuddered at the thought of these, but decided that it would be better to have it checked out. He looked forward to playing his cello for the rest of his life, so having his finger fully functional would be essential.

The poet's 90-year-old friend had sent him her new book. He would wait before opening it, to let it "age" and settle, a day or two. He liked to build up the suspense before opening a package or an important letter. He liked waiting, and looking at the unopened package, wondering what was in it was like. This would be an impossibly beautiful book, from this dearest old friend, and he would treasure and cherish it forever. What a kindness it was for her to have sent it!

He was enchanted by Ovid's story in Metamorphoses about Narcissus. The poet was impressed by the fact that both men and women fell in love with this beautiful boy. He had not yielded to their advances, but kept himself pure. Narcissus didn't know that his reflection was himself, and fell in love with the beautiful boy he saw in the pool's water. This was a clearly homosexual love, narrated by Ovid with sensitivity and naturalness. He had never realized this aspect of the story of Narcissus before.

The poet was moved when Narcissus realizes that his reflection is himself. The impossible dilemma he was in leads Narcissus to wither and die, and turn into the beautiful flower that bears his name. The poet found this story enchanting and magical. He loved the transitions depicted in Ovid, metamorphoses of one thing into another. He was amazed at the beauty and detail in this book, and how cleverly the stories were told.

Overwhelming entrances conferred with the best oracles to describe the intricacies of memory.

Fluttering feathers floated down from the ceiling, as they sucked cough drops on the roof of the building. Sensory extraneous moments converged into excellent representatives of fluttering moths, gathered at the screen door, attracted by the porch light at night. Like writing a novel, elephants drowned their sorrows in the pool of tears, laughing as they went along.

While waiting for the elevator, girl scouts sell their cookies to the waiting mob. Girl scout cookies, made from real girl scouts, for your eating enjoyment. The rampaging boys impale one another with their blue electric penises, stopping at nothing until their goals were achieved. No one notices mopeds, electric chairs, and licorice. The clergy had all retired to the coast, where they put their feet up on footstools and read the daily newspaper.

He wondered whether there were really such a thing as love, especially romantic love. Wasn't love a metaphor for getting one's needs met, physically, emotionally, psychologically? Wasn't all love an extension of self-love, as Narcissus found out? Self-centered lives impacting other self-centered lives?

The poet had been jaded, disillusioned about love, having given himself so fully and so often to so many, only to have it thrown back in his face.

He had loved too often, and it had drained him of his enthusiasm and intentions. He no longer looked for love, or desired it. He had found a way to live on his own, with his son, and this was good enough for him. Most of his old friends lived in other states, far away, and the only way he could maintain contact with them was over the telephone. These old friendships were precious to the poet, and he valued his friends as sources of hope, encouragement, and compassion.

The son was depressed. His birthday was coming up next week, and he felt he had nothing to show for his years of life. Things had always been hard for the boy; growing up had been painful. He had no friends, and longed to find love in the midst of his despair. He had given up hope of ever finding a mate for himself, and had no idea how to meet people. So he howled and moaned, screaming to the heavens for some relief from his misery. The boy wanted to die, and had been saying so for twenty years. This broke the father's heart to see his son so sad and hopeless.

So the son sought solace in sleep, retreating to his bed every now and then for a nap.

The father took this quiet, peaceful time to write, weaving fugues of words into symphonies of language. He would drain his brain of ideas, attempting to write a constantly interesting and intriguing pattern of words into his novel. A novel novel, this book would be the successor to his first novel, and would take its place alongside the other book with sibling pride and joy.

In the war, the people were starving to death, when they should have been fasting during their holy month. How could they fast when they were already starving? The bombs were dropping everywhere, and there was nowhere safe in their small territory. Children were terrified and cried constantly out of fear and hunger.

The parents grieved that they had no food for their children.

Babies were dying because their breast-feeding mothers had no milk, themselves starving.

Meanwhile, back at the ranch, the cowboys shot at immigrants, crossing into the country.

The hate they felt toward these foreigners was extreme. Xenophobia had taken over the land, and bands of vigilantes roamed the border, aiming to kill any immigrants they could find. There was a bounty out for those who killed them, and the marauding bands spared no one, intending to collect those fees.

It was open hunting season, and no license was required to kill.

So the flagrant vagrants tried to help the immigrants, bringing them water and food, much to the displeasure of the vigilantes. They cared instinctively about these poor people, who had traveled through jungles, thick with dense undergrowth and wild animals. They had been robbed along the way, raped, murdered. The compassion of the vagrants knew no bounds, since they had suffered homelessness and hunger themselves. They wanted to help these poor people in any way they could.

The silence was engulfing the poet, like a heating pad when he had a muscle spasm. He felt at home in the silence, which was comforting to him. He could hear his own thoughts, and concentrate on his writing this way. In solitary isolation he lived his life, considering the beauty of the all-engulfing emptiness. Like planning their suppers, this was all part of a plan for his life. He rejoiced to know that he was doing exactly what he should be doing.

"Vague semblances" was a term from the Tao Te Ching, and expressed the diaphanous nature of the mystery of Life. These filmy substances were barely physical, and came from another world. The poet thought of these as floating amorphously through the misty evening air. They danced and moved delicately through the days and nights of the villagers, awakening their unconscious minds to the vague consistency of everything that is and all that isn't.

Fingers fluttering like butterflies grasp hold of the night, and milk it for all it's worth. Empty rainbows collapse beneath the ceiling, calling for help from the assembled throng. Clashing crashing through the emptiness, they wander purposely against the grain of destiny. No one thought anything of this, and went on as though nothing had happened at all. Speaking through a megaphone, the mayor announced the closing of the community swimming pool. The children were so disappointed.

Like changing one's underwear, the symphony concluded with a crash. The audience fled the concert hall in a panic, demanding that their tickets be refunded. Blowing their noses, they tossed their soiled handkerchiefs into the air with aplomb. Rescuing the entrants, weeping began in the morning, and ended at night.

As a young poet, he had always played the passive role in lovemaking, with older men whose young lover he had been. He was comfortable with this role, and it seemed to fit his personality and nature well. He was able to maintain this ability throughout his younger years. But after his marriage, the poet had begun to play the active role in lovemaking, with younger men. This change had occurred over years of self-denial, and the poet was "feeling his oats," and enjoyed this new identity.

He had assumed every possible role in lovemaking

with both men and women throughout his long life. The poet's amorphous, fluid nature had enabled him to experience every form of love during his time in this world. He looked back on his history with amazement and mixed feelings, wondering how he had been through all he had experienced in one lifetime. Valuing all of it, he was grateful to have known love, in any form, at all.

The young poet had been the lover of his 90-year-old friend's former husband. They had all lived together in the city, and he had been the nanny to their two young children. One summer they all went to an island in the Maritime Provinces where the couple had a summer home. The poet and this artist made love often, and the young poet enjoyed their time together immensely.

But one night the artist wanted to make love, but the young poet wasn't feeling in the mood. So the artist raped him. This violent act was immensely disturbing to the young poet. He broke off all relations with the artist, and flew back to the city with the artist's wife and his poet mentor. This wasn't spoken of until years later when the poet established contact with his 90-year-old friend again.

He shared with her how her husband had raped him fifty years before, which she never knew about before this. She expressed her deep sorrow at this dreadful event. The book she had written, which she had sent him, contained material that she and her husband had created together sixty years before. When the poet saw the artist's name on the book along with his friend's he was shocked. To see this man's name took him back to that dreadful night so many years ago.

The poet had worked through his trauma over the rape with the Wise Woman, and thought that it was over, dealt with, and settled. But this awakening caused him to acknowledge the feelings he still had about this unpleasant event. He would read the book as though it were his friend's creation alone, and disregard the artist's participation in the work. He would find healing through reading this book, and peace over his trauma at last.

Climbing the mountain, the pilgrims wandered with a goal, to reach the summit together. But many of them collapsed along the way and could go no farther. So they stopped by a brook and admired the narcissus flowers growing there. Those who could, pressed on toward the summit together, and when they reached it, they sat down and admired the spectacular view. They took off their shoes and rested their tired feet.

Broken dreams colluded with pigeons along the way, opening their minds to unforeseen possibilities. Wending their weary way along, open theories captivated the vague entrances to close their open gates. Singing like an opera, their thoughts began to resemble open wounds. Close to nothing, tempestuous arousals grant proposals of marriage to the caged orangutans, blessed in their constant exposure to the elements.

Rowing their boat out onto the lake at dawn, the fishermen go out to fish for the morning.

Super colossal shrimp thaw themselves out from their frozen state and swim back to the ocean.

Crab cakes turn back into crabs, dusting off their breadcrumbs, and returned to the ocean again.

Lights go off all of a sudden, due to a power failure, and the people lit candles to be able to see.

Curtailing their trip abroad, the citizens return home, unhappily.

The poet's friend had been on his cruise with his wife for ten days, and would be returning home tomorrow.

He missed his closest nearby friend, whom he talked to on the telephone every day.

He would be glad to have his friend back again, since they were unable to talk on the phone more than twice the whole time that the friend was away. They would have much to catch up on.

He had had to be strong within himself, to get through these ten days without his friend.

The poet had instead called several old friends who lived far away while his friend was gone, just to have someone to talk to. And it was always beautiful to talk to these old friends of his. They all shared histories together, a body of friendship that had lasted a lifetime.

Caring and concern were important things, he believed, and compassion was essential to any relationship. It was these that the poet rarely received from his three daughters. This was a terrible disappointment. His friends cared more about him than his own female children did. At least he had some love in his life with his friends, or he would have withered on the vine, and disappeared.

Not letting himself think about unpleasant things, he protected himself from hostility and hatred, believing that Life was bigger than any of these difficult situations. He breathed in the fresh air of new life, and built his hopes upon a firm foundation, his poetry, his belief system, his life with his son.

Like ringing a bell to call one to dinner, he accepted his life, and went on with it regardless of his problems, opening the way to a better, more hopeful life.

Onward went the symphony, while encrusted temptations told people when they had misspelled a word. Orchestras on the radio, suddenly appeared on the village green. The collapsing roof of their tent fell upon the musicians, one of whose birthday it was. Luckily, no one was hurt. But they picked up their instruments and headed for their cars to go home. The audience was shocked but sympathetic. Only half the program had been performed, so everyone was disappointed.

Grim lunatics send telegrams to their mothers, while empty diners fill their plates with hopelessness. Back to basics, they emphasized the virtues of chewing-gum, courageously coughing up the remnants of their last meals. No one took photographs on a regular basis, and everyone was careful to maintain proper syntax as they spoke. Choking on their own heads, they laughed.

The poet mostly maintained traditional syntax, even when the content of his writing was obscure and nearly incomprehensible. He had learned this at an early age from reading Gertrude Stein, whose book, How To Write, he had just finished reading. An exercise of devotion, he reveled in her vaguely sensible language. In the literary tradition out of which he had emerged, incomprehensibility was considered a virtue.

He found that words can be used in a manner which divorced them from their meanings, nearly.

These words, liberated from their customary meanings, could then be free to exist on their own, and in combination with such other freed words. The words could then assume different aspects, given the context in which they appear, such as a sentence, or a paragraph.

Or, the words could have no meaning at all, and just exist as sounds, spots of ink on a page.

It was this that he had first encountered in the work of Gertrude Stein, and which he channeled into his own early writing. The poet had begun reading Stein's dynastic novel, The Making of Americans, intending to get through all 900 pages of it. This book had been written, amazingly, in 1906-1908, and tells the stories of Stein's own extended Jewish family. Composed while she was still finding her "voice," he found that this book was still written in her distinctive style, much like her *Three Lives*.

Reading The Making of Americans had been a lifelong dream of the poet. He had carried this book around with him for fifty years, intending to surely read it one day. Now the time had come.

He would read the book in the early pre-dawn morning, digesting her wonderful words before even taking food. This would be his aesthetic breakfast every day, nourishing his own poetic voice.

Unskilled workers begged for employment at the border. Hungry and homeless, they were willing to do any kind of work to survive. They were looked down upon, and employers were not eager to hire them, hating immigrants. When they were hired, they were taken advantage of, and given half the wages of native citizens. But they had no choice, they needed the work and the money.

Chunks of hopelessness floated down the river, like plastic polluting the waters. Only one period is necessary at the end of a sentence. Weary elderly residents of the besieged territory were crushed to death by falling humanitarian aid packages, as terribly ironic as that was. The army was refusing to open any of the other entrances into the land, thus starving the people stuck inside it. People desperate for food for their children were shot at by the army as they ran for their lives.

Close calls telephoned random numbers, expecting to get pizza delivered to their hungry stomachs. Entering unexpectedly, the remnants of the party left immediately after arriving. Vestments of clergy were turned into clothing for the flagrant vagrants to wear. They had settled into their renovated abandoned homes, and were living happy, contented lives at last. No one of them had any complaints to offer when asked.

The poet went out of the study to turn on the stove in the kitchen. He was making corned beef and cabbage for St Patrick's Day. Really, it would be New England Boiled Dinner (the title of one of his old poems), with the potatoes, onions, and carrots thrown into the pot with the corned beef. He tried to keep holidays by making festive meals, even though it was only for his son and himself. If he had been alone, he would not have bothered. But he did it for his son, and for his own enjoyment.

Walking through the living room en route to the kitchen, what did he see but on the couch, his son struggling to inject methamphetamine into the vein in his arm. This was not shocking, though always disturbing to the father, since his son had agreed to have one last bag of his drug before his birthday, after which he would quit. The father hoped and prayed with all his being that this would come to be true. It was all he hoped for in his life.

There was a terrible irony in the fact that he had dedicated his first novel to his children. And now, after being so happy and proud for him, they had all abandoned him, except for his only son.

This reality burned at his being, like a searing hot coal. After all he had done for them, caring for them throughout their lives, it had come to this. What a tragic ending.

But the poet went on with his life, accepting things that he could not change, hoping for better times ahead. He worked on his new novel every day, writing four pages each time. This discipline helped him to be serious about his writing, and kept his unpleasant thoughts at bay. He was writing a novel about a poet writing a novel about his life, who bore significant similarity to himself. Thus, we enter the hall of mirrors that is life and fiction, reality and art.

She had let herself go, the mother, and never washed her hair or rarely bathed or changed her clothes. She had given up on life, and spent her days and nights on the couch watching television, drinking her red wine. Her house was a mess, especially the kitchen, and she never got dressed unless she was going out somewhere, but stayed in her old nightgown all day. She had lost all motivation, and rarely even called her son on the telephone.

Both she and her son were so dysfunctional that neither one had the energy or motivation to reach out to the other. This was very sad for the father, who wished that the mother and her son would form a real relationship and spend time together once a week. She only lived in the next town, seven minutes away, so there was no reason why they couldn't see each other on a regular basis. But she had said that she would see her son on his birthday, this coming week, at least.

The tissue box on the shelf, the piles of books stacked up, two black bowls of the son's eaten meals needing to be washed, the empty glass ashtray, the cigarette lighter, the green cup, the pink water bottle standing at attention. The orange cap from a syringe, a chap stick, a toothpick, a candy.

Well, the same graceful entrances evoke startling news from the front of the wall, expressing violence and intended harm to the gardeners of the world.

Slowly moving in circles, the pilgrims left their homes and set out on their journey once again.

The milkman was just putting out fresh bottles for the villagers when they wake up. An Amish horse and buggy went slowly down the road, cars passing them every few moments. The Amish lived near the village, and would come into town to shop for food and provisions. The poet was always impressed by their simple, spartan lifestyle.

The village was a pleasant place, and the poet and his son were able to live their lives with privacy and security. The poet was content the live here, where he had his books, his artwork, his music, and everything needed for a comfortable life. He could write his poetry

and novels here, and enjoy the company of his son, when
he was stable and pleasant. It was an ideal situation,
since he had paid off his mortgage and finally owned
his home. In fact, they couldn't afford to live anywhere
else, since home prices were low, and the cost of living
was manageable.

"Heigh ho, heigh ho, it's off to work we go," the poet
would sing to his son as he went off to write for the day.
Beginning again each day was a sacred ritual: he would
read through the previous day's four pages, correcting
any mistakes with liquid paper, blowing on it to dry,
and then typing over it on his old black Royal Standard
typewriter. He loved this mechanism, and it inspired
him with its age to let his imagination run wild as he
typed.

Liquid daydreams confer with themselves as the
merry-go-round spins out of control. Painted wooden
horses flying off the carousel like Pegasus, suddenly
sprouting wings and soaring off into the sky. Luckily no
one was on the ride when this happened. All the rides
in the carnival were acting peculiar: most were going
backwards or upside down. The terrified carnival-goers
ran for the exit in panic.

The cost of living made life more difficult for the villagers: prices had soared, and groceries were very expensive. Families struggled to keep food on the table, stretching out meals to last a few days.

Gasoline prices had risen, so people only drove locally, avoiding any long-distance trips. No one had had a vacation in years, and people tried to be content with what they had. "Making do."

Most of the television and radio stations had been taken over by the government, so it was difficult finding news that expressed Reality. Only the public television and radio stations gave objective coverage of events. And the Arab station that broadcasted from the Middle East. It was these that the poet listened to and watched every day. He like the international news on the Arab station, in addition to their coverage of the war. They went to places in the world that no other station covered.

The poet felt compelled to know what was going on in the world he lived in. He felt a need to be aware of the suffering on the earth. He felt himself to be a citizen of the world, and felt no particular affiliation with his own country, whose policies he abhorred. Keeping a planetary perspective broadened his experience of life, since he lived as a hermit with his son, and had limited contact beyond the walls of his own home.

His friend had returned home from his cruise with his wife, and had mixed feelings about the experience. The ship had 5,000 passengers, and a crew of 4,000. The friend felt lost among so many people, with music playing that he didn't like everywhere, even on the deck. The poet had missed his friend terribly over the ten days that he was gone, and was glad to have him back home at last. Now they could resume their daily telephone conversations once again.

He would have to be careful to have consistency throughout his new novel, maintaining logical narratives and characters in his book without repeating himself. The poet liked its rhythm of alternating abstract passages and more realistic ones. This gave a variety to the work that would hopefully hold the prospective reader's attention. He hoped that his editor would want to publish this new novel when it was finished. At this rate, he might have it done in three or four months.

Flashing through the fields of horror, daffodils sprang unexpectedly open, since spring, dreadful awakening, had come a week early. The terror of spring frightened the poet in the past: the sudden onslaught of warmth, no longer being able to wear his overcoat and woolen hat for insulation from the world, suddenly being exposed for all to see in lighter clothing. The change from cold to warm, so relentless and overwhelming.

But since they barely had any winter at all anymore, due to global warming, there was really no sudden change this year. Winter had yielded to spring without a fight, and the day got light out an hour later, and stayed light an hour later. The poet had adjusted to this change gracefully this time around, and enjoyed the extra hour of darkness in the morning for his sacred reading time. He went to bed just as it was getting dark, to read in bed.

The poet liked the YIELD signs on the roadways. Its message was profound: he yielded to his Tao every day, but could use reminding every now and then. Renouncing his own will, to submit to a larger purpose, the poet aspired to be a sage, in the Taoist sense: a fully realized human being. He was being molded and shaped into a new form every day, yet he was consistently present through all of it.

The poet/father walked his spiritual life naturally. His path had become a part of him, in fact he was his own path. His spiritual life was no longer some separate compartment in his life, but the whole of his being. He saw the Tao as the "Way" it means, that which holds everything together, the fact of Life itself. The Tao, the Way, had become for him simultaneous with Life itself. Was this enlightenment?

We cannot say for sure, but he was faithful to his path, on which he had reached a happy state of mind.

"He who is contented with what he has, will always be contented," Lao Tzu had written once.

This was the central principle in the poet's life: being contented with what he had. Thinking about what he had, not what he didn't have. The glass is both half full and half empty, depending on one's state of mind at the moment. The poet reminded himself of this often, and tried to see the glass as half full.

The roses never opened: should he cut the stems again? Or return them to the supermarket for another dozen? The poet always kept fresh flowers in his kitchen, on the "island." This cheered him up immensely, and brightened up the kitchen. He also loved his living green plants, and often talked to them, telling them how beautiful they were, thanking them for coming to live with him and making him so happy. Especially his orchid, which had unexpectedly bloomed again, with three flowers.

Waxing and waning, sudden impulses surged through the streets, decapitating flowers along the way. Waiting for the locomotive to start, vegetables poured out of the freight cars, scampering off into the woods. Escaping prisoners ran out of the jails en masse, and the people were terrified to leave their homes. The gangs had let them out, demanding that the president resign. The gangs had taken over the island, and the police couldn't do anything to stop them.

Meanwhile: Claustrophobic enterprises waffled like jelly and prepared to take off from the ground. Lisping children walked sideways, entering their own bodies from the rear. Floating entrails desperately pleaded to be able to walk again. Separated bones congealed again, and were formed into zombies. Munching on rainbows, the unicorns cast off all fear and leapt into the void, together.

Normal people were a rare commodity at this point in history, but there were some.

People tried to paste their lives together with tape, staples, and glue. But their lives kept unraveling, again and again. They tried superglue, but this too came undone in the rain. Honking geese had returned to the village a month ago, and everyone wore rubber boots in their honor. Melting thrusts turn into badgers, escaping into the plains outside of town. No one was surprised or offended when the ice-cream man gave his wares away for free to the waiting children.

The alabaster albatross, the keys on the table, the mug on the tissue box, the wallet on the books, the photograph of his youngest daughter laid on its side so as not to be seen, cigarette ashes everywhere. Reaching his goal of four pages for the day, the poet finished up, adding a few sentences to his last paragraph. So the day was complete, and he would now spend some time with his son. A fulfilling experience, he could feel good about himself another day.

It had turned suddenly cold again, after the early spring, and there were snow flurries. It was the middle of Lent, with Easter coming in two weeks. Passover would be next month. The poet had spent so many years observing Lent: daily mass, Stations of the

Cross, purple vestments and hangings. Especially the Holy Week rituals were deeply meaningful to him: the chanting and incense, the ancient ceremonies. The culmination of it all in the Great Vigil of Easter Eve, with the vigil readings, the lighting of the new fire, the sharing of the light amongst the parishioners, lighting their candles.

His chanting of the Exsultet, which was the high point of the liturgy, to which he looked forward every year, was the most fulfilling moment in the Church's year. After his expulsion from the Church, and the resulting cataclysm, the father would get terribly depressed during Lent, especially during Holy Week. He missed the foot-washing on Maundy Thursday, the stripping of the altar and veneration of the cross on Good Friday, when he would prostrate himself before the altar.

The poet in him had entered into these rituals as a mystical experience; he was in an ecstatic state during these ceremonies, outside of himself, in an alternate state of being. When he censed the altar, moving slowly around it, swinging the thurible and wafting the incense over the altar, he transcended his own being.

Lifted out of his own body, paradoxically he was more fully present than he had ever been. Most of the parish were mystified by these rituals, but his faithful few adored them.

It had been painful for the father, especially on Palm Sunday, when his wife had broken down in church, and revealed his homosexuality to the parish. And then there was the Maundy Thursday when his youngest daughter had fallen and broken her leg: the father still had to go and conduct the service, while the mother ran to the emergency room at the hospital with their daughter. Officiating at this service was one of the most painful things he ever had to do, while his baby girl was suffering.

The father suffered for many years during Holy Week, reliving the pain of his separation from his vocation to which he had given his life. Every year it was the same, the doldrums would descend into his being, body and mind, and he would be rendered dysfunctional for that week. But over the years, this suffering began to subside, as the poet began to leave the Church's belief system behind in the dust.

Holy Week didn't hurt him now, he had grown so utterly far beyond its dogmas and doctrines.

He now had a general peace about him, which was not shaken anymore by painful memories. The poet had worked these all through in his mind, and with the Wise Woman over the past few years.

While seeing the beauty of religion, he also was aware of its dangerous nature, captivating people into beliefs that are contrary to Nature and Reason. Giving them a deluded hope of immortality, while Death is the final solution for all of us.

The poet looked forward, in peace, to death; he was ready to, one day, return back to the Tao, the unthinkable purpose which Life had in store for him. He looked forward to returning to the earth, becoming one again with all things, which had been the goal of his life while living. To be one with all things completely would be a wonderful blessing and culmination of his life. He had no fear of death, but hoped to life a long life. He grandmother had blessed him saying, "You should live to 130." He believed in her blessing, that it would come true.

The poet had read the story in Ovid's Metamorphoses about Hermaphroditus, and was enchanted utterly. This beautiful boy had scorned the advances of others, but found himself being pursued by an erotically overactive nymph, who had fallen in love with him instantly. When he refused her advances, she clung to him, wrapping herself around him like a snake. She prayed that their bodies would become one body, and the god answered her prayer. Hermaphroditus became a hermaphrodite, possessing both genders, being both, and neither, stuck in an inextricable dilemma.

The poet had always felt this way, possessing both genders, being both, while being neither.

He had heard that there are such persons as real, physical hermaphrodites, and was fascinated by this rare possibility. Was he himself an emotional hermaphrodite, feeling himself possessed of both genders? A psychological hermaphrodite? Tiresias had lived as both man and woman at different times of his life; this is what gave him such ability as he had to prophesy.

He had heard of "two spirit" people in indigenous cultures, whose nature spanned both the male and the female. Such persons were revered as mystical shamans, linking the earth and heaven, spanning and transcending all possibilities for being human. The poet was such a bridge spanner, including in himself all natures, all genders, as sexualities. He had been aware of this since childhood, and his early experiences prepared him for this role.

As a child, he had been born with a heart defect, which needed to be surgically corrected when he was only four years old. This was a frightening experience for the child, and he had vague memories of this time and this event. Having his chest cut open was traumatic: the surgery left a huge scar across his chest, of which he was to be self-conscious for the majority of his life. Only recently did he feel comfortable with his body, which had been violated at such an early, tender age.

When he reached the age of eight, further testing was required to determine if the child needed additional surgery. The parents took him to the nation's capital, where he had a catherization. The child felt the tube going up inside his arm to his heart, heard the sounds of cutting and sewing, since he had to be awake for this procedure. An additional trauma for the child, this experience left psychological scars as well as physical ones.

It was, perhaps, these early experiences of trauma

and loss that caused his nature to develop its spiritual capacity from an early age. At four years old, the same year as his surgery, his little cousin, a boy his own age, died tragically of leukemia. This must have made a deep impression on the child.

The same year, unbeknownst to the child, his mother almost died in surgery, but survived. The environment of illness and death made the child aware of the fragility of Life.

Random acts of kindness boil diapers in large pots on the stove. Entering entrants evoke evil designs upon the radiant microscopes that sit like salamanders on a rock in the sun. Milk turns into cheese after the goats are drained of their substance. Turning around in their seats, the listeners move circularly to hear the sound of the ocean in their conch shells. No one dislikes the sounds, and they take off their clothes and pretend to be at the beach.

Warm ideas control the universe, appealing to the better angels of their natures. Skipping the usual formalities, everyone went for the appetizers, set out for the flagrant vagrants to enjoy. Symphonies of conflict resolved themselves, openly advocating for the reimprisonment of the escaped convicts. The police had tried in vain to control them, but they were utterly unmanageable. Swift planes of buttermilk melted in the blazing sunshine.

The poet was halfway through his novel. He was writing a novel about a poet who was writing a novel. This, obviously, could go on forever, and will. He was encouraged by this achievement, and looked forward to writing the second half of his new book. He would work every day until the book was completed. This entire process was miraculous to the poet, who was amazed at how he had a seemingly endless well of ideas to put into his new book. This was a wonderful beginning.

PART II

Remembering particles of dust in the lunatics' asylum, reindeer fly through molasses, conferring with the highest authorities concerning the old gray barn along the road. Separated vestibules sign documents aligning with the particles of incest, flaming like torches. Upright books stand at attention, saluting their dead authors with applause. Carpets rolled up into orifices blame the standing committee for sitting down on the job. The actors in the play refused to perform.

The poet had been in psychotherapy for most of his life, having suffered from mental illness since childhood. It is likely that he would never have written the vast body of his poetry and fiction had he not so suffered. His search for his identity was heroic, and he dug deep within his psyche to probe the depths of his being. "To understand others is wisdom, but to understand oneself is enlightenment," Lao Tzu had written. Socrates had said, "Know thyself."

He had dedicated himself to this quest, and it ran through his life like his bloodstream. He and his wife-to-be were recommended to begin counseling with a Christian therapist. This woman listened as the young poet shared with her his constant homosexual yearnings and desires. She had told him to renounce and forsake these, and live his life as a heterosexual. In this she doomed him to extinction, in the tormented marriage that would follow. He was trapped like an animal.

When the marriage was at its worst, and the poet was beginning to lose his mind, he found an Anglican therapist who helped him come to terms with and accept his homosexual orientation. This therapist had liberated the father to live his true life, an inexpressible gift. This therapist, a portly man, had died after having a massive heart attack while ballroom dancing.

The poet had visited him in the hospital, where he lay unconscious, and had whispered a prayer into his ear, to let go and release himself from this life. This had been a very meaningful moment for the poet, and he hoped that his therapist had heard his prayer in some unconscious part of his being. He soon thereafter died, tragically. The poet's eldest daughter had accompanied him to his therapist's memorial service, where patients of his comforted one another in their loss.

His next therapist encouraged the poet's unhealthy relationship with his young companion, and actually supported their heroin use together, saying that he could safely use this drug without getting addicted. Of course, he did get addicted. The poet later terminated treatment with this therapist, and filed a complaint with the state board of licensing to get his license revoked. However fervently the poet pursued this, his effort did not succeed, sadly.

His next therapist was a very wise older man, whose office was filled with religious icons and symbols. It turned out that this man was a faithful Buddhist, and that was why he was so grounded in wisdom. This therapist encouraged the poet's Taoism and spirituality in general, casting a meaningful net over everything the poet would share with him. The therapist retired after a while, and the poet had to seek wisdom elsewhere.

His next therapist was slightly younger than himself, and the poet found a man who became an icon to him of what a proper, decent, integrated man could be like. He was impressed always by this therapist's wise and gentle manner and his integrity. He would quietly urge the poet toward a larger, more rich and rewarding life, and they would share deep talks together every week. The poet liked this therapist's office, where he felt comfortable to share his deepest secrets.

It was after several years with this therapist that the poet discovered the Wise Woman, who graciously assumed the role of his life counselor and mentor. He decided to give up his therapy with the last provider, since the Wise Woman had assumed such a central role in his recovery from trauma.

He had spoken on the phone with her this day, and always found her responses helpful and encouraging. He could feel her healing power through the telephone.

Coughing up faerie dust, the vague semblances proceeded to devour the remains of the orchestra's music while they were playing, entering suddenly, pressing their mouths against the glass of the window. Separately, the jars of jam in the supermarket exploded, scattering their contents on the startled patrons, covered suddenly with jam head to toe. The pharmacy woman wished his son a happy birthday as did the Wise Woman and the owner of his garage.

The son was having a terrible birthday. They had gone out to the store for a few things, and as soon as they got home, the boy started howling about how lonely he was, how he needed his drug but couldn't get any, how he wanted love, but couldn't find any. The boy was always rejected when he tried to make friends with anyone; they scorned and belittled him viciously. The son didn't understand why people responded to him in this way?

Bloody tissues in the waste basket, howling demons in the afternoon, waking up disappointed, hating life, wanting to die, howling to the heavens. The son woke up, depressed by his loneliness and isolation. His mother had tried to call him, but he missed the call since he was sleeping. He didn't want to see her in this horrible state of mind. So he went back to bed to sleep, avoiding life and feeling utterly hopeless. They had planned on going out to dinner, but not when the boy was so upset.

Open wounds bleed at the suffering of the world. Each wound is a person, his son among them.

The poet had to be careful not to let his son's suffering drag him down into despair. Caring compassionately and staying objective were essential in this situation. The father felt the son's pain as if he himself were experiencing this pain. He was like an emotional sponge, and had to work hard to maintain his own identity in the midst of his son's suffering.

The father had missed a day of writing for the first time since beginning his new novel. His son had asked the father not to write on the son's birthday, to which the father had agreed. But since the son had slept the whole afternoon, the poet decided to write after all. When the son woke up, he was annoyed that the father had written on his birthday, so they agreed that he would not write the next day.

This was a very peculiar sensation for the poet, not writing for an entire day. He was disoriented, and confused by this lack of productivity. A break in the flow of the novel. But, once the poet accepted the situation, he relaxed into it, and did other things for that day, spending more time with his son as he had requested. After screaming all morning on his birthday, and sleeping all afternoon, the son woke up calmly at last, and they had a pleasant evening together.

The poet had reached a realization: His intelligence quota was unspeakably high and extreme; he also loved reading incomprehensible poetry and writing, such as Ezra Pound and James Joyce. He had actually read the dreaded Finnegans Wake of Joyce three times in succession, when most readers barely made it through the first page. The poet had read all of the poetry of Pound, including the utterly baffling Cantos, written in multiple languages.

Was the poet drawn to these difficult works because ordinary writing bored him, not challenging his intellect sufficiently? Did he delight in seemingly incomprehensible writing, like Gertrude Stein's, because it stretched out his brain cells, making them work overtime, and stimulating his mind more than ordinary writing would? Did these writers, including the poet, write such difficult work as a disguise against their real desires, their rampant sexualities and passions?

Hadn't Freud written that the establishing of control of the sexual impulse is the food of civilization? Sublimating the sexual energy into a creative act forms the basis of culture, after all. All creativity emerges once the erotic impulse is brought under control. The poet had found this to be true in his own writing experience. The troubadour poets had made the most of their poetry writing to express the yearning of unfulfilled desire, turning their passion into poetry.

Was the poet writing in an obscure manner to avoid

writing what he really wanted to say? But maybe he was saying what he really wanted to say? Writing obscurely came naturally to the poet, who had fed upon so many challenging works. The Magnetic Fields of Andre Breton and Philippe Soupault. The Sleepers Awake of Kenneth Patchen. The Imaginations of William Carlos Williams. Books that took language to a new level, transcending the meanings of language in its customary usage.

The poet loved these books and poets and writers for their boldness and courage, their constant innovation, their commitment to their work, even though the readership for their books was very limited. The poet's book had not sold well, which was a disappointment to him. He hoped that his work would take its place in the canon of modernist poetry and fiction. He hoped that it would be recognized and acknowledged for the serious art it represented.

Bludgeoning through the wilderness, the vague semblances bounced echoes off of their heads.

Corporate windows open for the beginning of spring. Vessels of mercy bring bouquets of violets to the bold, inventive advocates and practitioners of euthanasia. Communicating vessels offer collapsed elevators to tune in the stations which the radio deleted. All the salvaged remnants colluded to bring offerings to the wilted salads in their wooden bowls.

Casting out their fishing lines, the flagrant vagrants hoped to catch something, but all they caught was a bad cold. So they went to the fish market and bought fish that they could take home to feel that they had caught something. The father wished that his son would eat fish. Catfish especially, which the father loved and missed. But the boy's stomach didn't like it, as well as his mouth. The father was tired of eating so much meat, and tried to make vegetarian meals more often.

The roses never opened, which he had purchased at the supermarket. What a disappointment. They withered whole on their stems, closed as tightly as the day they were bought. The poet's flowers gave him significant joy and happiness. They always cheered him up when he saw them in the kitchen.

This was an indulgence for the poet, since the flowers were dear in their price.

In the war, negotiations for a cease fire were stalled. The army was unwilling to cooperate and allow a cease fire to occur. They wanted the hostages released, but didn't want to give an inch when it came to reciprocation on their part. The resistance wanted a permanent cease fire, to which the army was unwilling to commit. They were determined to attack the last remaining area of the territory, where one and a half million people were sheltering for safety.

The army had no plans to evacuate the people sheltering there, and were proceeding in their plans to invade, not caring what happened to these innocent civilians. The army was utterly brutal in its determination to wipe out the entire population. This was pure, unadulterated vengeance on their part.

There was no mercy shown, even to the one million children trapped in the war.

The poet had written to the local university which had a poetry reading series, sending them his novel, and a cover letter describing himself and his work. He hoped that they would appreciate his writing and offer him a reading at their venue. This would help to put him on the map in his area, and would reach the students at the university, who might enjoy his novel and poetry. The poet was excited about this prospect, and looked with anticipation to their response.

Waffling through the syrup, with the butter melting, salvaging through the carpet remnants, the telephone rang, but no one was on the line. Buttercups surround the fields of memory, insisting that their followers would never agree to the terms of the contract. Savages protrude into destiny, eating their way through the endless temptations that surrounded the sacred circle. Enveloping the escalator, direct descendants forget what their names were.

Carpeted with moss, the bedroom caved in on itself, calling for reinforcements as the movie played backwards. Noticing the discrepancy, the director mentioned silent films, omitting their sound tracks for pity's sake. Alabaster pillars evoke nuisance at the store, inventing reasons for their failure to pronounce the proper words to the anthem. Failure to engage results in emptiness for everyone. So they countered with another proposal.

Given the time of day, the matter of course was disrupted, and the horns of plenty were blown.

Until the lunatics subsided, there was no point in eating in a restaurant at night. Frozen thrills continued to provide enough sensory stimulation so that the orphanage was reopened to the acclaim of the populace, relying on their underwear to achieve their goals and purpose. No one was disappointed with the results of the spring cleaning.

Numerous entities expressed their solidarity with the pension system, and were grateful for the opportunity it presented to everyone. Hot dogs and hamburgers were grilled on the village green, and the citizens were in a celebratory mood. The flag was set on fire as the villagers sang the national anthem together, robustly proclaiming the flaming reality of the proposal given at noon the day before.

The flag burned to ashes as the people clapped their hands.

Chopped eggplants with heating oil and natural gas. Opening their mouths, they offered sentences removed of words, mere breaths of openness, exhaling into the waiting silver bowls.

Mucous membranes exude vanilla frosting, and the elephants go on strike again. The exterminators spray their chemicals to eradicate the walls of the houses, infiltrating the bedrooms with sawdust and honey. Luckily, the windows were closed.

Queer boys, with their blue electric penises, penetrate one another exuberantly. The watchers brush their hair, parting it in the middle, for emphasis. The language of seals is refrained in its efforts, and vaseline is spread on the existing furniture for good luck. Expressing what everyone felt, they brushed aside the combs, and ran furiously into the water. Time for tea had not yet come, and the emphasis was once again on the latecomers.

Salamanders sunning themselves upon a hot rock, apportion their divisions into chopped liver.

Noticing the emptiness of the room, the movers decided not to violate its pristine purity with unnecessary furniture. So they went off to have their lunch, instead. The rampaging boys ride camels into the desert, racing each other to reach the nearest oasis of their dreams. The cream floats on top of the coffee, swirling like dragons in the abyss.

"It's time to put your clothes back on," announced the mayor, to the disrobed villagers on the village green. Everyone got dressed, and the children were brought out to play in the playground. An overcoat is good to wear in the winter. "The woods are the poor man's overcoat," Gertrude Stein had written. The poet loved his camel coat and woolen hat. He hated to give these up once the weather would warm up in the coming spring.

His coat and hat were like a portable hut he could go outside in, giving him warmth and protection from the cold and other weather, and also security, that he was safely enclosed in these garments. It would take him a while to adjust to the spring warmth, and the summer heat to follow. The poet embraced change, and the change of seasons was more of a gradual transition than a sudden metamorphosis, so he gracefully went with the flow of things.

The cycles of nature amazed him; how things naturally transitioned so gracefully from one season to the next. The seasons were arbitrary designations for something that was really a single uninterrupted flow. Like chapters in a book, the seasons were convenient divisions to make people more comfortable, giving them an illusion of humanly superimposed order. Or, as in a book, chapters, to make the work more approachable to the reader.

The poet accepted and rejoiced in all kinds of weather,

taking his morning walks every day throughout the year. He especially enjoyed walking in the rain with his umbrella. This took him back to his younger days when he would walk around the city in a raincoat with an umbrella, stopping at his favorite literary bookstore, where he would find poetic treasures to take home and read. He also haunted the other used book stores every week.

Walking in the rain was a visionary experience for the poet; he loved the sound of the rain on his umbrella, pitter-pattering gently on the black fabric of the slightly bent umbrella. The feeling of walking in the rain brought back his youth, when everything was fresh and young. It was like walking through a poem about the rain, to be walking in the rain. No one was about, and he could revel in his sensations, as the rain drizzled down around him.

Walking through the new-fallen snow was also especially lovely. The poet would walk in the street which had been plowed, since the neighbor's sidewalk had not yet been shoveled. He would hear the crunch, crunch, of the snow beneath his sneakers, a reassuring, comforting sound in the silence of the early morning.

And then come home to his nice, warm house, to huddle, like mice, around imaginary fires, in the cold of winter.

The poet was struck and moved by how Dante had been exiled from his native Florence, and been a wanderer for the rest of his life, composing his epic poem along the way. The poet had been an exile too, following the cataclysm and his expulsion from his home, his family, his vocation. He had also written an epic poem, a four-volume paean to his ill-fated relationship with his young companion and himself throughout their time together.

He had produced eighteen manuscripts of poetry and prose throughout his exile, and been as productive as he had been as a priest or musician. All these were a part of who he was: his priesthood was a central aspect of his identity, imbuing all his thoughts and actions with a measure of holiness. He saw his life as a sacred act, from more obvious activities to more subtle and seemingly insignificant ones.

He was blessed to be a vessel of blessing to others, and took this very seriously.

His vocation as a priest and poet was especially

significant to him. These two functions went hand in hand through his life. He loved how there were ancestors of this: George Herbert, John Donne, Jonathan Swift, Lewis Carroll, John Keble, and Gerard Manley Hopkins. The poet considered himself in their illustrious lineage, and thoroughly enjoyed being in their company. All had been, additionally, Anglicans, with the exception of Hopkins, who defected to the Roman Church.

The poet's spirituality was central to his life and existence. Yet he rarely indulged in such material in his poetry and prose, only alluding to it obliquely on occasion. He did not want to write devotional verse or fiction, but used his spirituality to inform what he was writing, always. He was a priest and musician who also was a poet. These functions had separate places in the father's life: convenient compartments to which he could turn in succession as the need arose.

The poet could not play his cello. His trigger finger on his left hand was still not fully healed, and this one finger didn't move as it should, refusing to cooperate and dance swiftly across the gut strings of his instrument. His other fingers were not moving properly either, as his entire left hand seemed to be effected by this problem. He had an appointment at the local hospital to have this checked out. The poet worried that he might need surgery to correct this injury.

He looked forward to playing his cello for the rest of his life, so this was very important to him.

Playing the cello was, along with writing, one of his greatest joys. He would practice his scales and arpeggios, play his favorite etude, then play through one of Bach's Suites for Cello unaccompanied, or one of Bach's Sonatas for Viola da Gamba, which gave him considerable happiness and satisfaction.

But now this injury had caused him pain and suffering. He was lost without his cello, playing his once a week practice sessions. This was so much a part of his identity that he almost didn't know who he was, missing this part of himself, not being able to play his cello. There was an emptiness that could only be filled by playing his instrument. He played for his own pleasure and enjoyment, and for his late parents, and for the healing of his son.

As a child, the poet had loved doing origami; he got very good at this, and produced several very advanced productions: a turkey, a mouse, an elephant, and others. These were challenging to his intelligence as a young person, and were deeply satisfying to create. The poet still had the red box filled with these origami creations, which he looked at now and then, to remind him of the happy times of his childhood. These were precious memories for him.

Singing knives opened the way toward the monkey-bars, pressing their emphases across the eyes of the beholders, grooming themselves like a lotus flower. Singing in German, they chanted songs of Schumann, enveloping space betwixt themselves, like an origami swan. Remembering who they were, the pilgrims evoked a solemn signal to indicate their oblique intentions. To persist, the galloping entrails tripped over themselves, in their haste to go to the bathroom.

Songs, like bleeding hearts, squeeze ecstasy into edible morsels, suitable for framing. Steering themselves in the direction of their erection, collapsing buildings sing gleefully as they fall down. Trying to make sense of it all, the mayor proposes an alternative concept: redo the mayor's office, decorating it in real Louis XIV antique furnishings, opulent bouquets of flowers in real Chinese Ming dynasty vases.

The proposal was, unfortunately for the mayor, rejected.

As a young poet, he had given a reading at an event featuring Christians in the arts. This was held at a large church in the city. When he was reading his modernist poems, he looked out at the audience and saw the most beautiful boy he had ever seen in his life. Catching himself up, having been told to renounce his homosexual desires by the church, he immediately altered his gaze to instead focus on the captivating girl he immediately also noticed.

They spoke after the reading, and the poet was struck by her innocent beauty; she looked like a boy, flat-chested with short cropped hair. It was, no doubt, the ambiguous nature of her appearance that had caught his eye. Perhaps he could channel his impulses toward this young woman, and find relief from his primary desire for his fellow young men.

In doing so, the young poet would submerge his true desires and nature, into a container into which it could not fit, having the wrong shape. He would be tormented at the sight of a beautiful young man, and tortured through the depths of his being. That would last until the cataclysm expelled him out of bondage into freedom to live as his nature dictated.

This young woman would appear at a dance held at the young poet's parish church. This church was known for having a significant number of young adults, and was a lively place to meet people. When the poet's friend saw him looking at this girl, he told him to dance with her. Thus, giving him away to this girl, rather than taking him for himself. More of this friend to follow shortly.

The young poet asked her to dance, and it turned out that she was actually a dancer herself. They really cut up the floor, dancing some crazy wonderful moves together, and got along splendidly.

They would begin dating, the poet living on turkey hot dogs at home, so he could afford to take her out to dinner. And then there would be the long train ride out to her borough, to see her home.

As they courted, the young poet felt that this girl was repulsed by him, disgusted by his appearance, manner, and diverse sexuality and gender. She looked at him as not being a "real man."

And yet it was his sensitivity and aestheticism that had attracted her to the young poet in the first place.

He pursued her as if his life depended on it, which it did.

He needed her to legitimize himself in life, to enable him to channel his impulses and desires toward her, and the family they might have together. He had always loved and wanted children. So this was the surest way to achieve that goal. She was a virgin, and intended to stay that way until her wedding night. The poet honored her position on this, and they refrained from intercourse, engaging in alternative forms of intimacy together, short of consummating the relationship.

The realm of physical love was new to the girl, whose innocence was central to her charm. The young poet was moved by the obvious fact that she was exploring love with him for the first time in her life. But he felt that she was not in love with him, and never would likely be. Nonetheless, he persisted in courting her, proposing marriage, which she refused. Not giving up, he kept at her until she finally gave in. Thus, the ill-fated union was begun.

To speak of his young friend who told him to dance with the girl: This was his bosom friend, closer than a brother, whom he loved more than his own life. They had both been homosexual, and were instinctively avoiding sexual contact with other men, conflicted as they were about this aspect of their being and its relationship to their faith. This dear friend was an artist, producing bold relief sculptures, influenced by his childhood in Africa, as the son of missionaries.

So the young poet and the young artist loved each other deeply, and would hold each other close in bed, passionately sharing love together, without ever making love. These beautiful, torturous moments of intimacy were ecstatic and agonizing, unable as they were to fulfill the nature of their desires. The young poet would marry, and the young artist married as well, to a charming artistic woman, much older than himself. The poet and artist would remain friends for life.

Looking back on this precious friendship, the poet wondered what the two of them might have been to each other, had their piety not kept them apart? What if they had been lovers, consummating their deep love for each other in a physical form? The artist's wife had passed away several years ago now, and the poet wondered: would this now be their time to be together at last?

But no, the Fates had not decreed this to be for them ever. The poet was completely caught up with his life in their house with his son and his writing and music. The artist was caught up in his pattern of life in the city, and his home at the shore on weekends. He scheduled musicians to perform in the train stations, and taught tai chi in the evenings.

The poet reflected that it had been better this way, that they had kept their friendship pure.

They loved each other and understood each other better than anyone, even their own families. This created a very deep bond between them that time had not erased, but only deepened. They had not seen each other for ten years, and the poet wished that the artist would come to visit him. But this did not appear to be forthcoming. Nonetheless, the poet continued to hope.

Wrestling in cream of mushroom soup, straight from the can, the rampaging boys had fun.

The onlookers couldn't believe the blue electric penises, erect and covered with mushrooms and cream. Savage remnants, dry salvages, infest the realm of dreams with orchestral music, heard through the static on the radio. They listened to it anyway, even with the static.

The marauding boys helped each other by licking the soup off of their friends' bodies. The onlookers were scandalized, and demanded their money back. Locomotives pressed on through the village, the cars stopped at the crossing for three hours or more. Laundry fluttered from the clotheslines, as blackbirds descended to drop their droppings all over the fresh clothing and linens.

Parting the curtains, the poet took a deep breath before proceeding. He had reach a new milestone in his work, inventing perceptions contrary to nature, describing acts of purity, intended to inspire a generation of readers. Into the future he would go, slowly achieving his purpose. Nothing would dissuade him from the completion of his monumental task. This could go on forever, and just might do that.

As he emptied the ashtray, his cockatiel suddenly began to sing beautifully. The poet had stepped outside onto his porch, descending the steps on which he had fallen, carefully, to stand for a moment in the sunshine of this late March day. He found the sunshine healing, and enjoyed raising his face into its bright rays. Parting the curtains, he let the daylight into the study, where he reviewed the previous day's work.

He had written to his editor about his new novel, and the excitement he had in writing it. The editor was glad to hear of the poet's new project, and congratulated him on this success. He valued all that his editor had done for him over the years, designing and producing his first novel. The editor had shown great respect and appreciation for the poet's work and efforts. Together the poet and his editor had produced a beautiful book that would endure the ages of time.

The United Nations Security Council had voted to approve a resolution calling for an immediate and lasting cease fire in the war. This was a huge accomplishment. His country, which had previously used its veto power to undo all the other resolutions of this kind, now merely abstained in the vote.

But would the leaders of the army and its colonizers honor and obey this resolution? Not likely.

They had ignored all the previous resolutions calling them to account. It was likely that they would do the same now, defying the international community and the whole world in their relentless pursuit of vengeance. Even the president could not stop them. And the world was waiting to see if he would withhold sending more weapons and money until they stopped their attacks.

The president was running for a second term, and it looked like he was going to lose because of his support for the war. He was a tyrant, and was hated by most of the country. The government had removed most human rights, and was supporting the war in all its horror. The people had had enough bloodshed and death; they sympathized with the suffering of the innocent civilians in the war. Huge demonstrations were held across the entire world against the genocide being committed.

The government moaned about the 32,000 deaths, not counting the thousands buried under the rubble. The president lamented that more must be done to protect innocent civilians. But the colonizers' army just ignored his pleas. Yet, at the same time, the president continued to send more bombs to the army with which to bomb and slaughter more innocent civilians. He was speaking out of two sides of his mouth. And the people weren't buying it anymore.

Platypuses cavorting in the creek, going for a swim on a hot summer's day. Flapping around and playing with their young in the water. Sinking floats abandon the entrance of the armory, insisting rather on waxing and waning like the moon in an elevator. Talking about the moon: Entering backwards, the flying chariot of the moon climbs to the empyrean, like a menstruating teenage girl. No one returned used tampons to the service desk that day.

Using obscure words, the poet delighted in invisibility, emerging only occasionally to take a breath of sunshine. He divorced language from its customary meanings, and placed words in unusual contexts, keeping syntax in his sentences, but substituting what would be expected with surprising alternatives. This kept the writing interesting, since no one could guess what would come next.

The poet's son was always resentful of the time his father spent working on his new book. The son wanted his father to spend time with him all day, while the father had many things to do and kept a strict schedule of activities throughout the day. The poet liked to write from two o'clock until four. This consistency of working helped him to be disciplined in his writing. He was careful not to sound like any of the writers and poets he admired, but always wrote in his own distinctive voice.

Clarifying spare ribs cling to the windows of the rectory; no one is at home, fortunately, since the baby was born and died shortly thereafter, sadly. Orchestrating the symphony, French horns played plaintively while the cows were milked. The cheese that they would make from this was green and mouldy, and smelled like dirty socks. No one wanted to eat it, so they fed it back to the cows.

Thinking outside the box, they decided to go to the bathroom in the sink. Everyone celebrated the opening of the new village gate. This gave the villagers a sense of protection, and also of being on the map at last. The mayor made a glorious speech, and everyone ate cupcakes on the green. The band played nostalgic tunes, while the children played with big balloons.

Occasionally the poet would slip in a rhyme when no one was looking. It was usually an accidental occurance, or at least an unconscious event. The characters in this current novel express themselves through the narration, not with dialogue. They rarely speak aloud, but more often think their words, in their minds, using the tools that nature had equipped them with, not without enthusiasm. Their silence is eloquent: they stand like statues that cannot speak.

One imagines them moving slowly, like actors in a Greek tragedy, or in a Japanese kabuki play or Noh drama, with solemn music playing as they move through the scenes of the play. It is their own play, their own tragedy or comedy, a little bit of both, perhaps. Or else, like a silent movie for which the reader provides the musical score, in the privacy of his own home.

Or better, to read this book in silence, respecting the silence of its characters. This is, after all, a work of fiction, and any resemblance to persons living or dead is purely coincidental. And yet, one knows these personages as if they were characters in one's own life. They have a vivacity and genuineness that makes them seem more real than life itself. A resilience and integrity that makes them more real and alive than living persons. Who knows? They may have emerged out of life itself.

Will they crawl back into life once this book is completed, and cease to be fiction, but reemerge like butterflies, or huge furry moths, to live another, fuller life than I am able to give them? Will they flutter off once their work is done, and be content to flit from flower to flower, sucking where the bee sucks, for the rest of their natural lives? What a heartbreakingly exquisite thought.

I have known these characters all my long life; they have haunted my dreams and waking days, waiting to be put into a book, so they can live and breathe at last. This is that book, and will be forever, once it is completed. The poet was aiming for at least three hundred pages, the same length as his first novel, and he was more than halfway to his projected goal. At the rate he was writing, this would take him three months to complete.

After this, he would attempt to write some new poems, perhaps another book, down the road.

The poet was glad to be writing again, working on his book every day. This was as fulfilling as cooking a good meal for supper every night. The satisfaction was the same: cooking and writing were both creative acts, and eating was like reading. The nourishment that one provided the body, was like that which the other gave to the mind. Both were equally necessary for good health.

Caterpillar crawling along a branch of a blossoming tree in spring. Walkers out for their daily bit of exercise. Colliding trains at the intersection fail to avert disaster.

Diapers are necessary if you have a baby. These were rarely available during the war, so mothers had to improvise. Castrated men become eunuchs in India, then turn to prostitution as women. They are both revered and reviled by the people putting offerings of food into their begging bowls.

The sliding door between the study and the living room had gotten stuck again, the result of a moment of the son's anger, slamming it in so it couldn't be moved. The son had broken many things over the years that he had lived together with his father. Many repairs had to be done to fix the things which the son had broken. Thankfully, the boy was more calm and contented these days, when he had his drug, that is.

The son now had what was to be his last bag of methamphetamine. He had told his connection that he was going to try to get clean, and would not be calling him again. This was a brave step to take.

The father was hopeful that this would mark the end of his son's active addiction, and that he would stay clean for the rest of his life. This would free up their life together, to be no longer controlled by this addiction and its cravings.

The father's life had been dragged into his son's addiction: the son had gotten his father actually to pay for his illegal drug over the years of his addiction. They would make crazed trips on the highway, with the old car ready to collapse, to obtain this terrible drug, with the father driving exhaustedly and panic stricken, wondering whether the old car would make it safely home again.

Eventually the father refused to make such crazed trips again, and the son would have to find people who could deliver the drug to his home, since the son didn't have a driver's license. But the father continued to pay for the meth, even though his conscience condemned him for this. He hated to see his son suffering through his withdrawal, howling for his drug, pleading to his father to get it for him.

So he had given in out of compassion, even though he knew that it was less than the best thing to do. But now, he expected his son to quit and get clean, if they were to go on living together. The father had begun a new kind of life, writing every day, getting published; he told his son that if he wanted to come along for this great, new journey, he would have to get his life together.

No more screaming and yelling, no more cursing and swearing, no more threats and attacks, no more calling his father by his name, but rather calling him Dad, showing respect for his father's role in his son's life and for his advanced age, helping more around the house, and the list goes on and on.

The son never picked up after himself, but left his bowls and dishes and cups on the bookshelves in the study for his father to collect and wash.

The father wanted his son to become more self-reliant, and less dependent on his father. One day, once the father was gone, the son would have to manage on his own. Since the son had been on disability since he was seventeen, the father needed to make provisions for the son after the father's eventual death. While the poet planned to live a long, healthy life, he needed to be realistic and arrange things so that his son would be able to manage when he was gone.

The poet had arranged for a special needs trust to be established upon his death for his son. This would be administered by the trust department at the poet's bank, and they would pay the son's bills for him. This was a great relief to the father, since his son would have had considerable difficulty managing paying all these monthly bills. Since they owned the house, the son wouldn't have to pay mortgage or rent in order to have a home to live in.

Approaching the castle walls, the pilgrims paused and took a cosmic breath. Their unconscious minds were not at one with their consciousness. Pleading for amnesty, the accused rent his garments, and vomited on himself. Paring the pear with a paring knife, no one was amused at the sight of pygmies picking their noses in concert with one another. So, the platypuses came out of the water and dried themselves in the warm sunshine.

Starting at the finish line, the runners ran backwards in the misty rain, exerting themselves beyond their capacities in the process. The elephants gave rides to the delighted children. It was a Tuesday, but it felt like a Sunday. For some reason, crowds gathered spontaneously on the lawn of the mayor's house. Fat rats ran through the property, consuming anything that they could get their yellow chattering teeth into.

Unpleasant things are a part of life; the trick is not to let them overwhelm you. The poet was trying to teach this to his son: that nothing or no one can "make you angry." One can choose how to react or respond to any circumstance or person. The poet had learned this from the Wise Woman, and tried to share what he had learned with his son. The boy recently seemed more open to learning from his father, for which the father had hoped and prayed for years.

Glamorous bathing beauties paraded about for the swimsuit competition, smiling their frozen smiles across the gaping audience and judges. They suddenly turned into marble statues, before the startled eyes of the beholders. They were such beautiful statues, though, reminding one of the workmanship of ancient Greece. Of course during that era, the male form was that of idealized beauty, so these sudden female statues boldly settled the score.

Timorous, the flagrant vagrants waddled across the field, picking wildflowers along the way.

Several of them were suddenly attacked with a fit of allergic reactions to the beautiful flowers growing in the field. They beat a hasty retreat back to their homes, and immediately turned on the air conditioning. They medicated themselves, used their inhalers, and sat down on reclining easy chairs to recover from their traumas, contentedly, in front of their television sets.

No talking in the library. Most books were banned, leaving only a precious few available to be read by patrons. People would bring their own books to read in the quiet of the library. Sudden peaches invaded the supermarkets, before their time in the season. The poet and his son were still eating apples and mandarins, since spring had only just begun. Not ready yet for peaches.

Salivating remnants processed through the rooms of the castle, adhering to protocol at all times.

The memory of distant events poured out into waiting cups, and overflowed their bounds. Waiting waiters waited on empty tables, pausing to take orders that would never come. The bus boys also waited to take away dishes that would never be dirty. Thankfully, no one objected.

Certainly everyone was very well pleased when the clowns and midgets played tricks on each other, galumphing down the tubes of the mechanism like there was no tomorrow. Applauding with one hand only, they expressed their enthusiasm by raising their eyebrows. Cotton candy flew out of its tubes, ascending to the heights of the circus tent. Again, no one was amused.

Tenderly tending the opulent shellfish, widows asked for spare change from the diners, who asked if they accepted credit card payments? Watering the garden of dead flowers, the widower bent over and couldn't get back up again. He sat down on a waiting bench and still was bent over to his knees. A bumble bee, flying by, kissed him on his nose, and suddenly he could get upright again.

Warm thoughts console the weary pilgrims, on their way to nowhere. The evangelicals swarmed over the audience at the movie theatre, warning of the coming judgment. The terrified audience tried to fight them off, but eventually gave up, seeing that the evangelicals were relentless and would not stop until they accented to their religion. So they headed for the nearest exit, and ran for their cars. No one ever found out how the movie ended.

"I go to meet my destiny," he said to his son, as he went off, new purple water bottle in hand, to the study to resume his great work, his new novel. He had been away from this book for six painful weeks. What his doctor had thought was a trigger finger on the middle finger of his left hand, persisted to trouble the poet; he was unable to play his cello, the fingers just wouldn't cooperate. He was barely able to type and thus work on his novel.

Having tried to correct the problem with the cortisone injection into the palm of his hand, which felt like his hand was exploding, the doctor then referred him to the local hospital for the orthopedic doctors to examine him. He went, and was treated by a wonderful, caring physician's assistant; she struggled with him to get his ring off his middle finger, so they could treat it; tying a waxed thread around the ring, she pulled gently and got it halfway off the finger.

Finally, the poet said to her "Just give it a good yank!" which she did, and the ring immediately came off! She then had the nurse wrap his entire left hand in a splint, which he had to wear for five weeks. This presented a challenge to the poet, who had to manage with just one hand for all that time. At least the thumb of his left hand was free, and could be utilized.

He was amazed at how quickly he adapted to these conditions, managing to do all his daily tasks: cooking, cleaning up after meals, caring for his son and their pets. But the two things which nurtured his life most he was unable to do: playing his cello, and writing his new novel. The old black

Royal Standard typewriter stood, forlorn, waiting for the poet to make use of it again. His left hand, wrapped in the splint and bandages, was unable to type.

The poet made use of the time as a "forced vacation," from the intensity of this work. After all, he had produced one hundred and seventy-six pages until this injury hit him, coming on gradually, getting worse by the day, and finally becoming intolerable. He read through the manuscript that he had already written, digesting it, remembering it, entering into it once again. And looking for errors that needed correction, which he did with white-out and pen.

This five-week hiatus forced the poet to slow down, even slower than he normally was used to being. It took twice the time to do the most menial tasks with one hand as it used to take with two. He became more mindful, and intentional than he usually was about the task he was engaged in at any given moment. He recalled the medieval monk, Brother Lawrence, whose way of holiness was in his tasks in the monastery kitchen. Sweeping was his favorite mindful task.

During the five agonizing weeks, he watched too much television, and read many books. He began reading through Gertrude Stein's dynastic novel of nine hundred pages, The Making of Americans, reveling in her telling of the stories or "histories" of the members of her extended Jewish family, written in her inimitable style and manner. He read this in the early morning, waking up at five thirty, and reading from six to seven each day.

The poet, at the time he resumed writing again, was nearly two-thirds through this masterpiece, savoring every word as he read along in the wee morning hours in his pink chair in the study. Sometimes his son would play quiet music, which provided a sympathetic environment in which to read. The father had purchased, to his absolute delight, a classic alarm clock with twin bells that ring him awake each morning. This delightful evocation of faeries provided an enchanting way to start the day.

So this went on for five weeks. To emphasize the point: it was not a trigger finger problem; the tendon on that finger had detached itself from the bone. The physician's assistant saw this right away, and had it confirmed by an x-ray. The purpose of the splint was to raise the middle finger of his left hand into a straight position, hopefully reattaching the tendon to the bone. Thus, his entire left hand, apart from his thumb, was contained, wrapped, tightly ensconced in the splint.

After three weeks in the splint, the poet returned to the physician's assistant, who unwrapped the hand, and saw that the tendon had not yet reattached to the bone. So she had the splint put on for another two weeks. Following the completion of the five weeks of bondage, the poet went to see the doctor this time. The doctor said that the tendon had not yet reattached, but that he was not recommending surgery at this point.

He kept him free of the splint and sent the poet for occupational therapy at the local hospital.

His therapist was a big, gentle bear of a man, bald on the head with a huge red beard. He made a splint for the poet, a small, thin one, just to wrap around his middle finger to hold it straight. The therapist took measurements of the angles of his fingers, and put a wonderful hot pack around his hand. Then he massaged the poet's hand in the most marvelous manner.

The therapist gave the poet putty to squeeze, to exercise his fingers, especially the middle one on his left hand. He was a specialist in therapy of hand injuries, and an expert in his field, having been at this hospital for twenty-six years. A most amiable fellow, the poet trusted the therapist implicitly, and believed that through their work together, his hand would be restored to health. Otherwise, he would have to face the prospect of surgery, either to reattach the tendon, or to put in a synthetic joint.

So when the poet came home from therapy, he decided that this was the day to get back to his new novel. "I go to meet my destiny," he had intoned to his son before entering the study to work.

Gingerly removing the slender, blue splint which the therapist had made for him, the poet sat down to write. He found that he was able to type at last! His fingers moved elegantly, not quite as fast as before his injury, but at a decent pace nonetheless.

Prior to this breakthrough, the poet had typed two

brief letters to his editor about his new poetry book. He found that he was able to type these, and thought that the time was approaching to resume his work on the new novel. His poetry book was now available for pre-order from the publisher, and the poet was most excited about this new book. This was the first book of poems he had assembled forty-four year earlier, edited by his dear friend, a noted poet and photographer.

Granular, glandular activity surrounds the captive audience, as, pummeling through the air, the frightened varmints eat their eager victuals, slurping up the remnants at the bottom of their bowls. Entering lightly, organ donors pay organists for their organs. The toast is burning when the bagel is too big. Empty your pockets of all extraneous items: pocket lint, spare change, rusty keys, unopened envelopes, personal lubricant, cigarettes, and chapstick.

Wetting their beds, the orphans sneeze orange juice over the resting vegetables in their trays. The captive audience begins a simple tune, and considers where the sardines swim before they are captured and put in tins. No one believes the report that coral are dying from bleaching. These beautiful, miraculous creatures are perishing because the oceans temperatures are rising. The ice bergs and glaciers are melting into the sea. Countless creatures will perish, and no one even cares about them.

But the poet had resumed his work on the new novel at last. O, frabjous day!! Back in the saddle again, as it were. Cooking with gas. Working on the railroad. Spending time with your favorite book, the one you are currently writing. Working overtime. At last he would begin typing his usual four pages a day, working each day for two feverish hours. Making hay while the sun shines.

But being released from the splint enclosing his left hand was a newfound freedom. He had his left hand back again! You never know how important something is until you lose it for a while, the poet mused to himself. Being able to do things with two hands was a sudden miracle. When they took off the splint, his hand was numb and swollen, stiff from not moving for five weeks. Gradually, the fingers began to move and regain their liveliness.

Still, his hand was weakened by this all, and it took some effort of intentionality to type the words of his novel. Nonetheless, he persisted, determined to resume his great work. The repeated appearance of the small yellow note, reading simply "Philippe Soupault." What did it mean? This prominent surrealist poet and writer haunted his waking hours.

He had begun rereading The Magnetic Fields by Andre Breton and Soupault recently. This book was his "bedtime story," as he read it each night in bed, his cup of peppermint tea by his side, and the new alarm clock with its twin bells that ring also there. This book entranced him: keeping conventional syntax, the poets replaced what would be expected with surprising, novel, surreal visions.

But the small, yellow note with Soupault's name on it appeared now and then, and just as quickly disappeared. This poet's voice spoke deeply to him, and his personality drew him like a moth to a porch light on a summer evening. He would seek further knowledge of this surrealist master, and look into his life and journey. A sympathetic soul, with whom he felt deep kinship.

The mysterious spectre of the French poet haunted him, as did the other surrealist poets, Breton, Eluard,

Desnos. Cocteau had been an early hero of the young poet, both in his sexual nonconformity, and his genius, expressed in every known medium of art. He felt an instinctive love of the French poets: Baudelaire, Rimbaud, Verlaine, Mallarme, Jacob, et al. Never having learned the French language adequately to read them, he was bound to translations, ever reading them.

In college, he had taken courses in French literature of the twentieth century, with a brilliant, eccentric professor who spoke of "the Almighty, with whom I am not on the best of terms," smoking incessantly his endless cigarettes as he lectured. Proust, Celine, Beckett, Camus, Sartre were heroes to the poet from an early age. His years in college were among his happiest ever, reading wonderful literature every day.

A lifetime of reading had nurtured and nourished his mind and spirit, encouraging him, out of this study, to attempt his own writing. As a young poet, he had produced voluminous bodies of work, and given public readings of his poetry and prose. He was noted as a young poet, and recognized for his work and efforts.

As he assumed his vocation as a priest, his poetry took back seat in his life. Having written so much poetry and his experimental novel, his marriage was a dry desert as far as poetry went. He poured his literary skills into his sermons and classes, spontaneously preaching and teaching from a mere few notes. He regarded this action as "prophesying," and saw it as a holy act, for which he prepared extensively throughout the week prior to Sunday.

He would enter into a mystical state while preaching, ecstatic and energized in spirit and mind and body. While he spoke in human words, these veiled a deeper reality, into which he invited his listeners to enter. He took this task of preaching and teaching very seriously, and prepared with a holy and open heart to what he would proclaim to his people.

The same state as he would be in at a poetry reading, this was the state he would be in while preaching and teaching. An out-of-the-body experience, transcending himself and his own limitations as a fragile human vessel, and yet at the same time embodied fully as in no other state. Now that he had reclaimed his life as a poet, he channeled all his energy into this new, yet ancient role.

He had been destined from birth to be a poet.

Nurtured on poetry by his mother through childhood, he developed early a love of verse, reading Shakespeare as a child with delight. His favorite play was A Midsummer Night's Dream. His mother had taken him to see an animated version of the play at the museum in the city. Then he had seen the old black and white film of the classic, and was utterly enchanted.

He felt, even as a child, a kinship with the faerie folk. It was a strange coincidence and violation of its beauty and magical qualities that he would be called "fairy" by vicious children at school. He didn't understand this name he was being called. Was he really a faerie? A magical being with supernatural powers, and a mischievous quality that made him endearing? But the children used this word in a hostile, hateful, malicious manner, desecrating the name of faerie every day at his expense.

In his present age, he relished the idea of identifying as a faerie, a real one, in his old age.

He could use some magic, to free him from the bondage of his disappointments. His birthday would be on Sunday next, and he would wait to see if any one of his daughters would acknowledge this event.

He did not expect that they would, and prepared himself for that eventuality.

He had begun planning his own funeral. He met with the funeral director at the funeral home in the village, and felt good about this action, and embraced the process with vigor. He had no fear of death, and wanted to decompose and return to the earth and be one with his Tao as efficiently as possible. He would not be embalmed, out of respect for his Jewish ancestors. He picked out the most beautiful, simple Shaker Pine casket, which was just what he had imagined choosing for himself.

The poet would pick out a plot at the cemetery in the village, and hopefully, one with a nice view. He would commission a grave stone, bearing his name, dates of birth and death, and simply the word "POET." He would plan a little gathering at the funeral home, with readings and music chosen for the occasion. He wondered who would even be there for his funeral? Would his daughters have been restored to him by then? Would they be at his deathbed? At his funeral?

He could not worry about these things, but went on planning these events without regard as to who would be attending. He needed to have these things in place concerning his death, so that his son would not have to deal with these matters in his grief after his father's death. He wanted everything in place and in good order, so that these events would occur smoothly and elegantly.

He would have read a poem by e. e. cummings, beginning "When God lets my body be"; the sixteenth chapter of the Tao Te Ching of Lao Tzu; and the Hymn to Death from Leaves of Grass by Whitman. As people are gathering, they will hear the Messe des Pauvres by Satie on the organ; at the end of the gathering, after the readings, they will hear the duet from The Pearl Fishers by Bizet.

At the graveside, those gathered will pray the Kaddish for his repose.

The poet felt so happy about planning his own funeral. This was giving him deep peace of mind, as he set in motion what he wanted for the end of his life. He hoped to pass away in his own bed, peacefully, and without benefit of clergy interfering. He hoped to be surrounded by his four children, and prayed that his three daughters would be reconciled to him and their brother by the time of his death, or, hopefully, long before this.

But who would do the readings? He had long imagined his daughters taking on the holy task.

Who would read them if his daughters were not there? What if nobody was there but his poor son?

He would then read the readings silently to himself. That would be so very sad. All of the poet's friends were ten years older than himself, and would likely depart life before him.

Nonetheless, the poet went on with his plans, hoping that when the day came, the pieces would fall neatly into place. He planned to live a very long time: his grandmother had blessed him, saying, "You should live to one hundred and thirty." The young poet took this blessing to heart, and believed in its promise of such optimistic longevity. This blessing had sustained him throughout the years, and he believed that it would fulfill its hopeful promise. He intended to be around for a long time.

The poet's son was suffering on two fronts simultaneously: His methamphetamine connection was not responding to his calls, and he was craving his drug of choice. Additionally, the young male nurse to whom the son had attached himself romantically was not returning his telephone calls either.

So the son was in the depths of despair, and the father had no way to alleviate his suffering.

The father and son had agreed to a plan for modified meth use by the son. He would use the drug on weekends, Friday night through Sunday evening. He would inject the meth once upon receiving it, and smoke it for the rest of the weekend. But the son did not adhere to this experiment, injecting the meth almost every day, and missing half the time, after which the son would explode in frustration.

The son's veins were shot and useless after all his injecting, and it was hard for him to hit a vein.

Smoking the drug was a totally different experience for the son than injecting it was. He loved the intensity, or "rush" of the initial hit. This was the only way that the son could feel human. His level of depression was so deep and intense that the use of the drug only brought the son up to the level of a normal, mentally healthy person, not even really getting him "high" anymore at all.

Smoking the meth was a more gentle, subdued experience, which just did not do for the son what he needed it to do. The understanding of the agreement was that the son would follow through with this plan, and eventually, after two or three months, taper off of the drug, and finally eliminate it.

The father wondered if the son would ever be able to fulfill this promise and intention?

Vague semblances protrude discreetly throughout the proceedings, enveloping themselves around the agreeable host parties. Drilling the point home, they expect numerous counterfeits to be exposed throughout the trials as they proceed. What would the mothers of the village think of this?

Test-tube babies float in formaldehyde as though they were some ancient, preserved vegetables.

Numerous flags were seen burning on their flagpoles, and entrances of ballerinas were performed in full view of the sight. No one perceived what this meant, and went back to their own private business. The vipers were stinging themselves out of hopelessness, and the ravens refused to utter a sound in protest. Usual seasons came and went, but the butterflies never returned from the south, to the dismay of the disappointed children of the village.

What smiles were wiped off of the sullen faces, now downcast into their own private oblivions?

What went away with them, cast off into endless smile-less solemnity? The poet rarely laughed or smiled for many years, during his daughters' absence, and following upon the disintegration of his affair with the young companion, and during his recovery from heroin use.

But now the poet smiled on occasion, and was even heard to utter a laugh now and then. His spirit had been restored through his years with his last counselor and his current work with the Wise Woman. Nothing could disrupt or disturb his peace of mind, and the center to which he strictly held.

Not even his friend, who had caused him considerable distress over several days.

The poet's telephone conversations with this friend had turned into extended therapy sessions, wherein the friend was speaking to him as if he were his therapist. The poet had to point this out to his friend, since their talks has become so one-sided, really monologues of the friend concerning all his conflicts, obsessions, and constant disappointment with his life and reality.

The friend did not take kindly to this suggestion that he seek therapy, but accused the poet of not caring about the friend. He accused the poet of being like everyone else, finding the friend bizarre and absurd, and not having the time to indulge his fantasies. The friend even accused the poet of suggesting therapy to the friend, so that the poet wouldn't have to talk to the friend anymore. None of this was true, and these were further neurotic reactions, to which the friend was prone.

The friend even suggested that listening to his negativity was therapeutic for the poet! So the friend hauled off all hurt and bothered. The next day the friend called the poet, but the poet was having a very busy day, and would call the friend back later on. But instead of waiting for his call, the friend went berserk, insisting that the poet just wouldn't make the time for him, and went off the deep end again, suggesting that it was time to end their friendship.

The poet had to reassure the friend and calm him down from his neurotic fantasies, always making a crisis out of nothing. Their friendship was precious to both of them, but the friend had surely developed a dependence on the poet, to which the poet was not always able to respond. His time was precious to him, and now that he was back writing his new novel, he would not always be available to talk to the friend when he might call.

The poet hoped that his friend would not have a mental breakdown every time the poet was unavailable to talk at a given moment. Finally, the poet had to tell the friend to stop harassing him, or he would refuse his telephone calls. This stopped the friend dead in his tracks, and no further discussion of this sort was engaged in from that moment on. The friend was awakened to sanity once more.

Claustrophobic entities embraced the remnants of the festival with bone-crushing intensity, threatening to break their victims' ribs in the process. The firemen hosed them all down, and broke up the party. Entering remnants exploded in enthusiasm, while their blood flowed helplessly onto the waiting, thirsty earth. No one minded the spectacle, but shielded their eyes from the horror.

Catastrophic beings, melting into the trees, gasped for air, and transcended their limits, molding themselves onto the bark in sympathetic moans. The Tree-People were now enmeshed in a sudden status of adventurous proceedings, asking nothing but answering everything. Using their fortitude as evidence, they climbed the limits of the mountain peaks, exuding their juices along their merry way. Barking like dogs, they howled at the moon, full and resplendent on high.

Sending messages, like moths, through the sullen air, the hopeful villagers insisted on being heard. The songs of yesteryear persisted in taming their enthusiasm, while pasta cooked away in huge pots of boiling water. The firemen retreated to their headquarters, and no one was the worse for the damages that cost the village dearly. The pasta boiled over and was fed to the waiting throngs, who turned their underwear inside-out before attending.

Filling up each page, the poet wrote with determination and elegance, turning phrases into thought-containers, sending out into the unknown endless messages from the earth he inhabited.

Writing of the same incidents as are recorded in this

current book, the poet persisted in writing the events of his extraordinary, long life for posterity to peruse and ponder deeply. This would be the legacy that he would leave behind, when he leaves this life.

Heartrending sorrows exude from decapitated veins, pouring out leprosy-infested memories of bleak substance, retaining the form they once possessed. At evening, the forest melted into mushrooms, while the faeries planted seeds to nurture overnight. These grew by morning, and were harvested of their ripe berries, as the faeries danced about, gathering them in their waiting baskets.

There was something protruding from the rafters, and its symphony extended life beyond its normal years. Remarkably, the cows came home, and flannel shirts were folded and put away for next fall and winter. Blown-up balloons floated off into the distant sky of doom, while active ants dug deeper holes to hide in. That reminds someone of something else they had forgotten about long ago.

Bleak corners send out thoughts which collide with the membranes and tendons that attach themselves to appropriate bones. The skeletal structure had become unhinged, and people were falling apart at the seams. No one knew what was causing this mass disintegration of the masses. The firemen were befuddled as to what to do; the doctors were at their wits' end. Everyone just gave up.

As to the effects of prosperous lunatics: they walk on all fours, and lie on their backs to have their bellies rubbed. Endless cans of tuna fish and sardines and tinned soups from foreign countries.

Shooting up forests of redwood trees like captivated monstrosities avenged by their kinsmen. In an alternate universe, a foreign reality system exists that would put all human advancement to shame.

The Alpine wilderness, the laundry in the clothes dryer, the various and sundry objects that infest the mind, clothing life with material substance, and excavating the rooms we inhabit. All the time, no one noticed the particles that float through your mind when you think. Marshmallows melting in the campfire, slowly falling off of the sticks into which they had been plunged. Glowing like embers, they revolve and split open, pouring out their melted insides into the fire.

It was his birthday, and his hearing aids were not

receiving his telephone calls. So when his 90-year-old friend called to wish him a happy birthday, he was unable to hear her, and said he would get back to her soon. Now he would have to motor down to the hearing aid place, to have this fixed. What other friends would call this day, and he be unable to hear them? Would any of his three daughters even acknowledge his special day? He shared his birthday with his eldest daughter; would she call?

He tried to stay focused, and worked on his novel instead of worrying. He had gone to the supermarket in the morning, gathering sushi, gyoza, seaweed salad, and cannolis for his birthday dinner with his son. He hoped that the son would be awake to eat with him, since he was unable to procure his methamphetamine. His connection was still ignoring him, not answering his calls, which was frustrating to the son to no end. And the father had to listen to his moans for his drug.

Crying "Help!" the son called out to an empty universe. A hopeless cry of despair. So, this was what his birthday was going to be like. He resigned himself to accepting the miserable situation, and went on with his writing. His son had been howling for days, and couldn't stop himself. Screaming "I'm sorry!" the son threatened to kill himself. "I will die! I can't take any more of this life! Everything is wrong! I must die to be at peace! This life is too much for me! I need to die!"

And so the music played on, the same incessant theme of cosmic disappointment. This is not a pretty story, but the truth hurts, sometimes. The swallowing vowels extremely corrupt the pains of vaulted enthusiasm, as the quiet resumes upon the scene. Enveloping entrails confuse the issue: people blowing their noses into their handkerchiefs. A distant bird, chirping in some tree.

Emptying their cavities of hidden jewels, they persisted in awakening the sounds of morning. In the rapture of this experiment, the followers in incest corrupt the morals of the village youth. Tumbling out of their beds, they put on their uniforms, and throw themselves out the window. No one would believe this if it were not real. Closing the doors, they forget why they came here.

Now entereth the poet's grandparents: His paternal grandfather he never met, his having died before the young poet was born. After immigrating from Russia, he kept a small farm upstate for a time, and then moved to the city and opened a Jewish dairy restaurant. He was a gentle, quiet man, and the poet wished that he had known him. His paternal grandmother lived in a slum in the northern borough of the city, in a walk-up tenement building in a bad neighborhood.

She was a thoroughly European woman, who came from Austria as a young woman. Her unmarried son lived with her there. She would serve schmaltz herring, the saltiest food imaginable, and bread spread thick with salty butter. She was a quiet, sturdy woman, not given much to physical displays of affection, but the young poet hugged her and kissed her mustachioed face with pleasure.

His maternal grandfather was an immigrant from what was then Russian Minsk, and was a thorough eccentric. He made a killing as electricity was being installed in stores and homes, and became quite prosperous. Having had only an elementary school education, he nonetheless had a natural gift for math, and was able to calculate problems in his head.

This grandfather was not especially religious, but became so when in the kitchen. He always wore a cap on these occasions, which they all called "Pappy's hat."

His presumption of religiosity was nothing less than amusing. He often spoke of his imaginary friend: "As I was saying to the other fella, ha hoo!" When one of the grandchildren was crying over something, he would gleefully say "Stop laughing, you'll be alright." Which would cause the child to stop crying and immediately start laughing.

His maternal grandmother was especially his favorite. A big, bosomy woman, given to much hugging and kissing, she was a constant delight to the young poet. She was American born, with parents from Romania. The young poet was able to know his great grandmother, during her final days in a nursing home. His grandmother made matzah ball soup, with boiled chicken, and kept an immaculate home. She always gave him a nosh to eat in the car on the way home: a roll with cream cheese.

The maternal grandparents were prosperous for a time, and owned their own home, and had a German maid. But after the Stock Market crash, they lost everything, and had to move to an apartment.

But they soon recovered, and led a happy, peaceful life. Later, they followed their youngest daughter, and moved out onto the island. The young poet would ride the railroad out to visit them often.

The maternal grandmother died first. And then the grandfather's diabetes got so bad that he had to have his leg amputated. The young poet visited him in the hospital on the island, and tried to cheer him up, encouraging him in his loss of his wife and his leg. He did not survive long, but died soon after this amputation. He just gave up on life, and decided to stop living.

When the poet's uncle came home from work, he found the paternal grandmother lying on the floor of the kitchen, groceries scattered around her. Was she robbed on the way home? Did she have a sudden heart attack and just expired? A mystery that was never solved. After her death, the uncle moved close to the poet's family. The poet's mother helped him set up an apartment to live in. Eventually, the uncle had to move to a nursing home, where the poet would visit him. He died there.

Captive domesticated fish swim helplessly in their pools, while antelopes range through the prairie under the moonlight. Pierrot stares at the shining round object, transfixed by its beauty and grandeur. Slinky think-tanks wander through the jello, exposing themselves to each other, as the blank orchids fade musically into faerie dust.

Telling the story, there is much more to tell. But backhanded whimsies press buttons that activate the antagonism of the putrid puddles. Went to the store, forgot what I wanted to buy there.

That's what he thought to himself, under the bedcovers. A soup made of tin cans, screwdrivers, and a chain saw. This would be served piping hot with a crusty bread.

The poet's father had another brother, who had estranged himself from his family for many years. A brooding artist, with a graceful wife, he took his own life, leaving instructions for his wife to destroy all of his artwork. The young poet only met this distant aunt after all this had happened. She was a sweet, dignified woman, who had suffered a terrible loss, indeed. How she continued to survive, the poet never knew. What happened to her? He wished that he had known this uncle.

Disruptions between family members was found

among the poet's relatives, on both parents' sides. His paternal grandfather, whom he never knew, had separated himself from the rest of his family.

His mother's sister didn't speak to their brother, nor he to her. Like a Greek tragedy, these dynastic curses enthralled these families, dooming them to extinction and disintegration.

And now, the latest tragic estrangement: his three daughters, none of whom called him on his birthday. And his hearing aids were not working, so he was unable to hear on the telephone when three dear friends called to wish him happy birthday. A solemn day, it turned out to be for the poet. At least his son got up from bed to eat the birthday sushi with his father. He thought that he could hear his son breathing in his sleep, upstairs in his bedroom. How was this possible from downstairs?

He had gone to have his hearing aids fixed, stopping first to his garage to get a bit of oil, before his oil change in two days hence. Driving down the highway, his car started overheating, as it too often did. He made it to the hearing aid place, and drove home terror-stricken, as the car overheated, instructing him to turn the engine off. But he was determined to make it to his garage again.

Mercifully, he got there, and after the car cooled down, the mechanic added coolant to the car.

What a panic that was, though! He loved his old plum purple Cadillac, but it always had some problem. The poet wanted to be secure, knowing that he would safely get to his destination, and safely return home again. This did not seem too much to ask for. Only safe travels, if you please.

Cockamamie biscuits have gone stale in their boxes, like oat and wheat with chocolate on top.

Thinking about salvaging unkempt tripods, when you ask for something, you always get something else.

Distinguished bedfellows walk hand-in-hand through the misty fog, entering the park with the crescent moon shining above them. There is no one else around to witness their love.

Draining the dregs, like squeezing out the last drops of tea from the teabag at the bottom of the cup. Talking of octopus: the grilled cheese sandwich with muenster cheese and sourdough bread was marvelous at lunch. Catching fireflies in jars, the children eat them, glowing in their stomachs now. They swallowed them whole, so as not to limit their luminosity.

Speaking of Greek tragedy: the poet had a sister, who was not speaking to him for several years.

He had repeatedly asked her to give him the addresses of his estranged daughters, so he could at least write to them. But she militantly refused. When the poet expressed his anger to her over her unwillingness, she broke off contact with him. This was one more act of the Greek tragedy that was his family life.

The poet's mother had a sister, of whom the young poet was extremely fond. She had given him two books by James Joyce: Ulysses and Finnegans Wake, which were to change his life forever. After his mother's death, this aunt told him a shocking story. His mother had been married briefly before to a man with whom she was passionately in love. But on their wedding night, he was unable to consummate the marriage, and it turned out that he was schizophrenic.

So, the marriage was annulled, and his mother must have grieved deeply over this disappointment. Because of this, the poet's father was not the great love of her life. He came in "behind the eight ball." The poet doubted that his parents much loved each other. There was little demonstration of affection between them, and his mother always complained that her husband was "cold." The young poet grew up in this unhappy environment.

The poet would often go to visit this aunt on the island where they lived. He would go to the beach while he was there, and sometimes would bring a friend along with him. The railroad train ride was always enchanting, the old trains chugging along with determination and fierce pride. He would bring a book along for the ride, and visit his grandparents while he was out there also.

He lost touch with this aunt and uncle for many years. She had come to his wedding with his cousin, and after that they slipped out of each other's lives. The next and last time he saw them was at his father's burial, which he conducted. There they were, the little old Jewish couple, huddling together at the graveside. His children were also all there, as was an old friend of his father's.

After the burial of his father's cremated remains, they all went back to the hotel where they were staying, and had drinks and dinner. It was a lovely time of gathering and remembrance, especially to see his favorite aunt and uncle, what would turn out to be his last time seeing them before they both died soon after this occasion.

After the poet's stepmother died suddenly, his sister moved their father to the northern state where she lived, so she could look after him. The poet and his children would travel up to see them every summer, combining their visits with pleasant times at the enormous lake nearby. These visits with his aging father with his children were precious times together.

When his father became ill, at age 92, the poet didn't know what to do. He couldn't face the long drive to be with them, and his resentment toward his father for throwing him out of the house at seventeen got the better of him. He couldn't face his father's death, and so did not go up there to be with him. The poet felt a sense of gnawing guilt over this failure and inability, but was resolved.

When his father remarried, he went to the museum to see the series done by William Blake on the biblical book of Job. This seemed a fitting substitution for attending his father's wedding. The young poet didn't visit his new parents' new home for one year after they married. He met with his father for lunch in the city now and then, and his father gave him money out of guilt and anguish.

After the wedding, his sister and young stepbrother moved in with the parents to a new, luxury apartment. His older stepbrother moved out, and the poet was thrown out. This new family was a typical American fantasy: two kids, both young homosexuals, doing drugs, partying in the apartment, while the adults wondered what on earth was going on?

So, the poet was evacuated for degenerate behavior, while the two children who were allowed to remain were doing the very same scandalous things. Life had been unfair to the young poet, and he soldiered on with fierce determination to survive and surmount these curses of Fate. He would go on to mold himself into the young poet he was destined to be from birth, and fulfill his promised heritage.

Hungering over the afternoon thoughts, the entryway was obstructed from the rear. When two opossums went walking through the fields, no one came to their defense. Open wounds were cleansed with water and vinegar, while the temptations of life went through the nose. Always there were troubles under the present platitudes, and entryways were blocked again.

The poet had another uncle, his mother's twin brother, named after a small furry animal out of whimsy. He was a large, corpulent man, who fought in the second World War, as his father had fought in the first World War. His wife was a demure, attractive woman of little intelligence. She was wont to say on occasion, "If I woulda know, I woulda go." The poet's mother delighted in mocking this aunt.

This uncle tried to reach out to the young poet after his mother's death. Only the poet's father and this uncle knew of his mother's cancer diagnosis. After her death, the uncle made several valiant attempts to reach out to the young poet, with dissatisfying results. The uncle wanted him to go back to school, stop smoking marijuana, and get a better circle of friends.

His efforts fell upon deaf ears, though. And the poet would go on with his journey, following it wherever it might lead him. After his mother's death, a close friend from High School invited him over to her apartment and gave him marijuana to smoke for the first time.

This was an enlightening experience for the young poet. She also gave him a copy of Kahil Gibran's book, The Prophet. This book impressed him tremendously and offered him great comfort. He read the chapter on death at his mother's funeral.

His friends from High School surrounded him with love and support after his mother's death. Somehow he survived, wallowing in the juices of his grief, and plunging himself into reading James Joyce, and spending time with his friends. This was a twilight zone for him then, and his despair was rampant, filling him with unspeakable terror and abandonment. He had been as close with his mother as any son and mother could possibly be. So the loss was profound.

Asking anybody for advice is a risky business. You have to know what you're doing all the time.

When the villagers saw the precipice involving the unwritten memoires of a student activist, the bother was not worth the trouble. Clicking their heels together, they danced through the sullen streets, abandoning all restraint, and indulging in produced satisfaction.

Abandoning all thoughts, the vague semblances reveal the most unusual aspects of time. All of the entrances were open, and the angels stopped peeling away lemons from the absent emphasis. You would think that no one will obtain the necessary patterns to close the cotton-wool chapters. They tried their hardest to make chocolate candies when the sun was in eclipse.

Darkened passageways expand in their limits, stretching out putty to strengthen their fingers.

When the topics were chosen for investigation, the elephants returned to the pond to drink. Everyone betrayed a hidden smile with frozen emphases and metamorphoses. It took three hours to cook the flesh of the animals that the hunters trapped and caught.

Dim vestibules radiate organized symphonies, caught in the middle of the sentence. With their hats on backwards, they looked like shark-infested waters, claiming to represent the interests of the commoners. Looking back, they thought again about what they were concerned with. Numerous contracts were signed and delivered, exposing the flairs that vanished in thin air.

So, the father and son lived on together. The son, grieving over the lack of his drug of preference, and the father not knowing what to do to help him. The poet's phone was now working again, and he was able to hear on the telephone at last. So, he called back the three friends who had called him on his birthday. They were dear friends, and they encouraged him to be happy.

The poet's three daughters didn't call him on his birthday. This was a devastating disappointment. What could be possessing them to abandon their own father in his old age? He felt, once again, like King Lear, forsaken by his daughters. Why did this keep happening to them? What anger and hatred had consumed them? There was nothing he could do about it, so he just didn't let himself think about the situation, or it would have disintegrated his being.

This book, a hall of mirrors. A novel by a poet about a poet who is writing a novel about a poet who is writing a novel. This could go on forever, and just might. The poet was writing about himself, beneath the guise of his character. All the events of his life were put into the life of his "poet." Thus, one enters into this series of reflecting pools, shimmering with faerie dust.

The poet worked diligently, now that his finger was working again. He wrote his four pages for two hours every afternoon as he had done before his injury. His occupational therapy was beautiful, and his therapist was a sympathetic, encouraging presence. He said that he liked the poet's "vibe." What a miracle to find a hand therapist in the next village over! What a gift to him.

The poet's therapist was impressed with the progress he had made, especially returning to typing and writing his new novel, after six weeks away from it, five in the splint, and one week recovering movement in his fingers. He was encouraged and hopeful that this therapy and his typing every day would reattach the tendon to the bone of the middle finger of his left hand, and that, thus, he would be spared surgery on the finger, if you please.

In the long-lasting war, the occupation had blocked all the border crossings, thus eliminating any source of food or medicine to the starving people of the territory. Famine had emerged, rearing its savage head, devouring the innocent, consuming them with Death. The humanitarian agencies had stopped delivering food to the besieged city, for fear of their own safety. The president had ordered a floating pier to be built, from which boats could deliver much-needed aid.

But this was not enough. The president's airlift packages had fallen and killed people rushing to obtain their contents. The occupation refused to open the border crossings, intentionally starving the people trapped in the territory to death. Hospitals were barely operating, due to lack of fuel and supplies. People were dying for lack of medical care, as the hospitals were no longer able to provide it.

The cobwebs on the wall flutter in the air conditioner's breeze. His shoes, brown Birkenstocks with buckles, surrounded his feet like two portable houses, ensconcing his feet in the safe, enclosed spaces they provided. These completely enclosed his black-stockinged feet, and offered comfort and contentment to him, as he sat and typed at the old black Royal Standard typewriter every day.

Black beauty like licorice or a crescent moon on an unexpected evening. You walk under the stars in your underwear in the backyard where no one can see you. The cicadas will be chirping as you relieve yourself, making water in the cooperative bushes. The simple gifts of life, moments clarified and syphoned out like butter, melting in the summer heat.

You ask, "What does it matter?" The answer will be revealed in time, at the appropriate moment, when you least expect it, when you have given up all hope, and suddenly, there it is: the unexpected answer to all your questions. Suddenly, it all makes sense. Even though you don't fully grasp the vast implications which evolve from this momentous revelation.

So the son slept on, through the entire day, waking up moaning for meth, his favored drug. His methamphetamine connection was still ignoring him. This seemed, to the father, so cruel, and inconsiderate. The son was just hiding in sleep, unable to face life without his drug. It was peaceful when the son was asleep, and the father was able to write during these times, without disturbance. But when the son would wake up, the peace of the home would be shattered once again.

The next day, the son was able to obtain his meth. Another connection had it, and got it to the son just in time. He was literally falling apart at the seams, and the drug arrived at an opportune moment. The son was so relieved to have his meth in his veins again. The fog was lifted from his mind, and his face lit up again with vibrant life. How amazing that this drug could create such happiness!

The situation was far from ideal, but the father was content to see his son contented once again.

How wonderful it would be if his son could quit this addiction and be freed from its cravings! But this did not seem to be in the cards for them at this moment. So, they went on with their unusual life together, blending-in thoughts and rescuing dreams.

The poet had written two hundred pages of his new novel, since his finger was recovering from its injury. It was splendid for him to be writing again, and he looked forward to completing his book at just over three hundred pages, since this had been the length of his first novel, Reap Violet Hiss. The journey of writing this novel would take him beyond his own capacity into a realm of fantasy and faeries.

Two hundred pages of insane ramblings, nonsensical phrasings, impossible images, cooked-up recipes for disaster. Why not implode the vegetables, and throw the fish to the cats? he wondered. Sudden emphases converged upon the greensward, enveloping with their fangs the openings that were previously closed for repair. Feather dusters flutter like peacocks on the front lawn of the courthouse.

The despair which consumed the soup on the stove recklessly protruded into the vat of steaming broth. Prolonged sighs extricated from bondage the empty voices of orphans, leaning on the parapet on the porch. The collapsing ceiling vents organized crime like sudden participles, inveighing against grammar through the open screen door. Thankfully, no one was looking.

When the organized criminals wet their pants, nothing was forgotten, as they were consumed by their incessant grief. When the remnants converged upon the village green, the purple flowers began to weep vanilla ice cream, liquefied in tears. Shooting the forest, the birds all fly away, and the catfish in the pond swim vigorously in the opposite direction.

Shaking his fist at the moon, the mayor disbands the flagrant vagrants into space. They stop to go to the bathroom before blasting off. The bank was closed for Memorial Day, and the startling sparkles suddenly illumined the distance. Taking off their backwards hats, the citizens applaud the angelic pronouncements exuding from the mouths of the invalids, speaking sideways in their chairs.

Cloud-infested pasta cooks, angel hair and fettucine, parting their garments like the Red Sea, open-coasted like toasted English muffins spread with butter and strawberry jam for tea. Opening the envelopes growing on the fruit trees, they read the obscure poems contained therein. The cryptic messages must mean something, and they took them to the poet to see if he could read them and interpret them to the villagers.

The poet read the messages, but could not interpret them for the people. So they made up songs with the poems as lyrics, singing with their guitars, banjos, and fiddles, the themes that the poems declared with such boldness. This turned into a regular festival, as the flowers around the gazebo bloomed scandalously, abounding suddenly in opulence before their very eyes.

Almost remembering his dream from the previous night, he fluttered in indecision, thinking what it was, and hoping to recall more of it. Dreams eluded the poet, since he could never remember them. What was this entire life he led while he slept? Wasted time, or useful material? Sleep was a great boon to the poet, resting in the arms of slumber for hours each night.

Cartoons like bleak, gleeful images dance upon the

roof of his skull. Flooding his mind with thoughts held captive in the dust, rearing the head of some snake, a python ready to strike at any moment. Backing off, they restrain themselves, coughing up stardust like there was no tomorrow.

Baking cookies, peanut butter, the bakers, dancing on the head of a pin, relieve themselves.

Standing at attention, the rampaging boys wave their blue electric penises at the audience, who disappear in a flutter of memories and warped enthusiasm. The boys never accept offerings, but put on their show with aplomb and serious verve. When they are done with their erotic games, the scent of lavender fills the air, with shades of eucalyptus following.

Like picking out a suitable wine for dinner, failures to engage lead only to desperate measures being taken. The fog had dissipated, and the laundry was hanging on the clothesline. Suddenly, a huge storm blew up, with rain pouring down in buckets. The streets were flooded, and cows floated off down the road, carried by the fierce floods of water. It took a week for the village to dry out.

The poet's contractor had installed bannisters on his stairwell, and railings on his outside steps.

This would be a great help to the poet, who needed assistance getting up and down the stairs. He was "old-age-proofing" his house, so that he would be able to live out his days in his home. He intended to remain in his house, never having to go into a nursing home, and die in his own bed one day.

His contractor was coming up with a plan to fix his porch: the ceiling of his porch was collapsing and need to be repaired. The insurance had refused his claim on the work, and the poet was going to have to pay to have this fixed. He would have to draw upon his investments, the nest-egg he kept for unforeseen needs. He hoped that he will have made enough money to pay for these repairs.

Next, his roof was being repaired. The insurance was paying for this work, and the poet was getting an entire, new, free roof. The roofer was behind in his schedule, due to the amount of rain that had recently fallen, and would get to the job after a time. The old house needed attention, and the poet was seeing to it that his home was well cared for. Nice improvements were encouraging to him.

The lasagna was in the oven. "Eating Your Lasagna"

was one of his most popular poems, written after a dinner with a charming young woman in a London restaurant. So the poet and his son would eat lasagna for supper tonight. With steamed broccoli, this would make a charming meal. The poet tried to feed himself and his son well each night. For breakfast and lunch they would fend for themselves, but the father made supper every night for his son.

Lunatics subdued for a season, the settlement extremely deserved better oysters than those provided to the diners. Slurping down the icy cold shellfish, they were delighted as they slid down their throats. Waiting for some response, the heads of the diners blew off, revealing their empty necks.

When someone fluttered into the room unexpectedly, everyone did a headstand instead.

Why not wait for some interruption to exclude you from the bazaar, entering like everything- bagels, pouring out tender thoughts of evenings in paradise. Looking out the window, the monstrosities conveyed their feelings, converging upon the scene of the crime with dangerous instincts. The old members dissuaded the entrants from eating chocolate.

Thankfully, everyone hates why the moon is not made of green cheese. And, explaining what they mean, they walk backwards their argument, flooding appearances with gleeful expeditions, into the unknown waters of exiled regions, pooling their resources so that no one is left out in the cold. When the partridges return to their roosts, the needles in the haystacks will be recovered once again.

Slicing through the distance, the horizon expands like the universe. Pretending to be someone else for a moment, you look inside your mind, exploring what remains of consciousness. Captivated by the fact of your own existence, you gaze endlessly into the looking-glass, mirroring your image in luscious hues. Your mental capacity expands like a balloon, blowing up, enlarging itself all over again.

The interesting principle, the one you forgot that you know, surrounds the enclave of your thoughts, pretending to explode into garments of the priesthood. The telephone rings, but he doesn't answer it, while he is in a fit of passion writing. He sneezes, twice, bending over suddenly with the thrust of the air's expulsion. Recovering himself, he goes back to writing once again.

The son was peaceful at last, enjoying the medication that his drug provided him. The father was able to write peacefully, since his son was engaged with life once again. A resurrection of sorts, the transformation of the son was remarkable; he didn't seem to mind anything, and went about his business, letting his father do what he needed to do throughout the day.

They would connect periodically throughout the day and evening, sitting together in the study, partaking of their marijuana, listening to the son's unusual music, talking to each other now and then.

Most of the time, these could be pleasant events of shared experience. This was when the son was high on his meth. Otherwise, it was like entering a pool inhabited by alligators, upon which one never knew when he might stumble.

When the son was frustrated, without his favored drug, he would take out his anger on his father, cursing him, calling him horrible names, saying unspeakable things to him. It was as though some inner demon was released on such occasions, vulgarity and profanity predominating. Some exorcism of hate and rage, anger turned to poison, venom flashing from his evil, possessed tender tongue.

Occasionally, the father would be on the telephone with a friend, when his son would suddenly start screaming; the friend would not believe the sound that came out of the son's wild mouth. The father worried what the neighbors would think: it sounded like someone was being murdered in the house. It had happened before that some passer-by would call the police, who would arrive wondering what was going on there. Embarrassed, the son would explain why he was angry.

So it was advantageous for the father to have the son medicated on his drug. At least there would be peace in the kingdom this way. It was not an ideal solution to the problem, but "getting clean" seemed a distant goal for the son. So he medicated himself out of the abysmal depths of his depression, up to the level of a normal, mentally healthy individual.

So this was to be their life: moving in and out of intoxication and hysteria. The son screamed at his father the same way the father used to scream at his wife. The son grew up in this hysterical environment, and learned screaming from his father at an early age. Throughout his childhood, the son would get upset easily, and had little tolerance for organized learning, namely school.

The hysteria had consumed much of their life together for twenty years, since the son decided to no longer live with his mother, but would live with his father. They moved into the big house, and began this new chapter of their life together. The son switched to the schools in the village, after living with his mother in the next town and attending schools there. And there was nothing but struggling for the son throughout his days in school.

He was unable to keep up with the work, and was diagnosed with a learning disability. However the school in the village refused to recognize his disabling condition, and was unwilling to accommodate the son's disability. So he struggled to keep up. Finally, he was put on a special program, but even this was too much for him to deal with, so the son eventually dropped out of school.

At the same time, the son went on government disability payments, which eliminated any motive for him to try to achieve any recognizable goals in life. He had never worked in his life, and had no desire to do so, not feeling that he would be able to handle the responsibility of working. So the son spent his time sleeping, drinking coffee, listening to music, looking at pornography.

Otherwise, he watched cartoons and horror movies, the scarier and gorier the better. The father had spent many nights watching such horrific movies with his son, but could no longer do this. He was scarred emotionally from watching these films, and could no longer let such awful images into his brain. The poet was a delicate being, and he needed to shield himself from violence and unpleasantness.

On the loose again, the pale-faced boys render satisfaction to anyone who challenges them in combat. Rampaging through the empty streets, their blue, electric penises flashing before them, they huddle to decide their next move. The movie theatre was closed for repairs, so people stayed home and watched old black and white movies on television, or on their VCRs.

Flashing like infidels against the Crusades, everyone present determined to write their names on their labels to identify themselves to one another. The cupcakes had pink and blue icing, so close attention was paid to who took which color of cupcake. Would the normal gender identifications prove what people did, or would they cross over categories, men choosing pink, women choosing blue?

Likewise, the manner of dressing was interesting and revealing. While women often wore pants, men rarely wore dresses, although the trend seemed to be arriving at last. The poet had purchased an elegant, black, floor length men's skirt, which he wore on occasion when entertaining friends. This provided a nicely gender-ambiguous garment for him to rejoice in and celebrate his nature.

The priest in the poet persisted, entrancing holiness into every facet of his life. The most mundane events and objects exuded divine life to him. He was a mystic, and saw in everything the great purpose of Life. His Tao penetrated and permeated all moments and things, encompassing life with a veil of purpose and protection that surrounded all beings at all moments.

Was he a saint? There were such rumors circulated, the villagers wondering who this hermit was, living in seclusion with his son. They knew he had been a priest in the next town over, and ended his tenure in suspicious circumstances. They also knew that he had been married, had children, and then come out as a homosexual. They didn't know of his current celibacy, though.

How ironic, that he would be thrown out from the Church for being homosexual, although he never had acted upon this nature. And now, after all these years, he was celibate and asexual. What he had given up in his life: was it all worth it? To end this way? But he was happy and very much contented, and needed no one's approval or permission to live his life as he saw fit.

Dabbling with ideas, the pilgrims took over a small, abandoned church in the village. With their long skirts and endless hair, they gave a certain quality to the place. The neighbors wondered what they were up to, with their doilies in their hair, and their little boys in suits. They would be seen walking together, one large, beautiful family, out for a walk. The poet had said "Good Morning" to them one day, and they responded in the most friendly manner.

The poet's neighbor had told him that these new neighbors had painted her arbor, over which spectacular, purple clematis would grow over the summer. He had spoken with this nice, woman neighbor, and shared with her the story of his hand injury, and the therapy and care he was getting. She was a physical therapist herself, and was most interested in the poet's story of his finger saga. It was reassuring to have such nice neighbors.

Flashing like strobe lights, the rampaging boys penetrated one another with glee, shooting their blue sperm all over each other. This was a monthly spectacle, under the full moon while the village was sleeping. What dreams did they have? the poet wondered. Did they remember their dreams? See them as significant? Illuminations to be treasured and cherished? Wanderings in the wilderness of their unconscious minds, they capsize, falling out of their beds, all at the same moment.

"Transcendent lunatics on parade!" the circus barker announced to the audience, as these filed in single rows to do their rambunctious tricks. Parking their cars behind the supermarket, teenagers engage in illegal drug deals and promiscuous sex of every sort. Snorting through their nostrils, they escape the bounds of their existence. Temporarily subdued like a happy platypus in the pond.

What with the momentary lull in the frenzy, open mouths flew moths into the waiting air, fluttering out through their parted lips. No one wears lipstick anymore, or even makeup, unless they are dressing up to go out somewhere. When the witches gathered under the crescent moon, they chanted sideways, evoking a remarkable symphony of blackened psalms to the dark side.

Going on each day, you wonder where it all is leading to? Questioning everything, the poet never accepted simple explanations. Simplistic thoughts bothered him, boring his intelligence and capacity for experience. However, he took notice of simple exchanges: a "Good Morning" to a total stranger going into the supermarket. A friendly wave of the hand to a passerby.

When the going gets tough, the tough get going. The inability of people to face down their problems incapacitates them, existentially. The poet learned through the years not to let things upset him emotionally. He was not in denial, but aware intellectually of circumstances and events, and refused to let them unravel him emotionally. He chose to keep an objective distance between himself and unpleasant situations, never succumbing to despair.

Learning to stop himself from thinking about some disturbing matters saved the poet from disintegrating emotionally as he had so often in his past. This new understanding and strategy for life helped him to stay on track with his progress and goals. His psychiatrist was amazed at his ability to live this way, and she said that he should teach this to others, giving classes and seminars about it.

While the poet was deeply flattered by this suggestion, he could never see himself in such a public role again, following his revealing of himself to his parishes, with dismal success apart from a faithful few. He felt that he still had much to offer, and wondered what the best way would be for him to share the gifts he had received from Life.

For the present, he was totally caught up with writing his new novel, and going for his occupational therapy for his injured finger. And with caring for his needy son, his days were filled up nicely. The holiday weekend was at hand, Memorial Day once again. This did not mean much for the poet, who grieved the losses of war, and war's relentless stupidity.

He did not identify with the muscular patriotism that revealed itself on national holidays.

The poet felt little identification with his own country, considering himself a citizen of the world instead.

The bombast and emotional hype of such celebrations offended his delicate sensitivity. He would spend the long weekend with his son, doing the things they usually do, and not specially acknowledging the holiday at all, really.

Today was the day that his middle daughter's second baby was due. Since she wasn't speaking to her father, he had no way of knowing whether the event had yet occurred. Left out of the process, he was on the outside trying to look in. Would he ever be able to be a part of his granddaughters' lives?

Would they ever even know that he existed? Know his name? Who he was?

This was enough to make a lesser man than the poet collapse in a puddle of tears. How did he stand such mistreatment? How endure such abuse? The poet's identity was now rock solid, and he knew his own strength to endure and survive. He practiced intentionality, surrendering to each moment, as though it were his last. Nothing could disrupt his peace of mind.

The flagrant vagrants, now settled in their new, renovated homes, no longer wallowed in the mud, but bathed excessively. In fact, some of them never left the bathtub at all. Eating their meals in the bath, watching television in the bath, sleeping in the bath, only getting up to relieve themselves.

Of course, one could not manage this living alone, but needed someone to bring them their food.

Now that that's settled, the movements of the vague semblances procure their own demise.

Wondering what was what, everyone assumed the position of ignorance, melting their dissolving limbs in a vat of oil. Their skin became porous, and they were very tender to the touch. In fact, they couldn't bear to be touched at all, some of them, indeed.

The price of grapes had gone up, and the last ones that the poet purchased were not even ripe, but were hard as rocks. He had intended to go grape-shopping when his car overheated once again.

The car was now in the garage, with the mechanics

trying to figure out why the car was always overheating. The tank had been full of antifreeze/coolant, so why would it overheat?

Bland vegetables, overcooked and soggy, sit vacantly in the bowl, waiting for someone to dare to eat them. But the meat-eaters prefer dead animal flesh. They devour this with enthusiasm, gnawing on their bones with savage teeth. No wonder no one went hungry that night. But there were leftovers, which they took home to eat tomorrow.

So much for the library books, overdue for years, on random shelves collecting dust and growing mold. Forgotten like memories, cavorting like lambs and young goats, all the extras were added for the sake of extravagance. Delectable appetizers proliferated at the reception, while waiters waited. All of the situations collided into dust, as envelopes bore fruit once again.

Thinking out loud, the centipedes removed their shells and walked across the poet's desk.

Reminding someone of something else, the truth is: which came first? One book is not as good as another, and waiting for recognition was slow and endless. Because of the collision, the folk remained in the hospital, awaiting news of their loved one.

Hopeless, the memories dissolve like flutter-dust, enlarging the capacity of onions. But there has to be a better way, like a knife slicing through soft butter, when the telephones are off the hooks.

No one was able to get through to anyone, and the panic set in. Escaping through the window, the criminal element went haywire, pasteurizing their victims like milk.

So no one was offended, as in previous incidents. Therefore, when the country falls apart, the government will be dissolved, and anarchy will prevail across the land. The landlubbers move inland, away from the coast, fearing their vulnerability will elude them. So they cast out to sea, fishing for vacant memories in the clear, blue water.

No, it's not over yet, although that would have been a nice ending. In the Italian opera, The Girl of the Golden West by Puccini, the cowboys sing "Hello" in English. Inflated like balloons, they quiver midair, a symphony of reluctance. Because he was writing automatically, as in "automatic writing," practiced by the surrealists and Gertrude Stein, he bypassed his conscious mind, drawing upon the ever-deep well of his unconscious mind.

The practice allowed thoughts and ideas to come naturally, in a limpid, languid manner that allowed him to type out these thoughts as they arrived. He listened to the opera as he typed away, clicking the keys with a pleasant rhythm. It was almost as though his typing mirrored the music playing on the radio. Almost as though his typing were part of the music, as it was in Erik Satie's ballet, Parade.

We will return momentarily, following a word from out sponsor: Cats wander through the alleys searching for food and love. One can hear them in the night, howling in agony and submission. So, we go through the motions, to quote a title of one of his books of poetry. In the arms of night, you express the endlessness of hope, baring your soul to the moon in the backyard where no one can see you.

Good night, moon, the poet thought, asking a blessing upon himself and his children. The opera slices time into roast beef, singing extra-unapproachable melodies that howl like wind through the air.

His car had overheated once again, with a full tank of antifreeze/coolant, coming home from the psychiatrist. He drove on, despite warnings on the dashboard to idle the motor, until he reached his garage in a total panic.

His favorite mechanic was going to look it over once it cooled down, but he never called to say it was done. So in the morning, the poet called his chiropractor to help him, since the garage was closed for the Memorial Day weekend. So the chiropractor called the garage owner at home. It seemed that they tried everything they could think of, but the car needed extensive repairs by the Cadillac dealer, which would likely be very costly. He would have to talk to his favorite mechanic after the holiday.

In the meantime, he could only drive locally, in the village, and to the next town. He dared not drive to the small cities surrounding the village, or his car would overheat again. What was he in for now? He dearly loved his old plum purple Cadillac, and would hate to have to part with it. It was like a part of the poet's being, and he would try to do everything possible to keep it running.

Since nobody asked, let us look at the possibilities that pertain the infestations of bed bugs.

When the son, a few years ago, went off in a taxi in the middle of the night to procure meth, he went to a very trashy trailer, sat in a chair, and didn't even get meth. But he did get a case of bedbugs on his clothing and body. By the morning he was covered with bed bug bites.

The bed bugs infested his mattress, where they would lay eggs and breed. So the exterminator service told him over the telephone to put a mattress cover on the bed. They did this and it worked for some time. But eventually the mattress cover got torn, and the bed bugs emerged once again, biting the son's ankles savagely. So the father bought another mattress cover that now sat in the son's room, unopened. This is how dysfunctional the son really was. He would rather get bitten than put it on.

The poet had spoken to his dear friend who lived in another state. She had been with him at the church he was received in, in the city. This friend had been an editor in a major publishing house in the city years before, when they first knew each other. She and her husband became very close friends.

They had lost touch over the years, and met for lunch after the poet had been "outed" by his church, and expelled. He shared with these friends his newfound hope in his homosexuality.

Twenty years later they got in touch again, and the friends drove up to have lunch with the poet in the small, nearby city. Time had taken its inevitable toll upon them all, but they recognized each other immediately and frantically embraced in the restaurant where they were eating. They had a deeply meaningful time together, catching up on their beliefs, their occupations, their lives. The poet brought them three manuscripts to read, and they gave him a book by another old friend.

The poet had written an Epithalamion for the couple's wedding, which he read in the gothic cathedral-like church where they were all members. They had danced at the poet's wedding also. Their friendship had sustained itself over their lifetimes, recovering immediately its intensity and depth even after many years disconnection. This friend took a great interest in the poet's publishing activity, what with his novel being brought out, and his poetry book in process.

He had purchased some very nice Swiss chard at the market, and a half-priced chocolate meringue pie. His son had bought some non-alcoholic stout, which would be fun for the father and son to enjoy together for the holiday. The poet never took a day off from his writing, needing to get out each day his required portion of writing: four pages written over two impassioned hours. The fact that he was writing of the same material as this current book contains should be borne in mind by the reader.

It is important that the author of the present work never reveal himself to the reader. The author's omnipotent voice must be acknowledged at all times, and it is irrelevant who his hidden identity might turn out to be. He is invisible, and has no secrets to reveal. One must trust him to provide the best information available concerning the poet and his activities, family, and being.

A cough in the midst of the opera: is someone sick, dying, suffering? Or was it an accidental cough by the singer, who couldn't help it? One may never know, as the opera steams forward full throttle, endlessly impassioning the air with helpless cries. Failing to exist much longer, the endless song protrudes, like soiled underwear, forgotten under someone's unmade bed.

The framed oil painting by his father, a still life of peaches, grapes, a plum, a pear, and a graceful pitcher, hung over his desk where he typed. He had all of his father's artwork, paintings and sculptures decorating his home. As a child, the poet would go out on the rocks with his father along the coast on vacations, and there they would both paint. He treasured these memories, and valued his father's artwork deeply.

His father's paintings had great depth and soul, produced by this quiet, gentle man out of the recesses of his imagination. The portrait his father did of the poet's mother hung prominently, watching over the living room. His father's self-portrait also hung there, with brooding eyes and balding head.

His mother's portrait made her look like a movie star to whom she was compared.

The painting of the old water mill, the landscape with two figures wandering down a road. The sculptures: the standing female nude, the praying slave, the long-faced woman, the small sculpture of a mother and child, a classical theme, which one of his friends pointed out must have been the poet's mother holding him close to herself. These were all the relics he had left of his father.

What would happen to all this artwork when the

poet died? What would happen to it all if his son decided to sell the house? He had hoped that one day his daughters would want some of these creations, but there was no telling whether they would ever speak to their father again. So this all remained in the hands of the vast Unknown, waiting to be fulfilled one day beyond his own life.

He had in his bedroom a beautiful skyscape that his father did, with misty clouds floating. It looked like a Chinese painting. There was also the huge mural-sized painting of roses, opulently blooming in colors of pink and pale purple which hung on the wall by the side of his bed. Surrounded by these works of art, the poet slept peacefully each night, in the aesthetic embrace of these works.

Lost in a hazy mist, the fog surrounding him, he floated off into a beautiful dream, enclosing him within such gracious arms. The left ventricle, the open casket, thread through a needle, infested memories, his belt is too tight otherwise his pants would fall down. An extreme set of variations, like in music, but with words. The laundry never gets folded, but remains in its baskets on the floor.

A place where laundry is sorted, people who actually do this for a living. A giant plant where thousands of people, mostly women, are sorting laundry, luckily clean. This goes on forever. They never take a break, but are fed through tubes. Their substances of elimination are likewise disposed of. Standing like this forever, their legs grow roots into the ground and become tree trunks. Their upper bodies remain the same as before.

Going nowhere slowly, we emerged from our cocoons, and went off to the supermarket, flying there with our newfound wings. You ask where this is all leading? And the funny thing is, we will never know until the book ends. This will happen when the poet ends his book. This book then will have no reason or ability to continue. Fancy that.

Luckily, no one was calling on the telephone today, so the poet was able to work in peace and quiet. The radio had static, so he finally turned it off. He actually preferred to work in silence, which enabled him to focus intently and exclusively on what he was writing. The intensity of his concentration was extreme: the full engagement of all his faculties, conscious and unconscious, to the act of his task.

Returning to his task, after a brief interruption from his son, he resumed work once again.

The son was actually angry that his father had to work, when the son wanted to masturbate in the study. The father had a strict work schedule: from two o'clock to four pm. He kept this strict schedule as part of his self-discipline. He novel was more important than his son's need to masturbate.

Spare me the details, he thought. Just the facts, ma'am. Please go through the revolving door. Only once. Stop going on and on! No one has any respect for decorum anymore. Screaming ceased, and there was peace in the kingdom once again. Loosen your belt, relax. Have a cup of tea. Listen to the sounds of the room, and of the world outside the window. Respect the moment.

Making a slow start, the pilgrims walked to their church on the corner. They were there for their Sunday gathering. What went on in their service? All the girls in long dresses, with doilies in their hair; the boys dressed up in their Sunday suits and ties. The poet was impressed by their integrity and peacefulness. He almost wanted to get to know them, be friendly as neighbors. But he thought not.

Sagging bunions, old dirty socks, tuna fish for lunch, parsley growing between your toes. He had taped together three precious books that were falling apart, taping back their covers onto the spines.

A huge, illustrated book of Chinese poetry, On the Nature of the Universe by Lucretius (which he was currently reading), and his mother's ancient dictionary, which he treasured and still used.

The rampaging boys, sleeping in each other's arms, breathe peacefully in their dreams. It was only when they were asleep that they were at peace. While they were awake, they were constantly on the move, following their instincts, and their blue electric penises. They only went out at night, and otherwise stayed in the old house they inhabited. In a state of disrepair and neglect, the house was what one might expect a brood of rampaging boys to live in.

There were orders within their ranks, based on age and seniority. The commanders were a rank of soldier-boys, who served under the pleasure of the chief commander-in-charge. He was the oldest boy, and had worked his way up through the ranks over many years. The boys had immortality, and stayed at the age allotted to them. They were hatched from pods that grew from blue seeds. Only a certain number of boys were hatched each year, so the population never grew over one hundred.

They slept in piles on a huge, massive bed, and would often awaken one another as they slept to fulfill the act of love, their blue electric penises glowing and quivering. The bed was stained with their blue semen, which they would lick up in the morning for breakfast. No females were allowed in their order, since these had their own secret societies. The boys would be boys.

Believing what they see, most villagers followed their own path. Since religion had been forbidden, the pilgrims were breaking the law by gathering in their abandoned church on Sundays. But they kept to themselves and didn't bother anybody, so no one seemed to care. Most people kept their beliefs to themselves, for fear of prosecution. So nobody knew what anyone believed or practiced.

The poet had decided to stop wearing only black, and had put on a colorful outfit for this day.

He was wearing pastel pink pants and a pale purple polo shirt, with his inevitable Birkenstocks on his feet.

This outfit lightened his spirit and mood, and made him feel as if he could take off from the ground.

His son had advised him to stop only wearing black tee shirts, so he had done so.

Covering their tracks, the weary monks trudged through the snow. They were on a secret mission that involved the True Foreskin of Christ. This had been preserved by Mary, and kept over her years, to be passed on to the Beloved Disciple, John. It had been transmitted through the ages through a secret lineage, and now the monks were in pursuit of this holy relic. Nothing would stop them now.

Outlandish messengers pursue the vain task of dismembering the prisoners, limb by limb.

The body parts would then be dissolved in acid, so nobody would know it ever happened. While the kettle boils, you eat a magical chocolate cake, which suddenly floods you with unabashed enthusiasm, carpeting your ride with floral scents and rich brocades. A symphony of platitudes, where no names are permitted, and faces need to be masked at all times for anonymity.

The drool from eating the cake trickles down onto your shirt and pants, suddenly staining them. You rush to the kitchen to sponge off the drool, and fantasize where the next cake will come from.

Several participants walked-back what they had initially proposed, contradicting themselves all over the place. The moderator declared a draw, and everyone made water on themselves.

The spirit of the entity would unveil itself like a grave stone, when no one was looking. Because the fence was open, the gate was closed, so no one could walk through the wall anymore. But the wall suddenly melted, and everyone ran through into the other room, celebrating this momentous occasion.

Participants ate pie and coffee, relishing the company of such an esteemed group of individuals.

The nitty gritty of salmon exhumes the carcasses of captives, on the principle of fair play. Bizarre doings in the hen house: the chickens are eating their own eggs. Loose-bandaged fingers drip honey like halvah on Sunday afternoons in summer. The turn of the season was imminent, and no one refused to acknowledge the supremacy of the mayor, who in fact was a manikin.

Eating a mistake for dinner, a mis-steak, or Miss Steak would you please step in here for a minute.

Taking off her wig, she was revealed to have a crew cut, and wore no bra. Miss Steak, will you please take a letter. Dear So and So, What did you have for dinner last night? Wishing you a good night's sleep. Yours, truly, etcetera, etcetera. So what's new, pussycat?

Eating your words, devouring the sense of them, transforming them in your mind into something else other than what they normally mean, removing words from their customary definitions and replacing them in a new, improved context, where they can breathe and just be words again.

This is what the poet did, and he revealed a new language as he wrote his new novel.

Used hypodermic needles in the waste basket amongst the cigarette butts and ashes. The new purple water bottle, a Tootsie Roll, a cigarette lighter, a pen, and several stray caps from syringes. Avoiding proper nouns, the poet never named the characters in his new novel, but left them, ghostlike, writhing on the page. Anonymous spectres, they persisted in spite of their lack of a name, inhabiting his novel as though they were real people.

He wrote about himself under the guise of "the poet,"

and included his son, his former wife, his wayward daughters, his friend, and other personages inhabiting his new novel. These he fictionalized, transforming them from mere images into living, breathing beings. No one would ever know that he was writing about himself and his life, since he had posited the existence of the one he called "the poet."

Breaking their fast, the pilgrims ate heartily when they came home from church. Country style meals where the plates and bowls of food were passed around the table. They didn't eat port though, abiding by the restrictions of the Law of Moses. They more than made up for this lack though, indulging in endless plates of meats and vegetables, mashed potatoes, breads and butter, pitchers of milk, and endless desserts: pies and cakes, cookies and ice cream. No wonder they were so happy.

Thank you, dear reader of the future, whoever you are, for reading this far in this current book.

Promises to you that it will be worth your while, following the history of the poet and his family and friends to the end, when the poet finishes his novel and this current book will cease. You are to be applauded for your persistence, determination, and commitment, and your reward will be great indeed.

It will have been noticed that none of the characters in this current novel are named. This is in keeping with the poet's own practice for the sake of consistency. Although this novel may have been based on living characters, it remains a work of fiction and the imagination. Any resemblance to persons living or dead is purely coincidental. Like pulling teeth by tying a string to a doorknob, the contents of the poet's novel and the present work are nearly identical.

Slumming through the city, the tourists were appalled to see the rat-infested neighborhood, and the vagrants, who were not flagrant or fragrant, sleeping on the sidewalks. Empty liquor bottles, used syringes, soiled sleeping bags, cigarette butts reproduced like rabbits in the encampment. The smell of urine and feces was prominent, and the tourists couldn't wait to get back to the suburbs. They climbed aboard their air-conditioned bus and returned home, disillusioned.

Tornadoes were threatening the region, and luckily the poet and his son had plenty of food and drink to sustain them. They hunkered down for the last day of the holiday weekend, Memorial Day. It was on this day when he was four years old that the poet's young cousin, who was also four years old, died of leukemia. This was a terrible tragedy for the family, especially for his favorite aunt, his cousin's mother. He couldn't imagine how she ever survived this devastating loss.

Tomorrow morning he would go to the garage to talk to his favorite mechanic who had worked on the poet's car, to see what he thought it needed. He would have to call the Cadillac dealer in the small city nearby to make an appointment to have the car fixed. He hoped that they would loan him a car to use while his Cadillac was being worked on. He never would be able to make it home after driving all the way down to the dealer in the small city nearby without overheating again.

He would then go meet with the funeral director, to finalize his plans for burial. This was in no way a morbid activity for the poet, but a beautiful embrace of life in its fullness, including death as our ultimate destination. This would give him peace of mind, to have these things planned out and arranged, so when the time came, all would work efficiently like clockwork. And, most of all, his poor, grieving son would not have to worry about any of these arrangements: all will have been planned for him.

In the afternoon, he would go for his occupational therapy, and work hard to recover from his finger injury, coaxing the tendon back onto the bone of the middle finger of his left hand so he would not need surgery for this problem. He trusted that through this therapy, his finger would be healed.

But today was an empty day, waiting to be filled up with writing and inspiration.

The poet had spoken with his former wife on the telephone to find out if his middle daughter had given birth yet; apparently, she hadn't. So he wrote her a brief note, saying:

"Hello. I am thinking of you, praying that you have a safe, beautiful birth, and that I can be a part of my granddaughters' lives one day. Blessings, Daddy."

His psychiatrist had suggested that he write her a simple, brief message, and he hoped that she would read it, and be assured of his care and concern, even though she was currently refusing to speak to him. This was a strenuous effort for the father, reaching out into his daughter's silence and distance.

But he was the better off for having done it. His conscience was clear now, since he wrote the note.

He refused to let his daughters' abandonment of himself and his son destroy his life. He intended to maintain his peace of mind, and not let their viciousness and resentment throw him off his horse again. He had had too many mental breakdowns over them, and would not fall through the ice again, due to their maliciousness. He had too much at stake, and needed to go on with his life. His resilience was remarkable; he kept going forward, no matter what.

Captivated gargoyles smile menacingly from the cathedral's flying buttresses, threatening anyone who looks at them with their delicious grins. Passers-by gaze with amazement at the melting telephone booth, a relic of history, now relegated to the pages of dusty tomes for reference. Applauding is forbidden in the holy place, for safety's sake. No one blowing their noses may attend the sacred ceremony, limited to those who can breathe without sneezing.

Secreting their juices, the audience waits in mystery for the forbidden performance. A man was going to eat a cucumber, as an exercise of art. A variation of the piece would be to eat a pickle. The choice is up to the performer. When the performance occurred, the artist was surprised to see the entire audience take out of their pockets and purses, green cucumbers and pickles, which they proceeded to eat at the same time as the artist ate his. What a festival of eating!

Plowing the fields, the farmers get ready to plant their seeds, expecting a successful crop this year. The composer and pianist sits at her instrument writing a new piece of music. The crawdads swim mercilessly to avoid the fishermen's nets. A young girl puts on her makeup for the first time, preparing to go out on her first date with another girl. She is the picture of perfection.

But the symphony was porous, and the cellist's bow ripped all four strings apart in the middle of the concerto. The principal cellist gave him her instrument and bow to finish the piece, leaving the stage demurely to wait in the wings. No one even minded to brief interruption, and the cellist finished the concerto with pizzazz. Everyone went out for pizza and beer after the concert.

The lovers break up, since there was no there there

to begin with, and thus, ending it was no surprise or trauma to either of them. Disappointments melt tears into sea salt, piled up for use at the table for dinner. The electrocutionist's song, bitter and acrid, burns the mouth of the prisoner to be deceased. Parting the curtains, they enter backwards, sideways plunging into the abyss.

Bloody tissues in the waste basket, evidence of his son's nocturnal methamphetamine use.

The spontaneous wound, coming out of nowhere, on the poet's left hand. He had gone to the bathroom at the funeral home, where he was meeting to finalize his plans, and when he came out there was this huge bruise on his hand, and it was oozing blood. He had no idea how this had happened.

So his funeral and burial plans were made at last. This was a satisfying feeling for the poet, knowing that things were in place. He planned to live a long, healthy life, but it was good to have this all arranged, because one never knows what's going to happen. He opened a Trust to pay into toward the cost of the burial, and would contribute to this as he was able over the coming years. The price was only guaranteed once it was fully paid up. So he wanted to pay it off as soon as possible.

Then there was the issue of his car: He stopped by the garage to see his favorite mechanic, to find out what he thought about the car. The owner said it was the head gaskets, a major expense.

He called the Cadillac dealer in the small city nearby to see what they thought about it. They said it would cost several thousand dollars to fix this, but it might be the air pump. So he made an appointment to go down there one month away, wondering if the car could even make it down there.

The poet then called his friend at the local dealer who had sold him the Cadillac. He said that it was most definitely the head gaskets. The poet then asked him to please find him a nice, big, old car; the friend knew what he liked. The friend then thought of an older couple who had an old Cadillac and another older car in mint condition. They had been interested in upgrading, but then decided that they didn't want to spend the money. This friend said he would contact them and see if they would sell.

This friend at the local dealer had found him several of his beautiful, big, old cars in the past, and he knew what the poet liked in a car. He like a big, old, car, because he could then have six feet of metal between himself and the next car. This had kept him safe over the years. Additionally, he loved the look of the older cars, their beauty, grace, and dignity. He loved the smoothness of their drive.

You would barely feel yourself moving in his Cadillac. It would be sad to see it go away.

Burning bonfires, like unnecessary words, spread like aioli on a roast beef sandwich. Your lunch is your underwear, clean and fresh from the dryer. You open a can of beans, and eat them out of the can with a table spoon, when you think that no one is looking. You admire yourself in the mirror, aroused by your own beauty. You touch yourself, there. Then suddenly stop, and go on with the laundry.

The scab had formed on his wound, the blood having rushed to the surface of his skin, the spot of blood on his tissue. The concern of the funeral director. The bewilderment of the poet as to the cause of this wound. He had had mysterious wounds before that suddenly appear out of nowhere. And then there were the bruises on his arms from his son grabbing him to tell him something in anger. The poet had worn long sleeved shirts to cover these bruises up, but now that it was warm he couldn't.

Captive angels dance on the head of a pin, Sufi-style, whirling like dervishes as though it were the most natural thing in the world. They danced until they dissolved into thin air, escaping the bondage that had been dared to be enforced upon them. You cannot keep an angel for very long; they like their independence. Like chocolate-covered strawberries, they vanish and are never seen again.

Savage savages whom we used to know, no longer invade our privacy. The lost telephone was found. Ostriches and giraffes stretch their necks, unknowing like clouds. They remove their heads, and speak to themselves in unknown tongues. Burning thoughts that strengthen as they are nurtured, finally explode, pouring out vengeance into the waiting open palms of the communicants. They bless themselves after eating and drinking the provided sacraments, kneeling at the altar.

Luckily, the choirboys are singing, they blend their voices with the organ playing, up in the choir loft. No one had infested the rudiments of cacophony like these choirboys. When they have free time, they play soccer, their knee socks revealing boney knees, as they run to catch to ball. Football, really, as the rest of the world calls it. Angels with dirty faces, as the old movie once called them.

Symphonic relations between similar persons are strictly forbidden. Only opposite types are permitted to mate, blending the powers of both energies at once. The resulting union will produce a hybrid type of organism, with characteristics of both ancestors, thus enriching the possibilities of an offspring who would have a rich blend of options.

Conjugal relations were forbidden outslde of state-authorized unions. For an exception to this rule, two people would have to go through a lengthy process of application, examinations, qualifications, expectations, originations, pacifications, operations, invitations, exclamations, exasperations, fascinations, inflations, dilations, captivations, and the quality of their teeth.

Since nobody asked, the flashing lights in the movie theatre alert the patrons to proceed immediately to the nearest appropriate rest room. There they are to actually rest, on inflated mattresses provided for their comfort. The sound of ocean waves was pumped into the rest rooms, and popcorn was provided, along with drinks. This was a happy alternative to the useless movies that were shown there, and the patrons emerged after two hours refreshed and rejuvenated.

The poet avoided explicit language as much as possible, but don't forget: he was seeing the words on the page and typing them in. So, there was very little editing involved in his process of writing.

These words emerged from some deep well in his unconscious; or were they coming to him from some external source? Some spirit speaking to him from the great Beyond?

Or was his mental illness a contributing factor here? Doubtless, he never would have written what he had, had he not suffered for many a day in order to write poetry, as Basho had insisted.

Now that he was healed of his illnesses, he wrote in a different manner. Alternating between very abstract writing and more realistic prose, he composed his novel, in a novel manner.

The poet's occupational therapy had been cancelled,

due to the illness of one of his therapists. His other, primary therapist was on vacation. That meant that he would have to go until the end of the week to have therapy for his finger. He was typing away like a madman, and the finger was cooperating beautifully. He hoped that this month of therapy would heal his injury, reattaching the tendon of his middle finger of his left hand to the bone, so he wouldn't need surgery.

Some of the women in the village were meeting secretly to engage in occult practices by night.

They drew a magic circle around themselves, and incanted obscure phrases at the moon and the stars.

No one knew exactly what they were up to, and no men were allowed into their ceremonies. There were rumors in the village that there were witches about, but no one was ever able to prove it. They worshiped the goddess, and drew upon the knowledge of herbs and plants.

When the forest was inhabited by faeries, these never showed themselves to people. Much as the children looked for them, they could never find any. So, the children played at being faeries themselves, scampering about with wings they had made out of crepe paper and wire hangers.

This charming spectacle occurred on the village green, and when the children came home, the faeries came out again, laughing at the children's impression of them, delighted to have seen it.

Soaking up inspiration, he began to write. Taking off his splint, his fingers fluttered like butterflies over the keys of his old, black Royal Standard typewriter. Like some great classical pianist of old, he was a virtuoso on the typewriter. There was something musical about the way he wrote his new novel, like playing a sonata on the piano, or better, the harpsichord.

Making no excuses, one wanders off alone. Like the time his first daughter wandered off while they were having a picnic in the park in the city with friends. Suddenly a woman came over with the baby, scolding her parents for neglecting to keep watch over their child. This was a humiliating moment for the poet and his wife, in the early years of their marriage. They never let their daughter out of their sight after this traumatic experience.

His son couldn't go out because he wasn't able to find his other sneaker. The son tended to lose things often, and was careless about where he put things. He rampaged all through the house and couldn't find the shoe. So the father went out alone, to the garage to see his favorite mechanic, who had ordered a sealant that would keep the coolant from being used up too quickly. This would make the poet's car much safer, until he could find a new car. He gave the mechanic his book, since he was sweet.

The mechanic told the poet to take the car for a drive, to let the sealant circulate. So he drove up the road to the next town, where there was a spectacular spot with the creek rushing through, and massive cliffs with a rock face and trees growing out of it straight up into the air, miraculously. He passed a man with a dog, three boys going fishing, and another man walking. They all said hello in passing. But the two huge lawnmowers were making such a noise that the poet left immediately.

It was rejuvenating to the poet to be out in nature, since he lived in the village itself. He regretted that the lawnmowers had disrupted his time at "The Rocks," but it was beautiful to just see this extraordinary example of natural beauty, five minutes outside the village, in the next town. He loved to see the trees growing out of the cliffs, seeming to defy all reason and sense, yet so miraculously perfect, like a Chinese painting on silk.

Strange, ambient music floats through the air: his son in the living room. The sliding doors between the study and the living room are open, at the son's request, so the father could hear the music the son was playing, as he wrote. The music is barely audible from the next room, and there was an almost perfect silence in which the poet could write peacefully.

A grilled Genoa salami and provolone sandwich on sourdough bread. Your thoughts and reactions as you read these words. You look up from the book and gaze across the room to see out the window. You take the time to listen to the sounds in the room and the sounds outside the window. A bird is chirping, there is sound of the traffic occasionally. You go get something to drink, and return to your reading, picking up where you left off.

Startling cobwebs reveal their spiders, spinning away, or catching some flying insect to devour for dinner. Running out of steam, no one goes overboard with shopping, since the stores were only open for one hour a day. There was a huge rush to get in and grab whatever things you could get before the store closes.

Panic-stricken shoppers grabbed up whatever they could, in desperation.

Distant thunder, the threat of rain, the sound of the air circulating, the blood in you veins moving along, your heartbeat regular and strong, your lungs breathing. The poet was in awe of his bodily functions, and wondered in amazement how he managed to be alive, after all these years.

Thunder overhead, rain pouring down. Wondering thunder over the house as he wrote.

Soggy biscuits, tea brewing in the cup, while in the war the suffering continues. The army had bombed an encampment of displaced people, burning them alive in their tents as they slept. This nightmare had occurred over the Memorial Day weekend, murdering more innocent civilians.

And yet the president still was sending more bombs to the occupation, with which to slaughter more women and children. This latest attack had killed forty-five people.

Slumbering bumpkins divide the spoils of entropy without exposing their faces. Looking at them, you would forget your troubles, and dig a grave for the dead. Noticing where you are can be helpful.

Disoriented, the figments move stealthily toward the end of the earth, the place where it stops and you fall off the edge. Places like that are just precious and cute, so don't forget to write.

Now that his car could only drive to the next town without overheating, the poet was unable to drive to see the Wise Woman, so they spoke over the telephone. She always had a helpful perspective to offer, and encouragement to the poet in the midst of the many challenges he faced. They would have to go on meeting over the telephone until the poet got a new old car.

The poet loved the sound of the rain, and the now-distant thunder. The worst was over. Please let the worst be over in the poet's life and his son's! No one can know what will happen to them next, so we shall have to wait and find out. The rain reminded the poet of how he would go walking in the rain in the city when he was a young poet. He would wear his raincoat and umbrella, and go out to the second-hand bookstores to hunt for treasures. These were his lovely, halcyon days.

Wend the weary way, looking through the glass to the world outside, and wonder, wandering in your mind through fields of wildflowers, a lush meadow, where the grass is thick, and lie down amidst the fruitful green, being embraced by the warm earth's loving touch. You gaze up at the sky, seeing the clouds moving, or is it the earth moving? Or you, moving in your mind to see the stars in the daytime.

Instead of bordering on the insane, they toast English muffins, overlooking any defects in the wallpaper. So, the tweezers pluck the eyebrows of infinity, the eternal dusting of rainbows, captive like snails turned into escargot. The garlic butter oozes out of the cracks, and the bread runs away with the butter knife. When no one is looking, a can of beans eats itself out of its own can.

Trying their hardest, who called on the telephone just before? Was it the milkman, wondering what we wanted to order for tomorrow? Never mind, our infestation is open, like a can of beer on a summer night, where insects dare to congregate. Playing at pretending to be someone else, the players perform their roles without a script. The spontaneous combustion explodes in their faces.

Quietly sitting, one learns to experience to fullness and emptiness of Life. Nothing can disturb you in this state of mind and body. Treat yourself and retreat into yourself. You are the only person you can ever truly know, so know thyself, as Socrates advised. That's why the poet gave his first novel to his favorite mechanic, as a gesture of appreciation for all his kindness and helpfulness.

The poet was reading Lucretius, On the Nature of the Universe, an insightful look at the way things are the way they are in Life. This scientific treatise from the ancient Roman world entranced the poet. He could only deal with ancient science, when knowledge was still blurry, and the imagination was often the means of finding out anything. He had always wanted to read this ancient book, so this was his new reading every morning before lunch, feeding his mind on these profound words.

He did not like modern science, which was able to explain everything in Life at once. The poet liked the mystery of Life, and didn't want to understand how modern science could explain it all. He wanted to stand in awe of Life's vast mystery, with the poet's eye, not the scientist's. He saw Life as art, and viewed everything through this aesthetic lens, perceiving beauty even in ugliness, and life in everything that lives. The poet was a born mystic, and viewed the miraculous display of Life with awe.

Medieval-sounding music, a torch lighter, the telephone, an ashtray, his splint, the purple water bottle, the lamp, the typewriter, the empty wastebasket, the marijuana pipe, the cigarette lighter. These exist in the mind of the beholder, an act of the imagination where you image in your mind the object seen, or see in your mind the object imagined. Which is which? Which is real? Both are real, really.

His closet had collapsed, the shelves fallen down, the clothes scattered in heaps. His contractor once again rescued the poet from disaster. He took all the clothes out and put them on the poet's bed and his youngest daughter's bed. He went out and purchased the necessary shelves and things to replace the ones that had collapsed. He came back and assembled the new shelves and racks, put all the clothes back in the closet. What an amazing, wonderful man; a real angel of mercy to the poet.

An amazing miracle: His friend at the local car dealer connected him with an older couple who have a vintage mint-condition Cadillac. The poet was very interested in this car, and hoped that his friend would drive him up to take a look at it. It was deep gray, a color that the poet liked the sound of.

Every time the poet had needed a new car, one just appeared. He hoped that this would be a similar situation for him, since he could only drive his Cadillac to the next town.

Force-fed imps limp lamely across the fields, wondering where all the flowers had gone. Young girls had picked them, every one. Sounds like a song, which had been forgotten for so long. So long, it's been good to know you. Camping out at the waterfalls in the town way up north where he used to live.

Politely excusing oneself, noticing the emptiness of telephone calls, he hung up before talking.

The way the symphony works, holding all the instruments together as one organism. The origami the poet used to do as a child. The wild trees that his grounds man had cut down amongst the lush vegetation. He hated to have these saplings cut down, but they gave a messed up look to the poet's home, which he tried to keep very neat, at least from the outside.

Thinking about cars, a necessary luxury where the poet lived with his son. Appointments to go to, shopping to do, a car was needed to do anything, living in the village. The flagrant vagrants had redecorated their new homes and were very proud of their living quarters. They visited one another, some played bridge together, some had coffee and cake together, some played golf together, some went fishing together, some went swimming together, some went out to eat together.

Violating the rules of etiquette, the rampaging boys ate food with their fingers, their blue electric penises fluttering and blinking as they ate. Following their leader, they went off into the woods to gather mushrooms, looking especially for the hallucinogenic types. These they gathered in woven baskets to take home to eat that evening. They took great risks, since some of these were poisonous.

Wandering through the forest, they frightened several small animals who came out to see what they were doing. Getting up their courage, they slowly approached the boys and, seeing that the boys were friendly, they made friends with them, letting the boys pet them like tame animals. Bunnies, deer, birds and butterflies, they all played together, and had a lovely time that day.

If you wonder what the story is, keep reading. As it unfolds, the secrets of many hearts shall be revealed for observation. Clicking their heels together, they returned home to bubbling pots of soup, cooking on the stove. On a winter's day, nothing can be more comforting than a bowl of hearty soup, accompanied by a crusty bread and butter, with perhaps some cheese to go along with it.

What would you think if this novel went on for nine hundred pages? The poet wanted his new novel to be as long as his first, just over three hundred pages. Tempting one another with disassociation, the weirdos walk sideways, rubbing their bellies and foreheads, breathing together on the bridge. You walk away from them, choosing to be alone, rather than in company.

The poet had read seven hundred pages of Gertrude Stein's dynastic novel, The Making of Americans. The remarkable book was just over nine hundred pages in length, and the poet read this book devotedly every morning from six to seven am. Absorbing Stein's words like a sponge, he read this book which he had always wanted to read, at last. The poet had been the young lover and personal assistant to the publisher of this book, so it was a sentimental journey for him to read it.

The poet had been to the occupational therapy, and received a beautiful hand massage from his therapist. He had given this man his first novel, and the man's wife had read him a few pages the night before. The poet loved the thought of his book being read by this wife to her husband. What a wonderful experience for his book to have, and for the couple to share in this way.

Insulting someone inadvertently is a shame, and no one expects it, but when it hits them, they fall down, unconscious for an hour. When they awake, they see things like a newborn child with new eyes, The poet's son like to wear a diaper now and then for comfort. it made him feel secure and safe. He had not given up his childhood yet, and clung to certain things that reminded him of that time in his life: a diaper, a baby bottle, a binkie, a onesie; these gave him great happiness.

The father had grown accustomed to these practices of his son's, and no longer worried about them. These things had become a part of their life together, and, though it might seem peculiar or strange, this was what their life was about. If only the poet could get a new old car, their life would be heaven on earth, once again. The poet prayed that this would work out for him soon.

Keeping on keeping on, that's what the poet did each day. Moving forward always. This was a challenge, when memories persisted, and disappointments threatened to undo him at every step. His was a bold venture, pressing ever onward, and never letting the past cripple his pursuit of his destiny.

His was a lonely road to walk, and he basically walked it alone. Yes, his son was with him for the ride, but the father did all the rowing in the small boat in which they traveled together.

What did we think we were doing when the forest consumed us? We got lost in the woods and wandered for forty days and nights, led by a flaming torch and a steaming pot. We never stopped to rest, but wandered on hopelessly, until we saw a light in the distance. it was a small, humble cottage, inhabited by an old woman who invited us in and gave us supper by candle light. Then she put us to bed on straw mattresses, and wished us goodnight.

The woulds that would wish for goldfish floating through the air, condensed like milk in a can.

Noticing that the words on the blackboard were backwards, the teacher erased them all, and started over again, writing them the right way. The students had already copied to backwards words, and had to start all over again. The teacher recited the words, but the students read the backwards words instead.

When the foster children dotted their i's and crossed their t's, the foster parents rewarded them with a trip to the carnival, where they happily rode on rides together. The entrance to the carnival was covered with flowers, and the children were delighted with the spectacle. They ate cotton candy, and had fun with their friends. This was an unusual treat for them, since they were usually locked in their rooms in between meals. No one knew how they were treated, or it would have stopped long ago.

"See my watch? See my entrails?" Thus a poem of his ended, suddenly. His poems defied the laws of gravity and poetry. He wrote with sudden twists and turns, opening the eye in the middle of his forehead to see beyond sight. The line between reality and imagination had blurred for the poet, and he responded with paintings on silk in words, revealing the thoughts of many, as the scriptures promised.

Peppered memories persist, drowning in their own misery, and washing their sneakers in the washing machine, since they had been pee'd on. The poet had an accident, hurrying up the stairs to pee, when he saw that his son was in the bathroom already, and the pee suddenly poured down his left leg onto the waiting carpet. How humiliating. But this had happened before, due to his enlarged prostate, and the poet was used to changing his clothes and putting the wet ones in the washing machine.

No one was looking when, suddenly, the roof collapsed. Partridges for dinner. Pressing needs make themselves known, and dissolve into the air, infesting eyes with apoplexy. Standard usage was meant for abandoned reflexes, like a word you never used before. Sponges with ridges to clean the stables of Hercules, on a summer's night, dreaming midst the envelopes from the fruit trees, that no one dares to open anymore, since no one could interpret them.

Poplars growing like cypresses, on an abandoned island. Ferns and mosses, lichens on the rocks.

An enchanted getaway, where no one blows their noses into their handkerchiefs on cue. The fellows who rented the cottage burned it down, from not watching their stove's oven. The gas leaked out and exploded, while the renters ran out in their underwear. The cottage was burned to a crisp.

Playing the tuba, the musician astounded the listeners with his virtuosity, playing Moon River, so that everyone burst into tears, tearing at their flesh until it bled onto their clothing. Starting to move across the room, everyone was enthused, and was motivated to eat their clothes. Wanting more, the festival goers rend their garments, and walk off in the nude.

When nothing seems to have anything to do with anything else, one must look deeper to find the connecting thread that links it all together. Perhaps, the connections will be made clearer as this novel progresses. It will all depend upon what the poet chooses the write, since this current novel duplicates what the poet is writing, as though it were the most natural thing in the world.

The simultaneity of events occurring at the same time stretches time out like taffy, elongating each moment with deep significance, as though there were no end to it all. So, pardon my French, but you look like yesterday's wilted salad. Take a shower and freshen yourself up. Reading this book is serious work, and you need to stay healthy and fit to endure it to the end.

Peeling away thoughts like lemons, as was once written by the poet, carves into space the twitching entrails of oversized baboons. Carving your name into your skin, you wish that you hadn't.

The teenagers of the village went in for piercings, and often cut themselves for fun and for the rush.

They experimented with drugs and sex, exploring the variety of possibilities available to them.

Multiplying their assets, the doomed veterans stood for nothing, and were adept at enduring much suffering in their bodies and minds. The wars had scarred their souls, and they felt empty as a cardboard toilet paper tube. Sent for rehabilitation, they worked hard to regain their strength, and never gave up, but kept going. There was no end to their persistence and stamina.

But when the orphans returned to the orphanage, they found chocolates and presents on their beds. No one ever knew where these gifts and candies came from. Restless images of ventricles opening and blood flowing through the whole body all at once. Like some movie where the action is intense, and an endless chase scene takes up the whole movie. So much for the wolves and bears.

Taking care of himself, the poet follows his rituals and routines every day and night. He had gone to see the new old Cadillac with his friend driving him up there. The old man who was selling the car came out and greeted him. They went for a drive in the car, but the air conditioning wasn't working. So the poet said if the man got the air conditioning fixed, he would buy the Cadillac, and made the man an offer which seemed fair. He looked forward to buying and having this beautiful car.

The car was deep gray, and had a wonderful wooden steering wheel. It had a CD player and cassette player, just like his old car, which the poet absolutely loved. The only thing was that the car started to lose power just as they were driving off. The poet wanted to ask the man about this. There was a signal on the dashboard to service something, but the poet didn't catch what it was. The man reset the dashboard and the message went away, and the car drove fine after that.

It was Sunday, and the pilgrim family was out for a walk in their Sunday clothes. The poet said "Good morning" to them, which they cheerfully returned. These people had moved into the neighborhood, and were often seen walking about, with their long skirts and the boys in suits. They added a touch of old world charm to the block, and an interesting quality to the neighbors' lives.

The poet's friend was very kind to take him to see the Cadillac. On the way home they stopped at the store, so the poet could buy food for his birds. They always had a lot to talk about, but on this trip they were both very quiet. The excitement of seeing the Cadillac had filled them both with suspense, wondering if this would be the car that Life was providing for the poet, miraculously enough.

Partridges on the grass, alas. Fragrant scents invade the waiting air, as mysteries unravel. A sullen force exhibits rare restraint, filling the envelopes with tropical fruit this time, when everyone had given up hope that such a thing would ever happen in their midst. The misty fog swallowed up all the festivities with one massive breath. The carnival of souls was starting, and no one was the wiser for having been there when it happened. At last there was an answer to their problems.

Like walking on water, or hot coals, the various barefoot emblems trade place with one another, exhorting each other to solve the mystery of existence. The suck on lollypops, and work their teeth into filters of emptiness. Vague semblances return, diaphanously emptying their contents into the open air, while being called to dinner. "Give up!" they encourage, as salt is poured into their wounds.

Awakening like breakfast, the movements of existence betray a false start, continuing what they had begun, but with a different attitude. Slumbering on their toes, the ballerinas dance, entranced. Faraway temptations refuse to acknowledge their feet, walking on their hands, instead. The bank is closed for Sunday, but the drive through is always open for the convenience of their patrons.

Catching wind of an idea, the thoughts of many are revealed. Enthusiastic, tender, temptations walk around the village green, saturating the landscape with rude awakenings. It was time to cut the grass again.

Centuries of philosophy have accomplished little in changing the habits of the human race.

Movements coordinated with mustard interest vague investors to refrain from buying in.

Wolves and bears wander into town, extraneously inventing new ways of surviving. All the used cars in the world converging on the parking lot at the supermarket. An infestation of used cars. Cars on the brain, cars in his mind. Cars to get where you are going, to take you to your destination and back again. A car to be your friend, your personal vehicle, your entrance into Life.

When the party is over, everyone goes home. But some people stay. The mess after the party needs to be cleaned up. Perhaps a few guests will stay to help the host clean up. Or they decide to leave it for the morning. No one objects when the motor starts, and the car drives off into the sunset. After the artichokes, one is too passive to move and inch. So the table remains as it is, waiting for tomorrow.

A nice turn of phrase, that; a suitable ending, really. Except that the book is not yet over, because the poet is still writing every day. Although he was not able to type yesterday, having misplaced his writing of the day before. He couldn't go on writing until he found these four missing pages. Searching everywhere for two days, he finally found the four pages at last. So he was able to read the previous day's work, as was his wont, and continue on where he had left off.

The poet's occupational therapist had given him a new brace for his left hand, designed to hold the fingers out straight, in order to coax his tendon back onto the bone of the middle finger of his left hand. It was one week from now that he would see the doctor to determine if his finger was healed. If it was, then wonderful; if not, then he would need surgery, either to reattach the tendon to the bone, or else to install a synthetic joint to replace the one on his finger. He dreaded the thought of this.

He hoped that through his therapy, his finger would be healed. He was in no pain at all, and the finger was working well, since he was able to type again. He had two more sessions with his therapist before seeing the doctor, and intended to work hard to recover. The therapist had given him some colorful putty, with which to do various exercises to help his finger to recover.

Stretching necks like flamingoes, like those he saw when he was four years old. Beautiful, endless pink birds in flocks, parading about with elegance and naturalness. He remembered birthday parties from his childhood, happy times to recall in the sweet silence of one's mind. Photographs that his youngest daughter had helped him put into an album, after carrying them around for many years in an envelope. Memories on a platter to be devoured with one's fingers.

Speaking of catfish: Sudden messages appear out of nowhere, as the page gets blurry. The poet nearly saw the words on the page of paper and typed them in. He was recording the promptings of his unconscious mind, drilling for oil in the depths of his brain. No sentimental greeting card, this work, but a bold venture into the hidden recesses of the human mind. So satisfying, so elegant.

So intelligent, the poet was too smart for his own good, although he was grateful for it. He read constantly, and exercised his brain muscles, so as to never acquire dementia. As long as his brain was working he was happy and productive. Observing the rules of grammar, he presented his work in a conventional format, with sentences, paragraphs, and pages of writing. But these he filled with the most extraordinary content, defying logic and reason.

He gave only the slightest, occasional hint as to what the subject was that he was writing about, or what it meant or signified. He liked the abstract quality of his writing, intentionally barely comprehensible, even to native English speakers. He pulled out all the stops, and lavished his future readers with glorious words, fit together in unusual fashion, to titillate the funny bones of those who would be actually reading his book one day.

Engulfed like a cathedral, the eggs fry in the pan, and you notice a fly buzzing around the room.

Swearing off profanity, the pilgrims speak in quiet tones, with muted voices that are barely audible to the hearing impaired. He turned off the air conditioner that was blowing at his head. Cashing in their chips, the tourists walk off with arms full of money. Now let that be a lesson to them all.

Blank checks walk off with emptiness, and no one bothers to sweep up after them. Like squeezing out the juice of a lime, their emphasis was soiled, and partially open. So no one was willing to use it, forcing cabbages to boil into soup on Friday. Thankfully, no one was injured in the course of these strange events. But the orphans prayed for real parents to adopt them, so they could have a family once again. Siblings hoped to be kept together, and not cruelly separated forever.

Sudden silence. The son was asleep, seeking solace in the rest provided by his bed. He was unable to obtain his methamphetamine, and was withdrawing. The poet's friend had found several medications that were used to treat meth withdrawal. The father called their doctor, and gave his nurse the list of medications, to ask the doctor if he would prescribe one of these for the son. The father hoped that one of these would provide comfort and help to the young man.

Applauding the performance by the funny clown, the children then went to get cake and ice cream at the birthday party. Molding their faces into putty, the grownups stretch their noses and ears, evaporating like destiny all at once. Clarifying what they meant, the somber spectres move silently, and in coordinated motion, toward the virgin spring in the woods.

Thankfully, the rocks remain silent, or else they

would split in half, like oysters. Using your ingenuity, try on the various articles of clothing that you haven't worn in years to see if they still fit.

The poet would have to do this one day, but not today. Most of his clothes he never wore; he had gained a good deal of weight a few years ago, and none of his clothes fit. Then he began taking his daily morning walks and lost all the weight again. So some of his clothes might fit him now.

The clothes which he mainly wore were in laundry baskets and in neat piles on the carpet by the dresser. His recently reclaimed pink and purple polo shirts rested in a pile on his bed. The poet took care with his appearance, and tried to dress in neat and clean clothes. He had taken to ordering his clothes recently from the various catalogues which he got in the mail. These gave him a dapper look, fitting for the village poet. He was eccentric, but traditional in his ways.

Saturated cows give excessive milk. His daughter rode a camel in the desert. Thank the people who help you in your life. Spending their savings on an octopus and its tank, the couple had barely enough food to eat. But the octopus was well fed. You never know what you are going to do next until you do it. Frozen catfish are spoken of in hushed tones until they defrost. Then they can be spoken of aloud. Never mind the hidden desires of the headmaster.

Similarly, the swimming team went to the competition, and won all the awards. Emphasizing their capacity for learning, they dissolved when they dove into the water. No one ever knew what happened to the boys. Sheltering in place, the inhabitants worried whether they would be able to order pizza tonight. Slicing through Life like mushrooms, they make room for differences, attempting to affirm all manner of people, sheltering from the storm.

But you said that you were open to friendship with her? Captivating walruses vent their spleen over the fountains and rocks where they live. Sending out condolences, they express their sympathy for those who have lost loved ones. Peppering their thoughts with acronyms, no one looked through the telescope in time to see the meteor shooting through the sky. But they ate fried chicken anyway.

The birds are singing outside his window. Something strange is about to happen, but he doesn't know what it is, or when it will appear. So he kept on writing. Catching rainbows, the flagrant vagrants moon like cream cheese over the cats and yard sales that accompany any decent form of livelihood.

Saying what you mean is not such an easy thing, especially when your mouth is sewn shut. But they didn't worry: no one spoke to each other anyway, so it didn't really matter.

Coursing toward to finish line, the racers run as fast as they can, keeping a steady pace along the way. The crowds cheer them on, as they race in this pointless competition. The requirement was that the runners run barefoot, and so this slowed them down greatly. They raced on dirt paths, so the ground wouldn't hurt their feet so much. Tearing down the path, they aggressively tried to run ahead of the others, forcing themselves to keep on going, even when they thought they couldn't go on.

Plastic polluting the rivers and oceans, forgotten memories captivated by excessive loss, images that float before your eyes when you think, obscure desires caught by the tail, investments producing the desired results, clapped-on roller derbies, egg timer perfecting its job, melting saunas with their boiled inhabitants, thankful well-wishers who clap their hands with glee, the unfortunate organist who never had conjugal relations with anyone, you know the rest of the story.

When classic cars parade down the street through town, you know it is time to put the chicken in the oven. The poet's occupational therapist lived in the village also, as it turned out. The poet had expressed to the therapist: "I believe that the doctor on Monday will see the progress I have made in my therapy and through typing my new novel, and tell me to continue my therapy, and not need surgery."

The therapist thought also that this would be likely to happen.

Baby Cakes pulls the strings on the surrealist umbrella, making love to a sewing machine, and everyone suddenly laughs. When the opera is over, the singers wash their faces, cleaning off their makeup, and get out of their costumes. But the costumes won't come off, and are stuck on the bodies of the singers. Try as they might, they couldn't get the costumes off. So they were forever doomed to live out their lives as the characters in the opera, whose identities they had assumed.

Working hard on the railroad, the men sweat profusely in their labor. Catching a cold like a baseball, the nerve endings were flattened, and turned to soupy substance overnight. Like adding an extra word to a sentence for color and flavor, like apple sauce. When you override the emphasis and equate substance with quality, then quantity is absorbed into the mix. Oil the parts of the mechanism and see how smoothly it will run after that treatment.

How did things get to where they are at present? The elegance of writing persists even when there is nothing to say. The poet clicked away at the keys of the typewriter as fast as his mind could think, recording the unconscious messages that came from the depths of his being. Castrated organs fulfill the remnants of disaster, excluding all manner of sympathy from the explanation offered. Blank checks given to those suffering most in the world to help them.

Taking out the trash, he threw in the garbage his two hanging flower baskets, which had withered out of not being watered enough. This happened to him every spring, when he would gleefully buy two hanging flower baskets to hang on his porch. Inevitably, he would miss some hot days, and forget to water them, so they would eventually die. It was a sad moment for the poet.

Rolling on merrily, the orchid had suddenly lost its blossoms. Fits of startling images confront the presuppositions of those involved in this mess. Capturing their vantage point, the seekers investigate the emptiness of the singular moment they inhabit. Investigating profoundly the deep recesses of the unconscious mind, they evaporate suddenly, and were never seen again.

Egg salad is always a pleasant surprise, when there are so many eggs to eat. Sudden revelations reveal themselves, opportunely addressing the cavity in the poet's chest. Sunken in, he was always self-conscious of this indentation. It was as though a piece of his soul had been carved out of him, leaving this empty cavity with nowhere to hide. His chest sunk in, and his belly stuck out, like some strange, exotic bird, with his prominent nose protruding as a beak. This was his body.

Birds chattering away outside the window, that is, in the open space alongside the poet's house. He would be getting a new roof put on tomorrow, thanks to his wonderful home insurance policy. And now, they would be doing the porch roof also and the gutters, since he had agreed to let them not remove the existing shingles, but layer the new ones on top of the old. So, the roofer would do the porch roof and gutters for the same price. What a wonderful deal!

Exploding windows with the glass blown out. Strangely flavored soup mixes that grow horns on your forehead after eating them. The depiction of Moses with horns holding the tablets of the Law. Based on a mistranslation of the Hebrew into Latin, saying that Moses had horns, when in fact, the text said that "his face glowed." Funny, the poet thought, how things happen sometimes.

This was when Moses came down from the mountain bearing the tablets of the Law. Some divine revelation had occurred up there, and he was transformed by this event. The poet had been to the mountain also, several times over the course of his long life. He had been progressively transfigured from the person he once was into the person he was now. His appearance had changed radically throughout his life, looking like one person, then looking like another.

Taking a break from his work, the poet went to obey

the call of nature, then made his afternoon cup of tea with two biscuits to revive his mind and body. He had begun taking tea at three o'clock every day, and enjoyed this pause in his writing. The tea and biscuits revived his spirit, since he only had one cup of coffee in the morning. He used to drink six cups of coffee a day, but switched to water after his morning cup. This helped him feel much better, and he enjoyed his cup of tea.

Orienting themselves toward the window, they covered their eyes so as not to see the proceedings, awkward as they were. The poet looked through his mail every day, hoping to find an actual letter from someone. But it was always all junk mail, which he recycled without opening.

But the cream cheese was all gone or spoiled, so he had butter on his bread, instead, along with two three-minute eggs for lunch.

Salt and pepper enliven foods on which they are sprinkled, titillating taste buds on your tongue.

At last, the symphony concluded, with a series of monumental crashes, endlessly spasming on, imitating the experience of the male orgasm. All the male composers do this. One thrust, then another, then another until the climax is reached. The poet always had thought about this in this way. Would female composers choose to end their works with an explosion and a crash? He wondered.

Vague semblances, those misty images that float before our eyes when we think, float mercifully through the room. Their presence is like eggplant; their hair is made of seaweed; they do not look you in the face; they are diaphanous like silk; they wonder who we are; they do not eat or drink or sleep; they rest in puddles, emptying their substance; they wink at you when you look at them.

Continuing on, the patrons express their dismay at the quality of the offerings given them. Picking up their belongings, they forget to whom they belonged, and rescue thugs from desperation as they open the orifice of midnight. Knowing who they are, they walk out backwards, not playing any tricks on anyone, but salvaging what they were able from what they had to deal with.

Honking their horns, they pull out of the parking lot simultaneously, and venture across the road like some memorable chicken who crossed it once. Thanking your lucky stars, you explode into pieces, ravishing twilight with your hidden weapons. In fact, the nose that got you here in the first place will probably get you home at the end of the day. A trumpet sounds: Asking for nothing, you wonder where everyone had gone, inquiring after their whereabouts persistently.

Pressing the issue, asking the question, rolling over in your grave, softball fields in the snow, tapioca perhaps, mowing the lawn, cutting the grass, trimming the bushes, chopping down the wild tree saplings, butchering carcasses, opening envelopes, printing your obituary, signing the contract, pulling no punches, rescuing doves, implanting sperm, asking the question again.

Luxurious music, wrapping itself around your mobile fingers. Expecting rain, you go out to do your errands before it arrives. Sacrosanct bushes are trimmed with a virus which burns through silk like a dishwasher. The rapturous music plays on, continuing the grief of exceptionalism. Thank you for correcting my spelling. Noteworthy exceptions warrant further investigation. The hold-up at the bank where the robbers gave money to the tellers, and then ran out again.

Thank the visitors for stopping by to see you. When the escalator goes backwards the patrons are confused. Insisting upon pastrami, the corned beef feels offended, so you correct the problem by ordering both of them. Nothing about one's personal problems. The kit that broke the camel's back. Their wanderlust conveys them across the mountains and rivers, sending trees to the pharmacy.

The idea vanished before he could write it down, so the poet mourned the loss of a pregnant phrase. Indenting paragraphs is a useful tradition. That way one can tell when an extended thought begins and ends. Useful reputations preclude the prelude, infesting night with bats and snakes. The period that comes at the end of a sentence is also useful, to show you the end of this brief thought.

Parallel universes are an interesting concept. The teenagers who all work at the skating rink.

What do they think about when they are alone? Hamburgers for supper with salad. Thinking of something to say, the poet drains his brain of excess fluid, parting the waves to reach the distant shore.

He always arrived fifteen minutes before an appointment, insisting on punctuality.

Women's breasts float on the pond, pointing upward. Strange music from the outside world.

Drastic measures were taken to prevent the ship from sinking. Man overboard! Buying a few things at the supermarket. Their doctor had prescribed a certain medication to help the son's withdrawal. The son was hesitant to take it, until he knew how it would affect him. So the father called the doctor's nurse who said it would help his anxiety and cravings for meth.

But the son came into the study and interrupted his father's working time. The son said that he wasn't going to take the medication, nor would he go to see the doctor in two weeks. The doctor was the only person to whom the son was accountable. He was the son's link to Reality, and the father was determined that the son would continue his appointments with the doctor. The son cursed at his father just because he was frustrated; this was the thanks that he got for trying to help.

The son would be screaming "Help me!" to his father, and the poet didn't know what to do. So he got out money from the bank to pay for the son's meth, if he was able to obtain it. He arranged for the doctor to prescribe the medication for the son's withdrawal. But the son was opposed to solutions.

He preferred to wallow in his misery, and didn't want a way out. He loved his misery. He didn't believe that anyone could help him, but felt doomed to this life of horror and disappointment.

Six men were crawling all over the poet's roof like long-legged insects. He was getting a free new roof, thanks to his wonderful home insurance policy. And they were putting new shingles on the porch roof also, and putting in new gutters. This was a wonderful improvement to the poet's home, and would increase the value of his property. This was a true gift of Tao to the poet and his son.

Placing their platypus on the table, the couple began to play with it and pet it. The platypus seemed to enjoy this attention greatly. So you wonder what will happen next? Octagonal shapes resort to optimum grape leaves to suit their tailor's measurements. Please do not suffer over unimportant things; it just makes things worse. So the poet had so many things going on: his finger injury, his son's addiction, his car needing to be replaced, the roof being done, the funeral expenses to deal with.

But he kept his peace and his center, not allowing himself to obsess over anything. He trusted in his Tao to provide for all his needs, and to continually lead him into the right things to do. In this way, his growth continued, ever progressing into the person he was becoming, and would be one day. His contractor had visited to see the roofing work being done, and said that he was coming up with an alternative plan for the collapsing porch, which would be more reasonable in its cost. How marvelous!

The poet liked feeling things growing all around him: his house growing, his finger growing, his roof growing, his porch growing, his car growing, his funeral growing. He was growing inside himself, deep within his being, growing each day into his full stature, engaging all of his potentialities and abilities, working each day to be healthy in mind and body.

He liked archaic spellings of words. This gave an antique quality to his writing. He used obscure words, and even invented words of his own, when the confines and restrictions of language were insufficient to express what he needed to write. His friend had called while the poet was writing; he did not stop to answer the phone, but went on working, intending to call the friend back when he was done.

His state of concentration was intense and all-consuming while he was writing. He had no time or tolerance for interruptions of any kind, which would disrupt his train of thought. Since this train came from his unconscious mind up to the level of consciousness, the poet would translate these images and thoughts into language comprehensible to a future, possible reader, mostly. This was certainly as close to giving birth as the poet would ever come in his life. His writing was his baby.

The poet gave birth to four pages of insane ramblings every day, through an arduous process of revelation of what had been previously hidden in the deep recesses of his brain. Dragging these images and thoughts out into the light of day was an overwhelming event. Occasionally being even comprehensible on occasion, as the subject warrants, he would go into labor, and breathe rhythmically, swaying back and forth as the words gushed to the surface.

Blank stares evoke dead stars, or starfish dying due to the increase in the oceans' temperatures.

Enough of ranting on behalf of social issues! But poetry and writing need to address the pressing issues of the day, in order to be credible and relevant. So the poet's novel took up arms against all forms of injustice to people, creatures, and nature itself. The environmental crisis ate away at his heart, not making this his primary issue, but caring profoundly about it nonetheless.

Caring was daring. It had become forbidden to care about other people. Shows or expressions of sympathy or empathy were discouraged and outlawed. People felt alone in their problems, with no one to help console or encourage them. Troubled teenagers were a special problem. They acted out in bizarre ways to get attention from someone, anyone. Their own parents were forbidden to care.

Teachers presented the day's lesson in a cold, distant manner, since they didn't care whether their students actually learned anything at all. Doctors didn't care when their patients were in pain, or had other diseases or problems, but coldly treated them without the slightest concern. Children had to grow up largely on their own, since parents couldn't be bothered to look after their own children.

Firemen and policemen took their time responding to emergencies, since they just didn't care.

Crashing cymbals awaken the dead, brain-dead patients, as they rise from their beds, thinking they are dreaming. Looking-glass wars evoke spontaneous combustion in the rear window, as the movie goes. Looking out the window, one sees a fabulous fountain, issuing forth in a plethora of colors and forms. The ostriches and emus dance victoriously, as satin dolls perform in graceful fantasies. You look at yourself in the mirror, and you have vanished from sight.

Playing with their toys, the toddlers prefer to eat the toys, rather than play with them. Thanking the audience for a terrific show, the announcer dissolves into a pile of his clothes and walks off, invisible at last. You come to your senses, and, like a puppet, you pull your own strings and perhaps belong in a mental institution for a period of recovery. The need for Dijon mustard is persistent, but questionable on grounds of morality. So you begin all over again with the same old song.

Everything was working out as if to some divine plan. The roof was finished and looked absolutely beautiful. The gutters would be replaced next week. And his contractor said that he was able to do the porch repair for half the price he had initially quoted, and would begin next week. How wonderful that things were fitting together at last. The poet was encouraged and inspired.

Walking along like a dog, their song was interrupted by cries of despair. Blowing dandelion seeds into the air, like frying catfish. Centered reflexes combine to outlast voluntary conclusions. Plastered walls collapse into seashells, advancing toward the sea. When the buttercups are aligned with plastic waste, the margarine begins to melt. Remembering to cut up anchovies, the telephone is ringing.

One knew that he had forgotten something. One knew that something was that he needed to buy, or wanted to buy. It had occurred to him only later that this would have been something nice to buy. He had not even thought of it when he went right by the place where it was, not thinking of buying it, when it would have been a nice thing to have. So he thought that he would buy it next time.

Placing the forest on one's head is like cutting trees out by their roots. Fallen escapades fade like a forest into pleasing vestiges of forgotten memories on toast.

Forgetting to be placed in the appropriate manner on the table, the silverware stood upright, as the cacophony closed in upon it. Nowhere was there any place for forgetfulness, when awakening, the promise of survival was enacted.

Necessary measures were taken to assure the preservation of aardvarks.

Blessing the many opportunities that had befallen them, the flagrant vagrants open boxes that are empty of any contents. Happily unwrapping them, they are not disappointed that the boxes were void of anything, but breathed in the air in the boxes as though it were some costly perfume or incense.

Camels move slowly through the desert, as a storm whips up the air into a frenzy. Bakers take off their aprons and wash their hands thoroughly before entering the ovens to bake themselves.

Reservations are made for the upcoming event, and the patrons eat their tickets, swallowing their attendance at the occasion. Nervous nannies press their temperatures into clay, warming the empty envelopes with whiskey and grapes. Closing in on the occasional rejections, they send their regrets to the hostess, bemoaning the price of asparagus, seemingly oppressed by guilt.

Avoiding proper nouns, the poet worked toward anonymity, not naming things or people as he wrote his novel. It was noteworthy that none of the characters in his book were named. He liked the empty quality of this practice, leaving open to the reader to define the characters as they might wish.

Breaking his own rules, he ventured into uninhabited territory, exploring the range of possibilities offered to the absence of definition. On a silver platter.

Posturing pleasantly, they contort themselves into pretzels, bending their bodies in the most archaic manner. Breaking through all precedents, everyone went crazy like artichokes inventing the wheel on a saint's day. Taking notice of nothing less than the utmost, weary bandits milk the anonymous cows of all their cream. Walking away suddenly, the wafting breeze absorbed the needy and their needs.

Needy knees sneeze fortitude, as waxing pavilions purchase new cars for nothing. When the sparrows number one hundred, they fly out of the poet's book of haiku. Caring about what happens to you when you die is useful. Playing the Victrola, the usual suspects bend cavities into open wounds.

Peeling away thoughts like lemons, the poems grow wings, and take to the sky, overwhelmed by their own innocence. Thankfully, the thoughtful people still survive.

Giving place to thoughts allows the mind to process its vital contents. Thinking allows the mind to unwind itself, pouring out thoughts like ice cream. When you are alone with your thoughts, you can embrace yourself in the totality of your being. Like a cup of tea, this is comforting to the mind, recognizing the abilities that the mind has to encourage and enliven the most worn out clothing.

Don't forget the three little things that need to be done. Reflexes working, the knees cooperated in their own exercise, advancing upon the lynxes as they slept. Forgetting what they came for, inanimate objects appear to have personalities of their own. Partridges for dinner again. When will the air conditioning in his new car be fixed? Then he will purchase it for himself at last.

Captivating rainbows blink hesitatingly at the night-blooming overcast witness, who proclaims that the centipedes are taking over the schools. Inflating their assets, the prancing dancers evade examination, on the principle that ancient manuscripts be translated into other ancient languages, for the entertainment of the clowns in the circus. Fostering an announcement, the sugar canes project an archaic enthusiasm that lends its profit to the ballerinas on point.

Used alleyways venture into no-man's-land, allowing the anonymous cows to present an alternative to dieting. Crashing like cymbals, the crashing stops and gives vent to more problems, as the windows' glass melts into the frames. Taking notice of this, the firemen start fires when there aren't any, just to have a fire to put out. The village found this questionable, and complained to the mayor.

So the firemen set fire to the fire house, and that was the end of that.

Honking their horns, the pilgrims made their presence known, as the parade of cars wended its way through the village. Peppered thoughts sent mobile sculptures into space, while the children played on the swings. The mail-art correspondents send art through the postal system. Trying to call his daughter's school in a dream. Prancing horses bemoan the embrace of embarrassment, calling upon the vanishing schools of fish along the road. Delicate thoughts included.

When writing, always be sure to type exactly what you are thinking at any given moment. Use your intelligence and ingenuity to place placemats where you expect to be eating. Given the wishes of dishes to fulfill their destiny, the diners respected the porcelain, and gave forth a hearty explosion of gas. The offended patrons picked up their dinners and walked out with them. Taking a slice of pineapple upside-down cake with your tea, but alas, you forgot to do so.

Invigorated stallions trot across the meadow, emptying their contents on the waiting flowers below them. Waiting guests prepare to receive television marinara, with a side order of pasta. Take your time with whatever you are doing. You and it are worth it. Devote yourself to the common tasks of daily living with a pregnant heart and a hearty spirit. Anything worth doing is worth doing well.

Parting the curtains of outrageous fortune, slowing down for a moment, you serve the tea and wish for companions to share it with. Sometimes you have to end a sentence with a preposition, against the rules of grammar. Please forgive this impulsive existence that colors the thoughts of the poet. End the contest where one needs to prove one's worth. This only leads to disappointments.

Catching wind of a passing thought, he reigns in his abilities momentarily, to examine and receive the contents of the letter that was never mailed. The emblem of the society was a round moon, full of itself, and staring right at you. In the emblazoned star, the arrows grow feathers and fly away on their own. No one was the wiser for the forgotten dreams of elephants.

Cautiously, he removed the brace from his left hand, and began to type. He had planned to watch a movie with his friend this morning, but the poet's son was having a very hard time. So he advised the friend that he had better not come over, alas. The son said that he was over his withdrawal now, but was just sleeping all the time. He would wake up after a few hours, smoke a cigarette, drink some coffee, moan and groan, screaming until he wore himself out and went back to bed.

He just couldn't stay awake. The father was going to

call the doctor on Monday to see if there was something they could give him to help him stay awake? There had to be a solution to this problem. The son and his father could not go on living this way; living was like dwelling beneath an active volcano: you never know when it is going to erupt.

The poet held onto the temporary peace that ensued once the son had gone back to bed, having worn himself out with screaming. This peace was precious, and the father could work on his writing. But he dreaded when the son would wake up next, since he entered the room like a whirling cyclone, scattering everything in its path. It was always the same old song: "Shoot me! I can't go on living! Somebody kill me!" And various and sundry similar ravings. It was really very sad.

Pouring out thoughts like candy on Halloween, the ideas transform themselves into popcorn, which they buttered, salted, and ate. Like the Oxford comma, his favorite grammatical device, the ice is frozen, but melting is on the horizon. Coughing up goldfish that, having been swallowed for a prank, got lodged midway down the gullet. Luckily both the goldfish and the victim survived.

The waystation of midnight: Golden thoughts melt like everlasting rainbows into burned toast with butter and salt. Thank you for the flowers; they are beautiful lilies that scent the kitchen with a pungent odor. The son did not like the scent of lilies, but the father found it arousing and sensual. He always kept fresh flowers on the island in the kitchen in either the red, beaded glass vase from his eldest daughter, or the blue, modern design glass vase from his mother. Having flowers cheered his spirit.

The poet rejected and repudiated the ideology of the occupiers in the war that God had given them the land that they claimed, expelling 750,000 of the natives of the land as they took control of it. By this logic, the poet thought that he could claim that God had given him Canada, and expel all the inhabitants of the country as he assumed control of it. Still, the native people dreamed and hoped for a country of their own, salvaged from the ravaged lands the occupiers had desecrated.

Crashing, clashing cymbals resound through the land, proclaiming the outburst of individuality, wherein those claimants exhibit their wares on the tables of the bazaar. In the desert, they wander, finding this oasis, they examine the objects for sale. Strong coffee in tiny cups, hookahs emitting scented vapors, rich hangings and draperies, oil lamps burning, incense wafting in mystical whirls, patrons reclining on pregnant cushions, time seeming to stop as the Arabic music plays on.

Loose clothing, men in robes, rich carpeting. Then the scene changes suddenly: Where are we? Entering the Forbidden Zone, where nothing makes sense anymore. The captive rangers are hung from the ceiling, subjected to various forms of torture. Not a pretty sight for sore eyes, the way you always misspell a certain word, perhaps reverting to a more archaic spelling documented well in various ancient texts and manuscripts. The word "eye" typed as "yey" for instance.

Papering the walls with endless notes, ideas come galloping off the wall, and run out the door before you can catch them. It's like making a sandwich you wish you had made before. The "Better Late Than Never" portion of the show. In this, the audience is the performer, and the moderator is the observer. So, the audience gets to perform whatever it likes: songs, comedy routines, recitations of poetry which had been memorized, dance acts, musical instruments, and so forth.

Catching himself up, the poet wondered how he was managing to write all of these endless words? Perhaps it was his nature to exude language the way other people exude their bowel movements? Sorry, that just slipped out. But seriously, writing for the poet was visceral, physical, all-engaging of his faculties and senses, all-consuming every time he wrote.

The poet was amused to find that Lucretius, in his The Nature of the Universe, proclaimed that the mind and spirit are located in the center of the human chest. Nonetheless, he claims that the mind and spirit grow within the body, and cease to exist after death, evaporating like a mist dissolving into the air. This belief stood in stark contrast to the more common conviction that the soul or consciousness survive after death in some manner. Lucretius is a bold poet for our time, the poet thought.

The poet found comfort in the cycles of Nature, wherein things are born, grow, flourish, wither, and eventually die. All things return to the earth from which they came: the vast cosmic composting process, through which all things become one. He looked forward to the completion of this cycle in his life, embracing death as he embraced Life. Not believing any longer in a personal God, he had no one to blame for sickness or death. It was all just part of the trip.

The father had called the doctor about his son's inability to stay awake. They were going to send the message to his doctor, who was at home for the weekend, to see what he wanted to do. The father hoped that the doctor would get this message and respond with a solution to this problem. Since the son had been taken off his medication for attention deficit disorder he had been medicating himself with meth to feel merely human. It was the only thing that would keep him awake.

The poet hoped that the doctor might put the son back on this much-needed medication. There was hope in the air, and the father was relieved to have told the doctor about this crisis. The son was having terrible nightmares about his absent family, which disturbed him profoundly. There had to be a solution to this problem. The father and son could not go on living this way.

Screaming varmints eat their victuals as the sun sets slowly in the west, or is it the east? Thankfully, the silence engulfs the proceedings once again. The tumult over the webbed feet of ducks revolves around the absence of anything the talk about. So, protruding out of the mouths of babes, comes wisdom needed for the survival of the fittest. Please belong to someone.

Hair-raising protrusions emphasize the alphabet in the instruction of blank verse. Do not disrupt the emphasis on clouds that float through the cereal in the bowl. They wander like daffodils across the remaining plains, asking for nothing, but returning everything. Please do not suffer on their account.

Black beauty is forgiving of mistakes, when no one expects to be brought up like children again.

Force-fed with Life, carrying on with death, making it up as you go along, the song dissolves into feather dusters, cleaning the lungs of smokers of the danger of cancer. When the lollipops explode, then it is time to fix the clocks. A lawnmower runs expectantly through the grass, colliding with stones that bend the blades of the mower. Transfixed by their own reflections, strange posters eliminate the faces portrayed on them. Counting on those who help, one hopes for the best.

Peacefully dwelling down the street, the pilgrims pray constantly. They work hard, then sit on their porch, sipping iced tea. Thanking their lucky stars, the congress invites the prime minister of the occupation to address them in joint session. The scandal of this is outrageous; he is the one perpetuating the war on the besieged territory. A warmonger, a megalomaniac set out to destroy an entire people. How desperately horrible that he would be granted such an honor.

One for my baby, and one more for the road. Blinking like a traffic light urging caution, you exit the Forbidden Zone, thanking your lucky stars that you survived. You go home and make supper. There is an octopus in the sink. How strange, but you decide to keep it as a pet, rather than eating it. Carefully moving it to the bathtub, you watch it gambol and frolic in the water, pleased to have found its new home. There are pygmies in the bedroom, watching television, thankfully.

Hope was on the horizon. The father had left a message on the son's meth connection's answering machine, telling him of the son's suffering, and saying that they had money and would like him to be a regular source of the meth. The guy responded, and contacted the son, so it was hopeful that he would be able to procure the meth. And the son said that he would begin taking the medication that the doctor prescribed for him.

There had been a power outage, just when the poet had sat down to start writing. He couldn't see what he was typing without any lights on, so he went and cleaned the bird cages for fun. He had kept birds over the years, and now had a parakeet and a cockatiel. He had another cockatiel that was trained and would come out to play with him and sit on his shoulder and give him little sweet kisses. This bird lived with him for twenty years, and was his constant companion through all his troubles.

She had been given to him just when he was thrown out of his life to console him by a dear lesbian couple who were close friends of his and his son's. When the poet found her dead on the floor of her cage one morning, he cried out, and was devastated and heartbroken. He wrapped her in a silk handkerchief and his son helped him bury her in the backyard, laying flowers on her grave.

He had had in the past also finches and lovebirds.

One of his cats broke into their cage and ate the finches. One of the lovebirds died, the female, and the male soldiered on alone until he too died.

The parakeet that he had now was very sweet and a beautiful sky blue color, but was unresponsive to any talking or sounds. The cockatiel was not trained, and the poet enjoyed talking to him, as the bird would respond with chattering chirps. When the poet said "Hello, baby," the bird would answer.

They had had two kittens which they adopted at the apartment where they had sought refuge from the storm. These were very sweet and playful. When they moved to the new house, they acquired two more cats, so now they had four. They all got along, and it was fun having so many cats at once.

Eventually, one by one, they all died, and they had no cats until their new kitten was discovered.

One day when the poet was opening the back door, he heard a tiny "Meow." He looked down and saw the sweetest tiny baby kitten meowing. He left her milk to hope she would be friendly. But she was afraid, being a poor, little abandoned kitten. So the poet called the animal society, and they loaned him a trap to catch her in. He put food in the trap, and she came in and was finally caught!

He had to then get a cage to keep her in for a month until she calmed down. The cage had cozy towels to sleep on, food and water, and a litter pan. The kitten eventually calmed down, and was let out of the cage. She ran around the house, darting here and there, and hiding inside the pedals of the old pump organ in the dining room. After a while she became more friendly, and settled into her new life with the father and his son. She grew to be a beautiful, big cat, and lived happily ever after.

She spent her days ensconced in one of the two chairs in the poet's bedroom in the alcove by the windows, coming down for food, or just to look around to see what was happening. She was a very cuddly cat, but reserved when she wanted to be. She often came into bed with the poet at night, and would come over to him, placing her paws on his shoulders, and cuddle with him in this manner. One time she climbed up onto his chest and just lay there for quite a while. This was pure bliss.

The cat was cautious around the son, since his

screaming frightened her. But she would let him pet her on occasion, and seemed to want to trust him, overcoming her fear of him. She loved to be petted by the father, stretching out on her back so he could rub her belly and chest and neck. The poet had always kept cats, loving their quiet, sympathetic presence. His cat was his Muse, and she inspired him every day just by her living and beautiful presence.

Wafting in the breeze, the overcast sky wanted to weep tears of rain, dropping on the waiting, thirsty earth. Enough of waiting, thought the poet, so he got started on his book. The fenced-in posters proclaim innocence on a stick, broiled to perfection. Monsters collude with one another, breaking their fast together, devouring pies and cakes by the mouthful.

Casting aside grief, the rainbows beg for mercy, discussing the antics of various feuds, as they enter an unexpected castle, variously musing over the color of the wallpaper. Cast-out castaways vent their emotions, buying into whatever caution is expected of them. New entreaties bang up against plowed driveways devoid of snow. Taking the temperature of one's temper is a good idea.

Telephoning destiny, you wonder what the results will be, so you understand at last the message being sent. Thank the operator for assisting your call. Long distance relationships cast off from the shore, expectorating mucous from their memory's vain cavity. You never would have thought to ask the owner of the club if you could be a member. Thrown-away thoughts collide with the truth.

You were expecting someone else, but when you saw him, something clicked in your mind's eye that told you you could trust him. Carried-away entrances break harmony with saws, excavating the mind of its cacophony entirely. In a manner of speaking, the terrors took off and fled the premises.

What were you expecting when the fathers and sons could no longer get along? Deep misery.

But the airplanes float helplessly in the empty, colliding sky. Emphasizing grief, the winds protect memory's gaze upon the flowers that bloom in the spring. If you had known they were coming, would you have arrived late? Testing the waters, no one expected the chocolates to melt. But the blazing sunshine, pouring through the windows, did its dirty work, abandoning hope all who enter.

Next of kin sit next to their kin, enjoying the captivity of forms, while the well-boiled icicle savors the remedy of nuisance, while slurping up the gravy remaining on the plate. Thankfully, no one was hurt.

You gave up your rights when you came here. Noticing the small print in the contract, you wonder if you will ever escape? Shut up in your room, you look for a telephone, but there is none.

Idiosyncratic poems tell the story of individuation, multiplying destiny with olives, dancing on the shore. When you take out the garbage, be sure to admire the new roof on the house. Taking advantage of the opportunity, the fencers relate small talk in plastic containers for lunch. Noticing the notice, your enthusiasm is baking in the oven, all to itself. You thank the oven in passing.

Taking stock of the inventory, the blend of story is enticing. One looks at the sun and is momentarily blinded. Bats in the belfry, socks hanging up to dry, spent dreams that wander off on their own, leaving the sleeper wondering where they went. Take two aspirin, and call me in the morning.

Taking off from the ground, the angels eat anchovies and chocolate, and then fly away.

Memory's gaze intrudes into your undergarments, seeking comfort in clothing. When the emphasis is on knowing, you wonder at the unknowing that is required of you. Taking away the distinction of parents toward their children, the ice cream is too frozen to eat once again. Thank you for listening. The marshmallows melt in the fire, burning up in flames before they can be eaten.

At last, the parallel universes claim prominence in the intergalactic plan of entry. They would blaze on like voices singing in French, when no one is at home. The television is turned off and sleeping, while the radio plays uninterruptedly. Sound of the symphonic poem, a hunt is colorful, performed entirely for your listening pleasure. No one stops to listen, so the music plays on anyway.

O frabjous day! The poet had been to the doctor for his finger injury, and the doctor was delighted with the poet's progress. He said that there was no longer any need for surgery, and agreed with the therapist that the poet should complete six more weeks of occupational therapy. The poet was ecstatic, and the doctor was thrilled. This was a blessing beyond belief.

The poet's son had gotten his meth, and was relieved and happy again. The meth was the only thing that would keep him awake, making him feel human at last. The son was pleasant to be around when he had his drug, and didn't scream and yell anymore. There was peace in their home finally, and the father was able to write in a quiet environment.

The contractor was hard at work on the collapsing roof of the porch. He happily had told the poet that he could now do the job for half of what he had originally proposed. This would make it possible to have this much-needed work done. The contractor was a dear friend now, and the poet was so grateful for all his beautiful help. There was nothing that he could not do.

The grounds keeper had his work cut out for him. When the roofers did the roof, they tore down the wild vines that grow up the side of the porch. These now were hanging down in the most droopy and depressing way. So the poet asked him to cut the hanging vines back. The grounds keeper also needed to cut back the huge rhododendron, so that the contractor could fit his ladder in the space next to the porch, so he could work on the porch roof. He did all this work beautifully.

A report from the front: Casting away grief that binds them, the architects peruse the plans for the new pavilion, keeping abreast of the ways that vegetation smiles. So they spend their thrifty pocket money on treats to relieve their hunger and thirst. Begging the question, the oranges forget their names, and, blending together with the anterior mixes, they spend their quadrupeds recklessly.

Orchestrating the symphony, pulling violets from the gripping earth, soundlessness evaporates into the aether, because of lunacy invading the underground tunnels where the effects of sin are removed. Thank the aether for its stinging benefits. The words grow blurry, as the snow falls helplessly from the sky. Your soup is ready, sir or madam, so beware that it is very hot.

Thinking out loud, no one will become active curtains, wending their way across the golden fields of wheat, shuddering in the breezy wind. The telephone sits there, waiting to ring at any moment.

Where the deer and the antelope play, the pardons are written to alleviate the suffering of the inmates. Elderly residents are especially effected by the ordinance.

When the exceptional students go on vacation, they

continue their studies on their own. Reading books prevents dementia, so exercise your brain every day. Tender shepherds corral their sheep into pens for the night. The ice cream sundaes melt in their bowls, as the cigarette burns down to its filter. Moose play gin rummy on the balcony, eating bologna sandwiches.

The insecticide is working on the centimeters of centipedes, pronouncing inviolate substances as remedies for the uncommon cold. Thinking backwards, the convicts examine the contents of the rainbows, exuding thoughts of nightmares into the washing machine of doom. When you will remember what you thought about yesterday, the Cadillac will be ready next week.

Ground-up memories turn to radiant dust, like the poems that you read when you were a child.

Paving the way toward a new understanding, the thoughts of many are transformed into concertos, to be played upon garbage cans, electric can openers, and toasters. When the right thought comes to you, you have to write it down, so you will remember it forever. Think about it, please.

For your own good, bleak pessimists extol the virtues

of snuff, pouring out their entrails as if there were no tomorrow. But when the district superintendent relates the openness of startling visions of entropy, the fish distinguish objects by name. Recognizing everything as what it is, believing in the sound of water pouring down upon stones of forgetfulness.

Tender remnants blow kisses to the audience, which responds with loud cheers and applause.

The shopping requires the vegetables, fish, and meat to reach the recesses of emptiness. Following their noses, they stumble upon an untended garden, overgrown with weeds and wild flowers. The gardener is absent for years, and will never return. So the garden grows wild and unruly.

Wishes comfort swordsmanship in the evening when the communicating vessels rest their case and retire for the night. Clashing blades of mercy beg to differ from the customary usage, preferring to cast out their hopes into no one's business but their own. Rescuing the babies, the comforters are ripped to shreds, and there is no milk to give them. So the song goes on, religiously.

Frogs and toads, croaking in the pond. The lily-pads float like homeless people on the water.

Cicadas soon will be chirping in the trees in the backyard of the house. Thinking persons prefer to advance their payments to cover the cost of their appendectomies, the preferred manner of speaking Chinese at home. Parsnips plead for mercy as the boiling water engulfs them.

When you come home, there is a surprise waiting for you in the parlor. Sit down and relieve your stress. Open a window as you read this book. Think about what you will have for supper tonight.

Mark with brackets your favorite passages of this novel, remembering to read them backwards. Risked solidity wreaks havoc amongst the elves residing in the next forest. Visit them when you can.

Pressing issues gain the attention of wolves in the throne room, as the empire collapses in front of your weeping eyes. Nothing will stop the advance of progress, pleading sympathy from the devils who walk sideways in the night, waiting to catch us unawares. Bleeding hearts proclaim the rest of the novel, as princesses sit on peas, to waken their reflexes in an exorbitant manner to please you.

Wintery weather will burst upon the scene: snow

in midsummer, rain in winter, clouds appearing on the horizon. So keep your captivity close by your side, and weather the slings and arrows of outrageous fortune. Send your pleasant membranes to the tendon on your finger that has, at last, reattached itself to the bone. Thank the tendon for returning.

Unaware of symptoms that would indicate a refusal to concede in the election, wiping their tears away, they lose their cool, and break into song. Whisking away on a flying carpet, the couple rides onward, gleefully exclaiming their delight. Wandering minstrels play their lutes and sing for their supper.

The miracles that keep coming make up for the losses which one has survived.

The old man from whom the poet was buying the new old Cadillac had the air conditioning fixed and a few other repairs done as well. He was ready to sell the car to the poet, and just needed to find the title to the car. The poet would purchase the car next week, and looked forward to owning this beautiful vehicle. He would finally be able to drive to his appointments himself!

He would have to send his old Cadillac to "car

heaven." This would be a very sad thing for the poet, who loved this car dearly. He had put so much money into it over the years, buying a new engine, and many other repairs. But the car had seen its day, and the poet couldn't see putting any more money into it, when it was already so old and used-up. So its life would soon come to an end.

Floating off into the cloud of unknowing, the poet partook of his excellent marijuana. This inspired him with wild, wonderful ideas, and released his unconscious to come bubbling up to the surface. These he would then type on the old, black Royal Standard typewriter, clicking away at the keys, his fingers dancing a marvelous ballet. From whence came these ideas, which had to be caught quickly?

Certainly his imagination was engaged and active in the process, and he had always been a very creative child, adolescent, teenager, young adult, middle-aged adult, and now older adult. And certainly he was aware of the circumstances, people, and events of his life, drawing subconsciously upon these mental resources to form the characters of his novel.

These characters would always remain nameless,

vague semblances, misty vapors, haunted spectres. And yet, the poet's novel had narrative, characters, events, and circumstances in it. So in some ways it was a very traditional novel. But it had these intervening paragraphs of surrealistic images, which often seemed to have no connection to one another. These abstract passages were similar to the ones in his first novel, *Reap Violet Hiss*, and were the way the poet liked best to write.

These passages, really all of the poet's book, were written in a state of automatic writing. As though in a trance or possessed by some spirit, the poet would click and clack away at the keys of the old, black Royal Standard typewriter as if there were no tomorrow. Totally enthralled by his work, his was a state of intense concentration, and totality of presence.

It was raining. He could hear the sound of the pitter patter of the rain on the window by the typewriter, and on the air conditioner in the window. The sound of the rain was comforting to him.

He enjoyed all kinds of weather, but rainy days were especially beautiful to the poet. He loved the gray grayness of the day, kindred to his spirit and to poetry. A day of the human mind.

The collapsing roof of the porch had been repaired at last. His contractor had done a beautiful job in less than one week, and his wife came along to help on the last day of the work. She was an utterly charming older woman, an artist who painted watercolors. So the poet invited her into the house to "see some art." He showed her his father's artwork, and she enjoyed meeting his birds.

When the job was done, to the poet's great delight and surprise, the contractor gave him a long embrace. This deeply moved the poet, since one time he had given the contractor a hug, and he seemed to freeze up in surprise. So this was a huge breakthrough, and it was a very deep, prolonged embrace, a lovely way to end the job he had done, as the poet paid him for his work.

He was ecstatic: the poet's first book of poems was published at last, and available for sale. He had written these poems in his late twenties, and they had been edited by his good friend, a noted poet and photographer. This friend selected the poems from a batch the poet gave him, edited them, and arranged them beautifully into four numbered parts.

The book, *Fresh Window*, was written in his tenement apartment in the city, and had a certain, real freshness, and newness to it, which made it approachable to almost anyone. The poet had circulated copies of this manuscript to friends long before it was published, and many had enjoyed reading it greatly. This was the first manuscript he had assembled as a young poet, and it was his first book of poetry to be published now, forty-four years later.

So he sent out a hopeful, wishful prayer to his new book of poems to "flourish, blossom, be fruitful and multiply! Go out into the world and be read by beautiful people who will be delighted by your contents. I send you out as my own beloved baby, now full-grown and going out into the world on your own. Have a wonderful life, and may you get the recognition that you so richly deserve!"

Waiting for the tea kettle to whistle, but it never does. Its whistle had deserted it. The crispy, creamy chocolate bar from abroad. The tea that is cooling off in the cup. Thunder rumbling above. The new, blue splint for his finger. The orange index card. The candy wrapper. The classic lip balm. The pen that doesn't write. The toothpick. The ashtray with two cigarette butts in it.

Blank verse, prose poems, all the varmints eat their victuals. Strange tendencies try to keep up with one's thoughts, and the visions fly out the window. A thankful pilgrim greeted the poet at the supermarket, remembering him as her neighbor. She had six little children with her in two shopping carts, and was very friendly. So much for the neighborhood, all friendly now, he thought.

Unpleasant things are a part of life. The best thing you can do is not let difficult circumstances upset you; this only makes things worse. Cultivate a neutral state of mind, where nothing can sway you from you path. Don't get too sad over misfortune; don't get too excited about something good. Keep a balanced, harmonious state of body and mind, adhering to your Tao. This is what the poet thought.

But had the tendon of the middle finger of his left hand reattached to the bone yet? This was the question that he had telephoned the doctor's office about. But no one ever called him back. He would have to call again before they closed for the weekend. This was an all-important piece of information, as he proceeded with his therapy and exercises at home.

His exercises at home were a lovely meditation, as he manipulated the stretchy putty into various shapes to exercise his finger. He concentrated deeply and would be in a very peaceful state to receive the healing that the exercises would provide him with. He did these exercises in silence, to be able to completely focus on what he was doing. And he could feel his finger healing.

Blank verse again, a prose poem is what the poet's novel really was, a symphony of sound and language, words dancing on the page in lively formation. Spontaneous prose that flowed like a river through his veins. Captive words transformed into clean laundry. Excavated ruins discovered to bear buried treasure. Trees fluttering in the spring breeze after rain. What you think you know taken away from you and replaced with something more interesting.

Galloping thoughts waiting to be corralled, while emphases are ready to explode into veracity.

Tender remnants transformed into practicality. Supermarkets overflowing with food. Starving refugees caught in the middle of the war in the besieged territories. Bands of settlers marauding through the territory, attacking trucks bringing aid to the starving refugees. Shameful doings all around.

Piecing together the pieces of the puzzle, the entrances were blocked, and will be opened if the peace agreement is ever agreed upon. Getting all sides to the table to reach a deal is difficult. Each had its own conflicting agenda, and no one wants to give up anything. And yet, Reality persists, and the starving children are dying every day, and no one can stop this carnage.

Puffy clouds in pink and blue flutter over the landscape of unicorns, fountains, and happy creatures of every sort portrayed in a rainbow of colors. The sickening puke of the lepers is gathered in buckets to dispose of quickly. Think of something nice, and forget about the rest. No, don't ignore the ugliness, when you enjoy the pretty parts. After all, it's all part of the trip.

Rough-housing together, the rampaging boys play games, their blue, electric penises fluttering in the breeze, blinking their lights and exuding their juices. They frolic, gambol, and some other word one cannot remember at present. Thankfully, they stretch their possibilities, arranging dances and romances fondly, like the way an orchestra all plays together. Their leader was the conductor.

Rambling on ahead, the fluttering munchkins blend silence with optimism, entrancing their doom into words' worth of mentioning. Think of the trust between actors and authors, when their fingers move silently over the strings of the instruments. Taking out the wash to hang on the clothesline doesn't happen anymore. And the strange sound of motors revving, while the albatross sleeps in its nest. What is best is really the worst in disguise. No one was the wiser for it.

Quaking ducks piddle paddle along the path, as acrimony descends from the rafters. The name of the person is marked on the ends of the beams, as the symphony finally concludes. When the parsnips are roasted, the end of the opera is near. Failing to adhere to the numerous weights that descend from the ceiling means that the musicians are on strike.

Cast-away fronds of violets standing in the lobby, waiting for a cab, pull their earlobes as a signal to the policemen that the play was in progress. Showmanship prevailing, no things were at cross purposes, so they went underground to play poker. Finally, you will center the thoughts of your brain into mud puddles, evacuating the train car before the crash occurs.

Gleefully proceeding, no one expects to get where they are going, because the ending of the book is getting nearer every day. When they went out on the roof, they saw the skyline and the air pollution encircling it. Expecting rain, the workers finished up the roof just before it started. Like sawdust, his thoughts were swirling around inside his head and never let up for a minute.

The paragraphs in the poet's new novel were all either four or five lines each. He liked the symmetry of the situation, and adhered to this discipline like water to a thirsty plant. No one could figure out what he did with his time; the neighbors were mystified by his presence and wondered what he was working on for all these months. They never knew it was his new novel.

He was getting his new car on Monday, and he was very excited about this event. His current vehicle was overheating even when driving from the next town, so he and the son were stranded at home for the weekend, not daring to drive the car in its delicate condition.

The son was having a visitor over: an encounter for sex, anonymous and satisfying. The father wrote in the study with the door closed while this was going on in the house. The son had needs, and found ways to fulfill them.

Plaster of Paris in the artist's studio, blank stares from the sculptures' faces, enormous mouths devouring everything in sight, partial dentures biting an ear of corn, semblance of reality appointed to pierce the veil of the temple, dangerous fibres vanishing into wakefulness, torn-up magazines depicting geographic formations, tax-evaders snacking on silhouettes.

Born-again mustard, vanishing parsnips, collections of clothes-drier lint in yogurt containers, partially blind inhabitants stretching to reach something on a shelf, pointed hats to wear on holidays, beans cooking in a stainless steel pot, chewing gum on the bottom of someone's shoe, ballet dancers opening cans of worms, blacked-out names on a list of discreet offenders.

Pudding in a giant can on the shelf in the supermarket, play-dough for infants non-toxic to be eaten, symphonies of psalms, back door reactions, taken-objects deferred by proxy, your urine taken as a sample at the doctor, blood drawn from your arm, awakened symptoms variously arranging themselves, crunchy raisin bran for lunch with milk. Taken unawares, they foster flowers in the middle of the road, when plastic containers are holding the invisible examples of radiance.

Dancing temptations react to fallen snow by eliminating the competition, meandering through the vestiges of parlance. Elephantine wings flap over the center of the room, enhancing the look of the entire scene with envelopes. Thanking the envelopes, you will have fallen over yourself by the time they will have been born. Wings flapping, they fly transparently through the infested air to the sky.

All of a piece, the princesses preclude the advance of introspection, as the ice melts in the ice trays, wanting to be frozen again. Then they opine over the pine trees evades capture, and sends its voice over the waves of the ocean, to hear the sound of the seashells put to your ear. Catching wind of a passing fancy, they open cans of sardines and eat them right out of the cans. Nothing could be further from the truth than how they acted in front of the audience.

So when the filters were removed, the mechanism worked smoothly, catching the insects from the air as they flew. Your voice is hauntingly beautiful, so sing when you want to, please. A musical interlude would be nice right about now. But the pot on the stove is waiting to be cooked. Answering the telephone, you talk to the person on the other line, emphasizing grief over partitions.

Right out of some movie, they pass on into invisibility, partitioning off their minds, and blinking their eyes rapidly from the substance they had imbibed. Crashing symbolism vacates the warehouse of enthusiasm, weathering the storm of life, excavating the dug-up ruins. Relics abound in the windows of captivity, wherein one wants to receive something in return. But no one does.

Singing the blues, the sinners proclaim their innocence, demanding that their cases be reviewed.

Endless water to drink, but the refugees in the besieged territory have no clean water to drink. They are drinking from puddles, and from seawater instead of clean water. Castrated envelopes peruse their contents, admitting the difficulty of just being alive one more day.

If you knew when you would succeed, it probably wouldn't ever had happened. You waiting, patiently, devoting yourself to the great work, and never stopped to see where it would end. So you were so engaged in the process that you didn't even notice the passage of time. When you looked up from your work, the entire day had passed, and you never even knew it.

Waffling down the alley way, the abandoned toilet is enveloped by weeds. The day lilies growing along the way, the yucca plants blooming. There are faeries in the alley, frolicking about. They look for some mischief to make, or someone in need to help. Looking at them, you are amazed to see their tiny wings and feet, so you make a promise to never tell anyone that you saw them.

Pandering to exquisite corpses, the bubbling wine that they awake each night to drink consumes them. Awakening their motor mechanisms, they infest the realms of grief with enthusiasm, capturing the rest of night with a butterfly net, and walking on water. Tanks of meaninglessness create an aura of temptation that no one can resist. So they walk on, disregarding the final scene of the play.

Playing the field, they notice that no one is wearing

shoes. So the opera continues, and the silence of the no-opera is deafening. The radio is off, and the new, blue splint is sleeping. The old black Royal Standard typewriter clicks away, and sends messages to the forest for the trees to hear. On their wings are rainbow-colored feathers which flutter as they fly off into the sky at night.

The propeller spins frantically, as the plane lands at the airport. The passengers have all changed into extraterrestrial creatures. They exit the plane to much acclaim, as the members of the press press into each other to get a glimpse of the space people. Their spokesman makes a moving speech, greeting the earthlings as they prepare for their interplanetary visit. Everyone is amazed.

When the flags wave, or are taken down, the entryways are closed for repairs. Catching themselves up, the toasters bleed prosperity, while the housewife bakes cookies. Nothing can stop them now. Wavering between this and that, the emphases revolt, enabling parlance between enemies, as the floating vessels communicate with one another, lasting the entire length of the opera.

Forced vestiges of times gone by intrude into the exceptionalism of entities benign in intention. Think of the lunatic fringe that heckles the pickled eggs in their vacant jar. Nothing is like the rumor of captivity which the orchestra refuses to play as an encore. Frankfurters fall suddenly from the sky and are caught in waiting buns by the passers-by who intend to eat them.

Preparing the room for visitors, the entities remove their shoes and flutter downstairs to make coffee. Thankfully, you will have put your shoes on by now, reading of the entities above. Wishing for better times, they are received into what will have been the opening of the artists' gallery. The protesters throw tomato soup on the Mona Lisa, which was protected, or course, by glass.

When will you have done what you intended to do so very long ago? No one is going to do it for you, so seize the day! Parking the car in front of the house, it is basically dead and cannot be driven. The poet would have to have it towed to the wrecking place, since the car would never make it there without overheating. He and his friend would drive behind the tow truck and get there together.

Now is the time for all good men to come to the aid of their country. And other such drivel which the government exuded on a daily basis. No one could be trusted anymore. The president continued to send bombs and money to the occupiers of the territory in their savage war against the refugees, starving in their tents. No one seemed able to wake him up to stop this genocide.

All in a day's work, the images explode and captivate the author. Vestal virgins offer the required sacrifice, promenading through the temple's court toward the altar and its high priestess.

He called an old friend with whom he had been out of touch for some time. This woman had tried to justify his daughters' abandonment of their father, saying that he was "overwhelming." Because of this, the poet had avoided talking to her for several months.

But she had left him several very kind messages on his answering machine, expressing support and encouragement to him through all of his challenges and successes. So he thought he would break through the ice, and plunge in and call her on the telephone this morning. They had a very informative conversation, and the poet was glad to be back in good standing with this woman.

Pressing matters press upon whom they want to, talking about the weather and the latest sports scores. North winds descend into the cavity of time, and wend their wintry way across the fields of snow. The end of spring was upon them, and the verge of summer was portending. Pretending to be someone else, the children play at roles, assuming different characters out of their imaginations.

One might prefer consistency of grief to unabashed happiness, but the latter is the final word from our sponsor. We wonder what the next thing will be that we have to suffer, but keep an expressive smile handy for emergencies. Thank the water before you drink it. Thank the food before you eat it.

Thank the merry lepers who protrude into hidden festivities on their own account.

If you wish for something, it may happen. If you are true to your Tao, you will meet the right people, and the right things will happen for you and to you. Expressing sympathy for someone in his suffering, will bring you blessings, as well as to the sufferer. Avoiding proper nouns, one invents improper language to express the same thing with different words.

This is all part of the process by which this current novel is being written, in alignment with the process used by the poet himself in the writing of his new novel. For sympathetic suggestion, this current novel is conformed to the events and characters of the poet's new novel. Whether this novel or the poet's novel was written first remains a hidden mystery. Both occur simultaneously, in truth.

A still life: The hard, blue splint, lying on its side, its white band relaxing, looking like some surrealist sculpture; the open pack of peppermint chewing gum, elegantly black in its box; a stray white cap from some bottle; various orange caps for syringes; the orange index card; a red cigarette lighter; the ashtray with a cigarette butt in it; a q-tip; the pen that doesn't write anymore.

Like breathing fresh air, the park is uninhabited, but the playground is empty. The walk through the woods, taking a stork for a ride, expressing a sentiment that had been forgotten for many years, opening a door where before it was closed, entering a new experiment, walking down the sidewalk, looking for a new purpose, wanting to go somewhere before the typewriter starts typing by itself.

It was almost as if the typewriter was typing the poet's new novel, or his fingers, on their own, separated from his consciousness, were typing by themselves. This was automatic writing at its best, which the poet excelled in exclusively. The images and words poured from his unconscious mind through his arms into his hands and fingers, which typed frantically to keep up with his inspiration.

Classic cars invade the experiment, concluding a deal with an elderly couple who have kept it safe in their garage for twenty years. If you look into your own mind, you will find limitless treasures there to explore and claim for yourself. Talking about windows: birds were singing on his morning walk.

There was still one dark chocolate bar left. They were stuck in the house for the weekend, because the car couldn't run anymore without overheating. Tomorrow, he would buy the new car.

The intentional corrections exude a tasteful officer who extols the virtues of a chance encounter between an umbrella and a sewing machine on an operating table. What ends the symphony is in part a portion of a thunderstorm in heaven. Taking care to blend the thoughts of many into one, the universal mind takes control of the proceedings once again. Taking their tea, they sip delicately.

A bird is heard through the window. Persisting with integrity over the voices of invisible participants. These walk on toward the center of the universe, taking time to notice the various entities pronouncing their names in a different language. Space people greet the earthlings with surprise, thinking that they look strange and ugly. The changes betwixt one variety of capsules and another preclude any reckoning amongst the universal order.

Inhaling Life like a cigarette, one moves slowly, participating in every moment, inhabiting the present, breaking down barriers, seeking something bigger, looking for largeness, hoping for the end to slavery and human trafficking, thank you for correcting my misperception. You help me through this jungle of words, to keep pressing on toward the inevitable conclusion.

The flagrant vagrants, flagrant or vagrant no more, play chess in their homes. This has caught on as a very popular game, and they enjoy the tense endurance it takes to make it through a game. They have settled into the rhythm of Life, and are enjoying their new homes, which they have decorated impeccably. Thank them for their beautiful existence, peacefully dwelling in the village.

So the typewriter says to keep going until one reaches the bottom of the page. What will you eat for lunch today? Have you showered and dressed? Brushed your teeth? What are you wearing?

Oh, invisible reader of the future, welcome into the world of this novel. You have read this far, and are to be commended for your fortitude and perseverance. Your reward will be great, indeed.

His son was sleeping through the morning, having been up early in the middle of the night. So the father was able to write peacefully in the willing silence of the study. It was almost time to finish for the day, and he had a satisfied feeling that all will be well. The world will go on, no matter who wins the election, and the poet will go on with his work every day, writing for two hours his four required pages, giving into his best impulses over the old, black Royal Standard typewriter.

MICHAEL COOPER was born in 1952 and raised in Queens, New York by an artist father and a poet mother. Upon age 17 he ventured forth to the East Village, where he quickly became immersed in the world of the arts. He attended the High School of Music and Art and New York University, from which he received the Thomas Wolfe Memorial Poetry Award. Michael was a frequent reader at the Poetry Project and other venues, as well as being a performance artist associated with the Fluxus group. An early disciple of John Cage from age 16, he served as personal assistant to the publisher, Dick Higgins (Something Else Press), and also to the poet Jackson MacLow. Michael was also Poetry Director of the New York Avant Garde Festival, as well as serving as assistant to the director of that festival, Charlotte Moorman. He was also co-editor of EAR Magazine. He went on to earn degrees from Hunter College (B.A., magna cum laude) and Union Theological Seminary in New York (M. Div.). Michael is a retired Episcopal/Anglican priest, having served parishes with a focus on contemplative spirituality. He also had a career as a professional cellist, performing with local symphonies. He is a committed philosophical Taoist, and is the father of four children. Michael is the author of 17 books of poetry, including *Fresh Window*, and two experimental novels, *Reap Violet Hiss* and *Vague Semblances*. Michael and his son live in Northeast Pennsylvania in a quiet, small town with a cat and two birds and several lovely green plants.

9 781963 908428